A STRANGE ALCHEMY

a Story of Today & Yesterday

SHEILA GEDDES

Pen Press Publishers
London

First published in Great Britain by
Pen Press Publishers Ltd
39-41 North Road
London N7 9DP

ISBN 1 900796 34 1

A catalogue record of this book is available from the
British Library

Cover design by Catrina Sherlock

Printed and bound in Great Britain by Antony Rowe Ltd, Chippenham, Wiltshire

'War is a strange alchemist.'
Alan Bennett (Forty Years On)

For my sisters,
Hilda Page and Rosemary Langford,
who share the memories.

Author's Acknowledgements

It would be impossible to list all the people who have given me information about their lives during World War Two. Some wrote letters, others gave me interviews or sent me cassette tapes telling of their experiences. Even the stories I have not used were valuable background information. I am well aware of the omissions of the work of various support groups. There were hardly any women who did not do something to help the war effort. To them all, my gratitude.

Books about the war are numerous and I have used many of them, but I must acknowledge my indebtedness to one above all. This is Eric Taylor's *Women who went to War*.

This is Now - 1

It was Aunt Julia who bought the summerhouse.

I have no idea why that sentence should come into my head as the only way to start my novel, but there was a compulsion that happens sometimes, and I suppose all the rest of it really starts there. Certainly, the summerhouse figured largely in the time which changed my life.

Aunt Julia and Uncle Reg had come to Norfolk to retire, back to their roots and, incidentally, to mine, though I had lived in London for ten years.

When she phoned, Aunt Julia was ecstatic, her long, involved sentences even worse than usual.

'My dear, we've had the most incredible luck – everyone's dream house – a cottage in the country, only it's a modern bungalow, thank heavens. Country cottages are pretty to look at, but hell to keep clean and much given to low beams, which would knock Reggie out every time he moved. But we do have a half-acre of ground, high hedges, even if they *are* cypresses and will need cutting twice a year – and nice quiet neighbours. Can you believe it?'

When she paused for breath I asked, 'Is it a village?'

'Even better, it's a hamlet – a mile from the village and three from the town – nothing much here, but we do have a post office so we can get our pensions without going into town.'

'But surely you'll be getting another car, won't you?'

She said vehemently, 'Not if I can help it, we won't. You forget we were brought up to cycle. We've got new bikes and there are four buses a day – they even go into Norwich. We got a bus once a week in the old days, so don't go putting ideas into Reg's head. It was a happy day when I persuaded him to give up the car. All those road accidents … Now, Jan, come and see us soon. Get out of that ghastly London and come into the fresh air.'

I put the phone down with a sudden pang of longing for the country, which surprised me. Perhaps it was the grey dankness

1

which hung over the town on that particular day. Normally I loved London – the buzz, the frantic pace of my job, even a sense of pride in the city. I was part of a team on an upmarket magazine, my career prospects were good and the shots of adrenaline kept me going. It was a life I had no wish to change.

Even when my partner and I split up the following February there was no reason to leave London. In fact, it was because I had refused to do so that the break came. Don had been offered a wonderful job in America and I knew it was not an offer he could turn down; but I couldn't see a career for me there, competing with plenty of well-established native journalists. What made the situation worse was that it had happened to me before. I had never met a man who considered my career equally as important as his. But Don had been with me for nearly three years and I missed him.

It was the silliest thing that got me out of London. I went on a skiing holiday in March. It was too late for the piste to be good; I broke my leg and sprained my left wrist. My mother insisted I come home.

'Darling, you can't stay in that flat all on your own.'

'It'll be a bit crowded with you – and with Easter so near.'

My mother lived in Cromer and provided bed and breakfast for visitors. My sister, Clare, was at the University of East Anglia and went home every weekend.

'We've thought of that. Julia has three bedrooms in the bungalow – it's gorgeous, you'll love it. She wants to have you – do come.'

I hesitated until I received the usual garrulous phone call.

'My dear, you must come. The place is crying out for company. Besides, I bought a summerhouse – with my own money, so Reggie couldn't say anything – and you can work from there when you feel up to it. I put electricity in, even if he did say it was extravagant, so now you have to come and justify it.'

It was very tempting. Even with my cleaner agreeing to come every day, being in the flat on my own induced feelings of panic. When my leg hurt the idea of being cosseted seemed wonderful.

Robert, who was my boss, was also a good friend and owned an enormous car. When he phoned, I said, 'My aunt wants me to go down to her, but I need someone to drive me down.'

'Down where?'

'Norfolk.' I hesitated, then said blatantly, 'You could stay the weekend.'

'Norfolk? Oh great. You won't mind if I disappear most of the time, will you?'

'What's the attraction?'

'The churches, of course. I haven't seen half of them – only the ones round the Fens.' It was his special subject and I had forgotten. At least the weekend would not be boring for him.

We braved the M25 on a crisp April day and ran thankfully into the country in a blaze of sunshine. We had been chatting about nothing in particular when Robert said suddenly, 'Look, Jan, you didn't hear it from me, but the mag's in trouble. In fact, I've got a new job. I leave at the end of the month.'

It wasn't too much of a shock – the market was overstocked with magazines devoted to gracious living. Every month some ceased publication and new ones started up. I didn't question how he knew – Robert was part of the hierarchy that would hear things first. Instead, I asked about his new job.

'Very hush-hush until the announcement is made. Let's just say it's a different branch of the media. Now what are you going to do? I'd like to have you with me, but I'll have to get my feet under the table first.'

'That's good to know. I might do some freelancing till we see what you can offer me. I suppose the mag will pay me until they have to tell us?'

'I'll see to that. You have a track record and your name's known – freelancing is a good idea.'

We left it at that.

'Just in time for tea,' said Uncle Reg, as we pulled up at a rather violently red brick bungalow. He was fixing trellis on the walls with his usual meticulous care. 'That should take some of the glare off it. Only five years old – still looks far too new.'

Already he looked the complete countryman, spare, tall and brown of face and arms with the leathery tinge that sometimes comes with age. He was fifteen years older than my mother, so that would make him 75 or 76.

Aunt Julia came to the door, hovering as Robert got me out of the back seat and gave me my crutches.

'Come on in. Don't let Reggie keep you, I'm sure you want your tea.'

We went from a spacious hall into a large, comfortable room and I introduced Robert. At her speculative look we both said 'No'

3

and I added, 'He's my boss – not a boyfriend or a lover,' and he added, 'Who happens to have a reasonably comfortable car.'

This brought anxious enquiries from Aunt Julia about my health and much fussing to get me settled. She was so obviously delighted to see us that I forgot any doubts I might have had.

We saw little of Robert the next day, but on Sunday morning he asked if he could take us anywhere – church, perhaps?

'Oh, my dear, we can walk across the fields, even if it is a bit muddy, but we both bought new wellies when we first came,' smiled Aunt Julia. She hesitated with her head on one side and looked at him coyly. 'What I would really like is to visit the nursery and choose some plants – it's not far, but if we go without a car it'll be days before they deliver it and the weather's perfect for planting right now. Besides, it's Easter soon and then they'll be so busy ...'

Robert's car, his pride and joy, filled with plants and their debris ... But he could hardly he refuse now. We took several large, clean plastic bags and I was packed into the back with them.

It was rather more than a nursery – smallholding might be a better description. I gave up any idea of seeing much of it, but there was a small tearoom behind the storeroom and I sat down gratefully with my leg supported on an empty chair.

Aunt Julia grabbed a fair, wiry man and said, 'Simon, I'm so glad it's you. I want clematis for the trellis. We just had to put trellis up on the front to hide that ghastly brickwork – and anything else you can think of. I need ground cover plants – evergreen if possible – once we've got the weeds out of the borders – then some conifers...'

He led the way out while she was still speaking.

Robert looked so pained that I had to laugh, but I said, 'Go after her and persuade her to have the biggest things delivered. She can't plant them all at once, even with Uncle Reg to help.'

'Will you all right?'

I nodded, just as a neat woman in an apron came through from the back. Robert went out gratefully.

'Lor, you have bin in the wars! Do you want something – or just to rest?' She spoke in the distinctive Norfolk accent which was my birthright and which I could still fall into as soon as I got home. I ordered a coffee. She brought it and then lingered.

'How d'you do that then?'

'It was a skiing accident.'

'Thass suffen I wouldn't have the nerve to do.'

4

She was a woman of about 35 and I assumed she was Simon's wife, but presently she said, 'We're that short-handed today. My son usually come in at weekends but he've gone to a Scout Church Parade. My husband, he say, if Jerry want to keep up with his Scouting he should set a example, and Simon agree with him. Course, we'll be up to our eyes come Easter and all the men will come in at weekends.'

'Simon is the chief nurseryman, is he?'

'Bless you, my maid, he own the place. That he do. He allus was the bright one of the family. Won a scholarship to Paston and then went to Agricultural College at Wye. He work hard and he done well, for all he got a bee in his bonnet about that there organic gardening. He's my cousin – three year younger than me but he know a helluva lot more.'

She didn't have to tell me that she had never been far from the village. Not many Norfolk people are that broad in their speech now. By the time the others returned I had learned a good deal about the neighbourhood.

Julia and Reg had been adopted without the resentment of 'foreigners who come in and push the house prices up so our youngsters can't afford them', because both were Norfolk born.

It was on the tip of my tongue to point out that it was the people who sold the houses that set the prices, but I was saved from this foolish tactlessness by a procession bearing plants which were unloaded around the counter.

'Heavens, I thought it was Birnam Wood marching on Dunsinane! Aunt Julia, where are you going to put it all?'

I had thought the garden well stocked, even overgrown, but she turned on me quite fiercely.

'My dear, it's full of marigolds – not French or African – just common marigolds. They're practically weeds – and ground elder and cleavers – and the brambles – I shall need a lot more before I get it respectable. How much is all that, Simon?'

The man at the till, still feeding in the amounts, flashed me a humorous wink as Julia turned to Robert. His dark brown eyes and lopsided smile gave his face a certain charm. It was impossible not to smile back.

'Now don't worry about these big ones. Simon will deliver them next week. If we can just take the fragaria – I know Reggie will say it runs all over the place, but it's easier to control than weeds – it makes nice evergreen rosettes and has bright pink flowers – and the heather and the herbs ...'

Eventually, we got back into the car. They covered my lap with the black bags and piled the plants on them. I sat clutching three clematis with their heads sticking out through the window and enjoyed the spicy smells around me.

After lunch we said goodbye to Robert, who had promised that he would try to let my flat while I was gone. Julia and Reg went into the garden and I wondered what I was going to do for the next six weeks.

I was awoken by my mother and Julia.

'Here she is, Sarah. We've taken good care of her – at least the nice, young man has. Sorry you missed seeing him, even if they both say they're only friends.'

My mother, in her sixtieth year, had the grace and elegance of a much younger woman. I had consciously modelled myself on her and had always admired as well as loved her. When my father died five years ago, a light had gone out of her life, but he had left her well provided for and as soon as she had been able to think straight she had bought the seaside boarding house and taken a catering course 'to keep my sanity'. Now she had been awarded a certificate for supplying healthy food and was doing well enough to afford help.

'Darling,' she said now, 'I'm sorry I couldn't put you up. I'm completely booked up for Easter, but you must come and get some sea air as soon as you can get about. Now what are you going to do while you're here?'

'I don't know ... I was hoping to do some articles for the mag, but Robert says they're in trouble ...' I tried not to sound too sorry for myself.

'It would be a good chance to start that novel you've always wanted to write.'

'I don't know ... I love the research and I can't do any sitting here.' I knew that I was sounding disconsolate, but I had slept awkwardly and woken feeling down. It was not a feeling that my mother would countenance.

She said briskly, 'The Gressenhall Museum of Rural Life isn't far. It used to be a workhouse, you know – fascinating history. Surely someone could take you.'

We were interrupted by Aunt Julia bearing a tea tray. 'That

period's been done to death, what with all these museums and theme parks. I've got a much better idea.

'I was so cross with all that hoo-ha about the 50-year celebrations for the end of the war. They practically ignored the women. Everybody knows they were in the three Services – to say nothing of the Land Army and the nurses and, of course, the volunteer services, but nobody knows about some of the brave and dangerous things they did. It really made my blood boil. Write about them and let's have some recognition before everybody forgets.'

It was the longest coherent speech I had heard Aunt Julia make, though I had realised long ago that, no matter how convoluted her sentences, she never lost the thread of her argument. Now I said feebly, 'I would need to go to the Imperial War Museum for that.'

'Nonsense. I know several local people with stories to tell – starting with me.' Well, it was something to do. I agreed reluctantly to let her wheel in her geriatric neighbours with little hope that they would remember anything worth printing, but I had always wanted to research the birth and growth of feminism, so perhaps I could get something out of it.

Aunt Julia installed me in the summerhouse which was complete with a convector fire, radio and standard lamp, provided a folding table and left me to it. Knowing how she rambled, I decided not to interview her in any formal way, but use her to fill up the gaps in my knowledge.

She had been in the ATS attached to an Ack-Ack battery, serving on the South Coast for most of the war. She was known as a telephonist-plotter and explained her role:

'When an air raid was on, we sat in front of a map of the area. We took map references from HQ on our headphones as to where the enemy planes were and plotted the positions with a cross on the map. The Officer would be prowling around behind us and he would have to decide which to take a crack at. Then the radar girls would give the guns the information they wanted. It was funny, you know – if the guns had been fired the boys had to clean them out before they could go off-duty – it made a very long shift for them, but they were always in good spirits. They only got fed up if they hadn't had a crack at Jerry.'

Gradually, I learned that she had had one failure before she went to the Ack-Ack battery. 'At first I got a wonderful posting. The Isle of

Man on a special signals course. That was because I had been a Girl Guide and knew morse. The Army had the weirdest reasons for what they did with you.'

She had had six months on that beautiful island which the war seemed to have passed by, except for Italian prisoners kept in a group of hotels on the sea front at Douglas.

'There was no rationing and you could get good meals in the YWCA and anything else you wanted. I even sent some of the Manx kippers home. The army meals were terrible there. I heard other girls say it was the same in Ireland where they could get good food outside. Once we had a pie which was stale greens with spud on top – no meat. We were entitled to an egg on Sundays but nobody bothered to get up for it. We could get eggs any time at the YW. Once we had some bread that was really mouldy. The messing Officer said there was nothing wrong with it, so we made her eat some – it got a bit better after that.'

On another occasion she told me how she had failed her final tests.

'I could read morse at speed, but as soon as we got on the machines where there was intercept noise I couldn't get a thing. How these young people can do homework with that music – heavy iron, or whatever they call it – well, I never could. Some of us were offered a hush-hush job and had to decide whether to take it. I decided against as they couldn't tell us anything about it. I know now that it was Bletchley Park – that would have been something to boast about, but then I would never have met Reggie.'

She had met him while training for the Ack-Ack job at Oswestry. She wanted to tell me all about it, but I was less interested in the details of her romance than in the fact that she was still in touch with a woman who had been on both courses with her.

But the first person Julia brought to me had been the village schoolteacher all through the war and for thirty years after. I expected her story to be background – what it was like on the Home Front for the women and very little more. Still, it would be a start.

Some of her story I heard from other people, but most of it came from the small grey lady with big brown eyes which were still lively though she was nearly eighty. Her name was Helen Rae.

That Was Then - Helen's Story

On the train from Liverpool Street to Cromer, Helen had time to think, at last, about the events of the past week.

Tomorrow would be September 3rd, 1939 and she would be twenty-one, but for all that she had only just had her first real holiday, and she had gone on her own. Certainly, the beaches of both Cromer and Sheringham were only a cycle ride from her home. But Eastbourne had been so different.

She had seen the advertisement in a church magazine and had booked to go to a house party for a week, based in a girls' boarding school. It had cost two pounds ten shillings, which was nearly a month's salary for a junior school teacher, but it had been worth saving for.

Apart from the organiser, Mr. Cotman, all the holiday-makers were aged from 17 to 30. They slept in rooms for three and each dormitory had its own bathroom with plenty of hot water on tap. This was luxury for Helen and both her room mates, Deirdre Sullivan from Coleraine and Jean Dixon from London. They all thought that the girls who were pupils here must be utterly spoilt – didn't know how the other half lived, as Deirdre put it.

Jean was tall and dark, with a carriage that might have suggested hauteur, but for her round, good-natured face and a tendency to plumpness. In her teens and early twenties she had gone through all the agonies of dieting and failing to stick to her regime many times, but now, at twenty-seven, she cheerfully accepted herself as she was.

She had grown up in a family where service to others was regarded as the norm and since she agreed wholeheartedly with the idea, seeing it as a natural corollary to her religious beliefs, she invariably became a mother figure to young people and a confidante to everyone.

It took Jean two minutes to recognise that Helen, with her sheltered rural background, was in some ways younger than her twenty years, despite her authority as a teacher. When she learned that it was the younger woman's first holiday on her own, she adopted her immediately.

Deirdre, the third occupant of their dormitory, was an Irish girl with flashing black eyes and a hearty laugh. She was fascinated by the shops in the town and would wander round them for hours if left to herself, though she usually accompanied the other two if they were going out walking.

Mr. Cotman, their leader, was a 30-year-old graduate. He usually held a service on the beach in the mornings when the tide was out. He was a good and amusing preacher and as such attracted a good audience, but Jean still felt in honour bound to go and support him and Helen usually went with her.

'That Mr. Cotman is just right for you,' Deirdre teased Jean after one of these sessions.

'Right for what?'

'Well, marriage, of course.'

'What nonsense will you talk next?' Jean sounded amused. 'You've only got to look at me to see I'll never marry. I've got 'Maiden Aunt' written all over me.'

The weather was perfect. The three women walked the Downs into Alfriston, visited Chichester Cathedral, swam and played cricket on the beach. Best of all, Helen's mind was stretched and stimulated by new people, and she hoped she might have made two real friends. Well, time would tell whether Jean or Deirdre would keep their promises and write to her.

She had been wondering all that week whether she could possibly save twelve pounds to go to Switzerland with the same group next year, but the news bulletins were becoming increasingly ominous.

Then, yesterday, *that* midday broadcast had come. Someone switched off the Home Service and there was a silence. Mr. Cotman muttered 'Poor old Poland' and a thin, nervy girl who chain-smoked sprang up shouting, 'Dear God! When are we going to *do* something? We promised them. What's wrong with this bloody government? I'm ashamed of us, I really am.'

After the first gasp of surprise there were murmurs of agreement. One of the young men said, 'I know. I've felt like that ever since Munich – but it can't be long now. Then we'll show them.'

A boy everyone called Ginger spoke urgently, 'I'll have to leave today. I'm in the Terriers. There'll be call-up papers at home, I expect.'

Some of the other young men agreed. Most of them seemed to be in the Territorial Army, but one was in the RAF volunteer service.

'OK, we'll find out about trains and get you to the station right away,' Mr. Cotman promised. 'Now, about the rest of you. I can't take responsibility for anyone under twenty-one. Some people would be going home tomorrow anyway and I really think we all ought to go. Trains will soon be packed with troops and some of you have got very long journeys.'

Deirdre said, 'I certainly don't want to miss the last boat to Belfast.'

It was agreed that they should all go home after breakfast the next day and Mr. Cotman had a final word with them.

'I think you'll all agree we've had a wonderful week. Lovely weather, visits to beautiful places, good fellowship – something to thank God for. Something to remember, whatever lies ahead. Now let's forget what we've just heard and make the most of our last day. Campfire on the Downs tonight. Sausages on sticks – cooked by you. Nothing will ever taste so good again – I promise you.'

They laughed and went off to make plans for the afternoon. Soon Helen was striding along the cliff-top with Jean and Deirdre. She remembered that they had heard and seen a lark. Jean had said it was a skylark and Helen had corrected her.

'No, it's a woodlark. Skylarks warble, they don't sing like that.'

They watched the bird fly out of a bush and spiral wider and higher. Deirdre was entranced. 'I never heard that before,' she marvelled, and Helen told her that they didn't go very far north, only getting to Norfolk in the summer. Then Jean and Deirdre teased Helen about knowing so much and being a proper old schoolmarm.

Yes, it had all been good. Helen smiled at the memory.

The journey to London was hilarious as most of the house-party were on the train. One or two of the girls were worried about their boyfriends and relations, but the boys were in roaring high spirits and refused to let them get despondent.

But once they had parted, reality broke in. Liverpool Street station, always busy, was now packed with young men, many in the uniforms of all three Forces and many more in civilian clothes. She sensed that they all shared a feeling – what was it? Not just excitement, nor fear – determination, that was it and, yes, relief that it had come at last. For surely the declaration of war must now be imminent. She thought of the girl who had asked 'When are we going to *do* something?' and realised that many people must have been feeling the same. The time for appeasement was past – the British have never been good at it – now there would be action.

Still, Helen thought, it would make very little difference to her life. Her cousin, Philip, was already in the regular RAF and other young men she knew would be joining up, but school teachers would be exempt from service. In her quiet country village, life would go on much as before.

Later she was to wonder how she could have been so naive. Nothing was ever the same again.

She saw Cromer Top station with a sigh of relief. It had seemed a long day, waiting about for trains and the bus to cross London, and then being squashed into a crowded train. But now she only had the three-mile cycle ride home.

Bob, the station porter, brought out her bike and asked about her holiday. Then he said, 'I am glad to see you. I'm going into the Royal Navy.'

'Are you, Bob? So soon?'

'Well, I was in the Reserve. We get called first. Dad gave me a message for your mum. Tell her to bring a big bag on Monday. He says we're bound to get rationing and he's going to make sure the staff have some groceries put by.'

Helen thanked him, wished him luck and cycled home.

Ken Rae had been invalided out of the Army, badly gassed, in 1916 and it had seemed unlikely that he would live long enough to father a child. So his wife, Sophie, thought it a miracle when Christmas 1917 saw him nearly well and soon after that she discovered she was pregnant.

Helen had been born the following September. Two months later, her father fell victim to the epidemic of Spanish 'flu which swept the country in 1918.

Sophie, who had long been the breadwinner, continued as a cashier at a large grocery store in Cromer, leaving the child with her sister, Ellen Lambert, who lived at the other end of the village.

It had been a struggle to bring up her daughter on her own, even though the rent for her cottage was small. It was one of two adjoining houses belonging to the Church Commissioners. They stood at the end of a long loke, well off the road and with plenty of land to cultivate. Sophie's brother-in-law Joe and her old neighbour had helped her to keep them in vegetables, but after old George died, the cottage had stood empty. Now it was to be let again to evacuees.

Sophie greeted Helen with the news. 'Sally is organising the evacuees. They've been arriving in droves while you've been away. I expect we'll have to take some.'

'What are they like?'

Sophie raised her eyes to heaven as if asking for strength. 'Mostly from the East end of London. I can't understand them – I suppose they can't understand us. The teachers that came with them seem to be able to keep them in order. Some of them look a bit doleful – never been away from home before. Oh, well, it's too soon to tell. They'll settle down, I expect.'

Helen was thoughtful. Next term was certainly going to be different – and challenging.

* * * * *

'Sally Wood is coming to see you tonight,' Aunt Ellen told her sister. 'We've agreed to take a mother and child in the back bedroom.'

'They'll have to go through yours – won't that be awkward?'

'Yes, but it's better than the other way round. We might wake the child.'

'Do you know where they're coming from?'

Ellen's warm, freckled face lit up with amusement. 'Yarmouth, I'm glad to say. At least they'll understand what we're talking about.'

'What happens when Philip comes home on leave?'

'I'll warn him. He'll have to sleep downstairs.'

Ellen's face looked worried. Her only son had joined the regular RAF as a photographer and reconnaissance expert, but she knew that he intended to volunteer for flying duties now that war had been declared.

It was the afternoon of Helen's 21st birthday and Sophie had arranged a little tea party to mark the occasion. All of those present had heard Mr. Chamberlain's speech that morning with no very great surprise, and had resolved to put it out of their minds for the rest of the day. That they had not succeeded was evident by the conversation, which avoided the subject directly but was full of related matters.

Stephen and Molly Painter, Ellen's next door neighbours, were talking to Uncle Joe about putting more of their gardens under vegetables, but he was reluctant to dig up his prize dahlias.

'Got to have something to keep our hearts up. We won't starve. Better off than townspeople.'

'We are that,' Stephen said. 'I'll have a word with the Squire tomorrow – see if we can do something about a pig. It'd keep us going for a while. I like a bit o' salt pork – and bacon.'

Uncle Joe looked doubtful. His meagre wages wouldn't stretch to the price of half a pig. But Helen had overheard. She said quickly, 'That's a great idea, Mr. Painter – perhaps we could split it three ways.' She smiled reassuringly at Uncle Joe. 'If you can arrange to get it cured ... ?'

Molly nodded. 'My brother in Sheringham would do that for us. Have to let him have a bit, of course.'

George Barker, Helen's headmaster, and his wife Sarah, were talking to Laura Thompson. The man's dark head towered over the two women, his bulk emphasised by the broad shoulders of the rugby player he had been with some distinction in his younger days. He owned a small car, but cycled everywhere on a high-seated ladies' bike, which looked as though it must buckle under his weight. His kind blue eyes looked down at Laura, courteously giving the village gossip all his attention.

Laura was fifty and looked sixty, partly because of her permanently aggrieved expression and her querulous voice. The village accepted her as villagers do, being sorry for her loneliness. They invited her to anything that was going on, knowing full well that she had a formidable will and would turn up anyway, and they mostly disregarded her gossip even though it was sometimes justified.

Now she was saying, 'I run the village post office in the last war – ah, and delivered telegrams too. That was awful. I knowed people dreaded me coming. And there was more than just the war casualties, as they called 'em. Ah, and there's more 'un one sort o' casualty. I mind one I delivered the Christmas after Armistice. It told this woman her man had taken up with a French girl and weren't coming back to her. She looked at me with tears streaming down her face and said, 'I'd rather it said he'd been killed.' Ah, there'll be plenty o' that this time too.'

George replied, 'That's what war does. It ruins lives in all sorts of ways. We're lucky in the country, though. We shouldn't be affected too much. Why, I remember when I got back from the last war, most of the civilians had no idea what it had been like for us.'

His face clouded and Sarah said quickly, 'It can hardly be like that this time, George. Not with all these new planes.'

He smiled down at her. 'Of course not – but we shan't see much of them, nothing worth bombing here. They might go for Norwich, or the docks.'

The door latch clicked and a fair girl of about fourteen appeared. 'Mum – sorry, Mrs. Rae – but them kids are fighting again and I can't understand a word they say.'

'Oh, lor, I better go and sort them out. See you tomorrow, Sophie, and thanks for the tea.'

Molly and Stephen left to 'sort out' their evacuees.

Soon after, the others went too. Sophie and Helen cleared up and sat down to wait for Sally Wood, the Squire's wife, who was still trying to find homes for people who wanted to get out of London.

Their house had two bedrooms, separated by the stairs. There was no bathroom and the lavatory was a shed in the garden, covered with ivy and honeysuckle which harboured insects. Helen and Sophie had a bedroom each, but would have to share a room if they were having evacuees. Fresh from her experience of proper bathrooms and plenty of hot water, Helen wondered how they would adapt.

'They'll be told 'There's a war on', I expect. That's what they kept saying last time if anybody grumbled,' Sophie said.

When Sally arrived Helen was struck, as always, by her tall, elegant figure clothed in the beautifully cut tweeds which had seen better days and which she always wore around the village. She looked the epitome of the Squire's lady, but there the resemblance ended. Although she had enormous influence, being the President of the Women's Rural Institute and the Chief Guide for the area, she liked to be called by her Christian name, thought nothing of mucking out the pigs if necessary and generally acted as if she were an ordinary villager.

Now she accepted a cup of tea, kicked her shoes off and produced a parcel for Helen and a birthday card. To the girl's delight, her present was a proper bag for her school books, very smart and capacious, and not to be compared with the old satchel she had been using. When they had discussed Helen's holiday, Sally said, 'Well, down to business. You're both at work all day and we've seen what havoc some of these London mums and kids can cause. What do you say to having a Land Girl? She'll only be here when you are – and anyway, I know her people. You'll be all right with Heather Francis.'

Sophie said, 'That's a lot better than we expected. Thank you, Sally.'

'Is she from farming people?' Helen asked.

'No. Her father Alan's a stockbroker, but Heather's mad on horses. She's always wanted a country life.'

'What about baths? Can she come to you for them?' Helen asked, thinking of the luxury of her holiday accommodation.

'Yes, of course. But I don't think she'll want to come to us every night after a hard day's work. Is it going to be an awful chore for you to heat the water for her?'

'No, but it's a bit infra dig for her – a tin bath in the kitchen – after what she's used to.'

'She's not asking for special treatment. I offered to take her as one of my evacuees, but she wouldn't have it.'

'I'm afraid she'll find it a bit primitive.'

'She's prepared for that and she's adaptable. Her father told her she wouldn't stick it through the first winter and that put her back up. My money's on Heather.'

When Molly and Stephen Painter reached home, they found Elisabeth Winter alone. She looked red-eyed and miserable but seemed unhurt. Stephen asked, 'Where's your brother?'

'I dunno. Wally went out.'

He turned to Molly. 'I'll go and find him. Have to leave this to you.'

Molly called upstairs to her young daughter, 'Make us a cup of tea, Joyce, while I talk to Elisabeth.' She sat down beside the skinny girl. 'What's been happening, my dear? We want you to be happy here. Are you missing your mother?'

The girl shrugged. 'I'm fourteen. I left school. They shouldn't of sent me away. I oughta be earning. There's nothing to do here and I ain't got a farthing.'

'There's a lot to do here, Elisabeth.'

'For God's sake, call me Liz.'

'Very well, but if you go back to school when they start next week, you'll get to know other girls and make friends.'

'Not bloody likely, I don't. Go back to bleedin' school again? Never.'

Joyce came in with a tea-tray and Molly sighed and poured tea for the three of them. 'Joyce, couldn't you let ... Liz ... meet some of your friends and join in whatever you're doing?'

Her daughter looked unenthusiastic. 'We can't understand what they say, Mum. Sometimes I think they talk in a secret language on purpose.'

'Her? She don't like me,' Liz broke in. 'It's *her* bedroom, not mine – Miss Toffee-nose. She'd be glad if I went home.'

'That's not fair! I have tried, Mum. The vicar said we should be friendly because they're a long way from home, but she won't be friends and,' Joyce added, suddenly vindictive, 'she leaves her stuff all over the place, not just her side of the bed, and some of it's none too clean.'

Outside, Stephen had found Wally. He was beating his fists into the trunk of a bullace tree, sending down a shower of little round, black plums that were Molly's favourites for making jam.

'Stop that!' Stephen shouted.

Wally swung round, red-faced and startled. 'I ain't doing no harm,' he growled.

'Use your eyes, boy. Look at all that fruit on the ground. You'll be glad to eat that before this war's over.'

'I ain't never see no fruit like that – an' I helped in the Garden plenty times.'

'You mean Covent Garden? Did you then?' Stephen picked up a handful of bullaces and held them out to the boy. 'Here. Try these. And when you finish them, you can pick up all the others and bring them in. Save us a job.' He turned to go and then swung round. 'We want you to fit in here. It might be years before it's safe for you to go home. We'll treat you right if you treat us right. No more fighting with your sister and don't be so ready with your fists – or you'll feel mine, and that's a promise.'

Left alone, the twelve-year-old put the plums into his mouth. Several were unripe and he spat them out in disgust. Frustrated and angry, he began to beat the tree again, without considering that there would be more fruit for him to pick up.

Like his sister, he had been in the habit of earning money when he was not at school – which was never more often than he could

17

help. There were always jobs to be had around the London markets. His father had a clothes stall in Petticoat Lane and he knew a lot of the traders.

He wasn't missing his friends. There were some down here but most of the boys he knew well had been in competition for the same jobs and street fights were commonplace. There was no fun here, no fights, nothing to do, no chance to earn money. And if he did, he asked himself angrily, what was there to buy in this place, where there wasn't even a fish and chip shop?

On the first day of the autumn term Helen went into school with the sense of anticipation which she had never lost. She loved her job and looked forward to seeing all the children together after the long summer break.

Her lessons were carefully planned to stimulate their young minds and she was quick to appreciate all the odd, quirky things they said and did, so that they were a constant source of surprise and delight to her.

This term there would be the challenge of the evacuees. She knew they would be feeling strange and lost and thanked heaven that one of their own teachers was with them. Joyce Painter had told Helen all about Liz and Wally Winter and she had heard other stories from women who were housing their schoolmates. Most of the grumbles had been about food. The London children would not eat fresh vegetables from the gardens or rabbit pies and were disgusted that there was not so much as a fish and chip shop. Some of the village people were sympathetic because the children were so far from home and it was obvious that some of them were really homesick, but others seemed to care very little and only wanted to cause as much trouble as possible.

Helen had dealt with disruptive children and knew that she would have excellent support from George Barker, so she was not unduly worried. But by the first break she knew that she was facing her greatest challenge yet.

She was sitting by the open window when she became aware that the usual playground noise had died down. She was alert at once. Now who was being bullied? The next moment there was a scream and she rushed out to find one of the village boys sprawled on the hard asphalt. He got up at once as she approached and

18

said, 'It's nothing, Miss.' He had skinned his knees, but was otherwise unhurt and was glaring at Wally.

'Go and wash your knees now. I'll put something on them when they're clean.'

They had fallen silent, but as Helen turned away, Wally yelled 'Country bumpkins! Clodhoppers! Know-nothings!'

The village children regarded him stolidly. He was a big boy, well-built and tall for his age, with large hands. They saw no reason to pick a fight with him.

'Don't even stick up for yourselves. Right lot of Charlies!' he goaded.

Then there was some jostling which the village boys returned. Before the situation could get out of hand, George Barker was bellowing and erupting into the playground. Dealing out boxes on the ears right and left, he restored a sulky peace. 'All right. If you've got that much energy we'll use some of it up. Get into three lines – quick.'

'But it's our playtime,' one of them objected.

'Didn't look like play to me – but all right, we'll make it a bit of fun.'

He took them through a brisk version of 'O'Grady says', catching out as many evacuees as village children. The girls beat the boys in both categories. Wally was one of the boys still left in at the end. Dismissing them for the next lesson, George said, 'Well, when it comes to being quick-witted there's not much to choose between country and town. As for how much you know – the exams will sort that out.'

He drew Wally aside. 'It seems you consider you know more than the village boys. You may be right. If so, there's a good way of proving it. Come top of the class and I'll be delighted to present you with the prize.'

George grinned as Wally scowled his way back into class.

Helen was nursing the fire in the living room by holding up a sheet of newspaper in front of the grate when she heard the kitchen door open. It was too early for Sophie, so she said, 'Damn', abandoned the paper and went to see who was there. She had not yet lit the oil lamp and, in the fading October light, it took her a minute to register that one of the two women was Sally.

'Sorry if we've come at a bad time, Helen, but Heather's just arrived and I have a committee meeting in Cromer.'

'Of course – that's all right, but I won't shake hands – I'm filthy – trying to get the fire to go, but you're very welcome.'

She lit the lamp and the two girls regarded each other, smiling.

'I'm good at fires – camping you know – let me have a go presently.' Heather's voice was low-pitched and friendly.

She was above average height with a rangy, athletic body and narrow waist. She had long, straight hair which shone in the lamplight, framing a pink and white complexion and grey eyes. Somehow Helen could not see this lovely girl coping with farm work, despite what Sally had said.

'Oh, were you a Girl Guide? We're looking for a Lieutenant for my pack. I hope you'll join us. You'll find our fire more temperamental than camp ones, but the range is OK – we'll have a cuppa in no time.' Helen moved the kettle over to the fire where it began to sing. 'Do sit down and make yourself at home, Heather. Thank you for bringing her, Sally. I know how busy you are. Have you got time for tea?'

'Well, I couldn't let her get lost – but, no tea. My meeting's in' – she glanced at her watch – 'Heavens! Half an hour. I must fly.' Sally gave Heather a quick kiss, said, 'You'll be all right with Helen' and ran.

'If you don't mind eating in here for tonight, I'll forget about the other fire,' Helen said doubtfully. 'This is always the warmest room.'

'This is lovely and cosy. If I were you, I wouldn't live anywhere else in the winter.'

'We don't,' Helen admitted, 'and everyone comes in at the kitchen door. I can't remember when the front door, which is round the back, was last opened. But it'll be a bit of a squash to eat here when my mother gets home.'

'Sally told me she works in Cromer and never knows what time she'll finish, so what do you do about meals?'

'I have a cup of tea when I get in from school, but in future I'll have it with you. You should be finished at five, unless there's something that has to be done. Then I'll make our main meal about 7.30 and we'll eat and keep Mum's hot in the oven.'

Heather stirred and looked uncomfortable, then faced Helen with a wide smile and said, 'I'm really asking because I'm ravenous. The London train was ever so late and I knew Sally had to go out, so I said nothing.'

When Sophie came in there was the good smell of a hot meal, but she saw the two girls still sitting over the remnants of tea and toast. They were chattering as though they had known each other all their lives.

That night, Uncle Joe came in on his way to the shop with the day's takings.

'This is my brother-in-law, Mr. Lambert,' Sophie told Heather. 'Joe, this is our lodger, Heather. She's in the Land Army.'

Joe looked at the immaculate girl and said, with a rueful smile, 'I can't shake hands, Miss. They smell of paraffin. I hope you'll take to the work and settle down with us. We aren't so bad once you get to know us.'

They all laughed and Sophie thought that Joe must be taken with the girl to say so much. In truth, he was horrified at the thought of this lady coping with all the dirty jobs on the farm.

He made it his business to see Stephen that night. 'Will you keep an eye on her? I know some of the men were against having girls. They'll likely try to get their own back. Mind, Stephen, I'm not saying they'll be as good as the men, but they ought to have a fair chance.'

'I'll put her right about a few things. Davey don't want Land Girls, I know – and he's none too pleasant to anybody these days – ever since his son joined up.'

Stephen introduced himself to Heather on her first day and told her to come to him if she had any trouble.

'There's one mean old sow – whatever she do, don't you punish her, or she'll allus have it in for you. Memory like a elephant too.'

Heather said warmly, 'That's really kind of you, but I'm not scared of pigs – or rats – though I don't like the idea of being chased by a bull.'

'No need to worry about them if they're in a field with the cows. They're on their best behaviour then.'

She came home on that first day looking like a ghost. She was covered in meal and flour and explained that she had been bagging up the cattle feed into rations, along with a girl called Aggie Taylor.

'She's only been here a month but she seems to know her way

around. She said we were lucky to be in a nice warm barn – it's only a weekly job, so we'll be out in the cold tomorrow. Now I must have a good wash – I've got cattle feed down to my toes. Can I put some water on to heat?'

'Well, hadn't you better have a bath? Sally did say you could go up to her ...'

'Heavens, I'm too tired to go trailing up there. What do you do?'

Helen decided it was best to be brutally frank. 'Tin bath in front of the kitchen range on a Saturday night. It takes a lot of water so Mum gets in after me – or vice versa – and strip wash in a basin the rest of the week.'

'Good – that'll do me nicely.'

'Oh no, you can have a bath every night. It's no trouble.'

Heather protested, but she usually found the hot water waiting for her.

'They're really good to me,' she told Sally. 'They go to no end of trouble to make sure I'm not deprived of all my home comforts.'

The next day they were picking up potatoes from the rows that had been turned up. It was hard work and they had been at it since 7am.

Heather stretched up and rubbed her aching back, then looked ruefully at her hands. The dirt was ingrained in her skin and under her nails.

Aggie smiled. 'You'll get used to it. Wait till we start sprout picking. The men say they get so cold they carry a tin bucket with coals in it along the rows to stop their fingers freezing. Never mind, it's gone four – time to call it a day.'

It was bitterly cold and the December light was fading fast. Helen put the poker in the fire, waiting for the damped down heat to blaze up again. Heather would probably come in frozen from the icy field. It was so near Christmas that Sophie's shop was extra busy and she had arranged to sleep at her Aunt Molly's in Cromer, since it was likely to be midnight before she finished cashing up. Helen put the kettle back on the stove as soon as she heard the door open.

Heather came in, dropped her dinner box on the table and moved at once to the fire, stretching out her hands.

'Don't,' said Helen quickly, 'you'll get chilblains. Here, let me,' and she dried the wet, cold hands and began to rub them gently.

'Thanks. My favourite job – picking sprouts with ice on them. Why must people have sprouts for their Christmas dinner?'

Helen smiled and passed her a cup of tea. 'Here, warm you hands on that. I've got some lentil soup for later.'

If Heather was grateful to Sophie and Helen, they were no less impressed by the way she had adapted to farm work and their home conditions. She had often come in exhausted or, as now, with a pinched, red nose and chilled to the bone, but had never complained.

'I'm determined to get Bob Davey to admit that girls can do the jobs as well as men,' she had told them.

Davey, complaining in the Haymakers about having to take the girls, had said, 'How are we expected to feed the country like that? Well, they'll have to do the same as the men, or there'll be trouble.' It was known that he gave the girls the worst jobs, despite having older men who had been used to such work all their lives. What amazed Helen was that Heather's privileged background had not only made no difference, but it seemed that she had welcomed the chance to escape from it.

'Dad would smother me if I let him,' Heather had once confided to her. 'He's worse than my mother. She's got an exclusive fashion shop and thank the Lord, she's too busy to worry. I had a fight to leave home, but he couldn't stop me once I was twenty-one.'

The two young women were already great friends. Heather was quick to appreciate the genuine warmth of Helen and her mother, shown by the many little kindnesses which made her new life less hard. She rejoiced in Helen's quick sense of humour and the way she savoured the odd things the children said and did, saving the anecdotes to pass on each night.

After a while, Heather got up, saying, 'I'm done this side, are you?'

They changed seats, Helen scowling at the scorch marks on her legs. 'I do envy you, wearing trousers.'

'Yes, they're very comfortable – when they aren't wet through.'

Presently they prepared their meal and started to talk about Christmas. Helen had written the nativity play and was now engaged in writing a pantomime for the New Year. Suddenly, she began to laugh.

'Charlie White didn't come to school until after eleven and then his mother was with him. I don't suppose you know her. She's enormous. She came panting up, dragging Charlie behind her. When she could speak, she said (here Helen's voice dropped into the vernacular), 'I'm right sorry he's late. I been that flummoxed this morning. I turned round and got the others off and, help my Bob, I just turned round and made a cup of tea and sat down for a minute, then I turned round and went to make the bed and there he was, fast asleep, in the middle of it.' '

'How could she have missed him?'

'She's got six more and they all share the same bed.'

Heather was quiet for a long time. 'Some of these people are very poor, aren't they?'

'Well, yes, I suppose so. We're all in the same boat. Agricultural wages are low, but we don't starve because every house has plenty of land to grow vegetables. I'm lucky because I'll be earning fairly well in my job, but look at Uncle Joe. He's out in all weathers delivering paraffin round the villages – then he has to see to his horse morning and night – and all for a few shillings a week. Their evacuees will help them financially and I think Philip sends them money when he can. The money for evacuees will help a lot of people, but it's the ones like Mrs. White and Mrs. Dennis who haven't got room for any who'll lose out. Most people can't afford to do more than feed their families and they buy what they have to have from catalogues, paying so much a week.'

Helen liked her new neighbour, Joan Dennis, a quiet, shy woman of about thirty-five. She was making a good job of bringing up four children on her own while her husband, Paul, was in the Army. They had been evacuated from London and, Helen guessed, from a good school. They were bright and well-mannered and George Barker thought they were all scholarship material.

She began to explain all this to Heather, but was interrupted.

'Look, Helen, Sally said something about organising a Christmas dance. Could we combine it with a useful present – food, coal, whatever? I don't want to seem patronising but I would like to do something – they needn't know it came from me.'

'Why don't you speak to Sally? If they thought it was coming from the Squire they'd take it gladly – especially if they were told it was because of the war.'

Presently, they had their meal and settled down for the evening. The paraffin lamp gave them just enough light for Heather to write home and Helen to work on the school pantomime.

'What are you going to call it?' Heather indicated the script.

'*Aladdin and the Forty Thieves.*'

'Shouldn't it be Ali Baba?'

'Oh, no, that's far too ordinary. If I have Aladdin, Mr. Barker can be the Genie of the Lamp. The kids love to see the teachers making fools of themselves. Then the forty thieves will give all the children a part – if you don't count too closely! If we get any more evacuees, I may have to write for a cast of a hundred next year.' Helen suddenly smiled. 'I've just had an idea. Jim – he's our vicar – he's got a nice tenor. It would be fun to write a part in for him.'

She shut the papers away, stood up and yawned enormously. 'I'm for bed.' After dampening the fire down, she made sure the doors were locked and lit a candle.

'Oh, by the way,' she said to Heather, 'my cousin Philip will be home for Christmas. You'll like him, I think.'

Heather had decided to go home for Christmas Day and Boxing Day only, so that she could go to the dance and the nativity play.

On the night of the play, Helen was busy behind the scenes so Heather sat beside Ellen, who gave her a running commentary. With them sat Mrs. Grice, Ellen's evacuee, a thin little woman with an air of constant anxiety. Ellen had explained to Heather, 'She's a nice person and we get on well, but she's torn between staying here with her little Rosie, and the rest of her family in Yarmouth. Her husband's a fisherman and she's got twin boys. Their school wasn't evacuated and they wouldn't come here, so their grandmother is feeding them all. She's found it hard, this bad weather, not being able to go and see them, but they're both going home for Christmas.'

'It should be safe enough. There's nothing happening, is there? I'm not surprised some of the London people have gone home.'

The nativity play, despite its religious theme, was hilarious. Apart from the minor errors, forgotten lines and mislaid props, the contrast between the Norfolk and Cockney accents had the whole audience suppressing laughter.

'That's Joyce Painter, playing Mary. They're our neighbours, you know – Molly and Stephen. Joyce is nearly fourteen. She's pretty, isn't she?'

Onstage, the graceful blonde gave a realistic stagger and gasped, 'Joseph, my man, I must rest.'

Wally Winter replied by leading her at a gallop to a baize-covered settle. 'Course you must, gal. Stay here. Oh, Gawd!' He went running off the stage.

Ellen whispered, 'He's a little terror. Helen can't do a thing with him. He's a real Cockney and thinks our kids are sissy because they're not always fighting.'

Presently, the baby was born and the angels appeared to the shepherds. The latter were identically dressed in striped deckchair material and looked very much alike, which was not surprising as they were four of Mrs. White's boys.

Among the angels were two little cherubs. Their plump, childish limbs and solemn baby faces brought an immediate murmur of appreciation from the audience. Mrs. Grice sat up straight and Heather assumed that one of them was Rosie. They stood shyly, eyes down, until the music started. Then they sang the first verse of *Away in a Manger* in high treble voices and all trooped off the stage. Under the wave of applause, Heather said warmly,

'What lovely little girls. How old is Rosie, Mrs. Grice?'

'She's four-and-a-half. You can see why her father wouldn't risk her staying at home.'

'And she's as sweet as she looks,' Ellen said. 'I've never seen a happier, more contented child. She's well named.'

Mrs. Grice glowed, her pinched face suddenly flushed with colour. 'You'd think she'd be spoilt with two older brothers and her father and grandma all doting on her – but she really isn't.'

At this stage, the three Wise Men came on all together, jostled for position and nearly dropped one of the offerings. Then there was an unexpectedly touching climax. As the kings knelt at the crib they were followed by children representing the five continents of the world. Finally came a Cub, a Brownie, a Scout and a Guide. Each in turn knelt to the baby while they sang *O, Come All Ye Faithful*. Heather had to swallow before she could join in with the rest of the audience.

* * * * *

'Old Billy Bates was in the Haymakers tonight.' Stephen was pulling off his boots, preparing for bed. Molly shot a look at Wally, but he was absorbed in a comic.

'That old scoundrel – what was he having to say for hisself?'

'The usual. We were daft to bother about rationing when there's game and rabbits to be had for nuthen. Mocking us for being feared

26

of Squire. He'd had a bit too much, but not so he didn't know to shut up when Bob Davey come in.'

Wally pricked up his ears. An old scoundrel who caught rabbits sounded just up his alley – might get a bit of fun here, after all.

He didn't have long to wait. On the following Tuesday, about half way along the country road between school and home, an unmistakable figure appeared. Wally knew him by sight but had never spoken to him.

He was a wiry old man, very erect, with a billycock hat pulled low over his face. He wore a very old jacket several sizes too big for him and carried a stout stick which he was switching at the hedges as he trudged along.

'Evenin', Mr. Bates,' Wally called out to him.

The old man stopped abruptly in surprise, summed up the sturdy boy, and smiled. 'Well now, thass a nice greetin'. I take that very kindly. You be the boy woz stayin' with the Painters. How do you like it?'

'It's OK – bit quiet – nuffin to do here.' Wally paused, then said meaningfully, 'Is there?'

'We-ell, I don't know as how I'd say that. How'd you like to come out wi' me some night? Can you get out on your own? Not say nothin' to them?'

'Easy – any time. I sleep downstairs. Tonight?'

'No – moon's too bright. Be about two weeks, I reckon, but I'll see you afore then.'

In the days that followed, Billy warned Wally to bring a torch, but not to use it near the houses and to wear plenty of warm clothes. They could start at 10pm. Farming communities were up early and would all be in bed by then.

The old man chose a pitch dark night, dry but bitterly cold. Wally crept out, locking the back door behind him and pocketing the key. He had often been out much later than this in London, but it felt much more adventurous in the country, with not a light to be seen and only the occasional hoot of an owl piercing the night silence. He was not yet attuned to the small sounds of the nocturnal animals, but he felt a thrill of excitement as he passed the last of the houses.

* * * * *

When he unlocked the back door again soon after 1am, Wally

27

had learned more in that three hours of country craft than he might have learnt in three years without the tuition of such a clever poacher as Billy. Their expedition had been successful and he was exultant. Quietly, he put the dead pheasant into the pantry. Molly would have a nice surprise in the morning. Billy had said that they were better eating than chickens any day.

'Much more taste to 'em. They need to be hung first – then they're fit for kings.'

All Wally had understood of the need for secrecy was that the pheasants could only be caught by night and that there might be other people after them, so you crept about, made sure you didn't step on twigs, and kept a sharp look-out. When Billy had stopped inside the wood and stood still until they had got their night sight, Wally had asked, 'Where did you learn all this?'

The old man allowed himself a quiet chuckle. 'Now thass a rum 'un. The Boy Scouts – thass where I larned a lot. My old dad taught me to catch pheasants without a gun.'

The Scouts! Wally had been asked to join and had refused scornfully. Perhaps he should think again.

The night had been so full of new experiences that it was an hour before he dropped off to sleep. Three hours later, Stephen Painter was shaking him awake and demanding, 'Where were you last night? Where d'you get that pheasant? I'll have no thieves in my house.'

Wally scrambled up, rubbing his eyes. Stephen stood watching him and glowering.

'What d'yer mean? I never stole it. Them birds don't belong to nobody. I thought you'd be pleased.' Wally was beginning to get indignant. This was a nice reception after all the trouble he'd taken to get them all something to eat.

Stephen said, 'Course they belong to somebody. Where did you go? Which wood?' But Wally didn't know. 'Who'd you go with?'

Wally stuck his chin out. 'I don't split on my friends.'

'Get dressed. We'll go and see what Joe has to say.'

When they got to Joe's house, the first thing he asked was, 'If you didn't think it was wrong, why did you sneak out and not tell anybody?'

'I was told to.'

'You weren't threatened?'

'No!' Wally was indignant. 'He wouldn't do that. He was kind –

28

showin' me a bit o' fun – first time I had any here,' he added accusingly.

Stephen and Joe exchanged looks. 'Ten chances to one it was Billy. I reckon that belong to Squire,' said Joe.

Stephen was grim-faced. 'Right. He come with me when I go to work and take that pheasant back. We'll see what the gaffer have to say.'

In the event, it was Sally who saw the culprit and she quickly realised that Wally had no idea of the situation.

'These are our birds, Wally. The man who took you out was stealing. He knew it, even if you didn't. This time you can take the pheasant back to Mrs. Painter, but if it happens again you'll be in trouble with the police. Do you understand?'

'No I don't, missus. How can wild birds belong to you? Not like budgies, are they? My gran got a budgie – my dad bought it for her – paid good money. That's different.'

Sally shook her head and tried again. 'You know lots of people keep hens in the country. They feed them and look after them. That's what we do with the pheasants.'

'What? In the woods? You don't go feeding 'em in the woods?'

'Yes, we do. Or, at least we employ a keeper to do it for us. He looks after them from the eggs until they're fully grown. Another of his jobs is to go after people like Billy Bates to stop them poaching our game, so don't you go with him again. If Mr. Skipper caught you, he'd take you straight to the police, so stay off our land in future.'

Wally asked defensively, 'How's anybody s'posed to know it's yours? It just look like fields to me.'

Sally said gently, 'You've got a lot to learn, Wally. Whether it's in the town or the country, most land belongs to somebody. Ask the village boys if you don't know. Now, off you go – I've got things to do.'

Wally went reluctantly, wanting to argue, and turned at the door to say, 'I bet you don't feed them rabbits.'

Early on the morning of the dance, Heather was driving the milk cart up to the stands where the milkmen would collect their loads.

Ellen Lambert had a churn and a half-pint measure, as she sold milk to the neighbours at her end of the village. Heather unloaded this churn and got back into the cart. Then she heard a shout and looked round to see Joe beckoning her. She stopped but didn't attempt to dismount again. Her horse was restive this morning, fidgeting every time she stopped and starting off so abruptly that she had twice been in danger of falling back into the milk churns.

Joe came up and behind him was a young man in an RAF uniform which bore the insignia of a Warrant Officer.

'Philip came home last night. I just wanted him to meet you.' This was a long speech for Joe.

Philip was a tall man of perhaps thirty. He had his mother's carroty hair and freckled face and an odd quirky smile that owed nothing to his parentage. But when he spoke it was in Joe's deep, slow voice.

'You're Aunt Sophie's lodger. Helen told me about you. How do you do?'

'I'm pleased to meet you, but I daren't stop. Dobbin's fed up this morning. He just wants to get on.'

The man stroked the horse's neck and said, 'Hello, Charlie. We're old friends, aren't we?' But the beast threw up its head and moved impatiently.

'OK, I'll see you at the dance tonight. So long.'

He sketched a salute and picked up the churn. Joe gave Heather his slow smile and followed his son.

Indoors, Philip said, 'What a looker! Pity she's a cut above us.'

Joe exchanged glances with Ellen and went to fetch his horse and cart.

Ellen said, 'Heather's father's well off, but she sets little store by that. She's fitted in well down here.' Then she added, 'You've got yourself a good job and had a good education – Nelson's old school – I don't think anybody's a cut above you.'

He kissed the top of her head and murmured, 'You're prejudiced, Mum, but thanks anyway' and took the bucket outside to fill at the well.

As clearly as if she were seeing the scene for the first time, Ellen pictured the eleven-year-old Philip, already shooting out of his clothes, standing in the doorway and saying sheepishly, 'Mum, I done a stupid thing.'

'What's that, son?'

'I got a scholarship to Paston Grammar School.'

Suddenly, it hadn't mattered that she was worn out with trying to stretch money, or that it would be years more before he was earning. He would have a better life than them. Thank God.

As Philip came back in with his bucket full, he was caught by the brightness of her smile, but she only said, 'I'm sorry Dad roused you so early this morning. I told him to be quiet and not disturb you.'

Philip grinned. 'Oh, he crept about all right, but he couldn't resist giving me a cup of tea at half past five. I can't remember a time when he didn't. He thinks it's the proper time to start the day.'

'Well, you can have a rest when he's gone. I don't call Mrs. Grice until eight, unless Rosie wakes.'

'Oh, no. I'm going the rounds with Dad. Must catch up on all the gossip.'

Two days after the nativity play, the school hall was transformed for the dance. The children had made masses of paper chains which were hung from the beams and draped down the walls. Flags of all the Allied nations were pinned in between. A large, glittering Christmas tree, the gift of the Squire, stood to one side of the temporary stage, the rest of which was occupied by the band. They were a group of four Cromer men who went to all the villages, not only playing but also singing and organising the entertainment for every local occasion. The plank floor had been polished and then liberally covered with Borax.

Helen and Heather, coming in from the sharp, frosty night air, gratefully breathed the warmer atmosphere. Heather said, 'Well, I never would have believed it – what a change!'

'All the same, it must be very different from your idea of a dance hall.'

'Yes, and I bet it's twice as much fun, too.'

Philip had seen them and now came over to Helen, who greeted him teasingly. 'And how did you wangle Christmas *this* time?' She turned to Heather. 'You've met Philip, haven't you? I don't know how he does it, but he always gets leave whenever he wants it.'

Philip said, 'Did Charlie behave himself this morning?'

'Well, I got back without falling into the churns.'

'Good for you. If you must know, Helen, I got leave because I'm not reporting back to my old base. I'm going on a flying course.'

This was said with the sheepish grin that Helen had known all her life. It meant that he was pleased with himself but didn't want anyone to guess. Now she replied, 'And how did you wangle that, I'd like to know? I should have thought your job was just as necessary.'

'There are ways and means. My age helps. Most of the fellows training now are in their teens or early twenties. They need a few of us older ones. With any luck, I'll be a fighter pilot before the party really starts.'

The band started with *Tiger Rag* and Heather was whisked away from them by one of the young farm labourers. Helen asked, 'Did you hear about our bit of excitement a couple of weeks ago? A Jerry plane ran into the radio mast at Beckham and crashed on Sheringham beach – or so we heard.'

'Oh, it was true. A Heinkel. All three killed. Not much doing yet, but it could hot up any time. Come on, let's dance.'

Presently he said lightly, 'By the way, I've fallen in love.'

Helen looked at him quizzically. You could never tell when Philip was joking. 'Who with?'

'A charmer called Rosie.'

'Aunt Ellen's evacuee? She turned you out of your bed!'

'I'd sleep on the floor for her any day. She's quite delightful. I should think she loves everybody.' He added thoughtfully, 'I never fancied being a father, but I wouldn't mind having one like her.'

Both Helen and Heather were in demand. Young people had come in from all the nearby villages, but it was an advantage to be on home territory and well known to the local men. It was nearly two hours later before Philip managed to get a dance with Heather. The band were playing *I Only Have Eyes For You* and they danced, for the most part, in companionable silence, at the end of which Philip said, 'Thank you. That was perfect', adding almost under his breath, 'and true.' Heather made no answer, but gave him a dreamy smile before turning away.

Among the Christmas post Helen had a letter from Jean. She had not written to Deirdre since leaving Eastbourne, but Jean had kept in touch with them both. Helen had become very fond of her in the week they had spent together, sharing the dormitory and going out as a trio.

Jean had seemed placid and contented with her office job but lately Helen had detected a restlessness in her letters. Surely that would be natural, living in London during such troubled times. Even so, her news came as a great surprise. Helen read:

'I had seen myself as the spinster aunt and was quite comfortable with the idea. I should have had a good career if I had stayed in this Local Government job – in fact, I've already been promised promotion when my immediate boss is called up. They would have to advertise the job, but it would have been a mere formality.

'Anyway, against all the odds, I've got myself engaged! Can you believe it? Douglas is a Naval Officer – Captain on a destroyer. He was in the RN before the war broke out. My father brought him home – he's the son of one of Dad's oldest friends. We were hardly alone together before he said, "Do you believe in love at first sight?" and I said, "Well, I didn't …" and that was more or less that. It happened so quickly, I still feel breathless.

'I don't know if I'll like being a sailor's wife, but I'm about to find out. No, we're not getting married yet, we thought after the war, for obvious reasons. But my second bit of news is that I volunteered for the Women's Royal Service Corps, so I expect the next letter you get will be from a Wren.

'I suppose there's no chance of seeing you before I go. Can you think why a journey to London should be necessary?'

Helen didn't think seriously about going to London, but she put the letter away thoughtfully, wondering how many such couples would survive and have a happy married life.

It was a great comfort to Sophie to find both the girls cheerful and optimistic, especially as her shop manager was perpetually worried about his son, Bob, now a radio operator in the Royal Navy. Like Helen, Heather often came home with amusing stories.

'I got a black mark today because I was missing so long,' she told them one evening.

'Did you get lost?'

'No. I was in the stables feeding the horses when an old bull came ambling in. I was in the hayloft so quickly, I don't remember climbing up! He sniffed around for ages and, of course, I wouldn't come down till he went. The men teased me no end, but Bob Davey was furious.'

The foreman had indeed been furious. 'Only a silly woman would be scared of him. I'll make sure she has something to be scared about next time.'

'If you do,' said Stephen quietly, 'I'll make sure Squire knows. She's a friend of theirs – or, at least, her people are.'

'My God! Isn't it enough I have to put up with women without having teacher's pets thrust on me?' Bob's face was scarlet.

The cowman said, 'I reckon they don't do a bad job. That Aggie now – she's a London girl – but she's a good little milker. Picked it up quick, too. I reckon you'd have nothing to complain about if that's the worst you get before this war's over.'

As they walked away, Stephen said to the cowman, 'I'm getting right fed up with Davey. He's always belly-aching these days. For two pins, I'd join up.'

'Ah. I reckon he miss his boy.'

'We all miss him. Bill was a good worker and always good for a laugh, but that's no reason to take it out on the girls. If it gets any worse, I'll tell Molly to drop a hint to Sally.'

* * * * *

It was in the Spring of 1940 that the first big change came to the village. There were still a few people living in the workhouse and the order came for them to be rehoused. Sally Wood was in charge of this and persuaded Ellen, as Secretary of the Women's Institute, to help her. They found the operation required a mixture of sympathy and firmness.

Old Mrs. Brown was moved to her daughter's home in the next village, where the departure of two sons into the Forces had left a room free. Others were fitted in similarly.

To everyone's surprise, Stephen Painter had volunteered for The Royal Norfolk Regiment, been accepted by the Fourth Battalion and was at Regimental HQ in Norwich. Molly was still tearful, puzzled and resentful.

'He would go. Said he was too young for the last scrap and he wasn't going to miss this one. As though it was a picnic! He's thirty-eight – he needn't have gone. It was selfish. He didn't think of me.'

By May, the workhouse had been transformed into a barracks for the Royal Engineers. With them came an unexpected bonus – electric light. The Army intended to use the village hall, but Colonel Green was anxious to be on good terms with the villagers and needed little persuasion (by Sally Wood) to agree that his men should install electricity in the school as well.

34

Once the work was completed, he lost no time in inviting everyone to a dance in the newly-decorated hall.

'Just listen to that band,' said Helen to Jim Crook, the vicar. 'They're as good as professionals.'

'I believe one of them is – I heard the drummer belonged to one of the well-known dance bands before he joined up.'

Jim was the vicar with the 'nice tenor voice' and his rendering of *Take A Pair of Sparkling Eyes*, sung to the young Aladdin and his girl, had been a highlight of the New Year pantomime.

He was a man of forty and a confirmed bachelor, living in the small rectory with his widowed mother. He and Helen had been friends for some time, sharing an appreciation of classical music which they indulged by listening to records on his gramophone, taking turns to wind it up. Old Mrs. Crook was something of an expert on tapestry work and liked the accompaniment while she worked on her latest project.

The other passion of Jim's life was fishing and he would cycle for miles with all his tackle if he thought he could get some good sport. He regarded this as 'thinking time' and said that the ideas for his best sermons came to him when he had a fishing rod in his hand.

Just now, Helen was missing her musical evenings as she felt it her duty to be there with a meal on the way when Heather came home.

They were dancing a lively quickstep when they realised that everyone was standing still. The next moment the drummer had launched into an exciting solo. He was certainly worthy of their full attention and got a great round of applause as he finished in a blaze of musical fireworks.

'That was marvellous,' Jim said warmly.

A young Sergeant replied, 'He's pretty good, isn't he, sir?' He held out his hand. 'I'm Johnny Keene – the men call me Ossie' and added, with a grin, 'that's when they're being polite, of course.'

Jim took the proffered hand. 'I'm Jim Crook, vicar of this parish – and this is Miss Helen Rae, who is one of our school teachers.'

Helen, mentally cursing Jim for such an introduction, smiled and asked, 'And are you an Aussie?'

'No. I'm a Yorkshireman by birth, but I've lived in Sydney since I was a kid.'

He was a well-built man, deeply tanned and with his fair hair, bleached by the Australian sun, he stood out a mile from the other young men. Helen decided that she liked his accent. When he came to claim her for the next dance she asked, 'Have you got a wife and children back home?'

'No. I've got a girl, but we're not engaged. It didn't seem fair with me going away, but she knows I fully intend to marry her after the war.'

Later he showed her a snap of Cathleen. She was as fair as he – a little slip of a girl with shoulder-length hair and cornflower-blue eyes.

'I thought all Australian girls were bronzed Amazons,' Helen told him.

'Oh, don't let that small frame fool you. She's very strong – in fact, she's got a wicked backhand and can beat everybody at the Sydney Tennis Club. Do you play?'

'Not much chance here. Just a knock about. I take the girls for netball and all the children for rounders. What with that and cycling everywhere, I get plenty of exercise.'

They had the last two dances and then Johnny asked if he could see Helen home. She looked round for Heather, but was told by Laura Thompson that she had already left. 'With a soldier,' she had added primly.

'I'm going home with a soldier too,' Helen told her – and you can tell that to the village, she thought. It wouldn't be a secret for long anyway.

Before he left her, Johnny asked, 'If I can get transport, will you come to the pictures with me?'

'What do you want transport for? We've got a spare bike – we can easily ride into Sheringham.'

'Bike! I haven't been on a bike since I was a kid.'

'You don't forget. It'll come back to you.'

'I'd better get some practice in – and I'll see if there's transport too. I don't suppose you know what's on next week?'

'Oh yes I do. *Tales From The Vienna Woods* – Paul Muni and Luise Rainer. I hope you love music as much as I do.'

'As long as it's not too heavy. Strauss will be fine.'

Back home, Helen found Heather and Sophie entertaining a young Private, who got to his feet as she came in, stayed long enough to be introduced as George Bell and then said he had to get back to barracks.

'Heavens, he looks too young to be in the Army!' said Helen.

'He's only eighteen,' explained Heather, 'but he was in the Terriers

36

so he got called up straight away. He's still feeling a bit lost, poor lad.'

'We must ask him for a meal,' Sophie said.

Heather was thoughtful. 'I've no intention of being seen as a kidnapper. If I can get hold of a couple of chickens, could we ask some of his mates as well?'

Helen laughed. 'Now I know why Laura told me you'd gone home with a soldier in that disapproving tone of hers. Strikes me that safety in numbers is likely to be a good idea.'

The girls were hoeing along the rows of sugarbeet and enjoying it because several of the men had told them that they were doing it well.

'Here comes Davey,' Aggie said. 'Bet he doesn't give us any compliments.'

But, to their surprise, Bob said grudgingly, 'You two girls aren't bad at that. There's a competition for hoeing sugarbeet on Saturday. Will you go in for it? Represent the farm?'

Aggie and Heather looked at each other. 'Do we have a choice?' Aggie asked.

'Well ... yes. I can't make you, I suppose.'

Heather shook her head.

Aggie said, 'We're doing no favours for you, Mr. Davey. You haven't got a good word for the girls usually. You'll get more out of us if you treat us better and don't give us all the rotten jobs.'

The blood rushed to the man's face, then he hesitated, closed his lips firmly on the retort he had been about to make, and walked away.

'He'll be worse than ever,' Heather said, not sounding very bothered.

'Not him. We should have stood up to him before.'

The kitten had stayed with her all night and Rosie felt its warmth against her as soon as she woke. She had been allowed to take him to bed with her because her mother had gone to Yarmouth for the weekend. She had no fear of sleeping alone, but normally her mother's body heat enveloped her and she had complained about the cold. These cottages were very damp and it was always difficult to keep them warm enough for comfort.

Gently she stretched out her hand and began stroking her pet, loving the feel of its soft fur. At once it started to purr. The vibration shook the whole of its tiny body. Rosie sat up and looked at it. On the honey-coloured coat were darker marks, five straight lines on the back of its head, concentric circles on each flank, tiny paws planted demurely together. Its beauty and precision delighted her. She considered a name for it, her head on one side. Its colouring reminded her of that toffee with circles of cream and treacle colours alternating.

'Toffee,' she said softly. 'Toffee, that's a nice name for you.'

She got out of bed carefully, not wanting to disturb it, but the kitten was instantly wide awake. She moved her fingers in front of it and it darted at them, then suddenly dashed out of the open bedroom door and down the stairs. Rosie followed, still in her nightdress. Auntie Ellen was in the kitchen.

'Hallo, my maid. You're up early.'

'I came for my kitten. I'm going to call it Toffee.'

'What a lovely name. You must thank Heather for bringing it from the farm.'

Rosie nodded vigorously. 'Heather's nice,' she agreed. 'What am I going to do today?'

Ellen Lambert smiled down at her and thought how well she had been named. Flushed from her sleep with skin as delicate as rose petals and with the bloom of childhood on her, she could only be compared to the flower whose name she bore. Mrs. Grice had told her that the family had a saying 'Happy as Rosie'. Her father had said it one day and it had passed into their lore.

'Uncle Joe is going towards Cromer today. Would you like to go with him?'

Rosie considered. 'On a bus?'

'No, with the horse and cart.'

The child capered delightedly. 'Oh, yes please!'

'Come and get ready quickly then.'

An hour later, Rosie was standing knee-deep in straw, while Uncle Joe saddled Major. The horse seemed huge to Rosie but she loved him and Uncle Joe had to keep her back until he was safely between the shafts of the cart. She liked the smell of the stable with its rich mixture of straw, leather, brass polish and horse, in the same way that she liked the grocery shop to which they were now going. It too had a queer variety of smells, selling paraffin, firelighters, wood and kitchen pans as well as groceries. All these Uncle Joe delivered to the surrounding villages, where he was known as the oil man.

The paraffin oil lamps fascinated Rosie. They had gas at her home in Yarmouth, but in all the villages there was only oil for light and heat, except for the coal or wood fires. Consequently, all that Uncle Joe carried was important to village life and he had to deliver it whatever the weather.

They loaded up the cart from Mr. Green's shop and he gave Joe some loose change and found a few sweets for Rosie. Then they were threading the country lanes perched up high above the broad back of Major. Rosie watched his shoulder muscles ripple as he clip-clopped along, enjoying the play of light which changed the colour of his chestnut coat, deepening it under the trees and making it glow red when the sun fell on it.

At the first village, Rosie saw children she recognised. They waved to her and presently an older girl called, 'Leave her with us till you've done, Mr. Lambert. We'll look after her.'

They took her down to the brook where they amused themselves by throwing pebbles at a saucepan that was in the water. Suddenly, there was a shout from the opposite bank, 'Hey, that's our dinner!'

There were three big boys – Rosie thought they were nearly as big as Philip – but they didn't look annoyed and the eldest girl shouted back, 'Why, whatever have you got there?'

For answer, one of them waded out, took the lid off the pan and held it upside down. Nothing came out.

'It's set now, all right,' he called to his friends. Then to the children, 'It's jelly. We couldn't get it to set, so we boiled it up again.'

The children shouted with laughter, Rosie joining in, though she had no idea what had happened. It felt so good to be part of the laughing group, playing in the sunshine with the stones in the brook gleaming. Presently, they waded across and helped the boys to eat the jelly.

It seemed that the three young men were camping on the farmer's land and cooking for themselves, with a little help from the farmer's wife. Rosie went into their tent and was immediately enchanted. She decided that this was how she would like to live forever.

Presently, Uncle Joe shouted for her and they were soon on their way again.

Their progress round the villages was slow. Most people needed to stock up as the oil man would not come their way for another week. The hedges were bright with honeysuckle, wild roses and haw blossom, but what Rosie liked best was to pass into the shadows where the trees met thickly overhead and she felt herself surrounded by their presence. Then she ceased chattering and became still, savouring the feeling of peace and safety.

Uncle Joe had no small talk. He was used to his solitary occupation and rarely said more than a few words to anyone. The first time Rosie accompanied him he had made an effort to amuse her, but finding that she could prattle on quite happily without expecting more than an occasional nod to show that he was listening, he reverted thankfully to his usual habits.

When, about lunchtime, they came to The Chequers and Major had stopped, as usual, of his own accord, Joe lifted Rosie down from the high seat and said, 'Don't go away. I won't be long.'

He picked up a large can of oil and a basket of groceries and disappeared into the dark interior of the inn. Rosie scuffled her feet and looked back to where the horse was browsing in the hedgerow. No-one was about for her to talk to and she fell into a dreamy chant of her own.

'Once upon a time there was a little cat named Toffee. It used to sleep on Rosie's bed ...'

She was interrupted by Joe returning with a woman from the pub, who turned to her and said, 'So you're keeping him company today?'

The child nodded, suddenly shy. The woman laughed and turned to Joe. 'She looks as though she's flourishing with you.'

'Ah, she's not too bad. Come on, my maid, up you go.' And they were off again.

Despite his silences, everyone wanted a few words with Joe. Had Mrs. Crouch had her baby yet? Was old Mr. Matthews all right after his fall? Had he heard ...? Rosie ceased to listen to their gossip and stayed quiet. But when Joe turned the horse for home and old

Major broke into a trot, sensing his oats and his bed, her tongue was miraculously unlocked and Uncle Joe heard nothing but 'jelly boys', tents and the delights of camping all the way home.

Helen picked up the post and smiled. The unmistakable Forces envelope was addressed to Heather in Philip's handwriting. Good, she thought, he's made up his mind not to let Heather's social standing get in his way – and that was right because she was sure Heather wouldn't care. Love was in the air – Heather and Philip, Jean and her Naval Captain. Helen was pleased for both couples, but she felt a little wistful. No-one on the horizon for her. And not likely to be, she told herself severely, as long as you go around with Johnny.

They had been to the pictures several times, sometimes with a crowd but more often on their own, and they were always partners at the frequent dances in the village hall. No doubt he felt safe with a schoolmarm and had written in those terms to Cathleen. Anyway, there wasn't anyone else who interested her. Johnny was by far the most serious-minded of his group and they had so much in common. He loved to talk about his home in Australia and Helen was only too willing to listen. Her class would know all about this far country once she had assimilated the facts. Still, it wouldn't be for much longer. He was taking his men away for further training shortly.

Her thoughts were interrupted by Heather, who spotted her letter and took it up eagerly, her face flushing. Presently she said, 'Philip sounds depressed.'

Helen's head shot up. 'That's not like him. Whatever has happened?'

Heather read: *'I feel such a fool – and a failure. I can fly the bloody plane, but I can't land it. It must sound stupid – God, it is stupid – but I don't seem to have the sense to know how far I am off the ground, and either land with a bump or keep hovering above it. Anyway, I'm never going to be a pilot, that's for sure. The only good news is that this means I'll be coming on leave in a few days. By then, I'll probably know what they're going to do with me ...'*

Heather folded the letter and said, 'I suppose it's a tragedy to him, but I can't help feeling relieved.'

'You're fond of him, aren't you?'

'Yes, I am, but I've got a feeling he won't commit himself until the war's over – and the ruddy thing doesn't seem to have got really started yet.'

Philip came to meet them from church the following Sunday morning, quickening his step as he saw Heather. Helen said, 'Ask him to lunch', waved her greetings and turned back to speak to Jim, so that the two could walk on without her.

'I'm sorry I wrote you that letter – feeling sorry for myself, when other people are worse off,' Philip told Heather as they went along, 'but I think I've come to terms with it now. They tell me I'm not the first to fail that way.'

'I'm quite sure you're not. Helen says I'm to ask you to lunch – corned beef and salad, all right?'

'Not today. Mum's cooking. The butcher left her a small joint because she told him she was expecting me home, so I'd better go and have it. Look, I'll just see Helen and then we can go for a walk.'

When they were alone again, Heather asked, 'Do you know what they'll do with you now?'

'I've been transferred to Bomber Command.'

'Oh, Philip!' She couldn't keep the tremor out of her voice. A fighter pilot had been bad enough. Bombers would be infinitely worse.

'I know. I tried to tell Mum that it's safer, but I don't think she was fooled, and Dad knows. The job isn't what I want either – no, not because of the danger, but because there's such a wonderful feeling of freedom flying a fighter. You're up there on your own and you can do whatever you judge to be best. Oh, of course the Squadron Leader's in charge, but it's not like being in the same plane. In a bomber, when the Skipper makes a decision they've all got to do it, whether they agree with it or not. Only, I'm the wrong type – I can see myself getting mad and arguing.'

Heather managed to strike a lighter note. 'That's your ginger hair, I bet. Has your mother got a temper?'

'And how! It's over quickly but fierce while it lasts.'

They wandered on, enjoying the summer day and presently he took her hand. 'It's not fair to ask you, Heather – I may not come through this – but I know it would help if I knew you were my girl.' He stopped and turned to look at her. 'Are you, my darling – will you be my girl?'

'I think I am already – no, listen – but you shouldn't have more personal responsibilities. You'll have enough on your plate ...'

He had drawn her close, and now he interrupted. 'No! That's not the way it is. If we love each other – don't you see – it's already happened. However far we take it – an engagement – a wedding – it's already a fact. You'll always be my care now, and I'll be yours.'

'Yes, I know.'

They kissed and clung, and kissed again. At last, he asked, 'What will your people say?'

'I'm free, white and twenty-one. If we both come through this, nothing and no-one will stop me marrying you.'

Until April 1940 the only privation the country had endured was the rationing of staple foods, but then the picture began to change. On April 9th Germany invaded Norway and Denmark and, as the war began to go badly for the Allies, Chamberlain was forced to resign.

George Barker, meeting Helen as she came into school the following day, said brightly, 'Things will go better with Churchill. He's the only one who had the foresight to see what was coming. We should have listened to him long ago.'

'I still don't understand why we were so unprepared,' she confessed.

A shadow crossed his face. 'That's because you don't remember the last war. The memories of trench warfare are unforgettable to my generation. No government would have dared to suggest to the people that we needed to re-arm so soon. The wounds were still too deep.'

On May 27th began the evacuation of Dunkirk and by mid-June the Germans had taken the town. The capitulation of France was inevitable. Despite the losses, the evacuation was hailed as a miracle.

Heather brought home a copy of a newspaper cartoon which showed a lone soldier hurling defiance at the enemy. The caption was '*Very well! Alone!*' It summed up the mood of the people. There was a new sense of pride in Britain, bolstered by Churchill's speeches to the nation.

In July came the German bombing which was intended to pave the way for the invasion of Britain.

East Anglia was protected by 11 Group RAF and the Coltishall Squadrons were made up of both Spitfires and Hurricanes. The girls heard snatches of information – Squadron Leader Douglas Bader had shot down a Dornier near Cromer, another was badly damaged off Yarmouth. Norwich had its first raid on July 9th when two factories of Colmans and Boulton and Paul were attacked and there were casualties.

This was serious warfare, but both Helen and Heather were affected more personally. All the evacuees who had gone back to their homes returned, together with many more. Sally and Ellen were kept busy trying to house them and the school had to take extra classes in the village hall.

Heather found herself sharing her room with a teacher from a London school and the loss of privacy was a source of some distress to her. Stella Doren was a young woman who had not long completed her training. She was rather nervy and talkative, being permanently worried for the safety of her parents, who lived in Clapham. She needed as much reassurance as the evacuees after the London raids started.

'Was there a raid last night? Have you heard the News?' she asked every morning at breakfast. When she sat over the radio all evening, Heather decided that something must be done.

'We need you desperately at the Red Cross. They're always short-handed and I'll soon be in the harvest fields till late. You must join – it's your duty.'

But she also sympathised with Stella and spoke to Sally, with the result that the girl could go up to the farmhouse every weekend and telephone her parents. Their neighbour had a telephone and would let them into her house to receive the calls.

Stella had brought with her several benefits. She was registered for rations as a vegetarian. This meant that the family had to forego her meat ration, which was less than two shillings, but her cheese ration was surprisingly generous and made a welcome addition to their diet. In her turn, she was delighted with the wealth of fresh vegetables and found great pleasure in picking her own.

'My father was badly gassed in the last war,' she explained, 'and my mother was advised to put him on a vegetarian diet. When she understood all the benefits of it she saved herself a lot of trouble by cooking vegetarian food for the whole family.'

Stella knew a great many of her mother's recipes and was

always happy to cook a meal for the four of them whenever the meat ration just would not stretch.

At school, George soon spotted that she had a gift for painting. She was actually a history teacher, but he involved her in scene painting for the revue which the village was putting on to entertain the troops.

The original idea had come from Sarah Barker.

'What are you going to do with the evacuees in the summer holidays?' she asked George. 'I suppose you realise they won't be interested in the things our children do. They'll soon get bored and start causing trouble.'

'You have a point,' he conceded, 'but I don't see that we can do much. They might come for a treasure hunt or a paper chase, but I couldn't organise something every day.'

'I've been wondering if we could get up a concert for the troops. We could have some of them rehearsing, some painting scenery and some making costumes. I would help with the dresses.'

George stretched his long frame, got to his feet and kissed his wife.

'That's a brilliant idea, and you are an exceptional woman. We might even involve the rest of the village. We could all do with a lift.'

Sally and Ellen were enthusiastic from the start. 'There's quite a lot of talent in the village. We see it at the Women's Institute,' Sally said.

'What about Laura Thompson?' Ellen turned to George. 'You would never guess it, but she loves the old Norfolk tales and the dialect. If you could write it for her, Helen, she could give us a mardle.'

Sally and George had agreed to co-ordinate the whole affair and Ellen, Helen and Stella formed the rest of the committee.

'But would she do it?' George asked.

'Tickled pink at the idea. She's done it for WI parties and loves making people laugh. No nerves either. Not like Mrs. Dennis.'

'What can she do?' Stella could not imagine their shy neighbour appearing on a stage.

'Didn't you know? She has a lovely contralto voice and has performed in public, but she says she gets so nervous beforehand that it isn't worth it.'

'I wonder if she could lead the chorus. We need a strong voice for that.'

'Let me talk to her,' Helen said as the meeting broke up, with

45

Ellen agreeing to see Molly and Mrs. White about the refreshments.

George was right. The Battle of Britain, as it came to be called, was relentless. Every day the newspapers put up the score as though it was a sports competition – so many enemy bombers shot down with only a few of our fighters lost. But, George reflected bitterly, each one of those fighters represented someone's son who would never return.

Heather was full of thankfulness that Philip was not a fighter pilot. When Churchill said that August, 'Never in the field of human conflict has so much been owed by so many to so few,' Philip had written to her, 'I should have been one of them but for my own stupidity. But at least I can tell you that I am now a navigator.'

He was qualified for perhaps the most difficult job on a bomber plane. It was his responsibility to get the Blenheim to its destination, guide the pilot on to the target and finally to release the bombs. He wrote to Heather that this last task gave him no satisfaction, though many of his fellow navigators rejoiced in it.

'Perhaps I shall feel differently when we've lost a few of the men I know. I'll probably get as bloodthirsty as the rest of them,' he told her on his last leave before his operational posting.

They were staying with her parents a few days prior to announcing their engagement.

The first thought on Alan Francis' mind as he was introduced to Philip was that this boy was absurdly young to be wearing the uniform of a Flying Officer. The hard-headed businessman had found himself touched by the vulnerability of the young men who were in uniform all over London. They looked as though they should still be in college or university.

He was agreeably surprised to find that Philip was nearly thirty and had a career behind him. Neither he nor his wife raised any objection to his engagement to their daughter, having no illusions about Philip's chances of surviving the war. Felicity Francis did say to Heather, 'My darling, is it wise to get engaged when he's in such a dangerous job? I'm thinking of your grief if anything happens to him.'

'It won't be any the less whether we are engaged or not, Mother.

I want Philip to be sure of me. If he has something to live for it may make him just a bit more careful.'

It was blindingly hot in the harvest field. Heather wiped the sweat off her forehead with the sleeve of her blouse before forking up the next lot of hay. The harvest had been good and Bob Davey, her immediate boss, had seemed pleased, but today he was back to normal – finding fault with the women whenever he could. He deeply resented having to admit that the girls could do as well as the men and today he had lost another good man to the Forces.

The man on top of the wagon, stripped to the waist, smiled at her and said, 'Why not take your blouse off?'

'What, with Bob in this mood?'

But one of the local girls was already stripping off. After all, she still had more on than she would have worn at the beach. Heather hesitated no longer. In a few moments every one of the women had followed suit.

Almost at once there came a bellow from the far side of the field and Bob came steaming over, yelling as he came, 'Get those blouses back on!'

'Oh, Mr. Davey, we're so hot!'

He came up to them. 'I said put 'em back on. You'll upset the men.'

One of the girls said pertly, 'I suppose it doesn't matter if they upset us.'

But they were already obeying his orders. To her astonishment, Heather found herself in tears.

She had been working long hours until the light faded, often under a blazing sun, hoping to exhaust herself enough to sleep. But sleep had not come. Night after night she had lain rigid for fear of waking Stella, imagining that she heard the drone of bombers going out and coming back, wondering if Philip was in one of them.

No-one mentioned her tears and she soon recovered, but one of the girls told Helen that Heather had seemed very upset by Bob and that it wasn't like her to take him so seriously. She added, 'It did just cross my mind that she might be pregnant, but she seems thinner, if anything.'

'I've been so involved with this concert, I hadn't noticed. And she's been working late, so I've hardly seen her. Thanks for telling me – I'll do something about it.'

When Helen told her mother, Sophie said at once, 'I *have* been a bit worried about her. I don't think she's been sleeping well. She looks drawn. I suppose she's worrying about Phil – it's natural – and there's nothing we can do about that.'

The Battle of Britain had mainly involved the fighter pilots, but now there were reports of raids over Germany every night. Women all over the country were worried for their men, carrying on with a grim determination and a hard lump in their hearts that they grew to accept as normal. Heather would have to learn to do the same. Nevertheless, Sophie decided to have a word with Sally.

Two days later, Sally came out to the three-acre field and drew Heather to one side. 'You're getting thin. Are we working you too hard?'

'No. I love the work. It's the only thing that keeps me sane.'

Sally laid a hand on her arm. 'Knock off early tonight. I'll tell Bob. Come to us for dinner. That's an order. Alan would never forgive us if we let you get ill.'

Wearily, Heather changed out of her uniform, put some water to heat on the stove, washed and put on a summer dress, scribbled a note to Sophie and left the house.

Sally took one look at her, poured a generous sherry and said, 'Now. Get that down and tell me about it.'

The girl dropped heavily into an armchair and accepted the glass thankfully. 'I tell myself I'm no different from hundreds of other women who are worried about their men, but it doesn't do any good. I can't sleep and, of course, I'm afraid of waking Stella.'

Sally seemed to understand this at once. She nodded. 'It's always difficult to share a room when you're awake. Well, I can help you there. You know Gertie, one of the housemaids, left recently? Now Betty has decided she can't settle without her. She volunteered for the ATS and I expect she'll be called up any day. So their room will be free. Come and stay with us.'

Heather frowned. 'That's a cop-out. Think what Dad would say – living in the lap of luxury with Sally, or something like that. Besides, I really don't want to leave Sophie and Helen. No, I've got to beat this on my own.'

'Yes, I think you have. There's only one way to defeat fear, and that's to face it. You know the worst that can happen, but in this war it's as likely to be you as him. Suppose you went home for a weekend and got bombed? All the same, I wish you could have a room of your own – at least you could move if you were awake without having to worry about disturbing anyone else.'

Heather looked up at that. 'It's a fearful cheek to ask, but would you consider having Stella? She's not reconciled to country conditions yet.' She laughed suddenly and unexpectedly. 'I don't know if you know, but we've got a double lavatory up the garden. The other day she sat down on one hole and a rat jumped out of the other. I've never seen anyone so panic-stricken! She was white and shaking for ages.'

'Then I think it's my duty to take her, if only to stop her going back to London, and George can keep a teacher he needs now that all the evacuees have returned. Come and have dinner. It's only shepherd's pie but I'm going to open a bottle of Chateau Neuf du Pape.'

At ten, Heather returned home. With sudden awareness, she realised that there was a brilliant Hunter's moon above. There would be no bombing raids tonight. For the first time in weeks, she slept soundly.

Helen had a letter, unmistakably Forces mail. It was from Jean and something about it struck her as odd – different surname. She opened it quickly and began to read:

'Dear Helen,

As you will see, I am now a married woman. Like everything to do with Douglas, it happened very quickly. He had been on the Atlantic run, up to Russia. Do you know anything about that?

Well, I did. I heard a lot of the men here talking about it. Cherry Garrard called Scott's last expedition "The Worst Journey in the World". Well, I should think the Atlantic run must be the worst voyage in the world – freezing conditions, lower than any we can imagine, dangerous seas and U-boats shadowing them all the time.

From the moment I knew Douglas was out there my heart was in my mouth. It was difficult to concentrate on my own work, I can tell you.

Anyway, as soon as he came on leave we both agreed to get

married at once and take whatever happiness we are allowed to have. We got a special Forces licence and got married quietly in my local church. All our parents were there but very few other people as not many of our age could get leave.

Our wedding breakfast consisted of tinned ham and salad and a home-made wedding cake, which was more than either of us expected. Both of our mothers had been hoarding dried fruit and points for the ham and Dad has been growing salads in the greenhouse though we could only manage tinned tomatoes – bless them all.

We spent our honeymoon in Blackpool, of all places, both feeling conspicuous out of uniform among all the RAF and Polish airmen. There were plenty of Civil Servants but all of the men seemed to be older. The reason for this venue was that Douglas has an aunt who owns a boarding house there. She is forced to take either Forces or Civil Servants, but she had a bedroom spare just at that time and offered it to us. I think she really wanted to see what sort of girl Douglas had married, not having much opinion of the morals of the WRENs.

The weather was gorgeous and we spent a lot of time walking in the country, which is lovely round there.

Now I am back at base and I don't know where Douglas is at the moment, but I'm sure I shall hear soon. It feels a bit bleak without him, but we are lucky that we ever found each other.

After all that about me, how are you? Do write and let me know what you have been doing. I hear Norwich got a pasting, so I hope all is well with you and yours.

Lots of love, Jean'

Helen put the letter away, feeling glad for her friend and wondering vaguely about a wedding present. Perhaps that had better wait until after the war.

Joan Dennis, Sophie's neighbour, was a happy woman.

The concert had been a great success and her beloved husband, Paul, had arrived on leave just two days before. Now she stood with him at the door and waved the children off to school. Ten-year-old Paul was inclined to be bossy and the twins, John and

Josie, to resent it. They were already forging ahead and he was shouting after them.

'Paul,' his father called sharply, 'wait for Babs!'

The boy turned and held out his hand to the little girl. They watched him and smiled as the young child gazed up at him in adoration. Barbara had been at school just a year. Joan missed having a child around but she had to admit that it was good to have more time to herself, especially since she had come to this friendly village and become absorbed into its many activities: the Women's Rural Institute, the Red Cross, some of the school activities, culminating in the concert.

George Barker had decided that this should be held on the Saturday before the children returned to school, so that he could keep them occupied through most of the holiday. The local youngsters, with a few exceptions, wanted nothing to do with it, preferring to chase rabbits in the harvest field. They were so contemptuous of the indoor activities that some of the evacuees had deserted the workrooms to sample the joys of country life. If anything, George was even more satisfied with them. He had arranged an afternoon paper chase, as he had suggested ,and several outings so that none of them were hard at work all the time.

But it was surprising how many of them had got so involved with their projects that they grudged any time away from them, being sure that this was worth doing because it was to cheer up the brave soldiers.

Joan turned to her husband. 'Did I tell you that Josie did a lot of those decorations herself and helped with the costumes? Helen says she's a good little needlewoman – and Paul and John have been painting some of the scenery.'

He smiled down at her fondly. 'I think you did just mention it – a few times. We seem to have a bevy of clever children.'

Over the washing-up, they continued the subject. They had great hopes for their young family, but Paul had been a long-distance lorry driver before the war and they knew it would take all their resources to give the children the chances they deserved.

'I've been wondering whether I couldn't start my own garage after the war,' he mused. 'I've got to know a few chaps who want to be their own bosses once it's over. I might go in with some of them.'

'Oh, Paul, you are clever! Young Paul may be nearly off our

hands and earning for himself if he doesn't want to go to college, and I don't think he will. He's good with his hands, like you.'

She gazed up in admiration at her husband. Sergeant Paul Dennis of the Royal Armoured Corps, tall, broad-shouldered and bronzed, was a man to be proud of. The Army had changed him – made him decisive, instead of leaving all the decisions to her. She had enjoyed introducing him to her new friends. Two weeks after his return to his unit, she was still basking in the remembrance of their time together.

Helen had been delighted to see that Johnny was in the audience at the concert. It had been well advertised and the hall was packed with members of all three Services.

It began and ended with the children singing songs familiar to the audience from their own school days such as *The Ash Grove* and *Early One Morning*, together with some rounds which the audience joined in heartily and with much laughter as George divided them into groups and several came in at the wrong time. Having got them laughing, Laura did her 'mardle', relating a humorous sketch in the broad Norfolk dialect. One of the farmers gave them *The Floral Dance* followed by *The Yeomen of England*.

Some of the girls, suitably attired in green, danced an Irish jig, and the first half ended with a chorus of children and adults singing a medley of patriotic songs, during which a large Union Jack was unfurled to much applause.

In the interval, Johnny came up to Helen. 'It's a fair dinkum show. Congratulations. You must have worked hard.'

'We have, but we've all enjoyed it and it's kept the evacuees happy in the holidays.'

'That's all very well, but what about you having a holiday? Come to the pictures with me next week.'

'Oh, are you back here for a while?'

'Can't tell with this lot, but I'm supposed to be training a new intake ... if they don't change their minds. What about next week?'

She grinned. 'Do you know what you're letting yourself in for? It's *Gone with the Wind*. I'm dying to see it, but it's three hours at least.'

'Then I'll have to get transport. Mustn't bike home with lights on after dark. I'll let you know when I can make it.'

She excused herself and went behind the scenes to help with the second half of the concert, noting with approval that Joan's husband was assuring her that, of course, she would do it splendidly.

'Why, I came home specially to hear you sing. You don't want me to go back disappointed, do you?'

Helen heard her reply, 'Oh, was that what you came home for?' There was a laugh in her voice.

The second half opened with a sketch written by some of the older evacuees, poking fun at the Norfolk people, with a rueful look at how they themselves had to come to terms with some of the strange habits of the natives. From the sketch George Barker learned that, when he was angry with any of them, it was best to keep him talking as he got increasingly cheerful the longer he went on.

'They'll regret that,' Helen thought. 'They've told him now and he won't forget.' But the next minute she was laughing as some of them attempted to speak the dialect.

This act was followed by Joan and Jim who sang the kissing song from *The Mikado*.

'Were you not to Coco plighted,' began Jim, gazing not at Joan but at Paul seated in the front row. Paul blew a kiss back at Joan and Jim continued, keeping a wary eye on the handsome Sergeant during the actual kissing. The sight of their bachelor vicar kissing a woman with every sign of enjoyment was obviously the highlight of the performance for some of the local women.

Then he stepped back and left Joan to sing Katisha's song, *Hearts Do Not Break*. The contralto voice was deeply emotional. For the first time the audience sat in total silence, then there was a storm of applause.

Jim sang *Titwillow* and then the two of them launched into the sprightly duet from Patience, *And That's What I Shall Say*.

Next, George and the Squire, Bill Wood, appeared as a rustic couple, cracking the corniest of jokes which had some of the Servicemen shouting 'The old ones are the best!' They ended by singing *The Lincolnshire Poacher* and *To be a Farmer's Boy*. Neither of them made the least pretence of having a voice, but they roared out the verses and encouraged the audience to join in the choruses. This was so popular, since most of them were dying to join in, that it was voted the hit of the evening.

Helen went home well satisfied. It had gone without a hitch, or at least none that the audience saw. And next week she would go to the pictures with Johnny again, and he would be there for the weekly dance. At that moment, she was not prepared to admit how glad she had been to see him.

One evening in the middle of October, Joan Dennis put the children to bed and sat down to think what she should do. She had hoped her family was complete. Four bright children were going to be difficult enough to educate; a fifth might bring real hardship. Besides, she didn't want any more. Just the idea made her feel worn out. One thing she knew. Paul must be told – and soon. Better to do it now.

She wrote:

'My darling,

I have some news which I think will not be entirely welcome. I am pregnant again, Paul. I feel a bit distraught. Write quickly and let me know what you think ...'

She watched for the post-girl anxiously, but Paul's reply did not come for almost a week. She opened the unmistakable Forces envelope with shaking hands.

'My dearest girl,

I don't know what to say. I'm sorry would be wrong. How can I be sorry that we love each other so much? But I share your anxiety. We must give the children as good a chance as we can. I know you can only just manage on the little I can send you. I didn't tell you, but I refused a Commission because the expenses of being an Officer can outweigh the advantage if you're not very careful.

How would you feel about an operation to get rid of it? I believe it's very easy in the early stages. I wouldn't dare to suggest it if you didn't sound so down. I think I can get an address from one of my mates, then it would be a day in London for us and no-one need ever know ...'

Joan sat down heavily. She felt frightened and relieved at the same time. At least Paul understands, she thought. We feel the same way about it ... but oh, it's a baby as well – and it's Paul's – and I love him.

After two days and three sleepless nights, she wired, 'Agreed. Let me know date.'

A week later they met at Liverpool Street Station. Joan's journey had been a nightmare. The train was packed, mostly with Servicemen, and subject to long delays. She felt ill and worried and became more and more agitated as they got nearer to London.

Paul held out his arms to her from the end of the platform and clasped her tightly. His voice murmured in her ear, 'Darling, we're not going to do this horrible thing. Cheer up and smile at me.'

The smile was shaky, but the sight of his face and calm voice steadied her. He took her into the lounge at the Great Eastern Hotel, which was almost deserted, and got her some tea and sandwiches. She began to relax.

'I've got some explaining to do and it's rather a nasty story, I'm afraid,' he said quietly. 'One of the ATS girls I knew – she had been engaged and her man was killed at Dunkirk. It seems she went out with one of my men. He took advantage of her while she was still in shock. It was a rotten thing to do, but he's been punished for it all right. She got pregnant and he arranged for her to get rid of it. She died of blood poisoning – septicemia – two days ago. She didn't deserve that – nobody does. Well, of course, that settled it – I couldn't take that risk with you. But don't worry. We shall have to muddle through somehow. Other people do.'

Joan had hardly spoken, but now she said, 'Oh, that poor girl – but I'm so relieved. I was dreading it – and not at all sure that we weren't doing a terrible thing. That boy must be feeling awful ...'

'Yes. It's just another war tragedy. I expect there'll be others – but it came in time to save us. I don't know if it can ever be right, what we were planning. Did you know that Beethoven was born to a syphilitic mother and a drunken father? You would think he would have been an ideal candidate for abortion, but think what the world would have lost.'

Joan laughed, a little shakily. 'I doubt if our fifth child will be another Beethoven, but it might have a very useful life. Oh, Paul – I'm so happy!' And she realised that it was suddenly true.

'Good. Now, what do you think we're going to do?'

'Now, you mean? I think you've got something planned.'

He looked at the station clock. 'There's a train home in half an hour – and I've got a 48-hour pass.' He laughed at her expression. 'When I knew that we would have the baby, I went and saw the Captain, told him you were pregnant and in need of reassurance. I said I was worried about you. That did it.' He added, 'I'm dying to see the kids. Let's go and tell them they're going to have a new baby brother.'

Joan shook her head vigorously. 'We'll do nothing of the sort. They'll be looking for him – or *her* – and pestering me every day, and it won't be till June.'

'Well, we can tell Sophie anyway. I know she and Helen will keep an eye on you. As for the rest – we have to live one day at a time, like everybody else.'

'Rumour has it,' said Stephen Painter, 'that I'm about to get my knees brown.'

'Going to help Wavell?' Philip asked.

'Could be the desert, I suppose, but the grapevine favours the Far East.'

'It's amazing how often the rumours are right. Makes you wonder how we keep anything from the Jerries.'

The two men were both on leave and were talking in Ellen's kitchen while she and Molly were at a WI meeting. Joe was in his usual chair, his pipe in his mouth and gazing into the fire. Stephen turned to him. 'I really came to ask you to keep an eye on Molly and Joyce – but I know you will.'

Stephen looked younger, more upright and at ease with the world. Uniform suited him and Molly was so proud that she couldn't hide it, though she still complained that he need not have gone.

'Yes,' said Joe in his slow drawl, 'I'll help them if they need me. And I'll tell you what. I wouldn't be surprised if young Wally didn't turn out to be a help too. He's fond of them both.'

'Where is he sleeping while you're home?' Philip asked.

Stephen grinned. 'On the floor. Same as usual. Good job his sister decided to stay in London. I reckon he's a lot better without her to fight with.'

'He's a lot better anyway – he's beginning to get some more interests. Even wanted to know what made my dahlias better than the Squire's. We'll make a countryman of him yet.'

Joe returned to his pipe, noting with satisfaction that Philip was more relaxed today. He thought his son had lost weight lately and he had certainly been too active and hearty when he first came home. It had fooled no-one, not even Ellen, who had said nothing but looked at him anxiously.

'I see you got yourself a car – nice little job. All right if you can get the petrol,' Stephen remarked.

Philip smiled ruefully. 'There are advantages in being part of a bomber crew – not many, but some. We get pampered because they know we won't last long – sorry, Dad, but we have to face it – so we get extra petrol, extra rations and so on. I bought the Morris cheap from the father of one of the pilots who copped it. I expect he got it the same way. Don't tell Mum or Heather, will you.'

They sat in silence for a minute gazing into the fire.

'Little Mrs. Dennis – her husband's in the desert. They don't seem to be having much trouble with the Eyeties.'

They discussed the recent successes there and the general progress of the war. Then Stephen got up to go.

'I'd better get back in. I shan't tell Molly this is embarkation leave – you won't say anything?'

'Course not. I won't even tell Ellen.'

'I'm coming too,' Philip said. 'Heather and I are going to give Rosie a surprise. Pick her and her mum up from the station. They've been home for a few days.'

Rosie was the first to see them.

'Mummy, there's Heather – oh, and Philip!'

She ran towards them, arms outstretched, to be gathered up by Philip and flung into the air.

'You mustn't do that any more. I'm a big girl now. I go to school,' she reprimanded him, as Heather explained to Mrs. Grice that Philip had a car and would take her home. She looked worried and Heather asked, 'Is everything all right with your family?'

'My mother has had a fall. It's not that serious but she can't look after two households and I think that may be why it happened – trying to do too much. I think I'll have to leave Rosie here and go home myself. I trust Mrs. Lambert and I know Rosie will be all right with her, but I don't like giving her the responsibility.'

'Don't worry, everybody loves Rosie. We'll all look after her.'

Philip, with the little girl clinging to his hand, had come up in time to hear this. Now he said, 'I'm on leave all next week. I'll drive you back to Yarmouth whenever you want.'

Once they were on their way, Rosie was full of her doings at school. 'And I have to call Helen 'Miss Rae' – don't you think that's silly?'

'Of course not. It's what all the other children call her, isn't it?'

'Yes, but they all know she's really Helen,' said Rosie scornfully.

Philip tried again. 'What's your name?'

'You know, silly – Rosie Grice.'

'But I only call you Rosie now. When you're grown up you'll be called Miss Grice.'

'Will I really?' Her eyes were wide.

'Really. All grown-up young ladies are called Miss.'

This intrigued Rosie enough to keep her quiet for a while.

At home, Ellen heard the story and willingly agreed to look after Rosie.

'She's really no trouble – and at school all day now. Helen will keep an eye on her at dinner time and I'll get Wally to bring her home.'

The next morning Philip drove Mrs. Grice back to Yarmouth.

'I'll come and see you soon,' she told Rosie. 'Auntie Ellen and Helen will look after you.'

'You mean Miss Rae,' Rosie told her.

In December of 1941 Heather was having one of her favourite days. Riding Charlie and leading Henry, she was taking the two carthorses to be shod. It would take all day and there was just enough nip in the air to make the warmth of the forge very welcome. She loved watching Arthur, the blacksmith, at work, gazing at the play of light on the coats of her charges and seeing what else Arthur had been making lately. There should be some iron sent in to him to break up for the war effort and some of this, like the ornamental gates to Sally's house, was very fine. It was a shame they had to go, but the war did not spare beautiful things.

The year that was nearly past had seen the blitz on Coventry which had destroyed the fine cathedral. It was ending with mixed fortunes in the Middle East, the German occupation of Crete and parts of Russia, and the signing of the Atlantic Charter between Churchill and Roosevelt.

What had affected the village most had been the letters of Paul Dennis from Tobruk and Stephen Painter from Malaya and, of course, clothes rationing.

Mrs. Dennis had had her baby at the end of June and he had been christened Douglas after Douglas Bader. His mother seemed as content as she could be with Paul in the Middle East. He seemed to be moving about a lot as the battles raged with gains and losses to the Allies. Paul wrote when he could, always cheerfully, and seemed delighted with the news of his young son.

Heather was pondering what the last year had brought in terms of changes to the village and to the war, and wondering what 1942 might hold. Against all the odds, Philip and his crew had survived and would soon be off ops for a while. There was talk of a better bomber for them too.

Soothed by the clip-clop of the horses, she let her mind ramble, dwelling on their last leave together. She was still smiling when she reached the forge.

The blacksmith came out to meet them, taking Henry from her while she dismounted from Charlie. He was a wiry man, not tall but broad-shouldered, and his bald head was covered with a billycock hat. He asked, 'Heard the news?'

Heather said that she hadn't heard anything that morning.

'The Japs bombed Pearl Harbour – never heard of it afore – just off Hawaii, they say. Reckon they sunk half the Yanks' fleet.'

'Will it affect us – so far away?'

'Wireless said it'll bring the Yanks into the war against Germany. Might have some over here afore long.'

'It might shorten the war.'

Arthur shook his head. 'Ah, that might. I got a boy in Singapore, you know. Japan's too close for comfort.'

'Oh, that's nonsense, Arthur. It's a long way. The Yanks will stop them getting that far.'

'Ah, well, thass no good worryin'. Come up, boy.'

He led Henry in and went to work, but was almost silent for the rest of the day.

Helen went home from school feeling depressed. A trying day had included a half hour of work with gas masks on. None of the teachers liked it and the children, without exception, loathed it. If they got notice of it, there would be a lot of absentees, but if it was sprung on them, as today, there were always some who had forgotten their masks and had to be sent home for them. They took their time returning. Today, Emily Saunders had wet herself at the thought of it and, being a girl of eleven, she had gone home ashamed and in tears. Bobby Smith had been sick, and Helen sympathised with him. The rubbery smell and the tightness of the mask induced feelings of claustrophobia.

And it all seemed so unnecessary. Surely if the Jerries were going to use gas they would have done it by now? But orders were orders, so they still carried their awkward cardboard boxes – most of them very battered by now – with the hated masks inside them.

Helen filled the kettle and put it on the fire then went into the garden. Spring flowers were beginning to appear and she felt her spirits rising a little at the sight. The winter had been fairly dry and her first thought was to give the vegetables a drink.

Engaged in carrying water from the well, she did not see Johnny until he was almost upon her. She had not expected him and her smile of welcome was wide. As she felt the warmth of feeling surge through her, she suddenly realised she loved him.

But Johnny had come with bad news. As he took her pail, he said, 'Singapore's fallen. The Japs seem unstoppable.'

'Oh, Johnny, so soon! Poor Arthur – Heather said his boy is out there and Stephen Painter.'

'Yes, and so is my best mate – and some more men I know.'

He looked so downcast that her arms ached to hold him, but all she said was, 'Come in. The kettle should be boiling by now.'

Over a cup of tea, he brightened and gave her the rest of his news. 'At least I'm going to have a crack at them, at last.'

'You're going out there?' Helen was horrified and sounded so.

'No. I think we're going to the Middle East.' Then he said bitterly, 'But anything's better than here. I'm fed up with training other men to go and do something.'

'Are you sure it isn't the Far East?'

'Rumour has it that Churchill can't see further than beating Rommel. He's pouring troops into the Middle East – not Singapore and the Pacific.'

For a while they sat silently, each busy with their own thoughts. Helen had to come to terms with her sudden revelation. There would not be a future with Johnny. He was engaged. He lived in

Australia and she could not leave her mother. None of this mattered, because he wasn't in love with her, but she had got used to the idea that he was relatively safe. And now this.

The man was back at home. How many of his friends were already involved, perhaps dead or prisoners? He came back to reality as Helen asked, 'Any idea when you'll go?'

'That's what I came to tell you. I'm on a fortnight's embarkation leave. I'm going to spend a week with some friends in Yorkshire, then I'll come back and we'll go out whenever you're free. Jim has offered me a bed in the Rectory.'

She forced a smile. 'I'll look forward to that, but what will you do all day?'

'Jim's anxious to take me fishing and if you'll lend me that spare bike, I want to see a bit more of Norfolk.'

'That's a good idea. There's so much worth seeing. I'll give you a list of places. Of course, some of the best, like the beaches and the cliff walks, will be out of bounds – and don't take any chances, some of them are heavily mined – but there's enough to keep you occupied, and there's the Friday dance as usual.'

When Sophie came in and heard Johnny's news, she suggested he should stay for the evening and share their meal, but he said, 'Thanks, but there'll be something at the barracks – I won't pinch your rations.'

'Oh, it's only a bit of Spam and I thought I'd do some roasted onions – we have plenty of them.'

But he couldn't be persuaded and went away, promising to see them in a week.

'He's sick about Singapore. I've never seen him depressed before.'

'Yes, it's bad news. Molly was bad enough when she knew where Stephen was. If I know her, she'll be frantic with worry.'

It was just the beginning of the most miserable of the war years for the village.

Molly came into Ellen in tears and shaking.

'Oh, Ellen, whatever shall I do? I never wanted him to go. He didn't have to. Why was he so pig-headed!'

'Now then, sit down and have a cup of tea. We must keep hoping. We can't know what's going on. Joe said, only last night, that they have to treat prisoners decently under the Geneva Convention – I think that's what he called it – and the Red Cross will let people know what's happened to all the boys as soon as they know.'

But Molly was in no mood to be comforted.

'It's all very well for you. You know where Philip is.'

'Yes. I do know. And I know he's in great danger every time he goes out on a raid. For all you know, Stephen may be quite safe.'

Molly was at once contrite and burst into fresh tears.

'Oh, Ellen, I'm so sorry. You must be worried out of your mind every time.'

'I try not to think about it. Time enough if the worst happens. Besides, I have to keep cheerful for Rosie and Joe. He's always quiet but sometimes I think he feels it more than me. He's on his own so much of the time.'

'So am I, now Joyce is working.'

'Well now, how would you like to do some work yourself?'

'What sort of work? We already go to Red Cross.'

'Sally's thinking about forming a working group in the village for people who can't go out to the factories. There are quite a lot going now all over the country and she thinks we ought to do our bit – and the money would help.'

'But what sort of work?' persisted Molly.

'Sally's looking into it, but it seems there are women making small aeroplane or gun parts at home. It only means learning to use a screwdriver.'

'Well, I've done a few things Stephen used to do. I dare say I could manage that.'

'If it comes off, we might all meet together instead of being on our own. That way we won't have so much time to dwell on what might never happen.'

At last Helen had a letter from Johnny. It read:

'Dear Helen and all,

Well, I am where I thought I would be. You know I can't say more than that. We are all safe and well but things are changing rapidly.

I have met a fellow Aussie. I didn't know him before, but we almost fell into each other's arms when we heard the familiar accent. We'll keep in touch as long as we can.

I often think of the good times we had together and wonder how you're doing. If I'm here when the war ends, I hope I can get demobbed in England so that I can see you all again before I go home.

I'll write when I can, but I hope all of you will write often. I'll be glad to hear from anyone. Tell Jim I can't get any fishing here, but I would like to thank him again for putting me up and taking me on the trips with him.

Much love to you all.'

Helen hardly saw his signature through her sudden tears. It had not occurred to her before that she might never see him again, that he might go straight to Australia from wherever he was stationed.

Then she thought: better so. She should put him out of her mind, but Jean's words 'bleak without him' seemed to sum up her future. On leaving, he had kissed her, but so he had done to Sophie and Heather. She meant no more to him than any of them.

* * * * *

Joyce Painter was a blue-eyed blonde. She was a small girl with the appealing face of a kitten so that she looked younger than her age, which was nearly seventeen.

At school she had always been chosen for the plays, chiefly because she had a pleasant, clear voice, and her ambition was to be a BBC announcer. But she was a practical girl and she had decided when she was called up for war work that she would go into a factory in Norwich, with the intention of joining one of the Women's Services when she was old enough.

The news that the Japanese had taken Singapore had hit her hard, partly because of her own anxiety for her father and Molly's distress, but also because she could not now leave her mother to join the Forces.

But neither, she decided, could she do factory work for very much longer. All the shifts were terrible – 8am to 4pm was the best, but even that meant getting up at dawn to be ready for the factory bus which went round all the villages picking up the women and girls (and a few men) and returned them to their homes about 6pm if they were lucky and didn't get held up by farm carts along the narrow lanes.

At least on that shift they saw daylight. Both the others meant blackouts on windows, an increase in the considerable noise, hot and stuffy conditions in summer and cold ones in winter. Lack of ventilation meant that the workers got increasingly weary as time went on. They were working on aircraft parts. Joyce had had a short period of training and found the work easy, thanking her stars that she was not in the paint shop where the fumes were overwhelming.

The women made the best of it, singing all the popular songs of the moment, cheering each other on – often with ribald remarks to the men – and reminding each other that they were shortening the war. But Joyce hated the conditions and the innuendos.

On this night in late April, Joyce glanced up at the big clock. Twenty minutes to midnight. She would soon be free. Then came the familiar wail of the air raid siren. The girls put down their tools, donned tin hats and prepared to go down to the shelter. Before they could get there came the sound of the planes and the first bombs began to fall. They were not far away. The ground shook under their feet.

'Into the shelter!' yelled the foreman. 'Hurry up!'

But already some were saying, 'Not likely – don't want this lot on top of us.'

And Joyce was inclined to agree with them as heavy thumps shook the building. She was at the door and staring up at a sheet of flame. Even as she watched, it spread rapidly and lit up the sky for miles around.

'It's the railway line they're after,' said one of the men.

'A railway line wouldn't burn like that,' replied a girl.

Then, suddenly, the whole of Norwich station was ablaze. Being mostly timber, it burned fiercely and its light showed wave upon wave of bombers coming in.

Without further warning, the machine gunning began. Now everyone was a target. The shelter seemed the safest place after all. They ran to it and listened to the menacing noises, ears strained to catch the first sounds of their own building collapsing.

Then someone started singing and others joined in with enthusiasm. This was better than having nerves stretched with the constant alertness. *White Cliffs of Dover, Paper Doll, That Old Black Magic, White Christmas* – then the old ones from the last war – *Pack up your Troubles* and *Tipperary* were sung loudly to drown out the noise outside.

It was nearly 2am before the All-Clear sounded, but by then Joyce was already helping at a mobile canteen, serving refreshments to the emergency workers, firemen and ARP personnel who had been working tirelessly all through the raid. There were even Girl Guides and Boy Scouts acting as messengers – on foot in most areas, because broken glass and twisted water pipes made the use of bikes impossible.

All through that night she found work to do. A church hall was opened for people who had lost their homes and she shepherded some of these poor bemused individuals back to this place of refuge where the Women's Voluntary Services were waiting to give them tea and blankets.

When the factory bus arrived – very late – with the 8am workers, she sank into a seat wearily, only to find that she had to give it up to an older woman, since there were two lots of shift workers returning home.

The second shift had been able to work most of the night, as the factory had not been damaged. They were lucky. They soon learned that twenty factories had been destroyed as well as many small businesses and Woodlands Hospital.

Joyce arrived home about half-past-nine in bright Spring sunshine. She could have four hours' sleep before the bus came back again to take her to work.

They never heard of any casualties from that raid, though over a thousand people were left homeless.

The next day, more than two-hundred-and-fifty guns were moved in to defend Norwich. They were just in time. The bombers returned on April 29th and all through the beginning of May, culminating in a pitched battle on the 9th. The noise of the guns was added to the racket of falling bombs and aircraft. Balloons had been hoisted to prevent planes flying low enough to hit their targets with the result that bombs were scattered over a wider area, so that several of the outlying villages were hit.

By now the village work group was up and running. As news of the homeless came in, the talk was all of what they could do to help.

'I phoned several of the WI secretaries from the villages which were worst hit,' Sally told them. 'They all want bedding – anything we can spare.'

Blankets had been in short supply ever since the evacuees had come, and the children had been knitting squares for extra ones until they ran out of the last scraps of wool.

'Could we do patchwork quilts? Can we still get something to fill them with?' Laura Thompson had not lost her thirst for gossip, but she had improved a great deal through her involvement in the war effort and often made good suggestions.

'I'll see. I think I have some kapok somewhere. There won't be a lot, but we should all see what we can find.'

And so, like millions of other women all over Britain, they undertook yet another job for the war effort.

There were spasmodic raids after that, but nothing so serious until the end of June. On the 25th bombers attacked Yarmouth and Ellen was worried until she knew that Rosie's people were safe. Although both the Town Hall and the police station were hit, only three people were killed.

Two nights later, Norwich was the target again, not only with heavy bombers but also with ten thousand incendiaries. This time, nine people were killed and one of them was Joe's brother, Bob, who had lived in Brook Place, where the whole block of flats had been hit.

Ellen was fond of her brother-in-law and this was the first death in the war which had affected anyone in the village since Dunkirk.

'I know it's silly,' she told Molly, 'but in a sense it makes Philip seem safer – I mean, when it can take ordinary people like that. I'm glad now that Bob was single – and the times I've wished he was married with a family. Helen is Philip's only cousin and I used to think it would be nice if there had been more.'

Molly sympathised. As the time went by and there was no news from Singapore she had become more resigned to waiting, but now she was worrying about Joyce.

'It's not just that she's in Norwich. It's the work. She's only a little thing, and this is heavy stuff they're dealing with. She doesn't get nearly enough sleep and I know she hates it, although she never says so.'

'I think she looks exhausted, but I don't suppose she can leave it. Sally will know, I expect. Ask her tomorrow.'

Before July was very old, Sally had seen Joyce and, with some difficulty, wheedled out of the girl that she really wanted to join the ATS, but felt she couldn't leave her mother.

'Well, my dear, thousands of girls have had to and the mothers have to put up with it. Would you go into the Land Army or Women's Voluntary Services?

'Either, if I could live at home.'

Sally arranged for Joyce to have a medical examination and the doctor was surprised to find a country girl so anaemic. She was exempted from indoor work and joined the WVS within a week.

When George Barker asked his wife if she thought the evacuees would like to spend part of their holidays preparing a revue again, she was not so sure.

'I think you should ask how many would be interested. You may find a lot of them would rather go into the harvest field with our children.'

It was true that some of them had taken to the country life. There was much less homesickness, especially in the summer holidays as the mothers were keen to visit when the weather was fine. But there were some who would enjoy using the time by working on a new revue – only there were no troops near at hand to make an audience for a concert. Helen suggested that they should concentrate on the Christmas pantomime.

Then, in early August, the barracks which the RE had vacated was taken over by the American airforce as a depot, holding spare parts for their planes. By now there were Liberator bases all over Norfolk and they had chosen the village as a safe place for their stores.

With them came an air of excitement. None of the villagers had met anyone like them. There were only a few men at the depot, but word got round about the Friday dances and soon there were lorryloads of men and girls coming in from the bases. They courted the girls with gifts of nylons and sweets and repaid their mothers for hospitality with tinned food such as they had not seen since before the war; some that was unknown but delicious. They seemed to be short of nothing, whether it was food, transport or money.

It was hardly to be supposed that the local young men would

take kindly to them – these smart, uniformed boys with money to throw around – while they could barely afford to take their girls to the pictures and had to wear whatever clothing had so far survived the war. But gradually, even they succumbed to the good nature and generosity of the newcomers, much encouraged by Jim, who never let slip an opportunity of pointing out that these boys were far from home and in need of all the friendship the village could offer them.

Joyce Painter had been one of the girls who cordially disliked their brashness and was not to be easily won over by gifts of nylons. It upset her to see some of the girls who had boys in the Forces 'fall down all of a heap if one of them so much as looked at her', as she put it to her mother.

But that was before she met Hank. This tall, broad GI had approached her for a dance and, as they finished a particularly boisterous polka, he murmured, 'Some fun, eh?'

She agreed, thinking that at least some of these boys had a simplicity which did not bear out their reputation for brashness.

'What's your name?' he asked her, and when she gave it: 'I'm Hank.' She had never heard such an outlandish Christian name and assumed that 'Hunk' was a well-merited nickname, and thereafter she never called him anything else.

Sophie and Helen liked him from the start – a naive country boy, like so many they knew – and were completely won over when Ellen told them, 'That young Hank actually asked Molly's permission to take Joyce to the pictures and promised to get her home by ten.'

It was true that many of the GIs were really shy and quite a lot were from small towns where church-going and deference to women was a way of life.

Under their influence, the dances became more and more informal. The Americans taught the English their country and western dances. Some of them were good 'callers', keeping up amusing patter while instructing the steps to take. In return, they learnt the Veleta and the Gay Gordons.

Joyce and Hank made a quaint-looking couple, this big man with a little slip of a girl in his arms, but everyone got used to seeing them together and Molly started to worry in case Joyce got hurt when the Yanks returned to America.

'You can't lead other people's lives for them,' Ellen reminded her. 'It doesn't matter how much you love them. They have to have their own heartaches and joys – just like we did. It's all part of growing up. Joyce is very young. She should have plenty of young men before she settles down. And she's a lot tougher after all she has seen.'

Jim was undecided, when he first saw couples dancing the Jitterbug, whether he ought to suggest that the committee should ban it. But one or two partners were so good at it that he became fascinated with the sheer excellence of their performances. So did the rest of the dancers, who stood and watched, applauding loudly, as though they had been seeing a stage show.

The men swung their partners off their feet, then over their shoulders, turning them in mid-air, through their legs and back to the ground again where both picked up the rhythm without missing a beat. It was a very slick performance when done well and soon there were contests for the best couple.

Laura Thompson shook her head and told everyone that no good would come of it.

'They said that about the waltz,' Sophie reminded her.

With all this new activity, both the children and the adults felt a lift to their spirits, but then came the news, via the Red Cross, from Singapore. Arthur's eldest son had been killed in the fighting. He took it philosophically.

'I had a feeling right from the time he left. Thank God he never got captured by them bloodthirsty Japs.'

Nobody repeated his words to Molly when she heard that Stephen was a prisoner of war.

Ellen reached for the packet of Force and poured the flakes into Rosie's bowl.

'Why has Sunny Jim got that funny bit at the back of his head?'

'I don't know, my maid. Perhaps it's a bit of his hat.'

'Why doesn't Toffee have kittens?'

'Now, Rosie, eat your breakfast. You'll be late for school.'

'Yes, but why?'

'Well, he's a daddy cat. Mummy cats have the kittens.'

'Can we get a mummy cat?'

Ellen heaved a sigh. When Rosie got in this questioning mood there was no stopping her.

'We'll have to see what Uncle Joe says.'

Luckily, Wally arrived. He said, as usual, 'Hurry up or I'll go without you.'

She hurried. Wally was a great favourite with her.

Ellen was joined by Molly as she watched them go.

'She was in one of her 'Why' moods this morning. I was glad to see Wally.'

'Good job she's at school now.'

'I suppose so, but I still miss her around the house. She gets more fun out of life than any child I ever knew. Everything is a great adventure, even if it's only going out with Joe.'

'When is Mrs. Grice coming to see her again?'

'Both of them are coming this weekend. I wish she could stay. Yarmouth's dangerous. I just hope they all survive,' she sighed.

'Well, Rosie's safe here anyway.'

Helen was just leaving for school when she noticed the packet of sandwiches on the table. She was not surprised. Heather had mislaid her engagement ring and had searched for it until she made herself late. She had dashed out of the house in a hurry, saying, 'I'll have a good look tonight. It can't be far away.'

Well, one of the children could take it to her in the break. She would be working in Bishops field near the school. Helen picked up the packet and put it in her bag.

At Assembly, George had a surprise for them.

'Our American friends are going to a concert given by our boys at West Beckham and they're going to take anyone from the village who wants to go. This is to thank us for the dances – don't forget to

70

tell your parents that, because they have had all the work of organising them. It's a proper concert-party which goes round entertaining the troops and there'll be a well-known lady from ENSA – no, I don't know who – they wouldn't tell me. So we'll go on Saturday. There will be transport of some kind, probably lorries.'

Rosie came up to Helen while the children were having their milk.

'Mummy and Daddy are coming on Saturday. Do you think they can come to the concert?'

'I should think so. Two more won't make any difference. That will be a nice surprise for them.' Then she remembered. 'Rosie, Heather forgot her sandwiches this morning. She's only over there in Bishops field. Would you like to take them to her?'

'Yes, then I can tell her about the concert.' She ran off delightedly, clutching the packet.

Heather saw her coming at the same moment that she heard the plane. It sounded heavy and the note of the engine was rough. One of ours in trouble? she thought. She shaded her eyes and gazed in the direction of the sound. There it was, low and making for the coast. Swastikas! Rosie was looking up at it too.

'Lie down!' shouted Heather and then – 'Oh my God, the school!'

But it was past the school and veering away. She breathed again. But there was something hurtling down from it. The devils – they had jettisoned a bomb. It seemed clear of the village – perhaps it wouldn't do much harm. All this went through her mind in the seconds before it hit the ground. It was well clear, even so the blast knocked her off her feet and winded her.

When Heather raised herself, Rosie was still lying down. She looked like a rag doll thrown away by a child – and as lifeless.

There was a stunned silence in the village that night. Hank, calling to take Joyce to the pictures, was met with a blank stare as though she didn't recognise him.

'Not tonight, Hunk,' she said colourlessly.

It was left to a subdued Wally to tell him the news.

It had been a difficult, busy day. George had decided to keep the children at school and to tell them only at the end of the day, but those who had gone home for dinner had come back with the news. What they wanted to know was whether it was true, so he called them all together before the afternoon session and addressed them.

'We have had some bad news today. This war, which is causing so much sorrow to so many people, has come close to us.

'You know that an enemy bomb was dropped this morning. I believe it was not intended for us and we were lucky that it didn't hit any building in the village. But some people were caught by the blast of the bomb and knocked off their feet. Blast has the effect of driving the breath out of your body. One person did not survive — little Rosie Grice.'

His voice broke. Some of the children burst into tears.

'It's right that we should grieve but this is wartime and we all have to be very brave, so I want you to go to your classes now and, later on, we will think what we can best do to remember Rosie.'

He could say no more and dismissed the children. He had already sent Helen home. Her first words had been, 'Oh, I should have gone myself. I should never have sent her.'

She sat alone in the house, shivering, weeping and blaming herself bitterly.

Heather, in a state of collapse after she had brought the news, insisted that she must tell Ellen, but George had refused to let her go until Sally had been summoned. She took the girl back to her home, gave her a stiff brandy and put her to bed. Then she put the bottle in her bag and returned to the working party. Taking Ellen and Molly on one side, she told them that Rosie had had an accident and that she would take them home in her car. Once there, she explained what had happened and left them to comfort each other while she went to see Jim.

Jim had telephoned the Yarmouth police and asked them to tell Rosie's family and their parish priest, asking the latter to let him know what arrangements were to be made. Then he went to comfort Ellen.

He was good with bereaved relatives but this was different because he was raging with anger inside. Wicked men had made this war and because of them a bright, young life — one of the happiest he had ever known — was ended before it had hardly begun. It was enough to shake your faith, he thought. Before he got to Ellen he had remembered the old saying that those *whom the gods love die young*. There would never be any suffering now for Rosie.

When Sally got back home she found Heather had already gone, leaving a note,

'*Sally – I have to get back to Helen. I know she is blaming herself. Thank you for everything.*'

Bill Wood found his wife red-eyed and exhausted.

'I was afraid you'd be doing too much. Let other people do more, Sal,' he said.

She gestured hopelessly.

'There isn't anyone else. Jim's doing all he can and the others who might help are the ones most affected.'

'Yes, it's a bad business. Is there anything I can do?'

She smiled. 'First of all, you can get me a drink, then I'll pull myself together and think about what else needs doing. Don't worry. I'll find you plenty.'

Bad news travels fast. Before she had cycled halfway through the village, Sophie had been told. Joe heard as he was bedding Major down and cried into the horse's mane. He was dry-eyed when he reached home, but one look at his face was enough to tell Ellen that he knew.

But now it was night and they were all in Ellen's little cottage: Joe, Molly, Sophie, Helen and Heather.

'Joe,' said Ellen suddenly, 'I want Philip.'

The Group Captain put down the phone and said, 'Get Flying Officer Lambert for me.'

The WAAF saluted and went out. She found Philip in the recreation room, watching a game of billiards, and gave him the message.

'What you done now, Pip? Haven't pranged anything lately, have you?' asked Avery.

'Not that I know. He'll be putting me in charge of the Squadron most likely.'

He went out cheerfully, their good-natured jeers following him. Groupie looked up as he came into the room and motioned him to a chair.

'Sit down, Lambert. I'm afraid it's a bit of bad news though I understand it doesn't affect you personally. I've been talking to a man called Jim Crook. I understand he's your rector.'

'That's right, sir. Is something wrong in the village?'

'Seems there was an enemy plane off course. Jettisoned a bomb. Missed the village, but the blast killed a girl called Rosie Grice.'

Philip felt as if he had been winded. There was utter disbelief in his tone as he said, 'Rosie. No. Not Rosie. My God, she's only five!'

'I'm afraid wars don't take account of the ages of their victims. Well, it seems your mother is very distressed and wants to see you. Was the girl a relative?'

'Closer than that. She was an evacuee and my mother had promised to adopt her if her parents didn't survive the war. I thought of her as my little sister. We were all very fond of her.'

Philip had a sudden clear picture of Rosie as she had been the last time he saw her. Laughing, hugging him, saying 'Come back soon'. This life had gone. This innocent lovely child had been wiped from the earth by those murdering bastards. Somewhere inside him a spark of pure hatred flickered and then flamed into life. He clenched his fists.

The Group Captain watched him closely, seeing the varying emotions cross his face.

'I'm very sorry. You've had a shock. I'll get someone to replace you tonight and tomorrow we'll see about some leave. I'll let Travers know.'

'No. Please. I'd rather go. Honestly. Please.' He spoke vehemently. He had to give the Jerries a taste of their own medicine. The Group Captain looked at him. He had got over the first shock and had himself well in hand. And sometimes it helped them to keep busy.

'Very well – and thank you. It won't be easy to find a replacement, so it would be a help.'

It was a help to Philip as well. The target was Dusseldorf and there was plenty of work for him to do. The moon was waning and there was intermittent cloud. It helped to conceal them but hindered him from getting a star sighting. Thankful to be busy, he concentrated all his attention on the charts before him. Luckily, the crew were used to his silence as they approached the target and, as far as he was aware, no-one knew of his trouble.

In fact, Groupie had thought it wise to tell Travers.

'I think he'll be all right or I wouldn't send him. I won't now, if you're doubtful.'

But Travers did not want a stranger in his crew and had said that he was sure Philip would be OK.

At last, Philip could do no more until they were over the target and he had time to think. The anger which he had been holding at bay came flooding over him and he was suddenly grateful that he had a chance of striking back. He felt exultant.

The first planes had hit their target. Dusseldorf appeared to be on fire as they approached and the flak was heavy.

'Bloody party they've got waiting for us,' grumbled Avery.

Then they were in among it. Travers couldn't keep on the course that Philip had given him or they would certainly have been hit. There were some very near misses. They tried a second time but had to get out quickly.

'OK, that's it. We'll offload on the outskirts. We might hit something worthwhile.' Then, a little later: 'This'll do, Pip.'

But Philip took no notice. It had suddenly hit him that they were over a residential area. There would be ordinary people and children like Rosie down there.

'Not here, Skip. In the country.'

'Don't be a fool, Pip. We're the ones at risk.'

Travers spoke sharply, but Philip was adamant.

'Sorry, Skip. I'm not pressing that damn tit to kill kids.'

'Scottie, release those bloody bombs.'

Scottie got up and made his way with difficulty to where Philip crouched over and snarled, 'Don't touch it.'

As he looked up, Scottie whipped his right arm back, then forward, catching Philip under the chin, then he put the lolling head up and touched the bomb release. The plane shuddered and lightened.

'Bombs gone,' Scottie reported.

'Good. You haven't killed Pip, have you?'

'No, Skip, he's sleeping like a baby. He'll be with us again before we get home.'

'Hell was that all about?' asked Avery.

So Travers told them.

'And you needn't tell the inquisition anything about it – not until I've seen Pip. It may never happen again,' Travers warned them.

They all agreed. Philip would have hit his chin when the plane was jinking to avoid the flak. That was all Intelligence needed to know. Luckily, the debriefing was short that night and after it Philip, nursing his sore head, went off without a word to any of them.

In the morning, the Group Captain sent for him again, but Philip asked to speak first.

'I want to come off operations, sir. I put my crew at risk last night and if I go out again, I know I'll do the same thing.'

He explained what had happened and why, adding ruefully,

stroking his chin, 'They had to knock me out to release the bombs.'

'I understand, but you know what this will do to your career, don't you? I'll have to record it as lack of moral fibre – that's the jargon – LMF. But it's not true in your case. This was no failure of nerve. Take some leave and think it over.'

'I shan't change my mind, sir. I think I considered everything last night. I'd rather settle it now.'

'Very well, You'll get your posting while you're on leave. I'm damn sorry to lose you, and for my money, you've got more moral fibre than most of us. It takes guts to make a decision like that.'

On the night before Rosie's funeral the family were gathered at Ellen and Joe's. Philip had gone to meet Heather and they went over to the church. The cut grass smelt of summer. Above them, a full moon turned it to silver. 'Bomber's Moon,' thought Philip. His thoughts with his aircrew, he said, 'These are the nights that show up targets to us and our planes to them.'

Heather shivered. 'I don't know how you can do it – after what's happened ...'

'I shan't have the chance in future.' He told her what had happened on his last raid and ended, 'But it's different when it's over a good target – munition works, railways. We have to stop them, darling. You can't let bullies get away with it forever.'

'I hate it,' she replied. 'Do you know how often the bombs miss? You know that schools have been hit?'

'It's inevitable.'

'But did *you* have to do it?'

He stuck out his jaw. 'Don't you think our way of life is worth preserving?'

'Oh, my dear, our way of life has gone forever. Whatever comes out of this, it can never be the same again.'

When they returned to the house, Philip told the others that he had something to tell them.

'Just as well now, while we're all together. You'll have to know sometime. You may not approve, but I don't think you'll despise me – though some people may.'

He caught his mother's eye and realised that she was afraid for him. He said quickly, 'In a nutshell – I've decided that I won't be responsible for dropping another bomb.'

Ellen said, on a deep sigh of relief, 'But that's wonderful. Why should anyone despise you?'

Joe patted his wife's hand. 'Some people might think he's a coward.' Then to Philip, 'Is this the end of your career, boy?'

'I expect so, Dad. They'll demote me and I imagine they'll find me something to do until the war ends, but then I'll certainly be discharged. Now you know the worst, let me tell you what happened.'

He related the whole story of his last mission. Joe drew his breath in sharply when he heard how Philip had disobeyed an order. Joe had been in Flanders. In that war, disobeying orders meant getting shot. But Ellen was indignant that he had been knocked out.

'No, Mum. They were quite right. For as long as the bombs were still there we could have been blown to bits if there had been even a minor incident, like a bit of flak which might only have caused minimal damage otherwise.'

'Oh, my boy – I haven't let myself imagine the danger you were in. Thank God you won't have to do it again.'

But Helen and Heather were both looking at him with shining eyes. Tears were not far away, but he knew they were on his side.

Heather said, 'Oh, darling, what a relief it will be! I won't have to worry about you on those ghastly raids.'

'But will they let you do it? What will happen?' asked Sophie.

'Oh, yes. They can't compel you – not these days. They will say I lack moral fibre – that's the jargon for being too scared to go on. LMF will go down on my record. I'll hear any day now where my next posting will be. But it's goodbye to a career in the RAF and that's all I know.'

'If this war's taught me anything,' Heather said, 'it's that you can't look too far ahead. The future must take care of itself. You're an expert camera man. You'll find something.'

After the funeral, Philip took Heather home in the Morris. As they passed Pretty Corner woods, she said, 'Let's stop and walk a bit. It's such a lovely day.'

The October sunshine still had some warmth in it and the fallen leaves were quite dry. They sat down in the middle of the woods and she said, with a catch in her voice, 'I'm glad it was fine for her

77

– and for them. At least they didn't have to go through it in miserable weather.' After a pause, she asked, 'You won't change your mind about the bombing, will you?'

'Never. Today I had no doubts – seeing her people standing there, hand in hand, rigid and dry-eyed at that little grave ...'

His voice broke and Heather burst into tears. He gathered her tenderly into his arms and, after a while, they comforted each other with the love that they both needed to heal their heavy hearts.

This is Now - 2

'And I,' said the grey-haired lady, who was Helen, 'went home and cried for Rosie and her people, for Aunt Ellen, who had loved her like a daughter, and for myself because Johnny was so far away and I had no-one to comfort me.'

I sat like a puppet – all energy gone. After a while, I said, 'Oh, that was all terribly sad. I hope you've got some more cheerful things to tell me.'

'Well, there was a war on, so there are more tragedies, but nothing that hit us so hard as Rosie's death. But, yes, there was fun, too. We had to get our pleasures where we could. Even in the village there was a sense of 'Eat, drink and be merry, for tomorrow we die.' The GIs were a great morale booster, with their generosity. I think it shocked them to see how little we had. But I'll tell you more next time. When do you get your plaster off?'

'Two more weeks, I'm afraid. It's been driving me mad, what with the irritation and not being able to get about. But, look here, I must thank you. You're so articulate and you seem to have total recall. It's amazing.'

Helen smiled and the brown eyes were soft.

'It's one of the compensations of old age. I forget what happened yesterday, but the past is vivid – and, of course, when Heather and I get together we remind each other.

'It was a very special time, you know. It changed so many lives – and we were proud to be taking part in such history. We still are. It's unforgettable. Which is why I'm glad to help you with your book. It will be worthwhile if you can get over to younger people what we did and how we felt. My generation has a special bond – we grew up in wartime – grew up, in more ways than one.

'Imagine, but for the war, our men would have lived all their lives in the village, going into Norwich for the cattle market, perhaps, but no further. Buses were sparse. You might have to walk a couple of miles to catch one, and only the rich had cars. Now these same men can talk of the Middle East and the Far East and of fighting with companions from every part of the Empire – and so can some of the women.

'There, I've talked too much again. I'll see you next week. You'll be wanting to get back to work soon.'

About this time, Aunt Julia had an unexpected letter.

'Fancy, Doreen and her husband are in Sheringham on holiday. She was with me since the Isle of Man days. Six is a good number for a dinner party – I won't have to extend the dining table. I've picked Simon's brains so much, I owe him a dinner.'

'So you can pick them some more?' suggested Uncle Reg.

I laughed, but I had had a horrid thought.

'You'll have to ask his wife, won't you?'

'Who? Oh, Simon. He's not married. You will make us something, won't you, Reggie?'

Matchmaking, I thought. Aunt Julia's at it again. When they lived in Richmond, she was always asking me to dinner and producing a male partner. I would have refused her invitations more often but for the food. Cooking was Uncle Reg's forte, and he was really talented – as long as he had the kitchen to himself. He became abrupt to the point of rudeness if he was disturbed. I had been snarled at once when I interrupted him, and though he apologised afterwards, I had learned to keep clear.

Now he said, 'There's a sauce I want to try. It would go well with a fresh chicken. When do you want to ask them?'

'Thursday or Friday – whichever they can all make. I hope Simon's not too frightfully busy. I better make it 8.30.'

After much phoning and many digressions, she settled on Thursday. I hobbled to my room and tried to decide what to wear. A long skirt would hide most of my plaster, but would it hamper me too much? Then I laughed at myself. This was the country. No-one would care what I wore and I certainly did not want to impress a country bumpkin, devoted to organic gardening who was trying to put the clock back when we were nearly into the 21st Century.

It was a splendid meal. We started with mushroom soup, thick, creamy and smooth, served with the lightest of plain scones and garlic butter. Lemon sorbet followed. The chicken had a flavour I had almost forgotten and would have been perfect even without the sauce. We identified wine, tomatoes, herbs and olives but Uncle Reg would not enlighten us further. Then he produced a beautiful Savarin filled with fresh fruit and topped with cream. I don't think anyone touched the cheese board.

As usual, the accompanying wine was a perfect compliment to the food, but Aunt Julia said suddenly, 'Wouldn't it be wonderful to have Chateau Yquem again?'

Doreen turned to her husband, George. 'Do you remember when we had some in Holland? Must have been thirty years ago.'

'I remember. It was about £8 a bottle then. I saw some the other day – it was nearly £100.'

Simon said, 'That would feed a few starving children.'

Something about this man was annoying me. My first impression at the nursery had been favourable, but for someone of my own age he seemed stuck in a time warp. He had been talking about organic gardening and companion planting for a lot of the time and I had been bored. This last remark nettled me. Undoubtedly, he would not approve of my lifestyle.

Perhaps some of my antagonism was also due to the knowledge that Aunt Julia had asked him there for me.

I said sharply, 'I suppose the vintners have to live, too.'

He looked surprised and Doreen said quickly, 'Well, Julia, that was a bit different from Smokey Joe's.'

'I thought that was a night-club,' I said.

'So it was. A long low barn of a place, thick with smoke, because Joe cooked everything in there. It was a favourite place for the Signals crowd. Cheap and cheerful.'

'He used to bawl out 'One *superior* pie' every so often. Doreen, was that where we had the talent-spotting contests?'

'Of course – we did a cockney mime.'

Simon said, 'I thought karaoke was a modern invention.'

'Oh, this was to an old wind-up gramophone. We had one of the men standing by all the time to see that it didn't run down.'

We went into the sitting-room. Uncle Reg excused himself to stack the dishwasher. I offered to help but he refused, saying that I should rest that leg, and not try to do so much. Julia and Doreen continued to reminisce, with much laughter. After a while, George disappeared in the direction of the kitchen.

Simon raised a quizzical eyebrow at me.

'Have I offended you?'

'You made it clear you don't approve of expensive items. It takes spending to oil the wheels of industry you know – and provides plenty of jobs.'

He replied quietly, but suddenly vehement, 'Unnecessary work when there are shortages in all the caring professions. Big money for fat cats and some people on the breadline into the 21st Century.

I looked at him pityingly.

'Yes, money rules, I'm afraid. Nothing much we can do about it.'

'We can try – if we care enough.'

I said fiercely, 'My uncle and aunt both cared enough to go and fight in the war. They've worked hard all their lives. Why shouldn't they have a bit of luxury in their old age?'

'I'm sorry if you thought I was criticising them. I wasn't – I like them both far too much. But I wouldn't feel happy eating a meal like that very often.'

'They don't either. This was a special occasion. Aunt Julia hasn't seen her friend for ages.'

He got up as Reg and George returned and made the excuse of an early morning start for leaving so soon, but I detained him while I asked, 'Uncle Reg, would you ever pay £100 for a bottle of wine?'

'What – over £15 a glass? – not in any circumstances. I'm not mean, but every sip would choke me. It's obscene.'

I shot a triumphant glance at Simon as he left.

In my room later, I thought of our conversation. Uncle Reg had been the chief accountant to a large London company and I assumed that his pension would be more than adequate. They had almost certainly made a nice profit from the house in Richmond. This bungalow was adequate for their needs, but certainly not luxurious. I knew that they had both joined the local golf club – it was one of their reasons for choosing North Norfolk – but I saw nothing ostentatious in their way of living.

I remembered, with a sudden feeling of guilt, that I had once been entertained by a stockbroker who had paid over £200 for a bottle of Sancerre.

The next morning Aunt Julia asked, 'What did you think of Simon?'

'Sorry to disappoint you, but I thought he was an opinionated bore.'

She frowned. 'I'm sorry if all the gardening talk bored you. We're both so interested in it.'

'Oh, no. It wasn't that,' I said quickly, 'it was the way he spoke – going on about companion planting and not using chemicals – he's living in the past. And not wanting people to enjoy themselves …'

'Yes, I suppose he could seem that way to you.'

She changed the subject, but I felt, for some obscure reason, that she was criticising me.

When Helen had gone, I found it difficult to drag my thoughts back to the present. Considering that she had been a school teacher and had written all their pantomimes, I suppose it was not surprising that she had been such a good narrator. She had certainly had me enthralled, but when I suggested that *she* should have written her story, she said that she preferred to write poetry – but only for her own pleasure.

It was a phone call from Robert that dragged me back into the real world.

'I'd like to talk to you. I suppose you're not mobile yet?'

'No. I should get the plaster off next week.'

'Well, could I come down on Sunday? I'll take you out to lunch somewhere and we can talk.'

Of course, Aunt Julia said that she would give him lunch, but I explained that he was coming to talk business.

'Well, what's wrong with the summerhouse? You can be on your own in there. It's ridiculous for him to drive you out somewhere. Poor man, he'll be driving all day – and you never know what you're eating in restaurants.'

I laughed. 'I've been eating in restaurants for the last ten years. You're just spoilt because Uncle Reg is such a marvellous cook.'

'Really, Jan, give me credit for doing most of the cooking. But we were both brought up in country conditions and with homemade food. There's not nearly enough hygiene these days – otherwise they wouldn't have all these food scares – and people buying all this convenience stuff when they don't know what's in it.'

We were never going to agree on modern day living. I dropped the subject, but there was sense in what she said. Robert would have enough driving to do, so we had our talk in the summerhouse after all.

'It's like this, Jan. I can offer you a job, but I don't think it'll be permanent. I've signed a contract for a year and I'll stick with it to give it a fair trial. But there's an atmosphere there I don't like. It might change, but if not, I shan't stay.'

'What's wrong with it? You're no stranger to intrigues and rivalries – and boardroom battles are two a penny.'

'This is different. It isn't jockeying for position – as you say, I'm used to that. No, it's this attitude to profits before everything. Management is completely orientated towards finance and anything creative comes a very poor second.'

I said that was common knowledge and I was surprised he hadn't been prepared for it.

'Oh, I was, but not to the extent that it exists. I thought I should warn you, but the job is there if you want it.'

We discussed, at some length, just what my role would be. It would be good for my career and I would have jumped at the chance just a few weeks ago, but I had been out of the rat race and living, through Helen, in another world.

At last, I said, 'Can I have a little while to think it over? I've got very involved with this novel I've started. I suppose it isn't really a novel – it's more faction – but it's really fascinating. Once I can get around I must do more research and interview other people …'

'I'd be sorry not to have you, but why not take a sabbatical and get it done? I might even be able to get you a grant – but don't decide today.'

We agreed that I would think it over and I prepared to do a final session with Helen.

That Was Then - Helen's Story

Molly Painter took the card from the post-woman and stared in disbelief. It was her first intimation that Stephen was still alive.

She had sent him parcels through the Red Cross, but with the understanding that she would probably never know whether he received them. She did not know now. The card said merely,

'Still here. All my love to you and Joyce.'

She could not see a postmark. It was impossible to tell how long it had taken to arrive. Molly sat down heavily, scarcely knowing how she felt. Shock, relief and anxiety were mingled.

Stephen would not have recognised the fearful wife he had left behind. The war had strengthened her in the same way that it had many housewives. Each had become head of her household and found that she could cope. Even more than the young women who had left home and gone into conditions undreamed of in their former lives, these older women had gained in confidence as they took on more and more of the work that had previously been done by the men.

They had all been helped enormously by the support they had received from each other. Even in the close community of village life, folk had tended to keep their troubles to themselves before the war, but now each of them knew that the others suffered as they did. The constant worry of having loved ones in danger, never spoken of during the day but coming back to haunt each lonely night, was a common experience. There was no need to talk about it – that would weaken them – but it was a comfort to know that everyone understood.

Equally, they rejoiced in the good news, whether it was a national triumph or just a village boy coming home on leave – safe for the time being.

Molly got ready to go to work, taking her precious card. Everybody would be pleased for her.

* * * * *

85

In the village hall there was the usual air of activity. The gossip only started when they had got down to work. Then Laura asked, 'Has anybody got any news?'

Rather shyly, Molly produced her card and passed it round the group. It was scrutinised with great interest and many expressions of gladness.

'Fancy that coming all that way! Thass a miracle,' said Mrs. White. And that was the general opinion. No-one remarked that it only proved Stephen was alive when it was sent. Molly would know that.

'And I've got some good news, too,' Ellen said, when the discussion had died down. 'Philip and Heather are getting married on his next leave.'

'When will that be?'

'Will it be here?'

'He thinks it'll be April. The wedding will be in London, but they're coming here for the rest of his leave and they've promised us a party.'

Heather had come back from a weekend in London and announced that she was getting married on Philip's next leave.

'And will you be my bridesmaid, Helen? It's going to be a very quiet affair – only about a dozen people, because most of our friends are in the Services – so I shan't be getting married in white. You will come and hold my hand, won't you?'

'Well, I'd love to, but what on earth can I wear? I haven't got enough clothing coupons to get anything new.'

But it seemed that was not going to be a problem. Most of Heather's friends and relations had promised her some.

'And the bridegroom's gift to the bridesmaid will be a new outfit – he's giving his mother one too,' said Heather, her eyes sparkling. 'And we're coming back here for the rest of Philip's leave, and we're going to give the village a party.'

Philip and Heather, like so many young people, had decided that the war was going on far too long to keep all their plans on hold. Now that he had received his posting and was doing reconnaissance work, Philip felt that his chances of surviving were much improved, and both of them wanted to be together whenever he was on leave.

Sally had not asked Ellen to take any more evacuees, feeling that she was not sufficiently recovered from the shock of Rosie's death, so Philip's room would be free for the newly-weds.

For once, Heather had decided to make full use of her money and to give the village a party to remember. There were several American airforce bases nearby and she persuaded Sally to lend her the car whenever she had free time and set off to purchase surplus food from our allies.

'The last time we went over to Horsham St Faith for a dance, I realised that they had food to waste. It's maddening when you think it's all brought over by our Navy and that we're kept on rations for the same reason, but as it's there, I don't see why our people shouldn't have some of it.'

From these forays, Heather returned with tins of fruit and other luxuries that British people had not seen since 1939, dried fruit and crates of grapefruit, oranges and bananas, and with the promise of more perishable food nearer the date of the party.

However, she found it difficult to stop the Yanks from donating the food when they understood why she wanted it and so she could only repay them by inviting some from each bomber station to the event. Matters were getting out of hand.

It was Jim who solved the problem. He had become friendly with the chaplain who served the base at North Pickenham.

'It's like this, Harry,' he explained. 'It's really intended as a blow-out for the village and any special friends of Philip and Heather, but your people have been so generous that Heather felt she had to invite them. The village hall isn't really big enough for a sit-down meal for that number.'

'And our GIs don't need any more food, for goodness sake. Leave it with me, Jim.'

The outcome was that the villagers would have their banquet and the Yanks would come along to dance after the trestle tables had been cleared away.

Ellen, Joe and Helen went up to London for the wedding. Heather was to be married in a beautifully cut blue dress which matched her eyes, but Helen and Ellen had both chosen suits, which would be the most practical garments for the future. Philip had contrived to get some parachute silk and they had made themselves new blouses, revelling in the opportunity to work on some quality material.

Joe had been apprehensive about meeting Heather's parents and of his own appearance. He wore his black Sunday suit, relieved by Heather's gift of a light grey silk tie. He need not have worried.

Almost the first words that Alan said were, 'These young people don't think about anyone else. I haven't been able to get a new suit to give my daughter away. Well, they'll just have to put up with it.'

'Who looks at the men at a wedding?' asked his wife.

Philip was complacent. He was relieved to be able to wear his uniform.

They were married by the family's local vicar, who joined them for the wedding breakfast at a nearby hotel. Heather, who had been nervous in church, was radiant once it was all over.

The only disappointment was the wedding cake. It looked magnificent but the icing was like concrete and the cake so heavily and artificially flavoured that no-one could taste what was in it.

'I expect that was the idea,' commented Joe. They all laughed and agreed that it was just one more casualty of the war.

Then they went home to prepare for the village party.

It was just the sort of boost the women needed. They were getting ever more ingenious at making the rations go round and producing nutritious meals out of very little – but, oh, they were so dull! The small ration of meat was stretched by the addition of oatmeal, potatoes, suet pastry – when suet was obtainable – and vegetables. The housewives in towns fared even worse when vegetables were in short supply and it was reported that a single onion could cost the earth.

Now they sat down to a real meal. There was as much cold meat of all types as they could eat, turkey with cranberry sauce (a new idea to them) and hot puddings bursting with steak and kidney in a rich gravy, 'like something out of Dickens', as Philip said.

He was astonished at what Heather, with the help of some of the villagers, had been able to do. Once they had got the basic ingredients, Laura and Mrs. White had made cakes and puddings in great variety, delighted at having icing sugar, unlimited eggs, butter and fine American flour with which to show off their skills.

'Oh, this is gorgeous shortbread,' sighed Sophie, 'I haven't tasted anything like it since Mum used to make it.'

'Yes, I thought of that, too. Molly made this one,' Ellen replied.

At the end of the meal, they were offered after-dinner mints – a commonplace for the GIs but never heard of in England until then.

There was still a lot of food left, so they cleared the hall for dancing, leaving a couple of trestle tables up to take the surplus.

It was then that Heather and Philip got their surprise. Jim carried in a two-tier wedding cake. It had been made by Laura and exquisitely decorated by Jim's mother, whose skill at tapestry work was, if anything, superseded by her skill at cake decoration.

They were delighted and started telling everyone how awful the cake at the wedding had been.

'Ellen told us,' said Jim, 'so the ladies decided that you should have a proper one. Laura made the cake and Mother iced it.'

Heather, of course, had never known the village when food was plentiful, and she could not believe the standard of the baking. As for Mrs. Crook's icing work, she could only say that it was better than many professionals.

'I love it,' said the old lady. 'I used to do a lot for the village fetes and WI activities – for all the villages round about.'

'And will do so again, I have no doubt,' said her son.

Soon after this, the Americans arrived, bringing with them buckets of ice-cream. They also brought a full dance band.

At intervals during the evening, mothers were taking the children home. They were loathe to go, but none went empty-handed. There would be plenty of good food in the village for a few days yet.

No-one was likely to forget Heather and Philip's wedding.

Despite continuing raids on London, there was a feeling that the tide was beginning to turn in favour of the Allies.

The Dambusters' raid on May 16th was received with great rejoicing. The dams which had been breached were all in Germany's industrial centre, so it was certain that their war machine would be seriously affected. Guy Gibson and his crew were the heroes of the moment.

In the Middle East battles had swayed backwards and forwards, but Sicily was finally captured on August 17th. Helen wondered how Johnny had fared and was delighted to receive a letter from him in September. As usual, he could say very little, but the letter ended, *'I am looking forward to seeing you all again'*, so he must be sure of coming back to England.

Heather watched her as she read it out and said, 'I wonder if that's a good thing.'

Helen didn't pretend to misunderstand. She replied, 'I don't know either, so I shan't think about it.' But of course she did.

In November, letters to both Helen and Jim revealed that Johnny was in the south of England. Jim wrote at once and invited him to spend his next leave at the Rectory.

'Johnny's going to be with us for Christmas,' Mrs. Crook told Helen, delightedly.

'That will be nice for him. You've been so kind. I'm sure he appreciates it, being so far from home.'

'He's an easy man to be kind to – just Jim's sort – and yours, too, I should think.' Helen stiffened. Surely she couldn't be that obvious? Did all the village know?

'Yes, we have much the same interests. I'll be glad to see him again,' she said formally. But the faint blush and downcast eyes were not lost on the old lady.

'Well, you must come for an evening of music when he's here. Jim wonders how he got leave for Christmas and thinks there must be a good reason.'

Helen pondered this on her way home. Why should Johnny be so favoured – unless he was going on a special duty.

The audience for the school pantomime was boosted by a large contingent of GIs and there were some in the cast. This year Helen had written, *Yank and the Beanstalk*, which included a scene where a Yank and a schoolboy argued over an old car. They got into hilarious misunderstandings over their respective names for the parts, the boy pooh-poohing the idea that a car could run on gas or that a bonnet was the same as a hood. They came to blows over a spanner and a wrench to loud laughter. Behind the scenes, Helen was busy, but amid the laughter she thought she detected a tone that she knew. From the steps at the side of the stage she peered down into the audience and saw Johnny seated with Jim near the front of the hall.

Good, she thought, I shall have to meet him in public. At least she was prepared.

In the interval, she went straight into the group surrounding him and offering her hand said, 'Good to see you back, Johnny.' But he ignored the gesture and swept her into a great bear-hug of an embrace.

'Come on, Helen, surely I rate a hug after all this time,' he said, laughing, then, 'This show's great. I suppose you wrote it as usual?'

He was even more deeply tanned, leaner and – what was it? – like a knife, she thought, honed to perfection. This was the ultimate fighting machine, fit, trained and at the top of his form. Suddenly she felt more frightened for him than she had ever been. What were the powers-that-be planning now?

More friends were coming to him and receiving the same hug of greeting and others came to congratulate her on the performance. Soon she was able to excuse herself and go back to her cast.

The Christmas holidays had begun and she was free to see Johnny often during his leave. As they caught up with each other's news she asked, 'How's Cathleen?'

'She says she's still faithful,' he grinned, 'but I've been away a long time and it's not over yet. We'll see what happens when I get home.' He spoke lightly and dismissed the subject. There was nothing to be deduced from that. She realised that he seemed to treat everything more lightly than he had done and wondered if he was facing something so dangerous that he thought he would not survive, which made everything else seemed trivial.

So she determined to enjoy her time with him and make it as happy as she could. If it was to be the last time she would see him she might as well have some precious memories.

But Johnny often found himself watching Helen dance with other men, especially some GIs who seemed to claim her quite often. On one of these occasions, he asked Heather, 'Are any of these Yanks keen on Helen?'

'Oh, yes – there's more than one – and who could blame them? She's friendly, warm – and so many of them are homesick – and they like her sense of humour. You saw how they reacted to that pantomime.' She paused and looked at him closely. 'Would you mind if she married one of them?'

'Too right,' he told her, 'but there's a war on, so they tell me. If I come through there'll be some sorting out to do – if not, better she never knows.'

'No, you're wrong there, my lad. Even if she doesn't care for you in that way (and I think she might, even if she hasn't recognised it yet) it's everything to a woman to know that she's loved.'

Heather spoke with great seriousness. Johnny had half turned away from her and she clutched his arm, so that he had to hear her out.

'Look, Johnny, suppose you don't come through and Helen never marries. It would mean all the world to her to know that she had been loved and wanted. Even if it's only in a letter, give her that gift. You could leave one with Jim. He would know when, and if, to give it to her.'

'I'll think about it,' he promised. 'That's a good idea – about Jim, I mean. He's been my best friend over here and I know I can trust him. Thanks, Heather. I know you'll look after her for me.'

After the Christmas holidays they went into 1944 with renewed hope. A Second Front was being talked of openly. The defeat of the Italians, scorned as a fighting force ever since they declared war, was still welcome news and the battle for Italy against the Germans seemed to be going well.

Helen had missed hearing from Jean for some years and wondered what had happened. She had been reluctant to write to the family home in case Jean was a casualty, but in February she sent a letter to the London address. Some weeks later, she received two letters and one of them was her own, marked DLO and with no other explanation. If it had come from the dead letter office the chances were that the house no longer existed. She hoped Jean's parents were safe, if it had been bombed. Possibly Jean had been on leave at the time and had not survived. It was to remain a mystery.

The other letter was from Johnny. He was coming on leave again in a few weeks. He had written to Jim, *'Don't think you have to put me up every time I get leave. I can stay here quite well, but I do want to see you about something important, so I would like to come to Norfolk and stay overnight.'*

Jim's reply was characteristic. *'Of course you must come and stay with us. Mother says I'm like a bear with a sore head in the closed fishing season and you should come and make me civilised. She wants to see you and so do all your other friends.'*

On a fine morning in early April the two men cycled out of the village and made for the coast road. Most of the coast was out of bounds to civilians, but Jim knew the side road in Sheringham from which they could get access to the cliff near the life-boat shed.

This was manned twenty-four hours a day now and they could see the men working on their nets and lobster pots. They sat down gratefully on the springy turf.

Below them, the sea looked calm and peaceful, hazy in the distance then blue in the sunlight with white waves creaming on to the sands and along the breakwaters. They were far enough away not to see the miles of barbed wire stretched along the beach.

'Looks peaceful enough,' Jim said. 'You wouldn't think there's a war on.' He paused and looked at Johnny, who was stretched out lazily beside him. 'But I don't suppose you can forget it for long.'

'I do though. Every time I get a chance. It's the only way to cope.' He sat up and looked out to sea.

'Jim – I've got to tell you a couple of things. It's no secret there'll be a second front soon. We can't beat the Jerries sitting here. We must get back on the mainland. Where and when I know no more than you, except that it has to be in the next few months, but what I do know – and you don't – is that the RE will be there first – and I mean first. We go in before the troops, before the tanks, before the infantry. We have to clear a way through the minefields. Until we've done that, nobody else can come in. We'll be carrying about twenty-four pounds of high explosives each – and, of course, we'll be under fire – sitting targets. I don't rate my chance of survival very highly.'

He stopped and Jim could find nothing to say that didn't sound like a vicar speaking, so he remained silent.

'There's another thing. When I was here at Christmas, I let out to Heather that I was in love with Helen. I said then, and I'm inclined to think now, that if I don't come through it would be better if she never knew, but Heather would have none of it. She thought Helen may care for me and said that it would mean a lot to her to know. But suppose it stops her marrying anybody else? I wouldn't want that.' He grinned up at Jim suddenly. 'What would the vicar's advice be?'

Jim found he was not quite in control of his voice but, after a pause, he said, 'I think Heather would know the way women feel about these things better than we do. And Helen is sensible – if someone else offered her marriage and she thought it would be for her happiness she would accept. And I don't think anyone is worse off for knowing the truth – not that sort, anyway.'

Johnny pulled a letter from his pocket. 'Please read it – it isn't sealed. If you think it's OK keep it and give it to her if I don't make it.'

It was quite short. Jim read,

'My darling Helen,

Those three words say it all. If I had survived, I should have asked you to marry me. I hope it will be a comfort to you to know that you were loved – so much more than I could write. But I hope it will not prevent you from making a happy marriage, though I must confess that I also hope you will never forget

your loving Johnny.'

Jim folded it up with a wry smile.

'Nobody could accuse you of undue sentimentality. Yes, you can leave it with me and I'll give it back to you next time you come. Then you can tell her yourself.'

'Sure – and thanks. Now I want to go and see if any of the Sheringham pubs have got any beer.'

Paul Dennis was home on leave at the same time as Johnny.

'That's a good little helpmate you have there,' he said one morning to Joan, nodding in the direction of his daughter who was playing with the baby, Douglas, now nearly two years old.

'Oh, Paul, Barbara has been so good. She was so upset after Rosie died, I really thought she would never get over it, but Helen persuaded her that I needed her help with the baby and now she's devoted to him. She helps in the house too. I don't know what I'd do without her now.'

'You haven't any regrets about Douglas, I can see,' he said, watching his wife gazing contentedly at the two fair heads so close together.

'No regrets in the world. I can't imagine life without him now. If I get you home safe, I won't have another thing to wish for.'

They were both silent, holding hands and wondering when, and if, that would be. Both knew the Second Front must be imminent and Paul knew that he would be involved from the first. Stationed near the south coast, it was impossible not to be aware of the build-up of military equipment in the area.

'I wish I had something to give the children. It feels wrong to come home with empty pockets instead of presents for them.'

'They know the war means they can't have things – and anyway, you brought them all your sweet rations.'

He shook his head. 'I want to give them things they can keep.' The words 'in case I don't come back' hung in the air.

Then Joan laughed suddenly. Paul looked at her quizzically.

'I had such a stupid dream last night. I've just remembered. You came home in an awful civilian suit and the most ridiculous trilby hat and said it was the best a grateful Government could do for you. I have a strange feeling that dream is going to come true.'

'Either way, we might as well make the most of this leave. Let's get the children ready and go out for the day. '

Helen had spent one evening with Johnny at the rectory and they had been to a dance with a crowd of friends. She saw no change in his attitude except that he seemed more relaxed than at Christmas. Jim foresaw that the last day of his leave would be difficult for Johnny and was planning to give him and his friends a social evening in the Church Hall, so that he could say goodbye to them all together.

Mrs. Crook asked, 'But what are you going to give them to eat? I've got nothing to give you – nothing that would be out of the ordinary for them. And Heaven knows that will be dull enough.'

'I don't know. I'll have a word with Sally.'

But the next morning brought a telegram for Johnny. The rest of his leave was cancelled and he was ordered to report to barracks immediately.

'Make my apologies and say goodbye to everybody for me. Don't worry, Jim, maybe it's better this way.'

They shook hands warmly and he kissed Mrs. Crook.

'Thank you for everything. You've been like a mother to me.'

He collected his kit and was gone.

Over the next weeks, many of the Army camps became deserted. Even the GIs started disappearing. No-one could doubt that the balloon was about to go up.

Then on June 6th the wireless news told the world that the Allies had landed on the Normandy beaches. General Eisenhower broadcast to the people of Europe 'Your liberation is at hand.' Soon it was known that the first objectives had been achieved.

The good news continued. The first footholds became a bridgehead, eighty miles wide. After that, the progress was slower but progress it continued to be. The Allies would not be dislodged from Europe again.

But in the village, as all over England, the lack of news from their own men was hard to bear. They realised that it meant nothing. The troops were pressing on, constantly on the move and it was not likely that Montgomery would devote any effort to mail collection.

So the village held its breath. Mrs. White's eldest boy, Paul, Johnny, friends from other villages – all out there, but no news from any of them.

However, there was someone who had a card from overseas.

'Ellen, look what I've just got – only I don't understand it, do you?'

Molly had opened the door, flushed and excited, and held out her card. Ellen read, '*Take care of Sicily for me. Love Stephen.*'

Molly said, 'Who's Sicily – and anyhow it's spelt wrong – but he's still alive – or he was.'

'Still is, I should say. If he's come this far he'll survive. I've always thought of Stephen as a survivor.'

'But what does it mean?'

Ellen thought for a minute, then said slowly, 'I think he means you to understand that he knows we've won Sicily and that he has access to a wireless, so he knows what's going on.'

'That's nearly a year ago, isn't it? Still, I think you're right. Please God, let him survive – after so long....' She broke down suddenly, then smiled through her tears. 'I don't know what I have to cry for. I feel sure he's still alive. I think I'd know if he wasn't somehow.'

At last, news started to reach them. First came a letter to Mrs. Crook from Johnny, very short and obviously written in haste.

'*All well so far. Please let everyone know. I won't be able to write very often, but things seem to be going well, if not so quickly as we hoped. I think of you all so often. You all made my time in England so very happy and I look forward to seeing everybody again.*'

Then Joan heard from Paul and Mrs. White heard from Alan. So far, so good. They began to say that, this time, it really would be over by Christmas.

Neither Ellen nor Heather had heard from Philip, but at last several letters arrived together – a proof of how the advance was continuing. His reconnaissance work meant that he was flying over terrain in front of the Allied troops, taking pictures of the area and then going back to base to interpret his photographs. Somehow, without incurring the blue pencil of the censor, he managed to convey something of this in his letters and there was no doubt that he was enjoying himself.

'It's great to be flying again,' he wrote *'and to feel that I am making a contribution to the advance.'*

Heather wondered how often his plane was under attack but she said nothing to Ellen. Perhaps, she thought, we have wiped out the bomber bases. Certainly there had been no raids of that type on Britain since D-day.

Instead a new danger had appeared, none the less frightening even if not so destructive. In mid-June and July the Germans launched pilotless planes – first the V1 and then the V2. They were directed at London but often fell short of the target so that the South coast and East Anglia suffered more than most. They were christened 'doodlebugs' but the derisory name did nothing to mitigate the fear that they engendered.

People had got used to seeing and hearing enemy bombers. Trained ears could tell which plane was overhead and 'it's only one of ours' was often said with certainty. But the doodle bugs came in low and at high speed. Alerted by the 'phut-phut' of their engines, everyone gazed up but could not see them until they were almost overhead, then a flaming tail was visible, followed quickly by the engine cutting out and the plane plummeting to earth. The ominous silence was worse than the noise.

The immediate effect on the village was the return of the evacuees who had thought it safe to go home.

One day in early September, Molly and Laura were on their way to the village hall when they heard the unmistakable sound. Both stopped dead and looked up. As they saw it, the engine of the V2 cut out. They flung themselves down, covering their heads with their arms. They heard the crump as it hit the earth and looked up to see that it had fallen three fields away, striking an elm and igniting haystacks.

They began to run, arriving to find men and Land girls already beating out flames and running for water, which had been kept handy for just such a purpose ever since the V2 planes had arrived.

'Thank God the harvest's in – we've lost a lot of hay though,' one of the older men said when they had got the fire out.

'You're a sight, Bob,' Laura told him. 'I reckon your missus'll have to get the tin bath out tonight.'

'Talk about the pot calling the kettle black. You take a look at yourself, my mawther.'

It was true. All of them were wet through and filthy, but no-one had been hurt and in their soaring relief it all became a joke, though Joe worried about hay for his horse when he heard about it.

To the Home Guard, manning a rocket battery in Norwich, none of it was funny. The V2 had a longer range and a more destructive power than the V1 and, on October 3rd, Norwich was lucky to get off with superficial damage in Dereham Road and Mile Cross. The main body of the plane fell on the Royal Norwich golf course, leaving a crater four feet deep where the seventh hole should have been. The dedicated golfers, who had continued to use the course even though it was criss-crossed with tank traps, were not amused. But, on the whole, Norfolk got off lightly compared with Essex. The damage the V2s did was more to people's nerves than their bodies.

Towards the end of Autumn, Sally and Bill Wood were having a meal together when the post arrived. Bill looked up from a letter, smiling.

'What do you think? We've been allocated Italian prisoners to come and work on the land. I must ring the Ministry and see what arrangements we have to make.'

He came back to her, still delighted.

'They're going to be billeted in the old workhouse. They're all used to farm work and we don't have to keep them under lock and key. They seem to have been hand picked for the job.'

The villagers liked the Italian boys right from the start. There were about twenty of them housed in the old workhouse, which the Yanks had made into luxurious accommodation such as they had never seen. Six of them were allocated to Bill Wood and the others worked in the adjoining villages.

They were good workers and very happy to be out of a war that was none of their making, but they looked thin and suffered greatly from the cold. Very soon they were on visiting terms with most of the villagers, sitting over the fireside and being plied with hot drinks. They repaid the women by chopping logs, bringing in water and doing any other jobs that had been neglected during the absence of the young men.

To the girls they were a godsend. Partners at dances since D-day had been, in the words of a popular song, '*either too young or too old*' – and these boys could dance! The weekly event was certainly brighter for their presence. They quickly picked up enough English to make themselves understood. It was not long before a few romances began.

Joyce Painter was missing Hank. She had told no-one that their attachment was serious. After all, he might not survive and if he did it would mean a life in America – and how would her mother take that? So she hugged to herself his final words to her:

'You know I love you. When I come back I shall ask you to marry me, so you better get used to the idea.'

So matters stood as events moved towards the last year of the war.

It was in late January that Sophie first mentioned pains in her legs. She always cycled the three miles into Cromer every day when the roads were passable. When they were not, she stayed with an old aunt who lived near the station. She had been living in Cromer for almost a week, so the first time Helen heard her complain, Sophie said, 'I had a job biking home. I suppose it's because I haven't been riding since Tuesday, but my legs didn't want to go.'

They thought nothing of it then, but soon she started having restless nights and by mid-February, it was obvious that she was in trouble.

'I'm afraid it's arthritis, Mrs. Rae,' the doctor told her. 'We don't know much about cures, but there are two or three things that seem to help. We'll get a dentist to have a look at your teeth. We might try some gold injections but they're expensive. Keep as warm as you can and I'll get you into hospital for a thorough examination as soon as possible.'

She struggled on into April, hoping that the warmer weather would help. Some days were better than others. Then she went into hospital where they stretched her legs and she came home feeling better for the rest. She was still going to work when the end of the war in Europe was declared.

Like everywhere else in the country, the village celebrated. Bunting and flags appeared as if by magic. Both the hall and the school were decorated, inside and out. Jim had a great banner outside the church. 'We thank God for Peace,' and there was a thanksgiving service prior to a tea and dance in the village hall.

The children had their own party at school with a conjuror and a sing-song. Most of the evacuees were looking forward to going home – some with mixed feelings – but they were all sure they were coming back for summer holidays.

'The beaches should be open by next year,' Helen told them. 'Both Sheringham and Cromer have lovely soft sand.' But even as she spoke, she wondered how many families would be able to afford twelve shillings and sixpence for train fares for each of them.

Suddenly, the village seemed quiet. Class sizes shrank and they had time to assess what they had gained from the children who had shown them a glimpse of a different life. Some of the village youngsters were inconsolable – they had lost 'best friends'.

Then, here and there, a house was decorated. 'Welcome Home' banners appeared as families prepared for the arrival of newly demobbed menfolk.

The first day back at school after the summer holiday had just ended when Johnny came to Helen. He had written that he would be returning to London to be demobbed and that he would see her before he went home, but she had had no expectation of seeing him so soon.

The children were still coming out of the school gate, so the pair met circumspectly, except that their broad smiles barely concealed their happiness.

'I need to talk to you. Will you come into the church?' he said.

It seemed a strange place to choose, but she realised that it was probably the nearest where they could be alone and unseen. But Johnny had another reason.

'I asked you to come here because it seemed the right place to ask you if you'll marry me, Helen. I've loved you for a long time but it wasn't fair to say anything when there was so much danger.'

She had never seen him so serious or so anxious. She said, 'What about Cathleen?'

'She isn't you. She's a grand girl, but I wouldn't be doing her any favours if I married her, loving you. Please say you love me, darling.'

He put his arms round her and she returned his kiss, but as he pulled her closer she drew away.

'Johnny – yes, I do love you, but there are ... difficulties. My mother ... '

'She can come out with us – I thought of that.'

'You are dear and good, but she's ill – I don't know. I need time. Just a little while. It's all been so sudden.'

'Victorian melodrama,' he said, with his old teasing smile. 'Oh, sir, this is so sudden. But don't worry, as long as you love me we'll sort something out.'

Helen left Johnny at the church and went towards Aunt Ellen's cottage, hardly knowing where she was going except that she didn't want to go home. Now she had to face the situation that she had been able to ignore while she thought that Johnny did not care for her. Her thoughts scurried around like mice. How wonderful that he loved her. And how comfortable his arms had been. Useless to pretend that she had never considered marriage to Johnny and a life in Australia. It would be a big change after the little village, but her resilient mind made nothing of that. She had always been open to new experiences – always wanted to see what was round the next corner. No, the problem was her mother. She was in no state to cope with a long journey and adjust to a foreign country.

Of course, Sophie would urge her to go, wanting her happiness above all, so she, Helen, must make the decision for them both.

The one living room of Aunt Ellen's cottage looked dark and gloomy as she entered. Her eyes, adjusting from the glare of the sun, could see nothing for a moment. Then Ellen said, 'Helen? What brings you here? Is Sophie all right?'

'Yes. I don't know why I came.' She put her hand up to her eyes, bewildered.

From the chimney corner, Uncle Joe said, 'Come you in, my maid. Sit down. I'll get you a drink.'

Ellen called to him, 'There's lemonade in the pantry.'

Helen sank down into the old horsehair sofa and drank gratefully.

'You haven't got a touch of the sun?' Ellen asked, concerned.

'No. I'm all right now. It was just coming in out of the light.'

'Then what's worrying you?'

Helen took a deep breath. 'It's Johnny. He's asked me to marry him – and go out to Australia.'

'Mm. It's a long way.'

'It's not that, Auntie. But how can I leave Mother?'

'You want to go?' It was Ellen who was doing all the talking. Joe puffed at his pipe and said nothing, regarding his niece steadily with those kind, brown eyes.

'Well – yes – I suppose ...'

'Then you must go.' Ellen spoke briskly. 'You have all your life in front of you. I won't stand by and see it sacrificed. Sophie can come here. We'll look after her.'

Joe nodded agreement. Helen looked at them with love. They had had her grandmother living with them for much of their married life. Now they were prepared to take her mother. She thought of Joe, out in all weathers on his open cart, getting home late and bedding down his horse before he could rest – and for a pittance. Now Ellen eked out their small income by serving dinners at the school, her only social life the Women's Rural Institute. If Sophie became bedridden she would have to give up both.

Helen had always thought of Joe as a perfect double for Joe Gargery – saying little, helping wherever he could and expecting no reward. What good people they were – salt of the earth. She could not put this burden on them. Her money would be needed to support her mother.

When she left them, her mind was already made up, but she felt desolate. Was this all that life was ever going to be?

* * * * *

By the end of the war Joyce had seen death many times. She had helped to dig people out of rubble, some still living, only to die shortly after. She had helped AFS men to fight fires after incendiary bombs had sent whole blocks of houses up in flames. She was always needed to take people to rest centres, to make them sweet tea, to lessen their shock and to stay with them to give what comfort she could to those who waited for news of family still trapped under collapsed buildings. She had heard stories from Air Raid Wardens and Firemen that the girl who had never known danger until the war started would not have believed possible. She thought she was immune from shock for evermore.

Stephen's home-coming changed all that. She had expected his gauntness and Molly had warned her that she must be prepared for other changes in him. Jim had said to all his congregation that they would never know what the returning men had seen and suffered. It would take them time to readjust to home life and every allowance must be made for them.

George Barker had gone further. He told everyone who would listen what it had felt like to return from the horrors of the First World War to find that civilians had no idea – and no imagination – of what they had suffered; and how he had found understanding only from others who had returned from the trenches. Of course, he conceded, this war had been different. All civilians had suffered to some extent and could imagine what some of our men had endured. But captivity – and by the Japs – that would be something no-one could conceive. Only those who had suffered it would ever know.

So Joyce thought she was prepared and her first impression was favourable. Her father's thinness was not as bad as she had expected after seeing pictures of Japanese POWs on the newsreel at the cinema. This was because he had been well looked after on the long voyage home. The troopship had stopped at various ports on the way and there nurses and girls from all three services had made much of the men. The women had arranged parties and entertainments and had let them talk freely, listening sympathetically to their tales of families waiting for them at home. This had helped to integrate them back into the civilised world.

And Stephen seemed to have lost none of his old manner. He had met them with delight – reaching out his arms to them both and holding Molly as though he would never let her go.

He stood back, beaming, and looked for a long time first at Molly, then at Joyce. Gradually his expression changed.

'Well, I'm damned,' he said, shaking his bald head, 'she look just like you when I first met you, that she do.'

'I'm flattered,' Molly laughed. 'Joyce is reckoned to be good-looking – or so the boys seem to think.'

He frowned. 'I don't want no boys running after her yet. Time enough for that.'

'Dad, I'm twenty,' Joyce said with spirit. 'Mum was only that when you married.'

But he shook his head and changed the subject. Later, he wandered out of the house, saying, 'I must go and have a word with Joe.'

'That's not like Dad. I hope he's not going to treat me as though I was still a kid.'

'Give him time,' Molly sighed. 'We'll all have some adjusting to do.'

All his friends were delighted to see that he had come back so well in health and so like the old Stephen they knew. With Joe among the prize dahlias one day, he said, 'You know, I used to dream about these. It helped me keep going. I used to tell myself I'd see Joe's dahlias again some day. Made me determined to come back'

'Do you want to talk about it?'

'No. Least said, soonest mended. As soon as I'm strong enough, I'll get back on the land – best cure I know.'

Joe nodded. Unlike George, he had never wanted to talk about his time in the trenches.

'Squire will be glad to have you. They've had Eyetie prisoners you know, but they've gone home – except one who wants to stay here.'

'Eyeties? Here?'

'Yes, Eyeties – and Land Girls – oh, but you know about them. Did anybody tell you our Philip is married to Heather?'

'No. I'll have some catching up to do – let's go to the Haymakers. I could do with a pint.'

Joe told him about Rosie and Molly talked a lot about Wally, who had gone home. Stephen seemed much like his old self and they all felt that he was coping very well with circumstances which had changed so much since he decided to volunteer six years ago.

At first Joyce was the only one who knew that he was different. She complained to her mother,

'Dad won't leave me alone. He follows me round everywhere – and yet he doesn't seem happy with me.'

Molly smiled. 'I think he is regretting the years he missed – not seeing you grow up. He'll get used to the idea that you're an adult now.'

The village had welcomed back the other men who were

demobilised. Paul Dennis had come home on leave but he was staying on in Germany in the British Army of the Rhine, an occupation force, with the intention of training for a better job before he was demobbed. At least he would get regular leave now. Joan was disappointed at the delay, but saw the good sense of the move. If he came out qualified for a profession it would be worth it.

Not all the homecoming was joyous. Sophie came home from work with the story of a colleague whose little boy would not accept his daddy because he was not in uniform and was even more upset when he was put into a separate bedroom while this strange man was allowed to sleep with Mummy.

'She's having a dreadful time with him. He was such a good boy and now he's getting into trouble at school and keeping them awake at night. His father daren't raise a hand to him in case he thinks this interloper is cruel.'

This was no new situation to Helen. It had been noticeable that some children had changed completely since their fathers returned.

'Tell her to go and see his teachers,' said Helen. 'They must all be coping with this sort of thing. If he knows he's not the only one who feels displaced it will help – and, of course, to have his own room is a sign that they think he's grown-up enough to be on his own at night.'

'I told her to let him have a night light,' Sophie said.

Helen was indignant.

'Surely they weren't expecting him to sleep on his own for the first time in a dark room? No wonder he keeps waking them. He must be terrified. Haven't they any imagination?'

Then there were husbands and fiancés who came back to less than the welcome they had been expecting. Some to other men's children, some to wives and girlfriends who seemed totally different from the women they remembered.

But, on the whole, the welcomes had been heartfelt and the normal pattern of life was resumed without much trouble.

One day Molly met the District Nurse, who stopped her to ask after Stephen.

'I think he's pretty well considering what he went through. He won't talk about it and I don't know whether that's a good thing or not. Of course, he hasn't got much energy yet.'

'No, I don't suppose he has. You mustn't expect him to resume married life for a while.'

'I'm too happy to have him home to worry about that yet.'

But she did worry that he was so restless in bed. One night, he told her, 'I think it's because it was so noisy in the dormitory with so many of us – and in pain. We all had to get up a lot in the night. You got used to it – now I'll have to get used to the sounds of the country again. Why don't I sleep downstairs for a while? And don't worry if you hear me get up and go out. I often used to do that when I had the strength.'

He took her in his arms.

'That's when I used to think of you. Please be patient with me. I'll be well soon now I'm home.'

After that, she heard him go out at dawn most days, but that was the countryman's way – look at Joe, always up by five – and Stephen was getting stronger. Presently he was able to go back to work doing some of the lighter jobs on the farm and this pleased him enormously. But he still continued to sleep downstairs.

It was Ellen who first remarked to Joe, 'Stephen's a lot quieter than he used to be. Sometimes he doesn't speak for ages.'

'Ah, I expect he's got a lot to think about.'

But nobody knew how much.

Hank was back in America and Joyce missed him very much. Every letter from him urged her to come out and marry him. There were ships sailing from Britain with GI brides, he pointed out, and why shouldn't she travel with them? At last, there was a letter which enclosed one from his mother. She wrote,

'I want you to know that we would welcome you as our son's wife. Hank is unhappy without you and that makes us unhappy too. Now that your father is home, I hope we will see you soon.'

There was no possibility of delay any longer. She showed the letter to Molly, who smiled, 'Well, my dear, we shall miss you, but if your happiness is with Hank then you must go. I liked him and I think he'll be good to you.'

'I have a feeling Dad will be difficult. You will back me up, won't you?'

But Stephen simply shook his head and said, 'It's your life.' Then he sat and cried.

106

When Molly tried to comfort him, he shook her off gently. 'It's only weakness. I cry more easy than I used to. Don't take any notice.'

That night, it seemed to Molly that he went out soon after they were in bed, but she fell asleep and never heard him come back in. He made tea and brought it up to her soon after six.

'I couldn't sleep,' he confided. 'I didn't think we'd lose Joyce when I've only just found her.'

'I know. It's hard on you, but we knew she would go sometime. The world has got smaller since the war – she could have settled anywhere. I'm sorry you don't know Hank – you'd like him. Perhaps he'll bring her home to see us sometime. He's only an ordinary boy, but all the Americans are better off than we are.'

He went off to work where he told Heather the news, adding, as he had said to Molly, 'So I shall lose her when I've only just found her.'

Ten days later, Molly did not get her usual cup of tea in bed. She dressed with a sense of foreboding, but began to prepare the breakfast and to call Joyce, who was going to Norwich to make arrangements for her passage to New York.

But by then, Joe had found him.

The horse was stirring restlessly when he got to the stable – wanting his oats, he thought. Then he saw the thing that was disturbing the animal. From a crossbeam something swayed backwards and forwards. A white paper on it caught the light.

Joe touched a dangling hand – quite cold. He led the horse outside before cutting down Stephen's body. Pinned to it was an envelope marked 'Joe. Private.' He stuffed it into his pocket and went for help. Only Joe and Jim knew the contents of Stephen's last letter.

'Dear Joe.

Sorry to do this to you, but its better than the women. You can let the rector see this – praps he pray for me. Its wrong but not as bad as my thoughts. I fell in love with Joyce – its been hell. And poor Molly. I could never love her again. So its better this way. Don't ever let them know. Thank you Joe – you bin a good mate.'

The coroner's verdict of suicide while of unsound mind was accepted by everyone. Most thought that Stephen's mind had been unhinged by his war experiences. Only Joyce wondered, but she kept her thoughts to herself.

She and her mother sailed for America six weeks after the funeral, and Helen learned the truth from Jim many years later.

* * * * *

On a bright June day in 1946 Sally came to see Ellen with a letter.

'What do you think? Wally has written to Bill and asked if he can have a job on the farm. Says he can't stick London any longer. Bill would have him, but he hasn't got a tied cottage with a spare room since all the boys came home. Who would be likely to take him?'

'I would,' Ellen said promptly. 'I got quite fond of him when he took such good care of Rosie. Funny, Joe said he'd never settle in London again.'

'No. He says he's tried for a year to please his mother, but they've finally recognised that he isn't happy and agreed to let him come back. Of course, they think he'll be just a farm labourer but Bill thinks he might make a gamekeeper eventually. And to think it all started with him poaching a pheasant!'

'Poacher turned gamekeeper – it's a familiar story,' Ellen agreed. 'Well, he can come as soon as he likes. Joe will enjoy having him.'

This is Now - 3

'But you can't leave it like that,' I said, as Helen rose to go. 'I've seen Wally, of course – and I shall see Heather – but I must know what happened to the others. Did you keep in touch with them all?'

'For quite a long time. Philip and Heather settled in London. He got a job with the Ordnance Survey people and, later on, Heather started a riding school, but she came back to Norfolk when Philip died, three years ago. When you see her she'll show you all the children's photos. My goddaughter, Helen, is the eldest. I'm glad you've seen Wally. He's still quite a character – proper old countryman, isn't he? Always moaning about the present day. You'd never think he was a cockney.'

'What about that couple who nearly didn't have their last child?'

'Joan and Paul settled in Yorkshire. Paul became a chartered accountant. All the children did well, but Douglas, the youngest, well, he's quite famous in his own field. He was a member of the team that did some of the first heart transplants.'

'How wonderful. So was it all happy endings?'

'Sally died quite young. The whole village missed her – Aunt Ellen most.'

'And Molly and Joyce?'

'Molly is unbelievable. She's a hundred and got her telegram from the Queen last year. She was very proud of that. Joyce and she were both happy in America right from the start – and Joyce still sends me a long letter every Christmas.'

I looked up at her. She knew what I was going to ask.

'And you never married?'

'No. Johnny married his Cathleen and she wrote to me for a long time. They sent food parcels until well after the rationing was over. I always wished him well and they seemed happy together.' She smiled down at me.

'Aunt Ellen said once that when you met the right man – the only one for you – no power on earth would stop you being together. I never felt so strongly about any man. It was children I wanted most, and of course like Mr. Chips, I've had hundreds of them.'

After Helen had gone I sat for a long time picturing life as it must have been before that devastating war. Flowering meadows, nothing to fear in the green woods and lanes – as long as the bull wasn't about. Freedom to walk anywhere and at any time – Helen had said that Joyce had never known fear or violence until the war came.

A hard life, yes, but with so many compensations. Long summer days in the harvest fields – Heather's favourite job, with the scent of the hay like honey, and the horses, placid and plodding through the long day. They had made their own amusements and were so much more involved in them than this present generation of TV and sport-watchers.

I thought of Robert in his new job, trying to cope with the trendy producers who were convinced that only they knew what the customer wanted and constantly under-rating the intelligence of their audience. I didn't see him staying there and was glad that he hadn't persuaded me to join him.

Many times I have said and believed that we can't stop progress and that we have to take advantage of all the benefits of the modern age. But Helen had made me feel a kind of nostalgia for those days, when cares were everyday ones, shared by the whole community. I could imagine now what that generation must feel. No wonder their memories were so clear, and so precious to them.

She had let me see some of her poems and there was one which stuck in my memory. It was to one of the Battle of Britain pilots and she had spoken of him going to fight for 'a way of life that cannot come again.'

Of course, that is true for all generations, never so much as now when the speed of change is so rapid. There is a sunlight which colours all our childhood memories, if they are happy ones. But the young people of Helen's day had been catapulted from their naive pleasures to a harsh reality which they could never have imagined.

In this mood, I was heartily sick of all the things that I deplore so much today: political correctness (muzzling free speech), trivialisation, people in authority who are ignorant of even the rules of grammar, a levelling down in all walks of life so that the incompetent are not made to feel unvalued, instead of giving them

110

goals to aim for and convincing them that they can achieve something.

Just then it seemed to me that the disadvantages of the present outweigh the advantages. We need a campaign, I thought, something to get people roused enough to say that they won't accept second best any longer. Where is excellence? Is it still revered anywhere?

A picture of Simon came into my mind. He and his ilk were trying to hold back the tide. I still didn't believe it was possible. Surely we couldn't go back that far, but I wondered what had given him the incentive to even try. Maybe I should ask him.

By early July, I had shed my plaster and crutches. Robert had helped me to get a grant to give me the time to finish this book and I was well enough to think of doing some first-hand research.

'I'm going back to London – I must see the tenants of my flat. I can't stay down here forever, being a permanent encumbrance –' I started to tell Aunt Julia, but was interrupted.

'Goodness, child, you're not well enough to go walking about London and anyway you can't go now – just when the summer's starting. It will be lovely in the garden soon and on the beach. And Doreen and George are coming back in August, so you can interview her.'

I let myself be persuaded. I still had to see Heather, who lived in Upper Sheringham, and I had plenty of work to do on the notes I had already taken.

Like Helen, Heather was still active and very talkative once she had got launched on her service in the Land Army.

'I wouldn't have missed it for anything, even though we had a pig of a foreman. He always gave the girls the job of sacking up the chaff after corn thrashing. It went everywhere – hair, eyes, nose and you got filthy.'

She went on to tell me about the day she took a bucket from some Italian prisoners to get some hot water for a drink. She gave it a good wash out as it was filthy. It turned out that they had put their cocoa in the bottom. She laughed at the memory and told me some more funny incidents and a tale about how she had hidden in a hayloft from a bull, but when I mentioned Helen, her eyes lit up.

'Helen was wonderful, you know. After she gave up Johnny she

111

carried on as though nothing had happened – one of the casualties of war, she said once. She put her whole life into those children, as well as doing everything in the house when Sophie's arthritis got really bad. All those little cottages were damp – and now Ellen's has got a preservation order on it. How she would have laughed.'

Our visitors had a surprise for us. They had been in Sheringham for two weeks and had been house-hunting. Julia was ecstatic.

'You're going to move down here? That's great. I'm sure you'll love it as much as we do,' enthused Uncle Reg, then asked, 'and have you seen anything you like?'

'We've put in an offer for a house in Castle Acre, so I'm going back home tomorrow to put ours on the market. I'll have to stay on for a while and see if anyone wants to inspect it, but Doreen can stay here. No point in us both going.'

'Of course not,' Julia agreed. 'And anyway, you must stay, Do. Jan wants to interview you for her book.'

So George went back to town on the following day and Doreen and I repaired to the summerhouse.

That Was Then – Doreen's Story

The atmosphere in the railway carriage was – peculiar. The girls were seated four on each side of the narrow compartment, each with a single suitcase or bag in the rack above her head.

As the Leicester train pulled out of London they glanced at each other and then looked away quickly. Three of them took out books and began reading. Presently one or two tentative smiles were exchanged and then somebody burst out laughing.

'This is ridiculous. We're all going to the same place – why don't we get to know each other. My name's Julia Lewis.'

She was a tall slim girl with straight, dark hair, on which was perched a little saucer-shaped hat, tilted over one eye, and no protection against the December chill and the unheated carriage.

'She looks a flirt,' thought the ginger girl opposite her, 'but she's got a nice, friendly smile.' So she offered Julia her hand and said, 'I'm Doreen Blackwell, but everybody calls me Do.'

'Bit premature, isn't it? We'll all be in separate units, most likely.' The heavily built woman looked up from her book. She was older than the others – 25 or 26 perhaps. Her tone was patronising and she returned at once to her reading without waiting for an answer.

'No, we all stay together for three weeks' basic training. Then they decide what jobs we do. I'm Mary Summers, by the way.'

There was a loud snore from a corner seat. Its occupant's head was thrown back and a magazine covered her face. There was some laughing and Julia said, 'I hope we don't all do that or we'll never get any sleep.'

The girl sitting opposite the sleeper, a little thing with a mop of black, curly hair that made her head look too big for her body, said in an unmistakable Cockney accent, 'The poor thing's been travelling all night, from the north of Scotland. I don't know why they couldn't find somewhere nearer for her to go.'

'That's the Army all over, my brother says. He's a long-distance lorry driver – and they need transport, but they posted him to the RE. They do the weirdest things.'

'Does anyone know if we get any say in what we do?' Doreen asked, 'I'm a shorthand-typist, but I want a change. No sense in joining up to do the same thing.'

'Like me,' Julia said. 'I love cooking and I've been working in a bakery, but I'm damned if I want to end up in an Army cookhouse, spud-bashing for the whole battalion. No, let's have some action if we're going to win this war.'

'I wouldn't mind doing my job in the ATS,' the Cockney girl said. 'I'm a tailoress. My friend says they do have them. It's to make our uniforms fit. She says it's a scream when you first get your togs – they only fit where they touch. I'd enjoy making the girls look smart.'

The girl who had spoken about her brother and had given her name as Audrey Miller said excitedly, 'I know what I'm going to be doing – or at least, I know a bit about it – it's a technical job to do with my training in Maths and Physics. I'm looking forward to it.'

Julia had certainly broken the ice. They were still chattering like birds when the older woman said to Joan Long, the cockney, 'You'd better wake that girl. We'll be in Leicester in ten minutes.'

Joan leaned forward and touched the girl gently, 'Scotty,' she said, 'sorry to wake you, but we're nearly there.'

A pair of hazel eyes opened and looked at them as if dumbfounded, then realisation dawned and she smiled. She had foxy red hair and a creamy complexion, her features were regular and Doreen thought she was the most beautiful girl she had ever seen. She said, in the soft accent of the Scottish highlands, 'Hello. I'm Alison Munro.'

There was an Army lorry waiting with an ATS Sergeant. She smiled at them and said, 'Hurry up. I want my grub and I expect you do, too.'

She let down the duckboard and turned to help the first girl in, but Joan hopped up easily and lent a surprisingly strong arm to Doreen, who reached out to help the one girl who had not spoken at all and now seemed quite bewildered.

'Up you come. What's your name?'

'Florence Young.'

'Good, oh. We're Do and Flo then. Sit next to me. Where are you from?'

The girl made a great effort and gave her dark curls a shake.

114

She was a little slip of a thing but her skin had a warm olive tone and she would have been quite attractive if she had taken trouble with herself and not worn such shapeless clothes.

'I'm from Yorkshire. I've been housekeeping for my dad – he's a vicar, and I've never been out to work or away from home before.' There was a slight quiver in her voice on the last words.

'There'll be a lot like that, I expect. You'll soon make friends. There'll be all sorts here. You're bound to find some you like.'

They were flung together suddenly and Julia said, 'Damn women drivers.'

They laughed and the Sergeant shouted back to them, 'Damn men drivers, you mean – he went right across the road. He's a menace. Hang on, I'm going to lose him. And you'd better not talk about Sergeants like that once you're in uniform.'

Laughing and chattering, they hung on tight until the lorry slowed and then stopped. The driver came round and let down the duckboard.

There was a silence, then Joan called out, 'Look out, Hitler. Here we come.' And they cheered.

It was 1942 and they had all been conscripted, so everything was in readiness for them, unlike the volunteers at the beginning of the war who had arrived to utter chaos.

Glen Parva Barracks was the home of the Leicestershire Regiment and there were still a few men there, including the bandsmen, but most of the accommodation was given over to ATS intakes – girls on the initial three weeks training – and their Officers.

The girls from the London train were taken into a large barrack room with ten double bunks in it, and were greeted by the Corporal in charge, who had separate sleeping quarters at the end of the room. She was a pleasant girl who told them that her home was in Leicester so she could tell them about buses into town. Then she shepherded them to the mess where they had their first cookhouse meal.

'I say, this isn't bad. There's plenty of it anyway,' Mary said, tucking into a cottage pie which contained plenty of meat and onion.

'Better than I expected,' Doreen agreed. 'Come on, Flo. Eat up. Got to keep your strength up.'

The Corporal smiled. 'Don't worry, she won't need any urging once you start training. You'll come in so hungry, you'll eat anything. The food's good here – better than you'll get in some places. At least you never need to worry about rationing.'

They started to ply her with questions.

'You'll always be called by your surname alone. You should call me Corporal Welch, but I don't mind just Welch if there's no Officers around. You call them Ma'am if you talk to them.'

'Ma'am!' jeered Joan. 'You'd think they were the Queen.'

'Well, they are in a way. It's because they hold the King's Commission. It's that you are supposed to be saluting – not a person.'

'Well, I never. Fancy that!'

'When do we get our uniforms?' Julia asked.

'You'll get all your kit this afternoon – bedding, shoes, underclothes, tunics, greatcoats, hussifs'

'What's that?'

'Its proper name is housewife – it has sewing kit in it.'

The older woman, who had told the Corporal that her name was Phyllis Styles, snorted audibly.

They all looked at her, and Audrey asked, 'What's eating you?'

It was the question she had been waiting for. She said bitterly, 'It's all right for you, but I've had to give up a good job. It's ruined my career to be called-up. It's not fair.'

'My God! Where've you been? There's a war on – or hadn't you heard?'

There were angry murmurs of agreement, then the soft Scottish voice said clearly and vehemently, 'Lassie, you talk like that and you'll be in big trouble. You don't know what the rest of us have given up. Think of the boys. My brother was killed in the Battle of Britain – and you think you're special! You're just pathetic.'

They started talking to each other again and ignored the woman who had offended them. Then another group of girls came in to the mess and Welch went to talk to them.

'She's nice, anyway, and so was the Sergeant,' Julia said, 'but I expect we'll get a few with rough tongues.'

'Talking of rough tongues – listen to that lot.'

It seemed that the latecomers had had a bad journey with a long wait at Preston and crowded trains. They were telling the Corporal about it and some of them were swearing in raised voices. Phyllis Styles looked up scornfully, but said nothing. Flo visibly shrank back and Doreen said, 'They're probably no worse than the rest of us when you get to know them.'

'We used to get plenty like that when we went hop-picking. Real rough types – not much education but that didn't matter when you needed some help,' Joan added.

The Corporal came over and told them that they could go back and choose their beds. Doreen told Julia that she felt she had to share with Flo.

'Yes, you're the only one she's spoken to – but it doesn't matter, I can take the bed next to yours and share with Mary or Joan.'

They soon sorted themselves out – Do and Flo, Julia and Mary, Joan and Scotty (as Alison was soon called). Phyllis took a lower bunk and looked round for her partner. Audrey, coming in last, sized-up the situation and deliberately dumped her suitcase on a lower bunk, opposite Do and Flo. She would take her chance with the latecomers and Phyllis would have to do the same.

When they came in it seemed that only two or three of them had been responsible for the noise. The others were only too glad to have arrived after their long journey. The girl who took the bunk above Audrey smiled and said, 'I could do with getting into that straight away. Did you come far?'

'Only from the London suburbs – our crowd all met on the train.'

'So did we. Some of them got on at Blackpool and had to change at Preston, but' she lowered her voice 'what's really eating them is that Blackpool's full of troops. They don't fancy being without men around. I'd say it will cut down their income a bit.'

It took Audrey a minute to understand this remark.

Julia and the others were watching to see who would take the bunk above Phyllis. She was a plump, fair, red-faced girl with a pert, turned-up nose. She glanced round to make sure there were no lower bunks vacant. She slapped her bag down and said loudly, 'Christ! How do I get up there?'

Phyllis flinched, lowered her head and did not reply.

'Oh, great. That's all I need – some snooty bit of work. Too good for us lot, are you?' And, when Phyllis did not look up: 'don't worry, luv, we'll soon knock you into shape.'

They staggered back to the room with stuffed canvas kit bags and arms full of bedding. Some of them gazed with horror at the

117

three biscuits – squares of mattress – which, together with the hard wooden bunks, comprised their beds.

Corporal Welch showed them how the beds were to be made up and told them, 'You're luckier than the men – they don't have sheets. If you feel cold put your greatcoats on top of the bed. I always sleep in bed socks and a hat. Don't use your ATS caps, though.

'It's your job to keep the fire going once you've lit it and it has to be blackleaded every day. Then you have to polish and bumper the floor. That's the minimum to keep the place clean. It has to be ready for inspection whenever you're on duty, so if you come in during the day make sure you leave it tidy.'

They gazed in awe at the pot-bellied black stove in the middle of the room, which heated the immediate area and left both ends to all the draughts of winter, and at the heavy polisher – a large solid block with a long handle – which Welch had called a bumper.

Phyllis was horrified. 'I can't do rough work like this.'

For the first time the Corporal frowned and spoke sternly. 'You passed your medical or you wouldn't be here. There's no-one else to do your cleaning and mending for you. As the song says, this is the Army.'

There was a chorus, started by Julia: 'You had a housemaid to clean your floor, but she won't help you out any more.'

They laughed, immensely cheered by their joint effort.

'Now listen. You won't find it so hard if you help each other. Most of you must have seen in civvy street how people are coping since the war started – when there's been bombing, or helping out with rations, offering lifts. Look at all of them sleeping in the London underground – it wouldn't work if they only thought of themselves.

'One of the greatest things about being in the ATS is the friends you make and how you know you can rely on each other. Anyone who comes in with a chip on their shoulder will get it knocked off pretty soon. We're all in this together and I'm sure you'll soon be proud to be serving your country. You'll get a pep talk from one of the Officers, but she'll only tell you the same thing.' She smiled and added, 'Now let's see you in your uniforms.'

The next half-hour was hilarious. Joan's friend had been right. There were greatcoats which trailed on the ground and khaki skirts which dropped to the floor and had to be secured with safety pins, but the khaki bloomers raised the most laughs. Welch told them that these were referred to as PKs – short for Passion Killers.

'They are that,' said Audrey's partner, who had given her name as Val Watson. Audrey looked at her consideringly. I bet you could teach me a thing or two, she thought. Some of the other girls were calling out in words that meant nothing to her. She guessed that the ATS would educate her in more ways than intended.

'Well, come on. Get changed into everything, then you can swap if it helps,' Lewis suggested. Doreen watched in surprise as Flo stepped out of a pair of peach silk French knickers.

'You're a dark horse,' she said admiringly. 'Where did you get those? I haven't seen any as good as that since the war started.'

Flo flushed and then giggled.

'Dad gave me some money and his coupons so I went shopping with the smartest girl in the parish. She got these from a GI but she said I could have them if I gave her some clothing coupons. I bought her some make-up, too – and some for myself, but I've never used it before and I daren't put it on before I left home.'

Do was jubilant. She knew she wouldn't have to feel responsible for this girl for long.

'Good-oh, I was thinking on the train you'd be very attractive in a smart uniform and make-up. I'll make you up tonight, if you like.'

Just then, there was a loud exclamation from one of the Blackpool girls.

'What the hell is this?'

She held up a denim garment which consisted of trousers attached to a long-sleeved top. There were buttons all down the front.

'Fatigues,' explained Welch. 'You wear them when you're doing the cleaning and dirty jobs.'

'They look like combinations,' Val remarked, 'but how on earth do you get out of them when you have a call of nature?'

'I know. They're a damned nuisance. You have to unbutton them and wriggle out of the sleeves before you can peel the trousers down.'

There was a horrified silence, then Joan laughed. 'Easy to see they're designed for men by men. Haven't they any imagination? But, look, this is 1942, surely someone ought to have complained and got them changed before now.'

'You'd think so,' Welch agreed, 'but they've probably got thousands of the things and can't afford to throw them away.'

'The things we do for England,' said Do.

119

Soon after this, the Duty Officer came in. She was a fair, pleasant-looking girl of about twenty-five. As Welch had said, she repeated much of what they had already heard and added, 'Tomorrow will be a busy day. You'll get your jabs for typhus and tetanus. Don't be frightened of them – it's only a needle prick, and the vaccination for smallpox is only a scratch. Your arms may be stiff for a little while, but it soon wears off. Then you'll get properly fitted for your uniforms. Some of you look as though you need it, but don't worry. You'll be very smart by the time you leave here. We might get time for a bit of drill or PT tomorrow, but if not, we shall start in earnest the next day.' She grinned suddenly. 'I know what you're thinking, but I'm hearing a lot of coughs. How many of you feel really well?'

About half of them raised their hands. Even the ones who hadn't got colds felt thoroughly chilled.

'That's what I thought. Now I'll promise you something. When you leave here you'll all feel one hundred per cent – perhaps better than you've ever felt. That's something, isn't it?'

She dismissed them and turned to Welch.

'Come down on them hard if they talk after lights out. They'll need their sleep tonight.'

She was as good as her word. By the end of the first week most of them were feeling much better. Long days of drill, good food, lots of laughs and getting used to being away from home all contributed to their well-being.

Joan was impressed with the work done on their uniforms and hoped she would be allowed to stay on at Glen Parva as a tailoress.

As well as the smart uniform of jacket and skirt they had battledress which they wore most of the time in camp. It was comfortable and blessedly warm in that winter of 1942 and the trousers were a revelation.

'Warmth,' enthused Alison, 'just look what the men have been keeping to themselves all this time! And why my countrymen should ever choose to wear kilts - and in our climate ...'

On Saturday they were told that they would march to church parade behind the band of the Leicestershire Regiment. They were all very impressed – the Regimental Band!

'It's a great honour and a recognition of all that the ATS are doing in the war. You know, the men didn't think we could do their jobs at first, but we've won their respect and we mustn't lose it. So let's see you march in step and with you heads high,' an Officer told them.

And it was great. They swung out behind the band helped by the beat of the Regimental March to keep step. They felt smart and looked smart, as the admiring glances of passers-by assured them.

'Good. I was proud of you,' Welch told them, 'and you'll do it even better next week.'

Besides the drills and disciplines the girls were being tested to see which of them would suit the various duties now open to women in the Forces. The range was being expanded all the time as the war took more men away and the women proved that they could handle more of the jobs that only the men had done.

There were some girls who had no difficulty in sharing a room but most of them had been brought up to be modest and were reluctant to undress in front of the others. Julia was almost prudish in this respect. She was to say later that nobody would believe how naive the girls in their early twenties had been in those days.

They were marched to the ablutions block about once a week and her heart sank the first time when she realised that she had to have a shower instead of a bath. She didn't trust gadgets and was sure that she would turn on the wrong tap and get scalded or drenched with freezing water. Neither happened and she had just got herself nicely soaped when she slipped on the tiled floor, clutched the rubber curtain which slid out of her hands, and went skating out into the corridor between the cubicles, yelling at the top of her voice.

The effect was immediate. A dozen pairs of eyes came round the curtains and, after the first gasp, there were hoots of laughter. After a stunned moment, she joined in.

'Well, now I've bared my all, you can see I've got nothing to hide.'

There were some ribald remarks, but she had broken a taboo for most of them. As Scotty said, 'We've all got everything we should have, or we wouldn't be here,' and Joan sang,
'Everyone wears what you see on the clothes line
So what does it matter, we'd all like to know.'

By the end of the first week they had all sent home for bed socks, nightcaps and hot water bottles. The barrack room saw some strange sights. Julia's cheeky hat was no good to sleep in and Scotty had lent her a mutch – a woollen bonnet which tied under her chin. Now that they had all had their hair cut to the regulation length, two inches above the collar, she could stuff all her hair into it. As it was flesh coloured it made her look completely bald. Scotty wore a tartan tammie and all the others had an assortment of headgear, some with scarves attached.

In the mornings, as soon as reveille was called, one of the Blackpool girls would sit up in bed and sing, '*Oh, the pity of it all!*" She was usually told to shut up and often had things hurled at her, but it was better than waking to tears and by the time they had thrown off their night gear most of them were good-humoured and ready for anything the day might bring.

Then came the day when they were told of their categories and given their postings.

To her delight Joan was to stay at Glen Parva as a tailoress. Mary, Julia and Doreen were to be sent to the Isle of Man to join the Royal Signals. The Blackpool girls were green with envy.

'It's as good as going home. Why couldn't any of us go there?'

Audrey told Julia, 'It's far better than Blackpool. Yes, it's a tourist area, but not so crowded and the whole island is so beautiful.'

Phyllis was posted to the Pay Corps in Preston.

'I think you will be in private billets there – so if you don't like your landlady, you'll be able to change her,' Welch told her.

Phyllis beamed. She wouldn't be doing any more housework. It was the first time anyone had seen her look pleased.

'Look what I've got – back to what I've been doing all my life.' Flo was disgusted. She was going to be an Officer's batwoman.

'You know what Welch told us. If we don't make the grade we come back here and remuster. Make sure you don't pass the training,' Mary suggested.

'How can I fail at making beds and cleaning?'

'You'll find a way – or perhaps you'll get a handsome male Officer and he'll fall in love with you,' Joan said.

Alison was being posted straight to an Ack-Ack battery training unit in Wales. She was not sure about the work but was delighted to be doing something that would actively help the war effort.

'What about you, Audrey? Have you got the posting you expected?'

She flushed and said apologetically, 'I'm going to OCTU.'

Phyllis's jaw dropped. In a tone heavy with disbelief, she said, 'You're going to be an Officer?'

Scotty said, 'Congratulations. Do you know what you'll be doing?'

'Yes, I've known all the time. I was recruited while I was still at university because I've got the qualifications they want. I can't tell you much because all I know is it's still secret at the moment.'

'Another dark horse – and a Mata Hari,' teased Julia.

'Oh no. It's not spying – it's just highly technical.'

'Will it be something to help beat the Nazis?' asked Mary.

'I suppose so, but I don't know the exact nature of the work. I'm looking forward to it, but I'm sure I'll feel a right twit when I start getting salutes.'

Joan was the only one who had noticed Phyllis when Audrey let slip that she had been to university. Now she said, 'The Pay Corps must be a come-down for you after your important work. Come on, tell us what it was.'

With as much dignity as she could muster, Phyllis announced, 'I am an Inspector in His Majesty's Government.'

'But surely that's a reserved occupation. Did they want to get rid of you?'

'Certainly not. I had only just been promoted and was under training for a new position, so they weren't allowed to keep me – my boss did try.'

'I say – don't Civil Servants get their pay made up?' Mary asked.

Phyllis said shortly, 'None of your business.'

'Well, you've got a cheek – moaning like that when you're better off than any of us.'

Then they ignored her and spent the rest of their free time talking about the show which was traditionally given by the new intake on their last night.

That night was a real celebration. They would be going home on leave tomorrow and spirits were high.

The concert revealed a remarkable range of talent as each barrack room made its offering. Two rooms had got together to form a team of dancers and another put on a one-act play. Joan did a Marie Lloyd sketch, complete with cockney songs which they all joined in. Alison had a small team of Scottish dancers, highlighted

123

by her own sword dance. Comedy acts were popular, particularly the ones which sent up the ATS training and two of the girls from Blackpool brought the house down with some Lancashire humour involving George Formby and his guitar. Finally, Mary, who had a strong contralto voice, led them all in a medley of popular and patriotic songs.

They said goodbye the next morning with many promises to keep in touch. Julia, Doreen and Mary would be sailing from Fleetwood, so they arranged to meet at Blackpool Tower the day before.

'I'll certainly write to you,' Alison told Joan.

'You must all write to me. I'll be the one who stays put and there's no danger you'll forget my address. Then I'll do a round robin and pass on all your news,' Joan said. They all agreed.

'And you might see some of us if we have to remuster,' Doreen reminded her. 'None of us knows what we're letting ourselves in for.'

Florence Young wondered if she dared go home with make-up on. Her face felt naked without it now. She decided to risk it. Perhaps Dad wouldn't notice.

'Young, there's a lorry going up to York – any good to you?' Corporal Welch asked as she was packing her kit.

'Wonderful – I was wondering how I was going to manage all this on the train.'

'Hurry up, then. He's got to leave in ten minutes.'

She rushed over to the cookhouse where she got some rations for the journey.

Corporal Reg Miller picked up Florence's kitbag and, flinging it into the back of the lorry as if it weighed nothing, said 'Up you get then'. He gave her a second glance and added, 'No, you better sit next to me. That stuff won't do your uniform any good.'

She climbed up on to the high step and settled herself. Presumably he didn't want to talk or he would have suggested this seat at first, so she said nothing.

They passed Joan and Alison as they drove out of the gate. The girls waved and shouted, 'Best of luck.'

She answered 'And you' then fell silent again.

The January morning was cold. After they had been driving about half an hour, Florence shivered. Corporal Miller stopped at once.

'Want your greatcoat, do you? Bit daft not to put it on, wasn't it?'

He got out and came back with the offending garment.

Florence said, 'Thank you. I couldn't manage my kitbag with it on – and I thought I was going by train.'

'Yes, they must be a weight for a girl, I suppose. Never thought about it before.'

The ice was broken. He seemed to feel that he owed her some amends for the thoughtless criticism.

'Where d'you live?'

'A little village just north of Selby.'

'OK. We can go that way. I'll drop you right home.'

'That's wonderful, Corporal. I'm very grateful.'

'Well, don't Corporal me. I'm Reg Miller – Dusty, of course.'

When they stopped for a brew-up, Florence got a better chance to have a look at her driver. Dusty Miller was a heavily built man of about thirty-five. He had a face full of freckles and a square jaw. His eyes were green – and wary. His marriage had been an early victim of the war. When Rose left him for an RAF Officer he had been devastated and then bitter. He had resolved that there would be no more women in his life.

Without knowing any of his story Florence sensed that he was a man who had been hurt and was still vulnerable.

What he saw was a slip of a girl with dark curly hair, brown eyes and a shy smile. She shouldn't be in this war, he thought – it wasn't a woman's place anyway, but certainly not for her.

'Where have you been posted?' he asked.

Florence grimaced. 'I'm going to be a batwoman so I don't know where I shall end up.'

'You didn't want that?'

So she told him how her mother had died when she was twelve and how she had kept house for her father, the parish vicar, ever since. Before they were into Yorkshire, he knew that she had dreaded her call-up, then found a new life in the Forces and now she had to go back to housekeeping again.

'It won't be the same at all,' he pointed out. 'You'll have young company, new friends and plenty of entertainment.'

'That's true – and I'll get more time off.'

'Did your father work you so hard then?'

'Oh, it wasn't Dad – or at least, he couldn't help it. It goes with the job. All sorts of church meetings and people wanting to see him at all hours. They had to have a cup of tea and something to eat. He's never off duty, so I wasn't either.'

'How has he been managing without you?'

Florence grinned widely. 'I've been wondering about that. He's got quite a following with the ladies of the church. They'll all be falling over each other to help him. He's not only the vicar, you see – he's eligible, too. He's been a widower eight years and only forty-six now – and rather a dear.'

Only forty-six, he thought, so this girl is nearly young enough to be my daughter. I'd like a daughter like her.

'What's your name?' he asked.

'Florence. The girls call me Flo. I rather like it. I've never had a nickname before.'

He grinned at her. 'Flo's awful. Make them call you Flora.' Like a flower and just about to bloom, he thought. 'Do you like dancing?'

Florence, who had loved the Scottish dancing which she had learned for the concert, told him about it and added, 'I don't know proper ballroom dancing. I never went when I was at home. I don't think Dad would have minded, but there are plenty of old dears, and not all women, who would have thought me fast.'

'It was time you got away and had a more normal life. Dancing's great and you soon pick it up. I love it.'

On the outskirts of Selby, he pulled up at a workmen's cafe.

'This is a bit primitive, but there's a Ladies here if you want to tidy up before you get home.'

In the little cubicle, she dabbled her face and hands in cold water then gazed into the flyblown mirror and deliberately renewed her make-up. Let the old women talk. She would only be home a week anyway. Something of her new resolution conveyed itself to him.

'That's better,' he said, 'let's go and shock the prudes. You realise your reputation will be in shreds, coming home in a lorry with a soldier?'

She laughed back at him. 'Time I lost it then.'

As she directed him down the village street, heads turned and she waved to some people. 'Hello, Mrs. Griffiths. How are you? Good afternoon, Mr. Prescott,' she called.

Then she turned to Dusty, laughing. 'Wasn't that what they call a double take?'

'Yes. You've done it now all right.'

He stopped at the house beside the church and jumped down

126

to heave her kitbag out of the lorry .By the time she had dismounted her father was at the door.

'Well, here you are. You must be tired, my dear.'

He bent to kiss her and his brown whiskers tickled her as usual. He looked well and familiar and – good. She was very pleased to see him.

'Not in the least tired. I got a lift all the way. Dad, this is Corporal Miller.'

They shook hands and murmured a greeting, then Dusty turned to Florence. 'Goodbye then, and good luck.'

But Richard Young would have none of this.

'Nonsense. You must come in and have a meal. I'm sure you could do with some hot soup.'

'Well, I can't stop long, sir, but thank you.'

He heaved the kitbag on to his shoulder and followed the vicar and Florence into the manse.

Despite the early start, Julia, Doreen and Mary enjoyed the sea crossing to the Isle of Man. They had had to get up at 5am and were warned that the journey took twice as long as in peace time because they had to avoid the known minefields. It had been a good idea to spend the previous day in Blackpool. They had slept at the YWCA in Fleetwood and had a good night's sleep instead of travelling up by train overnight.

Even so, they had a good old grumble about the weight and awkwardness of their kitbags.

'Thank the Lord we'll be here for six months and needn't take full kit on leave. Getting across London was awful,' Doreen complained.

'I got lucky. There were a bunch of RAF boys on the train to Liverpool Street. We were all standing in the corridor and got talking. Well, they were coming up north and they carried my kit from there. They'd been on leave, so they didn't have much themselves,' said Julia smugly.

'I don't know how you do it. You don't exactly look helpless, but you always get someone to carry your stuff. I wonder how Flo got on. Three weeks isn't long enough to develop muscles when you're as light as her.'

'She got a lift in a lorry – right to York,' Mary told them. 'Alison and Joan saw her go. Joan's the lucky one – she'll never have to hump all this stuff around if she stays at Glen Parva.'

They were pleasantly surprised by their reception at Douglas harbour. A crowd of girls disembarked to find themselves heavily outnumbered by the men, mostly Pioneer Corps and Royal Signals. The men flung their kitbags up to them as they clambered into the waiting lorries and they were driven along the seafront, stopping off at various hotels where they alighted as their names were called out.

The three friends were all in the same hotel, but the bedrooms were for two people.

A harassed looking Sergeant hurried them along.

'It doesn't matter where you sleep. You can change over later. Only hurry. Your boat was late and dinner's getting cold,' she said sharply.

They dumped their kit in two adjoining rooms and all congregated in one of them. 'Let's toss for who gets to stay here,' Do suggested.

'OK. Heads for here.'

Julia lost both spins and went back into the next room, where she found a fair, plump girl who looked up from washing her face.

'God, I wasn't half seasick,' she explained. 'Some fellers rescued me and took me up on deck, facing the wind – and now I could eat an ox.'

'I don't suppose you'll get that, but there's a meal waiting. Are you on your own?'

'Aren't we all? My name's Sylvia Harmon, by the way.'

'Julia Lewis. No, I've got some friends in the next room. You'd better come down with us.' All of them gathered over the unexciting half-cold meal, enthusiastic about their accommodation.

'How marvellous to have proper beds—'

'—and wash basins—'

'—and plenty of hot water.'

Julia turned to Sylvia. 'You don't snore, do you?'

'Not that I know.'

'Good, oh,' Doreen said. 'We should all sleep better than in a dorm. This meal's not marvellous, is it?'

From further down the table an unmistakable Welsh voice said, 'Get anything you like in Douglas, girls. There's a YW does beautiful meals. Only things on ration are marge and soap.'

The speaker had straight dark hair, cut in a bob, and bright blue eyes. She wore the two stripes of a Corporal.

'Oh well, we can do without both of them,' Julia said.

There was a general laugh, followed by a buzz of conversation. As they finished the meal, the Welsh girl got to her feet.

'My name is Corporal Evans and I'm responsible for this billet. Because we're not operational here and don't expect air raids, it's a pretty easy routine – not much different from office hours. You'll find plenty to do in your spare time and the rest of today is free. You've all been travelling so get a good night's sleep tonight and I'll see you at breakfast.'

'Sounds as if we've come to a holiday camp,' Mary said, as they went up to unpack their kit.

They all loved Douglas. Even in the chill February days they found the town charming with its open horse-drawn trams, the harbour and beach, the shops and the beautiful scenic walks.

They took the little railway to Laxey where they saw the enormous waterwheel, Lady Isabella. They climbed Douglas Head from where they could see over the bay in one direction and Snaefell in the other. They danced at the Villa Marina and met with many other Forces personnel for cheap meals and amateur contests at the well-named Smokey Joe's. The only thing that they regretted was that so much of the Island was out of bounds, because there were German Prisoner of War camps in the west.

The hotel on top of Onchan Head had been taken over by the Royal Signals and here the Regimental dances were held, but it was also used for training. The girls were marched up there to learn to read Morse and, later, to take actual messages in German on the Intercept machines. They had been issued with the Winged Mercury badge of Royal Signals – affectionately known as Jimmy – and wore it with a sense of pride. They found the training interesting and worked hard to get their speeds up to the required standard, but they also had plenty of free time.

One warm day in March, Mary and Do were sitting on the steps in front of their hotel, gazing out to sea.

'It's my twenty-first next week,' Mary remarked, 'and Dad has sent me a fiver. I'm thinking about having a party.'

'Good-oh. But we won't be allowed to have any men in the house.'

'I was thinking of the Villa Marina.'

'You were *what*?'

'Well, they've got a restaurant upstairs, haven't they? Why shouldn't I book it for the evening?'

'For heavens sake! How many were you thinking of inviting?'

'A dozen of us – six of each.'

'You're a dark horse! How many men do you know?'

'Only Ian and his friend, Ron – but all the girls will know someone.'

Well, thought Do, Mary might be the quietest of us but she's also the most unexpected.

'Yes,' said the proprietor of the Villa Marina, 'you can certainly book the restaurant if it isn't a weekend. I'll leave a long table in there and clear the rest of the room. I'll shift the piano in and you can stay till eleven.'

'We'll have to go before then. What about a meal?'

'You leave that to my wife. She knows what young people like – steak and chips and a nice pudding, eh? And we'll put out some sandwiches later. Five shillings a head, all right? Ten bob for the room.'

'That's a bit steep,' Julia said when she heard the terms. 'Wouldn't you rather buy yourself a nice present with that money?'

But Mary was adamant. She asked Judy and Ann to join the four of them and they all agreed to bring a partner.

Judy said, 'I know a boy who's a jolly good pianist. Only thing is he plays classical music, but I'll see if I can persuade him to unbend a bit.'

'That's a bit of luck,' Sylvia said, eyeing Mary suspiciously.

'I suppose you didn't know about that piano player when you asked Judy?' she questioned later.

'I may have heard her mention it – no doubt it was somewhere at the back of my mind,' Mary admitted, 'but he's a classical pianist.'

'Don't worry, we'll soon get round him,' Julia said.

She would, too, Mary thought. There was something about Julia that was very persuasive.

She had to use all her powers before they got the party underway. The girls were all ready to leave when Sylvia came in.

'I've just seen Bill. He says they won t get away for ages yet. Their Sergeant's got them on extra drill for something.'

'The food will be cold!' wailed Mary.

Halfway down the stairs, Julia flung back, 'I'll fix it' and ran to where the men were drilling in front of their hotel. She went straight up to the RSM and gave him her sweetest smile.

'Sergeant-Major, I've got a problem. Could you be very kind and help me?'

'Me? What can I do?'

'It's like this, it's my friend's twenty-first birthday. She's invited some of these men to a party and now she's crying her eyes out because the men will be late and the dinner will be spoilt. It's such a shame. After all, you only have one twenty-first.'

The RSM sighed. 'So you do.' He turned to face the squad.

'OK. You heard what the lady said. Same time tomorrow night. Dismiss.'

He started to turn away, but Julia said, 'Oh, thank you. You're a darling' and she kissed his red cheek. The men raised a cheer, but she shouted at them, 'Well, hurry up! Villa Marina in ten minutes.'

In fact, they had to wait for the first course, but it was worth it. A thick fish soup was followed by the succulent steak and then a chocolate pudding with plenty of cream. None of them could have afforded such a meal on Army pay. Truly, the island was blessed at a time when the rest of Britain was so strictly rationed.

As they were finishing the meal, Mary asked Donald, the pianist, if he would play *The Warsaw Concerto* – ease him in gently, she thought. He agreed and they sat and listened in silence. Here was someone worth attention.

Bill murmured to Mary, 'You *are* honoured. It really hurts him to play this stuff.'

So they started with party games, but presently Donald offered to play some dance music for them. Judy went to stand beside him and look at the piano music. It looked as if the pair might be serious. Doreen hoped not. These were not soldiers to fall in love with. They were destined for the Far East and who could tell whether any of them would come back?

Ron was only eighteen and was already engaged to a girl at home. No-one doubted that it was serious as he talked about her incessantly. He had a maturity beyond his age and they all liked him for his innate sweetness of character. At one of the Signals dances, he had delivered a rebuke to Doreen in the gentlest of ways.

That night some of the men in the bar, not drunk but certainly merry, had started singing their own versions of popular songs. They had enough sense to sing the most outrageous parts very quietly and Doreen had turned to Ron and said, 'Tell me what they're singing.'

He looked at her gravely, but with a little smile, and replied, 'Well, if you were my girl I wouldn't dream of telling you.'

She flushed and said, 'Then don't' and added, 'I shouldn't have asked.'

A young man to be respected, she thought, and his girl is lucky. She had asked him to the party so that he would know she had not taken offence.

As they danced, she asked, 'Are you all learning Morse, like us, or something more technical?'

'Learning Morse – yes. Like you – no. We're doing it in Japanese.'

'What's it like?'

'The alphabet is twice as long as ours, to begin with.'

'I ought to have guessed – I mean, if you're going to the Far East.'

'How do you know that?' Ron asked sharply.

'Is it a secret? It seems to be generally known.'

He shook his head. 'People can't keep their mouths shut. I hope no-one has told the Japs.'

Doreen shivered suddenly and hoped fervently that he would survive and come back to marry his girl. She prayed that night that they would all survive – decent and intelligent lads. The country would need them in future years.

Joan had a number of letters on the table before her and was trying to work out how best to co-ordinate them.

Flo had written that the nice Corporal who had given her a lift had taken her right to her door.

'*But don't get any ideas. He and my Dad got on like a house on fire, both being middle-aged.*'

She said she had quite enjoyed her training, though she didn't learn much she hadn't already known. She was now stationed in Preston and wondered if she would bump into Phyllis. She was sharing a room with a very nice girl from Sunderland, who was a dental nurse. And that was all for now. Love to all the others and she was looking forward to Joan's First Epistle.

Joan smiled as she read the letter through again. She had a postscript to add to Flo's copy of her letter.

'*That middle-aged Corporal asked if I had your address and I said I didn't know yet. I must say he didn't seem middle-aged to me. Shall I give it to him if he asks again?*'

Doreen had written for the three girls on the Isle of Man and had given an enthusiastic description of the island, their accommodation and their leisure activities, ending with an account of Mary's birthday party. There was no mention of their training.

It made a complete contrast to Alison's letter, which read,

'*The work I am training for is really interesting and once I get a posting I will really be doing something to help win the war.*'

Audrey's letter was the shortest of the lot. OCTU had been fun and she was now having further training for the secret work she expected to do.

As she had anticipated, Joan had heard nothing from Phyllis. She thought it was a pity that the woman had been posted to an office job and was in a private billet instead of a unit with plenty of other ATS.

She got down to the job of drafting her letter. At the end, she wrote,

'*I've got the most exciting news of any of you. Last week I got engaged to one of the Bandsmen. I don't suppose we'll marry before the war ends, but eventually I shall be Mrs. Albert Coles. I am very happy and so glad I got to stay here.*'

It was after their return to the island from leave that the trouble started. It began with a new Sergeant Instructor. They had been used to receiving Morse sent out in a straightforward way, gradually increasing speed, but Sergeant Davis broke up letters when she sent, so that the dot, dot, dot, dash of the letter V came over as two dots followed by dot dash. Most of them got used to her after a time or two, but neither Doreen nor Mary ever did.

She told them that most operators had their own style of sending and that they would have to get used to them all if they were going to be able to intercept German messages. Julia and Sylvia had no trouble with that but Julia got into difficulties as soon as they started using the intercept machines where there was background interference. She had never been able to concentrate against noise and now she could get nothing.

It was no surprise when only Sylvia of the four passed the training course. Then the Officer, interviewing them separately, offered each of the other three an alternative to re-training.

'I can't tell you anything about it except that you'll be using the skills you've already learnt. It's very secret and it will help us to defeat Hitler. But it's your decision. Let me know tomorrow.'

They talked about it with two other girls who had been given the same option.

'They say you should never volunteer,' one of them said, 'and I don't think I'm going to.'

Julia and Mary already knew their minds and, once again, it was Mary who surprised them. 'I'm going to risk it. I've enjoyed this course – and secret work sounds exciting.'

Julia was equally positive. 'I was thinking when I was at home. I don't really want to spend the rest of the war sitting down all day – too much like an office job. I'll go back to Glen Parva and see what they have to offer. I'd like some more active work.'

Doreen was undecided. She had got on so well with both Mary and Julia that she hated the idea of losing either of them. She would have dithered until the last minute but for the arrival of the mail. It contained another letter from Joan.

'If we go back to Leicester we'll see her and meet her fiancé,' Julia said. 'Wouldn't you like to see her again?'

But Doreen had focused on another part of the letter.

'I wouldn't mind doing Alison's job. Look, Julia, isn't that just the kind of active work you want?'

And that was how the two of them ended up serving on gun sites for the rest of the war.

* * * * *

Florence had arrived home on leave after a tiring journey from Preston to York. As usual, the railway carriages were crowded and there had been plenty of delays. She was sitting over her tea when her father asked how she was liking life in the ATS.

'I'm enjoying myself so much that I sometimes wonder if it's wrong, Dad. I can go dancing either in Preston or on camp any time I'm off duty. Then there's often a game of housey-housey in the canteen. We don't play for big stakes – nobody's got that much money, anyway, but I've hesitated to join in. I don't know if you would approve. I've got lots of friends so there's always someone to go out with.'

Richard Young looked down at his daughter's earnest face and bent to kiss her.

'My darling child, you've had such a dull time here. I'm delighted that it's a different life for you now. You've got young friends and a job worth doing. Of course it's not wrong to enjoy yourself. If you can get any happiness out of this war ...'

For a moment he looked wistful. 'If it wasn't for keeping a home for you, I'd be tempted to volunteer as an Army chaplain. I feel my own horizons need broadening.'

'Oh, Dad, don't think about a home for me – it'll never be ours, anyway. I've been thinking I might stay on in the ATS after the war. Surely they'll never go back to all men in the Services again. Not when the women have proved they can do so many of the men's jobs.' She clutched his arm and said, 'I think you should do it.'

'I'll think about it. If I'm honest I'd love to go, but the people here need me. They have sons and husbands in danger '

Florence broke in quickly, 'The Bishop would appoint someone else.' Her eyes danced. 'Perhaps a married man who wouldn't have to fend off all the parish spinsters!'

'There is that,' he conceded, colouring and laughing, then changing the subject.

'You'll never guess who I've seen. That nice young man who brought you home from Leicester.'

'Did you, Dad? What did he want?'

'Well, he brought me some stamps for my collection, but I think the real reason he came was to get your address. I didn't give it to him, but I did tell him you'd be home this week. I hope I did right.'

'I suppose so. But he can't be interested in me. I'm too young for him.'

'That's for you to decide. I wouldn't want to influence you in any way. I think he's a nice chap. He's been very frank with me and I thought that might be because of you, but I mustn't jump to conclusions.'

Richard did not think it necessary to tell his daughter that Corporal Miller had called on him, not once but three times since the day they had first met. It was no surprise to him when the man turned up on the third day of Florence's leave.

To her own annoyance, she felt self-conscious with him and blamed her father for putting ideas into her head.

135

'Have you learnt to dance?' Dusty asked, as they walked in the vicarage garden.

'Yes – and you were quite right. It's easy and I love it. I always go when I'm off duty.'

'There's a good place in York. If I can get up again this week, I'll take you.'

'That would be nice,' she replied rather primly. After all, there were lots of eligible men of her own age in Preston. She certainly wasn't going to be available just to suit him. But it was impossible not to give him her ATS address without being rude. He had mentioned the possibility of getting to Preston, but she could always be busy if he came.

Dusty didn't manage to get to York while she was still on leave. Florence found she was disappointed, but decided that it was because there was so little to do in the village in comparison with her full life in camp. She was also conscious of the need for propriety while her father was the vicar and thought that it would be a very good thing for them both if he became an Army chaplain.

Doreen and Julia went back to Glen Parva and met Bandsman Albert Coles. He was a six-foot, broad-shouldered man with fair hair and blue eyes and he looked younger than his twenty-six years. They both liked his ready smile and the way it softened when he looked at Joan. She was rather shy when she introduced them, but her happiness was plain to see.

When she was alone with the girls, she said, 'It all happened so quickly and I really wasn't expecting him to propose so soon, even when we started going out together – but he says he made up his mind straight away.'

'And did you say yes at once?' Do asked.

'Oh no. His Sergeant's awfully decent and he got Albert a twenty-four hour pass when I had mine. So we went home and he met my Mum and Dad. He's a lot like my Dad – same sort of humour – so they got on well, and the next thing I knew he got me into this jewellers and told me to choose a ring – and I did.'

She showed them the modest diamond with pride.

'Well, I don't suppose we'll see a lot of you now and we hope not to be here long,' Julia said, 'but it's been nice to meet him and lovely to see you again.'

When they were on their own, Julia said, 'I do hope it lasts – these wartime things are so quick.'

'I should think it's got a better chance than most if he's like her father. Don't girls often go for men like dear old dad?'

'So I've heard. Anyway, I've no intention of getting engaged before the war's over – that's if anyone asks me, of course. Would you?'

'Mm. There was a Hundred Years War, you know. I wouldn't be too sure.'

After a brief stay at Glen Parva Doreen and Julia were posted to Oswestry for training as Telephonist/Plotters. The camp, at Tonfanu, was a few miles from the town and was served by a railway and a slow, chugging train known as the Tinkers Green express. Their accommodation was in huts, but the men on the camp were in tents.

They found the training interesting. It comprised several aspects including learning to plot positions on maps, mastering the telephone switchboard and aircraft recognition by means of drawings of planes in all positions. They also learned how to recognise planes using the Telescope Identification instrument on the parade ground.

'This aircraft recognition is an eye-opener in both senses,' Julia said. 'I had no idea there were so many different planes. I'll never learn which is a Hurricane and which is a Messerschmitt.'

'You'll know when they are near enough for you to see the markings, but by then it'll be too late, so you'd better make sure you know the difference before you go on site. You'll be expected to do some spotting if need be,' the instructor told them.

They were working on the parade ground, taking it in turn to use the TI when a fighter plane with an RAF roundel marked on it flew slowly overhead. It was low enough for the pilot to see them. The Sergeant instructor threw up her arm and shouted, 'Easy one for you! What is it?'

'Spitfire,' they answered as one. There was no mistaking the graceful plane with the rounded wingtips. But Doreen was watching the instructor. Was she blushing? Had the pilot been looking for her? He flew back over them, waggled his wings and was away, climbing as he went.

They went into the NAAFI one Saturday night and found it packed.

Julia spotted a table with only a solitary Gunner in possession and made a beeline for it.

'Are these seats taken?' she asked, then stared in amazement as the young man actually got to his feet and remained standing until they were both seated.

'I'm trying to save one for a friend – he's on jankers – but the others are free. Can I get you a coffee or tea?'

'I think tea's safer,' Do replied and Julia nodded agreement, gazing after the tall, slim man as he went to the counter.

'What manners! What's he doing in the ranks?' she asked.

'Oh, come on, Julia. We've met plenty of boys like that. What about Ian and his friends?' But Julia was shaking her head as if to say, 'Not like him.'

When he came back, Do asked, 'What's your friend on jankers for?'

He grinned, rather sheepishly. 'We both skived off and Tom got caught. I can run faster than him.'

Doreen said afterwards that she never quite knew how it happened. He seemed a shy man but within a few minutes he and Julia were deep in conversation, so she wandered off to speak to a crowd at another table. Two hours later she went back to Julia and asked, 'Are you coming back?'

Both of them glanced up at the clock. Julia replied, 'Good heavens, is it gone ten already? Reg's friend hasn't turned up so I'll keep him company for another half-hour.'

When she eventually went back to their hut, she said, 'Sorry I didn't come back with you, but he's ever so shy and he was working around to asking me for a date.'

'When and where?'

'Pictures – tomorrow night.'

Do started to say, 'But you've already seen it this week,' then decided against it. After all, *The Gentle Sex* was a good enough film to bear seeing twice.

On the Monday, they were again on the square, using the TI when Do drew Julia's attention to what was happening on the men's side. Their TI was trained on the girls. The Sergeant gave an order and the next moment Reg was running round the boundary with a dummy shell on his shoulder.

'I do believe he was looking at you and didn't get away with it this time. Those things weigh a ton, but he's got off lightly.'

Julia said nothing. She had been aware for some time that Reg was watching her.

They met every night after that and at the end of a week he asked her to marry him. On the following Sunday, after Church Parade, she said that she would, finally reaching a decision during the sermon – a most relevant one as she had been asking for guidance – when the padre had spoken of taking risks in faith.

Of course, Doreen had seen it coming, but she couldn't help reminding Julia that she'd said she had no intention of getting engaged before the war was over.

'It was you who said it could go on for a hundred years,' Julia replied, unabashed, 'and, Do, now I come to think of it, he *is* rather like my Dad.'

Behind her back, more doubts were voiced. Some were not at all kind and Doreen wondered how many of the catty comments were inspired by jealousy.

'It won't last. Stands to reason, something as quick as that. And he's only a Gunner, anyway – no very great catch,' Doreen heard Lillian say.

She was about to respond when May, who was usually quiet, broke in. 'It doesn't follow. I've known my husband since we were kids. I've been married two years and I'm getting a divorce. I thought I knew him, but I was so wrong. I wouldn't have believed he could behave as he has ...' Her voice broke and they changed the subject.

Several times, while they remained in Oswestry, the lovers invited Tom and Do to go out with them, but although Tom was a pleasant enough lad there was no spark between them, and presently they found other friends and left the couple to their own devices.

Julia became more sure of her choice as she and Reg got to know each other better. They had so many interests in common and a similar philosophy of life. She found him a serious-minded man – so different from most of the ones she had met – with very firm ideas about how he wanted to see the country run after the war.

One evening, feeling that it was marvellous just to have met the right man for her, she said, 'You know, it really doesn't matter how long we have to wait to get married,' and he replied, 'So you know that, too.' She treasured that remark all the rest of her long married life.

It became automatic for them to walk hand in hand, a habit frowned on by the camp police, so they were continually being told to 'break it up' and Julia usually returned to her hut fuming about authority. They had so little time left together as the training for both drew to an end.

Both Julia and Do were looking forward to 'getting on with the war', as Do put it, but it would be hard to say goodbye to Reg. In the event, they were both posted to the south coast; he to Kent, the girls to Hampshire.

The gun battery was near Portsmouth and part of it was stationed on Southsea Common and the other part was just outside Fareham. They were in a hut of eight, each with a single bed. It was just as well that they did not have to scramble out of bunks as they had to race down to the Command Post as soon as the alarm bell went, if they were on standby duty.

They found that they had got into the war with a vengeance. Raids on the south coast were frequent and heavy. They worked in shifts in the large underground room with predictor and radar operators, where they manned the telephones and plotted enemy positions on a large map of the area. On standby, they got used to being woken by the alarm, grabbing tin hats and gas masks and stumbling into the Command Post, still half asleep and often wearing only a greatcoat or a pair of slacks over their pyjamas. Once they were on duty they were too busy to feel any fear, however heavy or long the raid.

They had not been at Fareham many weeks when Doreen got transferred to Southsea. She didn't want to leave the friends she was just beginning to know and she was even more annoyed when she discovered the reason for her transfer. It was because a girl at Southsea was too friendly with a married man and this was the standard procedure for dealing with the matter. No doubt the authorities thought this was the least they could do to prevent a disaster, but they didn't always get it right.

The girl who arrived from Southsea, Dawn, was equally indignant, quite unrepentant and determined to meet her Ernest in Portsmouth whenever she could.

'It's ridiculous,' she told Julia. 'He's getting a divorce and we're getting married as soon as it's through. Then I'll get pregnant as soon as I can and get away from all this nannying. Who do they think they are, trying to run our lives?'

'I expect they've had a lot of trouble – well, you know they have – with girls getting pregnant by men who haven't any intention of marrying them. I suppose they're bound to try and prevent it if they can. You can't blame them.'

'Huh,' said Dawn scornfully, 'they can't stop human nature and there's bound to be a percentage of trollops among the Services. Anyway, I'm going to see the Junior Commander and convince her that Ernest's divorce is going through.'

She must have been persuasive. A month later, she went back to Southsea and Doreen returned to Fareham with some news.

'You'll never guess who's at Southsea. Alison – she's a Corporal now. I'm arranging for us all to meet.'

It was some time before they were all off duty together, but at last they managed to meet at a roadhouse just off the main Portsmouth Road at Cosham. Despite rationing there was always a good meal to be had if you knew where to go, and it seemed that a Sergeant had taken Alison there. They celebrated their reunion with a bottle of wine. It made heavy inroads into their Army pay, but it was worth it for once.

Alison seemed more beautiful than ever. There was an extra glow about her that meant only one thing to Do, who remembered how Julia had been.

'Are you serious with this Sergeant?' she asked, and Alison admitted that she had been out with him quite a lot and thought that maybe …

'That's Joan, Julia and you all fixed up. Only Flo and me still on the loose – oh, and Audrey. I suppose hers will be an Officer.'

'You haven't had Joan's last epistle, then? Audrey's engaged to a university don who she knew before she joined up.'

'You've forgotten Mary,' Julia reminded them. 'Did Joan say anything about her?'

'Only that she's in a pretty isolated place and there's not much to do when she's off duty, but the work is a compensation. Apparently it's even more important than she thought and sometimes they're told that they've done a really good job which should help to shorten the war.'

'I don't think I'd find that much consolation if there wasn't plenty to do when I was off duty,' Do said. 'In fact, I can't think of anything I'd rather do than work in the Command Post. Then you know you're doing something worthwhile.'

Six weeks later, Doreen was transferred back to Southsea. Her language, as she collected her full kit together, was much more colourful than she had ever used in civvy street. Julia was apprehensive too. Whoever came would take Do's bed, next to hers. She hoped it might be Dawn again.

The girl who arrived, Vi Lumley, seemed pleasant enough, but it wasn't long before they all realised that she was one of 'them trollops' Dawn had been so scornful about. She made no secret of the fact and spoke as though all the decent girls were goody-goodies. Soon the men had labelled her as 'anybody's for a cup of coffee.' The other girls tolerated her without condoning her way of life and assumed, from her worldly air, that she knew enough to take care of herself. It came as a shock to hear from Southsea, after she returned there, that she had been discharged under Paragraph Eleven, which told them that she was pregnant.

There was no sympathy for her. They all felt that she had got what she deserved, although Julia did say, 'Perhaps a baby was what she really wanted.'

'She'll have it whether she wants it or not,' May replied. 'I only hope she looks after the poor little thing.'

Meanwhile, Doreen had gone storming into the office on her arrival at Southsea and demanded an interview with the Junior Commander. The Officer, hearing raised voices, looked in to the outer office, took in the situation and said abruptly, 'You'd better come in now.'

When Doreen stood in front of her she asked, 'Now what's the trouble?'

'Ma'am, I've had to cart my full kit over here from Fareham for the second time. It's not just a bloody nuisance – it's unfair. Just because other girls misbehave themselves and you want to get rid of them, I don't see why I should be picked on to move – I haven't been doing anything I shouldn't.'

The Officer, who had long ago come to the conclusion that this business of moving girls around was a complete waste of time if they were determined to 'act like floosies', soothed Doreen and promised that she should go back to Fareham as soon as possible and not be chosen to be moved again.

Her stay there wasn't all bad. To begin with, there was Alison. Then the camp itself was pleasant. They could roam the common and the sea was in sight. On warm days, they could sunbathe when they were off duty.

One day, Alison was on twenty-four hours' leave, which she was spending with a family who lived near to the camp. There were several civilians who had made friends with the Forces personnel and practically kept open house for them, but this was the first time she was to stay the night.

As soon as the air raid siren went they took her down to the Anderson shelter in the garden. It was nothing like as deep as the Command Post, but Alison found herself sweating with fear as the bombs started dropping, and felt shame as she realised that civilians all over Britain were coping with this night after night.

The Command Post seemed to be a place of safety in comparison to this claustrophobic, earthy dungeon – and there was work to keep your mind off the bombing. Alison made an excuse to leave, saying that the Battery was short-handed as there was a flu epidemic and she felt that she ought to report for duty.

Outside, she breathed freely. The 'epidemic' was a slight exaggeration, but she thought they might have a job for her.

'I'm a coward,' she thought. 'I couldn't stick in a shelter and not know what was happening.'

There was no evidence of bomb damage along her route and she reported to the Officer on duty and asked if she could be of any use. Doreen, sitting in front of the map with headphones over her ears, raised a hand in greeting and turned back to her work as the plots came in quickly.

'We're short of a spotter tonight,' Captain Holding told Alison. 'Be useful if you'd get up there and keep an eye open.'

So, for the next hour, Alison stood above the Command Post, completely exposed except for a tin hat, only too happy to be out of that stuffy underground shelter.

She heard a plane coming in from the coast but it didn't sound

143

heavy enough for a bomber. What were they playing at? Then she saw the fighter coming over very low and losing height rapidly. She was about to shout 'Messerschmitt' when she saw the RAF roundels. It was a Hurricane – and in trouble. She shouted 'Hurricane, about to crash,' and took off in its direction. Before she could reach it, there was a mighty noise and the ground shook as it pancaked then seemed to fold in on itself.

Then she was fighting to get the door open. The solitary pilot was unconscious and she struggled with the straps that were holding him. She never heard the arrival of the others or the shouting at her to leave him. She had partly dragged him clear when the plane went on fire. At first, the heat threw her back, then the flames reached her face and arms. Doreen arrived as the Officer covered her with a blanket.

The pilot was dead. The girl would live, but she would never be beautiful Alison again.

This is Now - 4

Doreen was tearful, after all these years, as the memories came flooding back. I felt shattered. The climax had been so unexpected.

I went into the house and asked Aunt Julia if I could make a cup of tea, as Doreen was upset.

'Alison?' she asked. I nodded. 'Go back to her. I'll bring it out to you.'

In two minutes she came into the summerhouse with sherry and glasses. 'I've put the kettle on, but get this down you first.' As we sipped the Amontillado, I asked Doreen, 'What happened to her? Can you bear to tell me?'

'It was a tragedy, of course – someone as beautiful as that, even though we knew it would still be terrible if she had been plain – but it wasn't as bad as it might have been. They took her to Portsmouth first but before we were allowed to see her, she was transferred to that marvellous hospital where Archie MacIndoe did such great work with all the burns cases. It was amazing what they did. Of course, only the least severe cases ever looked quite natural again – and it took ages, with lots of pain.

'When Alison was able to tell me about that night and how she felt a coward for not staying with the Campdens, I couldn't believe it – with all she went through afterwards, and so bravely. One good thing was that her Sergeant really loved her. He haunted the place every chance he got. Julia and I both went to their wedding about a year later. Of course, she had a lot more to go through even then, but it was one of the happiest weddings I've ever been to – everybody there was so pleased for them.

'After the war they went to Canada. I think he had some relations over there. We gathered from her letters that it was a remote part of the Rockies, but it was beautiful and she loved it. She was a grandmother before she died. She was only sixty – not a long life, but more than we ever expected when we first saw her.'

She was getting distressed again, so I suggested a walk before dinner. As we were leaving, Aunt Julia called from the kitchen, 'Are you going past the nursery?'

'Can do. What do you want?' Doreen asked.

'A packet of that stuff that stops leaves turning yellow. I can't remember. Simon will know.'

As we walked along, Doreen said, 'Sorry I got uptight about Alison. It brought all that dreadful time back. We just had to get on with it. No counselling in those days. They gave me twenty-four hours off duty and I felt I had to go and tell the Campdens and Julia. We comforted each other, I suppose. Now let's talk about something else. What's happening about your place in London?'

'It was let for six months so it'll be vacant again at the end of October and I suppose I'll move back then, but I don't feel like imposing on Aunt Julia that long.'

This was something to which I had given some thought. I was reluctant to move back to the flat. The present set-up was ideal for writing but I missed the facilities of the London office even more than I missed my friends. Apart from Robert, there was only one woman who rang regularly with a genuine regard for my welfare. She and I shared an interest in art and we had been abroad together for exhibitions. With my other acquaintances it was obviously a case of 'out of sight, out of mind'.

I used to meet them at frequent parties, for meals or to go to shows, but I had long realised that there was no depth to these relationships. At the moment, still walking with the help of a stick and needing rests along the way, I couldn't summon up any enthusiasm for getting back into the swing. But surely that was a lack of energy. I would soon start to miss the buzz of town, so when Doreen said, 'Why don't you sell it and move down here?' I laughed.

'I'm the complete Londoner. I'd miss all the things it has to offer. There's never a dull moment in my life there.'

'I must sound like a recent disciple, trying to convert everybody else. I suppose the country's not for most people. Good job, too. We don't want it to get crowded.'

We fell into house talk easily. Doreen and George had fallen in love with Norfolk themselves and decided that they would spend the rest of their retirement near Julia and Reg. Both of their sons worked in London but were often abroad, so they felt no constraint in choosing to settle where they liked. George wanted an old house – just the kind that my aunt had despised – and had found a three-hundred-year-old cottage in the beautiful village of Castle Acre.

Doreen had been dubious at first, but the discreet modernisation that George proposed had converted her, and she was now looking forward to moving in.

As we approached the nursery, the conversation turned naturally to gardening.

'What I want – and George agrees – is a courtyard garden with old flags or bricks, with old-fashioned plants and lots of herbs. It would suit the house well and some of it's there already. You must come over and see it.'

It being his busy season, I hadn't seen Simon for some time. We found him potting up some bedding plants. He was handling them with gentle care.

Unbidden, the thought crossed my mind that he would be equally gentle with a woman. The hands were as supple as those of a pianist, though strong and sun-browned. Can you fall in love with a pair of hands? I could almost feel them caressing my body.

Something must have communicated itself to him. He looked up, straight at me and did not appear to see Doreen. At once, I was crimson with embarrassment. It took an effort to regain my usual poise. We made our purchase for Aunt Julia and Simon said, 'You tell her she's watering her plants too much.'

Then Doreen asked, 'Can you recommend someone who could do a small courtyard? George has plenty of contacts but they're all in London. We'd like to use local people where we can.'

I left them to talk and wandered round the fruit garden. Try as I might, I couldn't get rid of the feeling of those hands on my breasts.

I wondered if Doreen's generation would consider me a 'trollop' or a 'floosie'. My affairs had lasted years and had not been without affection, but when it came to the crunch, my career had always come first and that was something no man I had yet met had found tolerable. I told myself that this feeling was merely a response to a period of celibacy since Don had gone to America.

That night, I thought of those women in the 1940s. How innocent they had been, yet most of them had stayed married to the same man for fifty years. Could it be that, because no-one had told them how they were expected to behave, they had no preconceived ideas and the marriages had thrived because that was their expectation?

On the following day, Doreen was quite happy to continue.

'Oh yes, I must tell you what happened to Florence,' she said. 'This is a bit sad, some of it, but not harrowing, like Alison.'

So we started on the book again.

That Was Then - Doreen's Story

In December 1943, Richard Young wrote to his daughter:

'I'm sorry you're not getting home for Christmas, but I'll come to see you before I join up. By January I'll be in the Army too. I'm still a bit worried about you not having a home to go to on leave if I'm abroad, but your Granny says you can always go to her. We'll find somewhere together after the war, if you're not married by then. Your Uncle Donald thinks I'm crazy, but then he never did understand how I came to choose this way of life. Grandad is surprised I should go when I don't have to, but I am really looking forward to it.'

Florence folded the letter with a smile. Uncle Donald was too busy making money to imagine how anyone could devote their time to anything else and her Grandfather had never taken a risk in his life.

There were other people who had been refused Christmas leave, but Reg wasn't one of them. He was still in Kent on a mobile Ack-Ack unit and would probably be one of the first on the beaches of France when the Second Front was launched. Everyone knew it must be in a few months and leave was granted as generously as possible to the men who would soon be in the thick of battle.

When she received his letter, Julia put in an application for leave. It was refused. There was a hectic exchange of telegrams. She sent, *'Leave not granted.'* Reg's reply was to the point. *'Will you marry me at Christmas?'* He knew they would not refuse marriage leave. She replied, giving nothing away to anyone who read the telegram, *'With pleasure. Julia Lewis.'* There was a special marriage licence for the Forces which only needed forty-eight hours' notice and Reg applied for it as soon as he got her reply, which made him smile. It was always a shock to see telegrams from a near relative signed with a surname, but such was the wartime regulation.

They were married by her local vicar the day after she arrived home. It was all so rushed that they both stood at the altar in uniform and the few people who could attend went back to a local restaurant for the wedding breakfast.

Never, in the years that followed, did Julia feel the slightest regret that she had not had a white wedding. It was all so unimportant when the only thing that mattered was to be together for whatever time was granted them.

She did regret that Doreen was refused leave, but Reg's young sister was so delighted to be her bridesmaid that her disappointment faded.

'Sheila was tickled pink, considering we didn't have time to get her a new dress, but she's a pretty girl who looks good in anything. I was sorry you couldn't come, but it gave her a lot of pleasure.'

'How many people were there?' Do asked.

'Reg's mum and dad and Sheila, my mum and dad and a couple of aunts, our next-door neighbours and an old school friend. That's all we could muster between us.

'Mum and Dad had a special surprise for us. Where do you think we spent our honeymoon? On the Isle of Man! They wanted us to be away from the bombing and they knew I loved it there. You know, it's funny, when I joined up, I was earning more than Dad, but now he's really making money. His engineering factory has turned over to munitions and he's a manager. They're on bonuses and goodness knows what else. So we went back to Ellen Vannin. Of course, it was pretty cold, but still beautiful – and peaceful.'

'Lucky you. And I think you've done the right thing, just in time. You should see the build-up of tanks and stuff – all round Portsmouth and Fareham. There's something under every tree and camouflage netting draped all over the place.'

Julia looked serious. 'Well, we know it's coming – and the sooner the better, then we can all settle down to a normal life again. Anyway, they can't take memories away, so I'll have no regrets whatever happens.'

Another person who had leave for Christmas was Dusty Miller. He spent some of the holiday with his parents, but the rest of the time he spent with Richard at the latter's invitation.

He had visited Florence as often as he could and they wrote to each other regularly, she knowing how everyone looked for the mail and was disappointed when there was none for them. He felt that she was always pleased to see him, but he was aware that he had never caused her heart to miss a beat. He was a good dancer, very light on his feet, and he knew that she enjoyed dancing with him, but that was all. His idea that he would like her for a daughter had melted away when he first took her in his arms. For months now he had been sure that she was the only girl for him. He said as much to Richard.

'I'm going to see her before I join up. I expect she'll be able to get a pass. Have you told her about your marriage? Are you sure you want to try again – and with Florence?'

'Never surer. Yes, she knows I was married and she's sorry for me. She doesn't think it's any of her business.'

Over the next few days, they discussed the war situation. Richard said, 'We both know something's going to blow up soon. If I cop it, will you do what you can for her? My people would give her a home, but they're both getting on. I've no doubt she would be a great help to them, but I don't want her going back to being an unpaid housekeeper again.'

'I'll do anything – only don't forget, it might be my number that comes up. That's why I don't want to say anything to her until I know we've got a future.'

'Yes, it's all in God's hands – and that's where we'll have to leave it,' said the Reverend Richard Young.

Doreen had a twenty-four hour pass in March and was debating whether to go home when she was offered a lift in an Army lorry, provided she was ready at 6am. She accepted with alacrity. London had been getting a pasting again and she wanted to see that her parents were safe.

'Thanks, Dave, this will do,' she said as they passed the station nearest to her house. The main road ran parallel to the railway line and her road was one of a number at right angles to it.

Almost at once, she realised that the area had been subjected to a bombing attack the night before. There was a gap of about four houses in the middle of every other road. The railway line was untouched.

Her mouth was dry as she hurried up to her own road. Intact. Thank God. But surely the house would not have completely escaped undamaged. She ran.

When her mother opened the door, she gasped, breathlessly, 'Oh, are you both all right?'

'Yes, love. Mind where you step. The windows went in again, but the sitting room is clean. No other damage, but the Brooks have lost their house.'

'But they're alive?'

Doreen picked her way to the room and sat down heavily. The window had been boarded up and the room tidied. The electric light was still burning.

'Yes, so the firemen said. As far as we know they were all in shelters at the bottom of the gardens. The Jerries only hit the houses. We've still got water and light, so we're a lot better off than some. The wireless says there were heavy raids all over London last night.'

Mrs. Blackwell was a stout, rosy-cheeked woman with plenty of energy. Now she bustled about making them tea and toast.

'When I've had this, I must go and see them. You won't mind if I leave you? I expect you're tired. You'd better sleep on the couch until I've cleared up the bedroom.'

'Heavens, no, Mum. I'll come with you. See what we can do.'

So they walked down to the next street, where they saw Mr. Brooks surveying the ruins. He was dressed for his work as a clerk in the Air Ministry, but explained that he had to wait for the rent collector.

'I've been asked to deal with him for all the ones who've been hit, so that the men could go to work and the women and children could go to the rest centre with the WVS. All the services were round here in no time – Air Raid Wardens, Fire Service, the lot. They all went away when they knew there was nobody buried under this lot, but the Fire Service are sending some people back before we're allowed in.'

'Is there anything to go in for? It looks jolly dangerous to me,' Doreen said.

'The wife wants to get the kids some clothes. They're going to my sister in Essex for the time being. I'll find digs till we can get somewhere to live.'

'There's Doreen's bedroom free when she's not on leave – she's only home till tonight – if it's any help to you.'

151

He smiled warmly, his rather saturnine features lighting up.

'That's very good of you, but I'll try for somewhere near work. Travelling isn't too good. It wouldn't be the first time I've slept on the office floor when I couldn't get home. We've got beds there for the watchers on night duty.'

'Where is Mrs. Brooks?' Doreen asked.

'They're all in the air raid shelter. They wouldn't go to the rest centre with the others. They'll go down to Effie as soon as they've got all we can save out of the house. The police are going to let her know they'll be coming.'

Doreen, thinking how efficiently all the civilian services seemed to co-operate, left them talking and made her way carefully across fallen masonry, glass and twisted pipes to the bottom of the garden. The two children came running to meet her.

'Hallo, Harry. Hallo, Ronnie,' she said, 'aren't you having an adventure! Now you're just like all the brave soldiers.'

'It was ever so noisy,' Ronnie told her, and Harry added, 'and it shaked and then it all fall down.'

Mrs. Brooks appeared, clutching her purse and the house keys.

'Mrs. Brooks – I'm so sorry,' Doreen greeted her. 'I expect you've lost a lot of your treasures.'

To her surprise, the little woman beamed.

'No. All my treasures are safe, thank God. None of us is hurt. Nothing else matters.'

They returned to the front of the house to find that a Salvation Army van had arrived to give them breakfast. The novelty of this procedure had the boys clamouring and asserting that they were starving, despite the ministrations of the WVS earlier.

'If you can't get anything from the house – if you need clothes, or anything at all, just let us know,' the young woman told them. 'There isn't much we haven't got by now. I m glad to see you had the sense to take day clothes down to your shelter. You'd be surprised the number of people who don't, after all this time.'

While they were eating, a grey-haired man turned the corner of the street. Mr. Brooks gave a sigh of relief.

'Here's the rent collector.'

The women drew away to let them talk. Mrs. Brooks clutched Doreen's arm and said, 'Do you know, we nearly bought a house last year. We had an insurance policy come out – not a lot, but we saw a nice house for twenty-five pounds deposit. Then we thought we might need the money for something for these two – they grow out of clothes and shoes so quickly. Now I thank God we didn't buy. It's the landlord's loss, not ours.'

A fire engine passed the bottom of the road, dropping two men off. As they came up, Mrs. Blackwell asked, 'When are you going to your sister-in-law?'

'Just as soon as we know what we can take. I'm hoping they can find a case and some clothes.'

'Well, you can't stand around here. Come back with me for now.'

Mr. Brooks, breaking off his conversation, said he would see that anything useful would be brought to her and that he would come and say goodbye before he went to work – if he ever got to work today.

'Are you coming back, Doreen?'

'I'll hang about for a little while, Mum. May be able to help.'

The young, lithe man with the deeply-cleft chin arrived just ahead of his mate, a well-muscled, greying veteran. In answer to her enquiry they both said, no, they didn't involve civilians if it wasn't a matter of life and death. Their job was to see that the premises were as safe as possible, all services cut off, and to save what they could from looters.

'I'm not exactly a civilian,' Doreen pointed out.

'Isn't that an Ack Ack badge?' asked the older man.

'Royal Artillery,' Doreen nodded.

'You'll have had your share of action. Leave this to us.'

She hadn't much choice. Ronnie had run back and was dragging at her hand. She turned and followed her mother.

The children, after their lively night, were thoroughly exhausted, their mother only less so. They all curled up together on the couch, while Doreen went upstairs to clear broken glass from the bedrooms.

It was nearly noon before Mr. Brooks came with the younger fireman. They carried an assortment of objects, explaining that most of the ground floor was ruined by water, glass and the upstairs rubble, but as there had been no fire, most of the contents of the bedrooms had been accessible, except where the roof had fallen. They had saved blankets, some clothes and some of the children's toys. As usual, there had also been some bizarre results, like the unbroken wardrobe mirror, though the wardrobe was spilt down the middle.

'If I could leave some here for now, I could take them down at the weekend,' Mr. Brooks said. Mrs. Blackwell agreed at once. 'Now, I'll take my brood off your hands and see them on the train at Liverpool Street,' he continued.

'Not until you've had something to eat, you won't,' she said, determinedly and, as the fireman made a move to leave, 'that includes you, my lad.'

She had made a soup, thick with vegetables, following it with Spam and fried potatoes. It was a valiant effort to feed seven people unexpectedly, with rationing tighter than ever, and they all appreciated it.

Doreen and the young man fell into 'shop talk' over the meal.

'Where are you stationed – or is it a secret?' he asked her.

'Not really. We're near Portsmouth. You'll know all the coast is heavily defended. What made you choose the Fire Service?'

He grinned. 'I'm a conscientious objector – and I didn't fancy being one of Bevin's boys. At least I'm in the fresh air. I think the ones who volunteer for the mines are just as brave as the Forces, don't you?'

'I suppose so – but I find it difficult to understand how anybody could object to defeating Hitler.'

'Oh, I don't object to that. I want to see him defeated, but it's not Hitler I'd be fighting, is it? It's ordinary people like us.'

She started to say 'but that's the only option we have' and decided that it wasn't worth it. They were never going to agree, and he wasn't exactly running away from the war, was he? Besides, he was too nice, and it was unlikely that she would ever see him again.

But when he left, he said, 'I hope I'll meet you again. When do you get leave?'

'That's in the lap of the gods. Once the balloon goes up I expect all leave will be cancelled.'

He scribbled on a piece of paper. 'Would you let me know? This address will always find me.'

She accepted the paper and smiled sweetly. But, of course, she would do nothing of the sort – running after a man like that. What did he think she was?

When they had all gone, she put the paper into her tunic pocket, glancing down at it first. His name was George Foster.

* * * * *

154

Florence collected her mail with a smile. Three letters – a record. There was never any doubt who had written them. Forces letters had to bear the full name and address of senders on the envelope. One was from Joan in Glen Parva, one from her father, Captain the Rev Richard Young, now a chaplain with the Royal Ordnance Corps, and the third was from Dusty Miller.

Something about Joan's letter was unfamiliar. Ah, yes Private J Coles – so she had married her Albert. Florence opened this letter first.

'Dear gang,

As you will see, I am now a married woman. It seemed wrong to wait with the Second Front hanging over us. We chose to tie the knot in the Leicester church, just so that we could boast that the Regimental Band played at our wedding. I was married in white, having received a present of parachute silk. I made the dress myself, of course – but that's enough about me.

Some of you will know that Julia is married, too. Julia, we all send you our good wishes. You and Doreen have been catching it on the coast, but so far, no casualties, thank God.

Alison is getting on slowly. We went to see her while we were on leave. She sends love to everybody and is interested in all the news.

Mary is still saying that her secret establishment is miles from anywhere and she can't tell us much, but I have a feeling she has found some consolation.

Audrey has married her don and is now Captain A. Oakley. She says her work is enthralling and hints that she may be able to tell us more soon.

Florence's father is now an Army padre and she is very proud of him. She hasn't bumped into Phyllis yet and of course I haven't heard anything.

Do keep writing. If you all stay in touch we can meet up after the war. What a party that will be!'

Dusty's letter was short and to the point.

'I shall be coming your way on Friday of next week. Keep as much time free as you can for me. I should be there about noon and will wait in the guardroom.'

She opened the letter from her father with a loving smile. He was having such a good time and she could only be glad that she had persuaded him to join the Army, despite the possibility that he might be in danger. He wrote,

'My dear daughter,

I hope you are still well and happy. As you know, I am really enjoying life here. I can be of help to so many men who need all the support that they can get, so I feel really useful in a way I never did in the village. They all expect to be involved in the Second Front and I hope I will be allowed to go with them.

There is one person I am concerned about and that is Dusty. Of course he will go too. I don't want to interfere in your life, but I believe that he loves you. I don't think he will tell you yet, but I hope you will not dash his hopes until he has come safely through – if you feel you have to dash them then. You know he has been hurt in the past and it would be good if you could give him a cause for hope. I can trust you to handle this well, I know ...'

There was more, but after a brief glance down the page, Florence laid the letter down thoughtfully.

Just recently she had been at a dance with her roommate, Susan, and for the first time she had been insulted by a soldier. She had danced with him on several occasions and thought him a decent boy, but at the end of their dance he had invited her to sleep with him – and as though he was doing her a favour. It happened that Susan was sitting out and watching her. She saw Florence go scarlet and look down. She guessed what had happened and thought that the flush was a sign of embarrassment, then realised, as Florence's clenched fists whitened, that her friend was furious.

Florence raised her head slowly, looked the soldier up and down and then said in an incredulous tone, 'With *you?'*

It was the soldier's turn to go scarlet and confused. He scowled at her and retreated. Susan had said, 'Beautifully done' loud enough for him to hear.

Florence was thinking of this incident as she folded the letter. She was well aware by now that most of the girls had had to fight off wandering hands and even more amorous advances. There were men with whom she would not dance twice, but this was the first time for her that it had been so blatant. She had wondered how she would cope with it and thanked heaven that it had not happened when she first came into the ATS straight from the village rectory.

In comparison with some of the men, Dusty felt safe. She was comfortable with him and perhaps the difference in their ages was not too much. Like most girls, she longed for romance, but she saw no reason why she should send him away without a ray of hope. Who could tell whether he would survive the coming battle?

When they met the conversation turned at once to the imminence of this.

'I know Dad's hoping to go with the men. I hadn't thought of that when I persuaded him to join up, but he's having the time of his life. Surely it can't be long now.'

'No doubt about it. The signs are all there. I don't know if I'll be among the first, but they're bound to want drivers pretty soon.'

As he left her, he said quietly, 'You know I'm very fond of you, Flora, don't you?'

'I'm fond of you, Dusty. Take care of yourself and come back safe.'

She reached up and kissed him gently on the cheek.

Doreen was on duty on the morning of June 5th when the phone from HQ rang and a voice said, 'Strawberries on sale. I say again, strawberries on sale.' Then the phone went dead.

The Officer on duty that day was a silly little woman. All the girls wondered how she had ever got her commission. She had made some frightful bloomers including giving the order to the guns to 'Practise Fire' when they were engaged in a real battle. Now she said, 'Well I never. Fancy HQ telling us that!'

Doreen, who had already spotted the coded SOS gazed at her in amazement.

It was lucky that the Company Commander came in at that moment.

'HQ have just told us that there are strawberries on sale – isn't that delightful?'

He gazed past her, murmured something that sounded like 'silly cow' (but surely couldn't have been) and jumped for the alarm bell.

It was the signal for everyone to muster. When they were all on parade he told them, 'It looks as though the balloon's about to go up. All leave is cancelled and you are all confined to barracks until further notice. Most likely it will only be for a few days. Dismiss.'

They fell out, some of them grumbling about missing dates they had made for that night, but all feeling excited and relieved. Julia, frantically trying to conceal her alarm, said to Doreen, 'Say a prayer for Reg tonight.'

'Every night,' Doreen promised, squeezing her arm.

In the clear light of an early morning, a group of girls stood together and watched huge gliders going out over the coast. It was the next day, D-day, as it came to be known. There were no grumbles now about their confinement to camp. They stood in silence, each busy with her own thoughts, everyone wishing their boys a safe return. Only a fluffy blonde young woman Officer murmured softly, 'God bless them all.' They waited as if time itself had been suspended, gazing up at the sky in a trance-like quietness, until the last of the aircraft disappeared from view. There was a great sigh from the group as they turned away and dispersed. It was an experience that they never forgot.

The days that followed were filled with anxiety. Julia, Florence and Joan all knew that they could expect no news for some time – unless it was bad news. Doreen, seeing Julia watching wistfully when the mail was handed out, felt grateful that she had no-one close to worry about. Even though the news was good, with the men securing the coast and then pushing further into France, it was obvious that they were too busy to write letters. It would be a weary wait.

But soon they had something else to worry about. Hitler launched his pilotless planes – the V1 and then the more deadly V2 rockets, which the British christened 'doodlebugs'. They came unheralded, making no noise until they were near, then the engines cut out and they hit the ground with a 'crump'. They appeared to be indiscriminate as to targets, so it was impossible to find any means to counteract them.

One day in August, Julia was asked to go down to the Command Post with a telegram for the Duty Officer. She liked Captain Symons and was glad to take the news that he was now the father of a son. Pleased with her errand and the bright, peaceful day, her ears caught the first menacing drone of a V2. It came into sight, fiery tail blazing, and she dived into the Command Post, just as the engine cut out. It was down almost immediately and the first shuddering impact was lost in the terrific explosion which deafened them and which went on and on. The noise continued to reverberate for what seemed a long time and was followed by smaller explosions.

The Captain, who had gone out as soon as the first explosion happened, looked in and said, 'Number one gun's caught it. Get the First Aid and CO – and phone the hospital.'

But the girl at the switchboard had jumped to her feet and run for the door.

'Come back!' shouted the Officer.

'No. You come on!' she shouted, and disappeared.

He hesitated for a minute, but Julia had taken the girl's place.

'You go. I'll get the Emergency Services.'

At the door, he looked back, but Julia was already talking. Well aware of what he must find, he went reluctantly. The telegram remained in Julia's pocket.

The girl who had deserted her post, Ada Mitchell, had gone straight to a scene of carnage, where the eight men of the gun team had been doing maintenance, surrounded by high explosive shells. They were all dead, bits of their bodies scattered among the pieces of metal. She had taken one look and had run to the next gun pit where she got to work on the living, stripping shirts for bandages. She was applying a tourniquet to the stump of a man's leg when help began to arrive. She continued working with the medical orderlies until ambulances and doctors came. Afterwards, shivering and crying, she had been taken into sickbay and sedated.

Julia was still at the phones when the Colonel arrived. He came into the Command Post with the CO. They both looked grave but the Colonel thanked her for taking over and the CO promised to send her a replacement, so that she could have some food and rest. By then, she had remembered the telegram and she asked the CO whether he would be kind enough to see that Captain Symons got it. The CO glanced at it and said to the Colonel, 'Well, this should help him.'

Julia asked, 'Is he hurt, sir?'

'No. Just shocked at the loss of all the men.'

And that was how she heard of the tragedy that had befallen the whole camp.

* * * * *

159

Leave was arranged for as many people as possible. Some of the huts had been damaged and the girls had to double up, carrying their bedding to other huts and sleeping on the floor. Julia and Doreen opted to sleep in the Command Post which was less crowded. The camp would not be fully operational again until another thirteen men had been drafted in. The casualties had been eight men killed and five injured. One of the injured died soon afterwards. In a self-contained unit, everybody knew everybody else and the feeling of loss was palpable. It was, perhaps, for this reason, as well as the fact that the heavy guns were no answer to the rockets, that the girls found themselves posted to Brighton until it was decided what was to be done with them. By this time, Julia, Joan and Florence all knew that their menfolk had survived the first battles of the invasion of France and were alive and well at the time of writing.

Despite some delays, there was no doubt that the boys were getting there. Dusty Miller wrote to Florence,

'For me the worst part was going through the Falais Gap and seeing all the dead horses. The Jerries killed them when they couldn't feed them any more. Poor brutes, what did they know of war? Still I suppose it's a good sign if they are that short of food.

Have you had news of your father? I'm always hoping I might meet him. It sounds unlikely, but yesterday one of our men ran into his brother – neither of them knew the other was anywhere near – so you never know.'

Florence had had several letters from her father. He was always optimistic and full of gratitude to God for being allowed to serve with men for whom he had the greatest regard.

'Even the worst of them never lets the others down. I've seen them go into mine fields to rescue a man who has been wounded – even if they think nothing of pinching each other's cigarettes, or going out to 'win' a chicken (though there aren't many of those about now). At the same time they will give all their sweet rations to the children. We British are a soft lot, really. I wonder if the Jerries would do it for ours, but perhaps some of them would. They were always good family men, before this dictator hypnotised them.'

Just like Dad, Florence thought. He would always see the best in everyone.

She had become accustomed to the idea that he was safe and thought nothing of it when the Junior Commander sent for her one day in September.

'Sit down, Private Young,' she said gravely. 'I'm sorry to say I've got some bad news for you.'

'My father?'

'He has been killed – my dear, I'm so sorry.'

'Oh, no, not Dad!' Florence groaned, and then, 'How did it happen? Do you know?'

'They were taking a village and there were still a few Germans trying to defend it. He got shot by a sniper. He died instantly.'

'That's a comfort.' She tried a fleeting smile, then burst into tears.

They brought her tea and left her alone for a while. When an Officer returned, she had arranged compassionate leave and made out a pass and rail warrant so that Florence could go to her grandparents.

She loved them both, but she knew that their own grief would be no comfort to her. She thought that if there was only somewhere else – someone else … But there was nowhere and no-one.

During that miserable leave she found her uncle, with his practical ways, was a surprising help to her.

'Your father wrote to me – in case this should happen. He was concerned that you shouldn't make your home here and be a housekeeper to the old people. What did you think of doing?'

'Staying on in the ATS.'

'Mm. I wonder if they'll keep the girls on after the war. A lot of men will be looking for jobs. You should get some training. Something you can use in civvy street if you have to. What about shorthand and typing? Look, you don't need to make your mind up now. You'll probably marry. Whatever happens, I'm going to get Mum and Dad a housekeeper. I know a young war widow who hasn't got a home now. I'll keep in touch and let you know if she takes it.'

So Florence sought an early interview with the Junior Commander to discuss a career for herself.

'If possible, I want to stay in the ATS. And I'd like to get away from here now. All my friends are treating me so gently, I could scream.'

The Officer smiled. 'I can imagine. Would you like to go to OCTU?'

'I don't think so. Being an Officer wouldn't be my style – and I doubt if I'd make the grade.'

'Well, I'll see you in a day or two when I've had a chance to get your test papers and see where you did well.'

When Florence was summoned again, it was Captain Hewson who saw her. She was one of the most popular Officers because she was so easy to talk to.

'We have discussed your problem, Private Young, and we all think you should get some useful training – something that will stand you in good stead both in the ATS and in civvy street. You did well in the road tests. How would you like to be a driver?'

'I'd love to be able to drive, but I think I'd be too nervous. Do you think there will be jobs for women drivers after the war?'

'I think it's a skill that may be desirable for a lot of work. As for being nervous, confidence comes when you've been properly trained and know you can do the job well. You've had nothing to stretch you so far. The ATS owes you training for something.' She glanced at the doubtful figure before her. 'It will be good for your soul,' she said with a smile.

The few words, though lightly spoken, had an echo of her father to Florence. She said immediately,

'Yes, I'll take it, Ma'am, and thank you.'

She was posted to Chester for training and fell in love with the quaint, old-fashioned part of the town, with the Tudor buildings and the shops on overhead balconies, even while she cursed the steep hills where the Instructors yelled '*Stop*' without warning.

Florence was trained to drive utility vans (Tillies), ambulances and staff cars. The engines were all supposed to be governed at twenty-five miles an hour, but the instructors, frustrated by crawling around, removed the governors and encouraged the girls to go faster. They were even more frustrated by Florence, who was only happy when she was driving slowly. She got used to finishing her turn with a sigh of relief from her instructor and a comment to the next trainee to 'take over from Young and let's get a move on'. She thought they would be bound to fail her and wondered what else she could do. Was there anything, or was she just stupid?

Then, quite suddenly, and for no apparent reason, everything clicked into place and she was driving confidently. For the first time in her life, she felt a glow of pride. She had achieved something on her own.

The course also taught her First Aid and map reading. She was brilliant at the latter and the other trainees liked to have her as their navigator.

Flushed with success, she waited eagerly for news of her

posting. It was to an Officer's training camp at Oswestry. She would be attached to the RA, like Doreen and Julia.

'Cor, Flo, you'll be driving Officers in Staff cars. Won't you be toffee-nosed!'

'Where are you going, Elsie?'

'Abroad, I hope, as soon as I can. I'm driving ambulances.'

Florence loved driving the staff cars and welcomed the opportunity to see new places. She found most of the Officers pleasant but remote. They were on their way to inspect camps or to high level meetings in London or Cambridge, engrossed in their own affairs. As soon as she reported back to base there would be another assignment waiting. It was good to be busy and feel useful.

She had to be completely self-sufficient. Very few of the Officers thought of her needs once they got involved in their own affairs. She got used to taking her bedding, picking up rations where she could and sitting in the car for hours at a time.

There were interminable waits at meetings which might end in the next few minutes or after midnight. The worst of the Officers would be sure to come, bawling, 'Driver, driver, where are you?' if she had got out to stretch her legs or made a dash for the nearest toilet. She got used to reminding them gently that she had certain needs herself.

She serviced the cars before each day ended and was happy when she was actually driving. Every day was an adventure. She never knew where she would be sleeping that night. If it was a camp, she was reasonably sure of a bed. In London, it was usually the Union Jack in Waterloo. In both places she would find contemporaries.

But she had not reckoned with the loneliness. There were days on end when she spoke to no-one from morning to night. Her passenger might be at a meeting all day, but she would not be free unless he had told her that she could go and get a meal, which would be a nice change from eating sandwiches in the car. Sometimes the Officer would say, 'You can lose yourself for a couple of hours' or 'You needn't come back till four – we should be finished by then.'

The more considerate ones would make sure she got a break and let her know their movements. It was one of these who came to her outside an Oxford College where there was a meeting with a lot of Top Brass.

'Private Young, I'm very sorry, but you'll have to sleep in the chapel. Everywhere else is choc-a bloc.'

So Florence dragged her bedding into the huge, cold, cheerless place. It was gloomy and faintly sinister. She thought, 'It only needs an air raid.' She lay restless and depressed. It was weeks since she had seen any of her friends. She was due to go on leave soon and there was nowhere to go – nowhere she wanted to go. She considered staying at the Union Jack, but London in wartime ... Everything seemed miserable.

Gradually, the light of a full moon filtered through the end windows of the chapel, casting the muted colours of the stained glass on to the floor. Florence sat up. Soon moonlight was flooding everywhere. The windows glowed, light shone on the gilt of the lectern below the altar and illuminated the granite carvings. It was impossible to be downcast with this glory around her.

She went and stood before the altar. Her faith had always been part of her – less because of her Christian upbringing than because of the example of her father, a simple, wise man. She thought of him now and how he had gone gaily into danger, only rejoicing that he could help so many men at a difficult time for them. Service – it was the only life worth living. It brought its own rewards of satisfaction in a way that nothing else could.

Florence resolved then that it would be her life, too – in the Forces, if possible. If not, there would be other opportunities. At the same moment, she knew that she was completely self-reliant. Friendships she would always treasure, but she did not need other people to help her. In that moment of insight she thought, 'Every human spirit is uniquely alone in the deepest sense – except for God – and that should be enough.'

Brighton was something else. They were billeted in beautiful bungalows on the seafront towards Rottingdean. There were rumours that one of these belonged to Elsie and Doris Waters, the much-loved comediennes Gert and Daisy, whose programmes were often used by the Ministry of Food to give housewives hints on using their rations to the best advantage.

'Good-oh. It'll be a pleasure to keep this clean,' said Doreen, glancing round their immaculate bedroom, 'and two bathrooms, and buckets of hot water.'

Brighton boasted several good restaurants with seemingly no shortage of food. The Dome put on concerts with first-class orchestras and there were plenty of picture palaces. And there was the Canadian Legion.

It was Julia who found out about this. She was returning to Brighton from leave and the train was crowded, but she found a compartment with one empty seat. The other occupants were all Canadian soldiers.

They started talking at once, then one of the boys offered her a bar of chocolate. She accepted it gratefully and put it in her bag.

'You can tell it's rationed here. At home, the girls would have broken it up and shared it right away,' one of them remarked. Julia flushed.

'Oh, it's not for me. I shall give it to our neighbour's little girl. She's only seven and she doesn't see much in the way of sweets.'

The effect was instantaneous. Chocolates came at her from all directions. When she protested, they said, 'It's nothing. We can get all we want at the Canadian Legion.'

They told her that she and her mates would be allowed in there and could get a good meal for next to nothing. When she told the others, Doreen said, 'Trust you. I bet you flirted with them.'

'I did not. I don't even remember what any of them looked like.'

Two weeks later, when they decided to try the Canadian Legion, they found it as the soldiers had said. They were served with a very good meal for one and sixpence each.

'I feel horribly conspicuous. We're the only girls,' whispered Doreen. They were being ogled by every man in the room.

'It'll be wolf whistles next. We'll finish this and go ... Oh, look out, one of them's coming over. '

The man who was approaching them looked very amused. 'How did the kiddie like the chocolate,' he asked.

'Oh,' gasped Julia, 'oh, I'm sorry. I didn't recognise you.'

'We're an ordinary lot. Come over and talk to the others.'

That was the first of several pleasant evenings. The girls found these boys charming and generous – always pressing on them things they had not seen for years and some which were completely new, such as the bouillon cubes which made delicious bowls of soup.

'What's your husband doing?' Julia was asked on that first night.

'Over there – in the thick of it. He's on mobile guns.' She looked suddenly older. Letters were few and far between.

'It'll be over soon now. They're only waiting for us.' And that was the only indication they had that these Canadians might suddenly disappear.

Julia and Doreen had both elected to learn shorthand while they were being held at Brighton, but long before they were proficient the postings came through. They were both going to the Pay Corps at Preston.

Once again, they said goodbye to friends who had been with them on the gunsite.

'It's the worst thing,' Doreen complained, 'you get to know people really well and then you never see them again. I've almost forgotten what Audrey and Mary look like. I wonder if we'll ever meet again.'

'What about our shy little violet, Flo? I bet she's a different person – pity she's moved from Preston. Still, we might meet Phyllis. I wonder if the ATS has changed her.'

'Not her. That sort don't change, you'll see.'

They went on leave before going to Preston. Julia planned to spend some of her time with Reg's parents, hoping they might have more recent news of him, though she doubted it.

Doreen, walking through the door of her home, was surprised to find George, the fireman, with his feet under the table and looking very much at home.

'Been keeping an eye on your mum and dad,' he told her.

'Do they need keeping an eye on?' she asked, tauntingly.

'Well, you never know. These old houses are pretty tough, but a lot of them have been weakened by the bombing – doesn't do any harm to be careful. Besides,' he admitted with a grin, 'your mum makes a good cup of tea.'

'Don't take any notice of him, he's been very good to us. He's always looking in and bringing us things.'

He's got a nerve, Doreen thought, as it became obvious that George had been intent on finding out exactly when she was coming home. Still, you had to admire his initiative and, of course, it was flattering. She went out with him once to the Stage Door in Piccadilly at her suggestion, which was a big mistake. He was conspicuous, both as a civilian and as an Englishman among all the Yanks. She apologised and let him take her to the pictures twice to make it up to him.

* * * * *

There was a surprise for Florence in the post. One letter was from Dusty, but the other was in a civilian envelope and she did not recognise the writing. She opened it first.

'Dear Miss Young,

Our son has told us of your sad loss and that you do not have a home of your own. I expect you have many relations who would be glad to see you, but we would be very pleased if you would come to us for your next long leave, and bring a friend if she is on leave at the same time.

We understand that Reggie was very friendly with your father, and for his sake as well as your own, we would like to make you welcome.

There is so little we have been able to do for our brave boys and girls, and we were considered too near to Coventry to take evacuees, so we try to open our home to people on leave whose own homes have been damaged.

I do hope you will give us the pleasure of seeing you.

Yours sincerely, Jennifer Miller.'

Florence felt stunned. She had been the recipient of hospitality from civilians before, but never on this scale. These people were offering her a week's holiday without ever having seen her. She read the letter through again. A very tactful letter, she realised. They were leaving her no room to suspect that she was being asked as

Dusty's girlfriend, but could she go, without giving that impression?

She would like to go, no question about that. The warmth of the letter, reaching out to her at a sad and lonely time, drew her to the writer immediately – and it would be nice to see where Dusty lived. She opened his letter .

He couldn't tell her much about where he was, but they were pushing on fast. It shouldn't be too long before the whole conflict was over. Then came the passage:

'I hope you will have heard from my people by now. They are intending to invite you to spend your leave with them. It was their idea as soon as I told them about Richard. They love having people. They had a woman and her two children for six months after they were bombed out. They look on it as their war work, so I hope you will feel able to go. I'd like to think you had met.'

Yes, there it was. He would like them to meet. Florence thought about it for a long time. Were they near enough to Glen Parva for her to see Joan? Suppose they didn't get on? Not a week, perhaps. She wrote:

'Dear Mrs. Miller,

Thank you for your very kind invitation. I am due for some leave shortly, but I think I should spend some of the time with my grandparents. Could I come to you for 3 or 4 days, perhaps? I have a friend at the Leicester barracks who I would like to see, so would you mind if I spent one day with her? I had a letter from Reg by the same post as yours, so he was safe and well then ...'

An immediate reply assured her that she would be welcome at any time and must feel free to go wherever she liked.

Dusty had said little about his people and the fact that he had preferred to spend part of his leave with her father made her a bit apprehensive. Well, nothing was unbearable if it was only for three days. She would go.

'Good morning. Delighted to see you.'

The tall, greying man stooped over Florence and took the hand she extended. 'My wife is in the car.'

He led her from the station platform through a short sandy path and out into a square lined with small shops. There was an ancient car opposite the greengrocers and beside it stood a tall, slim woman in a grey suit. Her rather sharp features were relieved by a generous mouth. She looked to be in her mid-fifties, but the scarf wound round her head barely concealed a mop of silver hair. She held out her hand and said, 'How nice. Now, can you eat cauliflower? He's got some fresh ones in' – with a nod towards the shop.

Florence laughed.

'Oh, Mrs. Miller, I'm in the ATS. We don't get a choice of what we eat. Yes, I love cauliflower, but please don't go to any trouble for me.'

'Call me Jenny, there's a good girl. I don't like being Mrs. Millered.'

The car, a Morris Minor, smelt of animals and antiseptic.

'Sorry about the smell. We have tried to smother it, but it's my runabout for work and I can't do much about it,' Dennis Miller explained.

'You work with animals?'

'Good heavens! Didn't Reg tell you I'm a vet?'

'No. At least, I don't think so.'

'Typical. He has no interest in it. More likely to open a garage when he comes home.'

This was at once better and worse than she had expected. They were welcoming and easy to talk to, but she was not their class. Florence supposed that her father could have been classed as a professional man but he had always been a poor country vicar. Nothing that she knew about Dusty had prepared her for this. Perhaps it explained why he had preferred her father's company.

The next day, Mr. Miller invited Florence to accompany him on his rounds. Out of politeness, she accepted. It was a time of unutterable boredom, consisting of long waits at farms or sitting in parlours while he attended to domestic animals. But even worse was the torment of being driven by a man who took the twisty roads at a rate of knots and jammed on the brakes sharply if anything impeded him. She longed to take the wheel out of his hands. No wonder Dusty didn't stay long at home if he was expected to do this. She decided that she would go to Leicester tomorrow

But when they got home, a white-faced Jenny was waiting for them at the door. Dusty was in a London hospital. Her husband telephoned and, after a lot of delay, was told that his son had shrapnel in his shoulder and arm. As far as they knew, it was not life-threatening, but they would know the extent of his injuries better very soon – and, yes, they could visit him.

Jenny turned to Florence. 'Will you come with us? I know he would love to see you.'.

Florence hesitated. How to ask if they would be driving up? She didn't think she could stand that.

'We'll pay your train fare, of course. I don't have the petrol to do journeys like that, I'm sorry to say.'

'I'd like to come – and thank you.'

Florence hung back as they entered the ward. She wanted Dusty to see his parents first. He was sitting up in bed, propped by pillows behind his left shoulder, which was heavily bandaged. The pain lines were etched on his white face and the smile did not reach his eyes. She had never seen him so vulnerable. Her heart went out to him and she suddenly knew that this was the man she wanted to love and cherish for the rest of her life.

Then he saw her and his eyes said everything.

'Flora. Oh, my darling.' He held out his right arm and she walked straight into his embrace.

'Well now,' Jenny said 'have we been entertaining our future daughter-in-law?'

'I hope so, Mum. Have they, Flora?'

'Yes.'

This is Now - 5

That was a good way to end,' I said, 'but you'll have to tell me what happened to the others. Can we have another session?'
Doreen heaved a great sigh.

'I don't know. It takes it out of me – re-living some of those days. And I only know what the others told me after the war. The reason I knew so much about Flo is that we were neighbours for a while in the 50s. We had lost touch and then met, of all places, in an ante-natal clinic.'

She laughed at the memory. As I saw the lines deepen round her eyes I realised that the young woman I had been picturing as Doreen was old and tired now.

'Well, thank you for all you've told me. I'll get Aunt Julia to fill in the gaps – but you never said much about your own romance.'

'Not much to tell. George made sure he was always there when I was on leave and I hadn't met anybody I liked better in the Forces. I'd had all the usual let-downs – fellows making dates and then not turning up, though, mind you, I've done a bit of that myself if something more appealing beckoned. Then there were the really handsome ones who thought they were God's gift to women. I told one of them that he bored me stiff all evening, just talking about himself. There were the downright liars and con-men, and, of course, the ones who couldn't keep their hands to themselves. Oh, the ATS completed my education all right. George seemed so safe after that lot and my parents thought he was great.'

It didn't sound like a wonderful romance, but she smiled at her memories and I left it at that.

Aunt Julia was delighted to give me the rest of the story and promised not to ramble.

'The Pay Corps was just office life,' she told me. 'We were working out payments for the men who had been invalided out and

171

gearing up for all the demob payments to come. I liked the work but neither of us liked being indoors all day, so we spent the weekends walking when it wasn't actually raining.

'We saw Phyllis and she hadn't changed much, but she seemed happier. She was a Corporal and was in charge of a group – not ours, thank goodness – and I think that suited her, She wasn't at all interested in what any of us had been doing, so we didn't bother with her,

'We were there when the war ended. The whole company were giving a concert the night before and the Colonel announced from the stage that tomorrow would be VE day – Victory in Europe, you know – and a holiday.'

'It must have been a great relief to you, with Uncle Reg still out there. So how did you celebrate?'

'We went to a thanksgiving service in the morning. It was a lovely day in early May, so we spent it wandering around the Ribble valley. It was so quiet and beautiful you could forget the war, but we didn't feel like celebrating – there'd been so many of our friends killed and injured, and there was still war in the Far East.

'But we did go and see *Arsenic and Old Lace* in the evening – Cary Grant, you know – and laughed all the way home. One of us would chant "I'm the son of a sea cook" and start us off again. Our landlady thought we were drunk when we first came in. '

'Did you find out what happened to all the others?'

'Oh, we had a marvellous reunion in London – in 1948, I think. Joan organised it. She did a great job in keeping tabs on us all wherever we moved. When you see London now you could never imagine what it was like. The worst of the rubble had been cleared by then, but there were gaps – sometimes huge ones – between the buildings, but the weirdest thing was to see weeds growing everywhere there was a space – mostly willow herb and London Pride. Noel Coward wrote a song about it, you know.'

She leaned back and started to sing, '*London Pride has been handed down to us, London Pride is a flower that's free* – oh, it's no good, my voice sounds just like my grandmother's used to.'

'But what happened to the other girls – Audrey and Mary?'

'Audrey had been working with Radar – not like the ordinary operators, though I believe she taught some of them – but on the technical side, much too complicated for us to understand. When the doodlebugs started, they knew as soon as the things were

172

launched and kept tracks on them. I understand that the other services were doing it as well. Anyway, it helped the RAF to shoot them down and sometimes to turn them round and send them back. She was very proud of her work on that. She lived in Cambridge after the war and she did some good research work, but we lost touch after a while.

'As for Mary – well, everybody knows about Bletchley Park now – you can even go and visit it and see what they did. She was there all the time and got official praise for her work, but she still had a surprise for us. She married one of our gallant Allies – a West Indian, no less. We kept in touch until she went out to Jamaica with him and even then we wrote every Christmas. I saw her twice when she was home on holiday. She died about five years ago.'

Aunt Julia sighed and then laughed.

'Well, we're all pretty ancient now, so we should expect it, I suppose. Norfolk may help, though – people around here often reach their hundred – they say it's selenium or something in the soil. That's if they haven't poisoned it all by now.'

I changed the subject hurriedly.

'Anything else? What about Florence and Joan?'

'Joan's an Army wife. I suppose they're retired now, but she's been all over the world with her husband. I bet she never expected that. Oh, I forgot – Ada, the girl who went over to the guns when they got hit, she got an MBE. That was a dreadful time. We knew all those boys so well.'

She closed her eyes and I asked quickly, 'When were you demobbed?'

'About July. I was one of the first because I was married. The idea was that we should make a home for our husbands to come back to – but, of course, there weren't any houses and I lived at home till Reg was demobbed in 1947. He was kept on in BAOR – The British Army of the Rhine – they were helping Holland and Germany and disposing of weapons.

'It was hellish being at home after the Forces. I'd been with so many good friends every day and it was hard to take up life without them. All the same, I wouldn't have missed it for anything.

'Apart from the comradeship, you felt you were doing something to help. A purpose to life and good company – no wonder we all think of that time as special.'

'Well, thanks, Aunt Julia. That just about wraps it up. Did Florence's Dusty recover fully?'

'Oh, Florence – I forgot. Her father was awarded the Military Cross. Apparently he was leading a party of stretcher bearers through heavy fire when he got hit. They didn't tell her that at the time, but the citation said that he showed the utmost bravery and calmness under fire. She had to go up to the Palace to get his medal and Dusty was recovered enough to go with her. She sent us the pictures.

'Dusty died about ten years ago, but he was healthy until the last few months. She's still alive and kicking and says she's had a good life. She's just been to Australia to see her daughter and grandchildren. Fancy, it took six weeks in the last war. Plenty of the girls served abroad, you know – in all three services.

Then Aunt Julia stood up and patted my arm briskly. 'Look, you've been taking notes all day. Give it a rest and help me with the dinner.'

Next morning at breakfast, Uncle Reg answered the phone, said 'Hang on' and turned to Julia.

'Simon is asking if Jerry can come and see me. He wants a reference for his gamekeepers' course.'

'Tell him to come about eleven then. He can have some coffee with us.' She turned to me. 'He likes my Nelson Squares. His mother's no cook – none of them are these days.'

'Oh, I remember them. Like bread pudding between pastry.'

'Jan, that's blasphemy! It's good fruit cake. You crumble it and soak the crumbs in milk, then put it in a pastry case and cover it with more pastry – only a thin layer, of course.'

'Sorry. I do remember it was gorgeous – Gran used to make it. Tell me about Jerry. I thought he was one of Simon's employees.'

'Oh no. He only helps out at weekends if they're busy. He's always known he wanted to be a gamekeeper. He's a very hard working, nice young lad – always doing something, and not always for money. You met his mother in the shop. His father's a farmer and he's been brought up to work.'

'And he doesn't want to take over the farm?'

Aunt Julia shook her head and looked concerned. 'There's no future for these small farms. They know they'll get taken over by bigger concerns. Even now Jerry's father is working with another farmer. They've just bought a new tractor between them – couldn't have done it on their own, Simon says.'

'It puzzles me how country people can want to breed birds for others to shoot.'

'Ask him when he comes. He'll tell you. Now I must go and do some baking.'

He was a tall young man of about sixteen, with dark hair and eyes, slim built but with well-muscled arms and broad shoulders. He was not at all like his Uncle Simon, except for his lopsided grin. He said very little but devoured three of the Nelson Squares – which were wonderful, but very filling – and two cups of coffee.

'Now, Jerry,' said Uncle Reg, 'what is it exactly that you need? Have you got some forms for me to sign?'

'No. I got a letter. Just a character reference. With your address and signed and your profession, it said.' Jerry flashed his crooked grin. 'Say I ent cruel to animals and hent bin in clink.' He spoke in a low drawl.

'All right. I'll go and think up something. I won't be long. You might as well take it back with you.'

Left alone with the boy, I said, 'Why do you want to be a gamekeeper?'

'I love birds. They're lovely when they're young, Miss. All fluffy, like baby chicks. And they all got their own ways …'

'But how can you bear to breed them for slaughter?'

He sat up at that and became animated. 'Oh no, Miss. You got it all wrong. If we didn't look after them, there wouldn't be any. They got enemies. A third of 'em get eaten, Mr. Wright say. Then plenty of 'em don't survive anyway. It's only our lot have a chance. It'd be a shame if they all disappeared – they're such lovely little birds.'

'But the shooting …' I protested.

'Well, the gentry, they like their sport and pay well for it – and that keep a lot of us in work and make sure the birds survive. And they're food – same as beef – for them as can afford it.'

And who are you, I thought guiltily, to criticise, when you've eaten them yourself? I seemed to be getting the worst of the argument and I was impressed by his enthusiasm. The country drawl had quickened and deepened as he tried to impress on me how much I had been in error.

I said, 'Well, thank you for telling me. I hope you do well.'

I got Simon's lopsided grin again and a 'Thank you, Miss. My

175

Uncle Simon, he say "she's a looker, she is" and he worn't wrong.'

I had accepted many compliments gracefully, but this one threw me. I felt the blood rush to my face. Uncle Reg came in, right on cue. I had never been so pleased to see him.

'Will this do?' He handed the boy a letter. Jerry read it through and I had the satisfaction of seeing him blush in his turn.

'It's brill. You don't think it's OTT, do you?'

So this country boy still managed to know all the up-to-date jargon. Reg smiled and shook his head.

'It's no more than you deserve.'

Jerry got to his feet. 'Thanks a lot – and for the Squares – they were brill.' He turned to me. 'Goodbye, Miss.'

The smile he gave was decidedly mischievous. The devil – he had meant to make me blush, and would probably tell Uncle Simon that he had done so.

July was going out in a blaze of heat and the night was sticky and humid. I had fallen into a restless sleep and was roused from it with the sensation of hands on my breasts and all my desires very much awake.

I slipped into a cotton dress, just in case Uncle Reg should see me, and let myself out of the back door and into the blessedly cool summerhouse. The moonlight was strong enough for me to see well and I thought I might be able to do some writing. Nothing relevant to my novel would come, and I knew that I must start scribbling the first thing I thought of, to get my brain moving. I wrote,

'Simon is available and near. This is his only attraction. He is a wimp who lives in the past, despises modern life and has chosen to opt out. Life with him would be boring, boring, boring. And anyway, he doesn't know I exist.'

Then I threw the pen down and burst into tears.

By the end of September I was walking well enough to go up to London. My tenant, Myrtle, had written to ask if I was prepared to renew her lease. I was torn between the need to move from Aunt Julia's cossetting atmosphere and a reluctance to return to London while I was still devoting so much time to my novel.

'I understand you're doing freelance work, so do you need to come back here just now?' Myrtle asked.

'I don't have to, but I can't live with my aunt forever. It's six months now.'

I looked around the living-room and it seemed unfamiliar. Of course, Myrtle had left her own mark on it – that was to be expected – but it didn't feel like mine any more.

'How long do you want? Have you been looking for somewhere else?'

'Yes, Jan. But I've faced the fact that I'll never find anything as perfect as this for me. I'll be honest with you. I'd buy it like a shot if you would sell it.'

I left her with nothing settled. She had another month and I would let her know my decision before that. Then I went on my other errand.

Helen had asked me if I would try to find out what had happened to Jean. I had the details of her last posting and her home address. Telephone calls to the Imperial War Museum and the National Maritime Museum confirmed, as I had expected, that queries by post could not be answered for ages.

Before I went to the museums, I visited the site of Jean's former home. I was prepared for what I found – a side street of modern houses with a combined paper and grocery shop, bearing an Indian name, and a large garage on the corner. I knew this part of London had taken a pasting during the war. Unlikely that there was anyone left who knew of Jean's family, but I could ask.

'No,' replied the young man at the garage, 'we've only been here about ten years. Don't think any of my customers were here during the war. I heard all the houses were so damaged they moved everybody out – land mine, I think.'

He scratched his head, thoughtfully. I was about to thank him and leave when I saw that he had an idea.

'I just thought – that Paki in the shop – he only bought it about a year ago, from an old man. He'd been here as long as anyone could remember. They had a send-off for him. If the Paki has got his address ...'

And it was as easy as that. I didn't have to go near the museums except for checking dates later on. From the grocer I got David

Jones's address and found a sprightly, spare man of about seventy tending his garden in Wimbledon. When I told him my errand he smiled and said, 'Yes, I can help you. My sister served with Jean in the Wrens. Come and have some tea.'

I heaved a great sigh of relief. It was hot and I seemed to have been walking pavements all day. London had temporarily lost its charm. Getting soft, I told myself, been pampered too long. It was surprising, I realised, that in spite of so much transport most people who worked in the City still did a lot of walking. So often it was the quickest option.

Mrs. Jones, a slim blonde-going-grey, set tea and some homemade cake in front of me, while her husband went to the telephone.

And that was how I met Pamela Humphrey, who was Pam Jones when she and Jean joined the Wrens together.

That Was Then - Pamela's Story

There were many reasons why girls rushed to join the Women's Services soon after the war started. Pamela's was one of the commonest. She was twenty-three years old and she wanted to get away from home.

In many ways, women who lived with their parents were subject to the same sort of restrictions as girls of the Victorian age. They might go out to work but at home they were still the daughters of the house and expected to conform to their parents' way of life. Pamela's father was even reluctant to let her go dancing at the Hammersmith Palais once a week.

'Don't know who you might meet at them places,' he complained.

'Oh, Dad, you know I always go with the girls and we share a taxi home.'

But he made a similar complaint every week, so she gritted her teeth and tried to ignore it.

She had won a scholarship to a very good girls' school and left with a Matriculation Certificate which, she knew, would be no good to her at all. University was out of the question. The paper shop which provided them with a home and an income did not generate enough profit to put her brother, Jack, through his apprenticeship as an electrical engineer without her contribution.

Reluctantly, Pamela had gone into the Civil Service with the intention of writing in her spare time. Her English teacher, who thought highly of her talent, had said, 'You can only write with authority about what you know, so take every opportunity to get new experiences.'

The remembered words increased her frustration. Fat chance she had of getting experiences.

For people like Pamela, the recruitment posters for the Services glowed like a beacon in the darkness. This was a way of escape.

One foggy November night, she walked home from the station, using her torch judiciously, and let herself into the house. She passed through the shop into the back sitting room where her parents sat over the tea table.

'Ah, there you are. The kettle's on.'

Her mother jumped up and kissed her. Her father looked up from his paper to receive her greeting. The family was in the habit of kissing whenever they met or parted. It made what she had to do more difficult. She took a deep breath and said, 'We were talking about the recruitment posters in the office today and I'm thinking of joining up.'

Her father put his paper down, pushed his glasses up into his hair and stared as if he had never seen her before. The blood rose in his face.

'Good God, girl! Are you mad? Throw up a good job with a pension to go in with a rackety lot? Mixing with all sorts – and most of them no better than they should be. No, by God, I won't let you.'

'I'm sorry, Dad, but I'm twenty-three. You can't stop me.' Her voice was shaking. This was so exactly the scene she had anticipated.

'P'raps I can't, but I should think you'd have more thought for your mother. How do you think she'll feel – and with Jack sure to be called up soon. This'll be the break-up of the family.'

'Oh, Dad, of course it's not a break-up. I'll come home on leave. Where else would I go? And Jack will go into REME and finish his apprenticeship there. He'll come out with a good trade – and you'll still have David at home.'

Her mother said, 'But why? until you have to.' And there was no answer to that which would not hurt them, so she put off taking action from week to week.

It was Jean Dixon who broke the deadlock. The two families had known each other since the children were small. Both the men were passionate bowls players and the girls had become closer since they started travelling to London together. Before that, the five-year gap in their ages had stopped them from becoming intimate, but now Jean seemed like an older sister, a little staid perhaps, but sympathetic to Pamela's situation.

It was on returning from one of the bowls evenings that Dennis Jones dropped the bombshell. 'What d'you think Dixon told me? Cock-a-hoop he was. Jean's engaged to a Naval Captain.'

'Jean? Jean's engaged? But when?'

'All very quick, so he said. Don't suppose it'll last – one of these wartime affairs. And who's to say he'll survive – bit dicey if you ask me.'

Her mother said, 'Fancy. She's usually such a steady girl. I never thought she'd marry.'

Pamela couldn't wait to hear the story from Jean herself. The outbreak of the war had meant earlier hours and overtime for her, so they hadn't seen each other for some time. She set out to the Dixons' house early on Sunday morning and met Jean coming to tell her the news.

'I didn't want you to hear it from anyone else, but Dad's so delighted because Douglas is the son of an old friend. He keeps telling everybody.'

'How did it happen?'

'Love at first sight! I know it sounds corny, but that's what it was,' Jean said, glowing.

'What does he look like?'

'That's corny, too – tall, dark and handsome. He's three years older than me and thought he'd never marry – married to the sea, he says – so we're both a bit staggered. Oh, and I've got another surprise for you. I'm going to join the Wrens.'

Pam caught her breath and grabbed her friend's arm.

'Jean – have you signed up yet?'

'No. I thought I'd go on Saturday.'

'I'll come with you.'

Even Pamela's father was mollified that she was going with Jean and she forbore to tell him that they might not be together for more than the initial training period. There was no guarantee that they would have to report at the same time and place. But it turned out as they had hoped. Both were accepted and waited impatiently for their call-up papers.

They almost ran towards each other as they met one morning in February.

'I've got to report to Campden Hill on Monday week,' Jean said.

'Thank God! So have I.'

Pam heaved a great sigh of relief. Freedom. Experiences. She was on her way.

Mrs. Margaret Lawson had joined the Wrens in a mood of frustration and self-disgust. Her marriage had ended after barely eighteen months and, although the ostensible reason was Brian's infidelity, she knew that there was some justification in his contention that she had contributed to the breakdown.

'Of course, you must come and live here. There's plenty of room,' her mother had said. It was just before the Munich crisis of 1938 and her father's opinion was that war was imminent. Brian was in the Royal Naval Reserve and would certainly be called up immediately, so Margaret might as well stay at home.

It had seemed good sense at the time, but the outbreak of war was delayed by a year and inevitable conflicts had occurred. Even if Mrs. Mann had not been the strong-minded woman she was, the fact that it was her house left the young couple with no status in it. Margaret was still treated as the daughter of the house and, as she was coming to realise, had meekly accepted the situation.

Brian was as self-willed as his mother-in-law. It was one of his traits that had attracted Margaret. She liked to have a quiet life and, if that meant accepting what other people wanted, it was a price she was prepared to pay. Inevitably, the 'other people' were always strong-willed.

'Why don't you tell her what we want?' he said frequently. 'You're a married woman. She can't boss you around all your life.'

'But, darling, it's her house. If she can't sleep till we come in then we can't stay out late.'

'She'll have to get over it,' Brian replied, setting his lips mutinously.

It was the beginning of many arguments between them, and Brian had gradually taken to staying out after Margaret had gone home, going back to a friend's house to sleep, or going to his parents for the weekend if his wife could not accompany him. She was fond of Mrs. Lawson and was always glad to visit her, but too often her own mother would complain that she liked to have her daughter at home for weekends, since she was at work all week.

'Brian leaves you alone too much,' Mrs. Mann complained one night as they prepared for bed at 10 o'clock. '

'He can't sleep if he goes to bed this early and it only disturbs you if we come in late, so he goes back to Ben's. We don't like it, but it keeps the peace.'

Her mother chose to ignore the implication. She pursed her lips.

'It's not natural in a young married man. He should be with you. You don't know what he gets up to.'

'Mother!' Margaret was suddenly angry. 'Now you listen to me. I left Brian at the pub tonight, finishing a game of darts. I came away at nine, simply to please you. If you weren't so hide-bound about bedtime ...'

'Don't you dare to speak to me like that, girl! I do as I please in my own house.'

'Then I wish we had never agreed to live here!' Margaret burst into tears and rushed up the stairs. It was beginning to dawn on her that pleasing other people did not always make for a quiet life.

'She's quite right. It never works,' her father said sadly. 'All the same, there'll be a war before long and she'll be glad to be here then.'

But by the time the war broke out Margaret's world had been knocked sideways. Brian had come to her asking for forgiveness. He had been unfaithful to her and was full of remorse.

'It's you I love and always will. If I'd been able to come home more often, it would never have happened. Say you forgive me.'

But Margaret was too shaken to think straight.

'I don't know. Give me time. You'll be going into the Navy – will I ever be able to trust you again?'

Even then, all might have been well. She loved him and would have liked to save their marriage, but once her parents knew, the end seemed inevitable. Her father was shocked. Her mother was triumphant.

'I told you how it would be. I never liked him. He's far too domineering – always telling you what to do. Get a divorce. An attractive girl like you will find someone better.'

It crossed the girl's mind that she had been told what to do all her life and she had never fallen out with anyone – until now. Perhaps her mother was right and Brian was too forceful for her. When she told him that she would apply for divorce, he said bitterly, 'I thought you loved me. Was this your idea, or your mother's? The old bitch – she's always wanted to keep her little girl to herself. No-one will be good enough for you. We might have had a chance by ourselves. Now she'll be happy.'

Margaret said, 'I'm sorry, Brian. I'd have liked to try again.'

'Then why don't you?' he pleaded, but when she shook her head, he said, 'You know the best thing you could do? Get away from her. Stand on your own two feet. Find out what you want from life. Join one of the Women's Services and learn about the real world. You might make some man a good partner some day – but not if you stay here, relying on other people to tell you what to do.'

She thought a lot about what he had said and admitted the truth of it. The day after she heard from his mother that Brian was in the Navy, she went into a recruitment office and volunteered for the Wrens. She told no-one until her call-up papers came through; by then it was too late for them to stop her, whatever her mother might say.

But Mrs. Mann said very little and maintained a hurt silence on the subject, even when Margaret kissed her goodbye.

* * * * *

Violet Allen and Josephine Colman both came from families where daughters were not expected to work. They stayed at home until they married or drifted into the life of spinster aunts. They were of the class which gave rise to the idea that the WRNS was exclusive, only accepting the 'best' girls and, for their part, it would not have occurred to them to volunteer for either of the other Women's Services. There may have been some truth in the supposition that all the Wrens were of a 'better class' at the beginning of the war, but recruitment rapidly became more widespread as women were needed for many categories of work which had been done by men.

Neither Violet or Jo (only her mother called her Josephine) was unduly conscious of class and they went into the Wrens with no qualms about mixing with other women. There the resemblance between them ended.

Violet had creamy skin, dark, shining chestnut hair and blue eyes. She walked with a fluid grace and radiated a confidence which was inbred. She had been brought up to believe that it was her duty to cherish her looks and her make-up was always immaculate. It was typical of her that, on the outbreak of war, she had stocked up on her favourite powder, lipstick and cream in case there should be a shortage.

Her father was the chief partner in a firm of City accountants and the family lived in a large house in Richmond, Surrey. Here Violet led the life of a debutante, 'doing the season' with her friends and driving everywhere in her nippy little sports car – the pride of her life.

The outbreak of war affected her only gradually as friends joined the Wrens or became busy with voluntary services. Many of her men friends were called up and her brother Robert, who was a regular Naval Officer was immediately in the thick of it.

Her mother, Marion, who was a Town Councillor, enlisted Violet's help to deal with the requisition of properties, but she soon found the work tedious and wondered if she should join the Wrens. Marion asked, 'But what have you got to offer them?' when Violet raised the question, and for the first time in her life she felt inadequate. She was catapulted into action in early 1940 by two unrelated events.

Taking a telephone call in his study, her father came to tell them that Robert was home and had shore leave.

'He'll be here at the weekend and wants to bring a friend – a Naval Officer called Geoffrey Bartlett. Is that all right, my dear?'

'Of course. Good job we've got plenty of room at the moment. I expect we'll get some people billeted on us later.'

Geoffrey was a dark-haired young man with a rather solemn expression, but his brilliant smile lit up his face and gave it a fleeting charm. Violet warmed to him when she found that he was a good tennis player and she enjoyed his time with them.

Less than two weeks later, she was first shocked and then furious to hear that his destroyer had been blown up by a mine off the coast of Harwich. He was one of the thirty casualties.

Raging against Hitler and all his works, she learned that the WRNS were desperate for drivers. This was something she knew she could do well. She volunteered within the week.

Jo's family had a large farm in Devon where they bred Jersey cows. It was a busy life, but there were plenty of farm workers and the three children were not expected to get involved. Jo, however, enjoyed the life and spent much of her time looking after the horses. That was when she was not crewing for her Uncle Mike, who had a six-berth yacht, the Girl Susan, in his boathouse at Plymouth.

She was boyish looking, deeply tanned, with very short black hair and black eyes. Her face was round and usually placid, but she had a surprisingly obstinate chin. Just now, her mouth was set firmly as she listened to her father's plans.

'We'll have to turn more of the land over to crops. If I don't do it the Government will soon make us. We've got to feed ourselves in wartime – can't rely on getting much from overseas. I'll get rid of some of the horses and get a tractor – plough up the five acre to start with.'

'You won't sell my pretty Jerseys?' asked his wife.

'Not all of them, but they're a luxury item – some will have to go.'

Jo was tight-lipped as she drove down to Plymouth for the weekend. Michael Bales took one look at her face and asked, 'What's up, Jo?'

'Dad's going to change everything. It won't be like home any more.'

Gradually, he got the whole story from her. His suggestion was completely unexpected.

'You're a girl who'll never be happy unless you're doing something – preferably in the open air. Is that right?'

'I suppose so. I hadn't thought about it.'

'Well, why don't you join the Wrens? Only don't let them put you into an office. There are bound to be jobs around the boats.'

She was immediately enthusiastic.

'That's great. I'd like that more than anything.'

Five different girls with five different reasons joined the WRNS in early 1940 and began the adventure of their lives.

Much later, Pamela was to laugh at the idea of freedom.

'Bossed around from morning till night,' she told her younger brother David. 'If it's not PT or Medical Inspection it's tests to see what you're good at. I've told them I don't want clerical work – I can do that at home.'

He looked at her, wistfully.

'Do you think it'll last long enough for me to get in?'

'God, I hope not, boy. Mum's worried enough by Jack being in France. If the war ever starts over here, you'll need all your wits to look after her and Dad.'

David shrugged and turned away. It would not do to let him know how much she was enjoying it. For, of course, there was freedom of a sort. Freedom to be herself without the constraints imposed by her father's ideas of propriety, freedom to take complete responsibility for herself – and, later, the freedom of confidence, knowing that she had been well-trained for the work she was to do and was thoroughly capable of doing it.

Of course, the initial training meant a complete upheaval for them all. None of them had been used to a communal life, except Violet who had been at an exclusive boarding school, but they brought a spirit of goodwill and co-operation to everything, realising that their problems were common to all.

There was never a day that did not bring laughter as well as work. Medical inspections were embarrassing at first, but also the source of hilarious exchanges which led to a growing intimacy between them. Only Violet was completely unruffled. She had submitted to having her beautiful hair searched for lice and her body inspected in intimate detail without losing her poise for one moment. Pamela envied her that self-confidence. Sensing her admiration, Violet was drawn to her and came to respect the intellect of this working-class girl who had obviously been strictly brought up and whose manners were at least as good as her own. So when Pamela said, 'I envy you, being able to drive. I was once on a friend's motorbike and loved the feeling of freedom', Violet had no hesitation in replying, 'Come and stay when you get a long leave and I'll teach you.'

By the end of the second week, Pamela and Violet, along with Jo, were a recognisable trio.

Jo had been a surprise to them both. A well-to-do girl with no 'side', she got on with everyone and was helpful and pleasant. But with a one-track mind. She would be part of a boat's crew or nothing and she had already been warned that competition for that would be fierce.

'But, Jo, you can't just leave if you don't get it,' Pamela protested.

'Yes, I can. There are ways and means.'

Violet agreed. 'There's not much they can do if you won't stay – not at this stage, when we're all volunteers.'

'What would you do though?' Pamela asked.

'I dunno. Join the Land Army, perhaps. But it won't come to that. I'll get what I want.'

The end of the third week loomed and with it the postings that would decide their future employments. Pamela had a very satisfactory interview and was made aware that her Matriculation Certificate was being given its full value.

'You've got Maths and Physics, I see,' the Officer said. 'We would like you to train as a radio mechanic. It means some initial training at Battersea Polytechnic and then a further course, but eventually you'll be servicing radios on ships or aircraft.

'It's a vital job – communications are everything in this war – and we think you will do well. What do you say?'

Pamela said 'yes' emphatically. It would be totally different from Civil Service work and let her use the other subjects she had enjoyed at school. She went back, glowing, to report to the others.

There was no doubt about Violet's position. She had volunteered and been accepted as a driver. She now learnt that she would be based at the Admiralty in London. She had to find her own digs and then have them approved. That was easy. She had a barrister uncle with a house near the Middle Temple and her aunt was keen that she should stay with them whenever she was in town.

The two of them waited for the outcome of Jo's interview together.

'Do you really think she'll quit if she doesn't get what she wants?'

'No. Not now. She's as proud of being a Wren as we are.'

'Isn't it funny? There are plenty of us. We're not unique.'

'Robert – that's my brother, you know – regular Navy, he says it goes with the Service,' said Violet, 'Its reputation's so good and it attracts the right types. There's a lot of tradition to being the Senior Service – and we're part of it.'

When Jo came to them she looked quietly pleased. 'The bad

news is there's no training for Wrens on boats yet. The good news is I'll be based at Portsmouth and do visual signalling and morse. She said the Navy is accepting girls to do more men's jobs every day and she's sure the time will come when Wrens will be crewing boats and I could be one of the first. She'll give me a strong recommendation, anyway.'

Jean had been glad to see Pamela adapting so well to her new life. She had felt some responsibility when Mrs. Jones had whispered, 'You will look after her, won't you?'

But it was soon obvious that this was not necessary

It was at an impromptu concert at the end of the first week that Jean first really noticed Margaret. The chorus on stage consisted of anyone who wanted to sing and who knew the words. They led the audience in a medley of popular wartime songs.

I'll Be Seeing You In All The Old Familiar Places and similar songs were interspersed with the more rousing ones, such as *Wish Me Luck As You Wave Me Goodbye*.

At the end, one girl stepped forward. She had a rich contralto voice. All her songs were applauded rapturously. The audience repeatedly shouted 'Encore' and would not let her go. Then she announced, 'This is positively the last':

'*When day is done and shadows fall, I dream of you ...*'

The voice throbbed with emotion. There were one or two gulps and Jean, longing for Douglas, wiped away a tear. By the time the last line came – '*I miss you most of all when day is done*' – Margaret had tears streaming down her face and her shoulders were shaking.

Jean knew that Margaret was a married woman and assumed that her husband was in the Forces. Surely she had not had bad news? These were no ordinary tears. This sounded like mourning.

Margaret crept out and, after a moment's hesitation, Jean followed. The girl flung herself down on her bed in the deserted quarters and sobbed. Jean sat down beside her.

'Oh, what is it? Have you had bad news?'

She put her arm across the tense body. Margaret gave a great gulp and fought for control. Presently, she raised her head and said, 'No.'

Jean waited, then she said, 'I don't want to pry, but sometimes it helps to tell someone – especially if you're not likely to see them again.'

189

'It's just – I've made such a mess of my life. I thought I had a good marriage, but it's all gone wrong.'

Gradually, the whole story came out. Margaret blamed her husband and her mother but, most of all, she blamed herself.

'I've been so weak. I let everybody tell me what to do, just to keep the peace.'

Jean searched for the right words. 'As I see it, it's like us and Hitler. You learn the hard way that sometimes peace isn't worth keeping and you have to go to war. And – don't you see – that's what you've done. You're already stronger for being here and not at home. And you must learn to forgive yourself. We all make mistakes.'

She changed the subject, asking Margaret, 'What do you want to do in the Wrens?'

'I don't mind, as long as it really helps. I'd like something active, I think.'

'You may feel you never want to talk to me again after telling me so much but, if you like, I'll keep in touch with you, wherever we go.'

For the first time, Margaret smiled.

'You've done me good. I'd like that very much.'

* * * * *

Jean was offered the chance to stay on at Campden Hill where there was a course available on Wireless Telegraphy. She decided to take it and found it very much to her liking. After becoming a Wren W/T she was posted to Liverpool.

Margaret went to Portsmouth as a Maintenance Wren, for which she would receive training on the job. It was a bit too near to her home in Portslade, but her confidence was rising with every week that passed. She knew she could cope with her mother now.

Violet sank back into the armchair with a sigh of satisfaction. Her aunt, Ruby, looked up quickly.

'You sound exhausted. I hope they're not working you too hard?'

'Heavens, no. It's just nice to have a comfortable seat. I've driven miles today – which I love, as you know – but it was an awful old Ford V8 van. It rattled like mad and the seat was split.'

'I'm surprised you have to do that when you've got your licence.'

'It's not enough, Auntie. I'm responsible for whatever vehicle I'm driving. I'll be on my own when I'm qualified to drive for the Wrens. I have to learn to cope with three-ton lorries, ambulances – whatever, and I have to be able to service them. Can't rely on some nice man coming along to change a tyre!'

Charles Allen looked up at his niece, amused.

'I'd like to see you change a tyre on a three-tonner,' he said.

'Well, I have, and I've dismantled an engine and put it together again. We have to learn all about the lubrication system as well.'

'Better you than me.' He left the women to talk and retired to his study.

'Do you really like it, Violet?' Ruby asked.

'Love it. I always liked driving and I can see the point of learning how to look after the car. It's one of the things that women will have to do with so many men away .' She looked down at her hands, frowning, and continued, 'except for my poor hands. Cream doesn't seem to do them any good. But then, I don't suppose I'll be able to look after myself like I do once I'm on the job. I gather the MTs are busy all the time. I only hope I pass the written exam – just a week to go.'

She went up to her room and spent an hour studying her notes before preparing for bed. It had been a tough two weeks.

Violet's initial training had ensured that she got her hands dirty, but scrubbing and polishing had not had the effect on them that servicing vehicles was having. She creamed her skin all over before retiring, sighing over heels which had chafed in her new driving shoes, and thought that she ought to be toughening her hands instead of creaming them. What good were soft hands going to be in the job she had chosen?

Suddenly, a picture of two men playing tennis at home in their garden at Richmond was clear before her eyes. Her brother and his friend – all that life and vigour – gone for one of them in a matter of minutes. It was what had driven her into the Wrens. What did her looks matter in comparison?

A week later, Violet had a driving test on a lorry. This was a piece of cake. She sat down with less confidence to do the written test and it was a great relief when she learned that she was a Wren M/T and could wear the coveted blue badge.

* * * * *

191

By chance, Pamela and Jean were home on leave at the same time. Jean was now fully operational, but Pam was still getting training. The exams at the end of each stage were tough but she had found that her good brain and her schooling enabled her to cope while others were struggling. In fact, she spent some of her free time helping her friends with the various problems.

'Do you know where I'm going tomorrow, Jean?' Pam asked one day. 'Back to school. Yes, really. I'm going to see Miss Brown who taught me Maths and Miss Crawley – she gave me no end of encouragement with my Physics. I want to tell them what I'm doing and thank them.'

'What a lovely idea,' Jean said warmly. 'It's such a pity that so many teachers never know that we have cause to be thankful to them – sometimes for the rest of our lives.'

'And I must see my English mistress and tell her I haven't written anything yet, but I'm collecting experiences.' Pam laughed. 'I wonder just how many experiences we'll all have before this thing is over.'

Jean said, 'You really should find time to keep a record, you know. I expect she'll tell you the same.'

But she did not comment about experiences. She knew that Douglas was on the Atlantic run and, talking to sailors in Liverpool Docks, she was not left long in ignorance of what that meant. It was the toughest of voyages in sub-zero temperatures, where a slip could be fatal and exposure to the icy waters meant death in minutes.

Like millions of others, she prayed every night for the safety of her loved ones, but it was no good worrying. She returned to Liverpool, thankful that she had a job to keep her mind occupied and was doing something to help.

Pamela went to Warrington to complete all her training and it was there, a few weeks later, that she received two letters by the same mail. She had promised to keep in touch with both Jo and Violet and had been too busy and absorbed to write to either. Now she saw that Jo had written and that the second letter was from Jean.

She opened Jo's letter first.

'Dear Pam,

Well, you are a good one! Who was going to write regularly? Do you know you've owed me a letter since May? Never mind, I forgive you – on condition you answer this.

I am still enjoying myself here. There's always something going on and I've even had a chance to go on boats in my spare time. Last week there as a destroyer in, so I chatted up some of the men and got an invitation to go on board. That was an eye-opener, I can tell you.

I've been going out quite a bit with Margaret. Do you remember her? I always thought she was rather dull and miserable, but she's a different person here. She drives tractors and uses cranes in the shipyard, in between bouts of welding in the engineering shop and stripping paint. She's the only girl I know who looks good in dungarees. I do wish we could get our uniforms.

I don't suppose you saw anything of the evacuation of Dunkirk? We didn't either – too far along the coast, but I've heard a lot from the men who brought the soldiers back. It seems most of the ATS and nurses got away before the end. The men make light of what they did, going back time and again into the barrage of bombs to pick up the troops, but they all seem to be haunted by the ones they couldn't rescue. Churchill may call it a victory but they know better. All the same, it's made them all the more determined to crack Hitler. One of them said "We owe it to the ones we had to leave behind."

I'm buttering up one of the Officers to see if I can get more work on the boats. Sometimes I envy Margaret, but it will be more important to know signalling when I get a boat.

Write and let me know what you've been doing and when your leave is due – you never know, we might be able to meet.

Love from Jo.'

When Jo had heard of the call for the little boats to go to Dunkirk her first thought was for her Uncle Mike. She knew that the Girl Susan would be among that motley assortment of small craft and regretted bitterly that she was not free to join him.

On May 28th she made a telephone call to home. Her mother answered in a voice sharp with anxiety.

'Is there anything wrong, Josephine?'

'Not with me. Do you know if Uncle Mike has gone?'

'Yes. He left word with a neighbour to let us know and said he would ring as soon as he returned.'

It was hard for Jo to keep her mind on anything else in the days that followed. Miracles were being wrought by the 850 pleasure boats, yachts, fishing boats and other small craft which had put out for Dunkirk. They were to rescue 340, 000 British troops from those hellish beaches, but 100 planes were lost and 235 of that gallant flotilla were never to return.

On the first day of June, Jo rang home again. This time her father answered.

'All we know is that Mike got home safely yesterday, so tired that he could hardly stand. He told us he intended to get a few hours' sleep and then go out again. I told him he had done his part but he said he couldn't leave men in that inferno – he would never be able to live with himself if he did. He sent you his love.'

So she could only wait, as hundreds of women were doing. When the rescue attempt ended on June 4th there was no more word of Mike.

Sadly and wearily, Jo faced the fact that she would never see him again.

Jean's letter was brief and to the point.

'Douglas and I are going to get married on his next leave – should be in August. Everything seems so dangerous, especially at sea, we both feel we must grab what happiness we can. If you are still at Warrington, or anywhere within reach of London, I'd like you to come. Hope you can get leave at short notice.

I've had a bundle of parachute silk given to me – never ask from where – all I was told was 'it's surplus to requirements', so I am busy making a trousseau – something I never imagined doing in my wildest dreams!'

Pamela folded the letter, feeling vaguely depressed. Dreams are all we have now, she thought, and who could tell what fate held in store for Jean and her sailor? Yes, they were right to take what happiness they could.

She was still at Warrington when the telegram came. '*Wedding Saturday from home. Hope you can come.*'

Luckily, she was due a 48-hour pass. She could make it if the trains weren't too delayed.

As usual, the train was packed. Servicemen and women stood in the corridors or sat on kitbags. Pamela resigned herself to standing all the way to London and thanked heaven that she was not travelling with full kit. Normally, she would not have thought of going home for such a short time, but it would be worthwhile for Jean's wedding.

'Are you being posted?' she asked a WAAF, adding hurriedly, 'but perhaps I shouldn't ask.'

'Oh, no. It's all right – I think.' The girl, smart in what was obviously a new uniform, turned an excited little face up to Pamela. She was sitting on a kitbag which looked far too heavy for her slight figure. 'I joined up and did my training in Belfast, so I'm on my first posting south.'

'You've carted all that stuff from Belfast? How on earth did you manage?'

Blue eyes sparkled and her head tilted to one side as she said, 'I had some help. There were a couple of sailors ... '

They grinned at each other. Despite their claims to equality with the men there were definite advantages in being feminine. So far, neither of them had experienced the disadvantage, when resentful men would deliberately load the worst and heaviest work on to the girls, often with a comment that, since they wanted a man's job, they could get on with it.

They talked for the rest of the journey, Pamela explaining that she was nearly at the end of a long course of training and didn't know where her permanent posting would be. The Irish girl, Marie, said that she would be learning to handle barrage balloons.

'Make sure they don't take you up with them,' Pam teased. 'I should think they need stronger ballast than you.'

'I know it looks like that, but I'm a strong swimmer – go in for competitions – and my arms and legs are very strong – and I'll be part of a team.'

The train was only held up for an hour, which was something of a miracle. The two girls parted with mutual good wishes and expressed the hope that they might meet again. It seemed unlikely, but the world for them, which had once seemed so huge, was getting smaller all the time.

Jean's wedding was typical of so many wartime ones. The local church was sparsely filled with both families and a few neighbours. Pamela's mother had taken an hour off, leaving her husband in charge of the shop. A small reception was to be held in Jean's home.

Pamela, hastily roped in as the only grown-up bridesmaid, marvelled at the serene way in which the couple took their vows. She was far more nervous than they. It was obvious that it would take a lot to ruffle the bridegroom. The habit of command sat lightly on him, but it was unmistakably there.

'He's a dish. Whatever did he see in Jean?' Pamela thought. Then, 'But who knows what anybody sees in the people they marry?'

As she had been told, Douglas was tall, dark and handsome, with a generous mouth and a formidable jaw. It wouldn't do to cross him and Pam was not sure whether she envied Jean or not. She looked at the bride in her beautifully cut blue dress which successfully slimmed the solid figure, and decided that her friend's placid disposition was probably well suited to that of the Captain.

His best man, also a Naval Officer, was thickset and ginger-haired, with powerful shoulders. Their uniforms looked impressive in the church and Pam wished that the powers-that-be would get on with providing the Wrens with a smart outfit and do away with those awful pudding basin hats.

She mentioned as much to Jean while some of the guests were taking photographs.

'Yes, I suppose so, but it doesn't matter. We're married and that's all I care about.'

'It's a shame you couldn't have a white wedding, though.'

Jean laughed at her.

'Oh, Pam, can you really see me in white? No, this is much better. I shan't ever regret doing it this way.'

Andrew Sadler, the best man, devoted himself to Pamela in the time honoured way, as to the chief bridesmaid, and she was pleased to hear him say, 'How nice to see a lovely girl in civvies. That's a pretty dress – I've been admiring it.'

'It's a pre-war garden party one. It'll be hopelessly out of date soon.'

They were interrupted by Douglas and Jean who had come to say goodbye, as they were catching a train to Blackpool, where Douglas's aunt had a boarding house.

Pam felt rather flat when they had gone and Andrew asked, 'Would you like to go out for a drink – or up to the West End?'

But she decided that she didn't feel like coping with her father's criticism if she did any such thing, so she said that she ought to go home and spend some time with her family. Andrew did not try to persuade her or ask for another date and she was not surprised nor disappointed. He had been a pleasant acquaintance, but he was not in the same league as – well, the bridegroom, for instance.

In September, her final exams passed, Pamela's posting came through. It was to Speke Airport in Liverpool, where she would be attached to the Fleet Air Arm. She wrote at once to Jean and the two arranged to meet the first time that they were off duty together.

'I'm still servicing radios in the workshop at the moment, but next week I'll be checking them in the planes, and we have to test them in flight. I feel a bit scared, but I suppose I'll get used to it,' Pam said.

'Lucky you. You'll be flying over the coast, I expect. There's an experience for you to write about.'

'If I ever get time. We're so busy. Fancy me going up in a plane!'

'I wonder if we'll think nothing of flying when the war's over,' said Jean. 'Imagine all the lovely places in the world we could go to.'

'Oh, I don't think I'd want to go out of England. Would you – really, Jean?'

'I certainly would – and, what's more, I'm going to if I get the chance. Douglas says I should see other countries while I can. He's liable to turn up anywhere and, after the war, he could be based wherever Britain "maintains a presence", as they say.

'Anyway, I've volunteered for service overseas. '

Margaret picked up the letter from her mother-in-law and disappeared with it into the heads. Her hand shook a little as she opened it, but the first sentence banished her worst fears.

'My dear child,

It was so good to hear from you. We hope you will not apply for a divorce from Brian. Dad and I both think you are well suited and this war will change everything – not least the people in it. If we all survive you may be able to make a new beginning.

Brian is still very bitter and blames himself the most. He was very well when he wrote last. It is up to you, but I think he would

197

welcome a letter, if only to say you forgive him, so I enclose his address ...'

As Margaret put the letter away, a longing for the feel of her husband's arms around her was so overwhelming that it left her trembling. It was only with a great effort that she managed to shake off the weakness and return to her work in the engineering shop.

Noticing her quietness that night, Jo asked her if she had had any bad news.

'No. I had a letter from my mother-in-law. She wants me to write to my husband.'

There were very few secrets between the girls who had been thrown together, far away from home and with no-one else to confide in.

'Well, that's what you want, isn't it? You want him back, don't you?'

'Yes,' said Margaret emphatically. 'Yes, I do. I've made up my mind.'

But it was not easy to write the letter. Should she start 'Dear Brian' or would that sound too cold? On the other hand an endearment – oh, darling, darling man – no, that was impossible. Finally, she wrote,

'*My dear husband,*

Your mother has given me this address and has persuaded me not to apply for divorce while the war is on, so you are still my husband and I hope you will be pleased about that.

She says you are still blaming yourself, but I want you to know that I now appreciate how much I contributed to our break-up and that I forgive your part in it. I am finding it more difficult to forgive my mother, though I know that she was only thinking of my welfare. Unfortunately, no-one else can judge what is best for anyone.

Whether we will get together after the war – if we are both here – I can't say. I have changed a great deal and perhaps you will not like what the Wrens has done for me. I am working in a shipyard, welding, painting, driving cranes – can you imagine it? And getting more confident all the time. My next big test is to tell mother my decision about us. That is, of course, if you agree? I look forward to hearing from you. Keep safe. My prayers will be with you.

Margaret.'

Now the post became something to watch for eagerly, but weeks passed without the longed-for letter. Brian's mother confirmed that she had heard nothing but added, *'There is always the possibility that a mail boat has been sunk, so I have written again and told Brian that you wrote to him, in case he didn't get it.'*

Towards the end of March, Jean came to meet Pamela with an air of excitement.

'I think I must be in the next lot to go abroad. I start leave on Saturday and I'm not due for it yet.'

'Oh, Jean – do you know where?'

'Haven't a clue. Rumour says Hong Kong. I hope it's true. Douglas said it was fascinating and quite beautiful.'

'It's a long way from home,' mused Pamela. 'Better you than me, though I wouldn't mind the voyage – better than flying all that distance. I get quite enough of that, testing the radios on the planes.'

'You're not still afraid of it, are you?'

'Not now but it just gets me mad sometimes. Some of the men are OK and realise I've got a job to do. But too many of them think it's great fun having a girl aboard. They make it as awkward as they can – jinking the plane around just as I'm ready to test. I've had some good old rows with two of them.'

'I know what you mean,' Jean said. 'They don't like seeing a girl in authority. I expect they see the writing on the wall.'

'You mean we'll never go back to being the little woman at home where the master's word is law? I won't, for one.'

Jean frowned.

'I've got a male Officer who's got his knife into one of my girls – I can't think why. She's a little dolly of a thing and quite inoffensive. He's going to be a vicar after the war and I told him it wasn't a Christian attitude. What do you think he said? I couldn't believe it.'

Pam shook her head.

'Said it was only a job. I told him if he felt like that it was wicked to go into the Church.'

She sounded so sad that Pam hastened to say, 'I should think he's a one off.'

Jean laughed suddenly.

'In a way he's done her a good turn. She wouldn't say boo to a goose at first but now she's started to stick up for herself. He wrote in the log book that she hadn't passed him a signal and she wrote under it: "Signal passed. Officer replied 'shut up!' " I took that for an acknowledgement.'

'Good for her!' Then Pam added thoughtfully, 'I think it's the same with me, as well. I can't believe how much I swear at those pilots. My father would have fits.'

Jean squeezed her arm.

'Don't let the Service coarsen you. It's difficult not to, but I always think of my father's phrase if any of us get out of line. He says, "It doesn't become you" – I like the idea that I'm someone to be respected and shouldn't let myself down.' She gave a sheepish smile. 'Sorry, I'm preaching again. I get sarcastic with them myself – I don't suppose that's any better. Though it seems to work,' she added with a wry grin.

The two girls met again after Jean's leave, but they both knew it would be the last time before she sailed.

'As far as I know, we're going in a ship that's escorting a convoy, and we are to be issued with "appropriate kit" before we sail, so it sounds like a hot country.'

'Are you excited?' asked Pam.

'I don t know what I am. I'm looking forward to seeing a new country and there's always the possibility of meeting Douglas, but I don't know what sort of sailor I'll be. I hope I'm not like Nelson – always sick at sea.'

Jean was happy. Her mood was always tempered by anxiety for Douglas, but on this beautiful day she had pushed it deep down and was rejoicing in her wellbeing, following her brief sea sickness off the Spanish coast. The sea was calm, there was real heat in the sun and they would soon be in Gibraltar.

Three of the seven Wrens and two nurses were sunbathing on deck, having found a corner where they were out of the way of the crew.

'Do you think we'll see the Barbary apes as we sail in?' one of them asked lazily.

'Don't know, but they'd better be somewhere or we'll lose Gibraltar.'

There was a general laugh.

Jean said, 'I never thought I'd see any of these lovely places. Aren't we lucky?'

She turned over and felt the warmth of the sun on her back. She sighed with bliss. Pure heaven.

Seconds later, the torpedo struck. She heard one almighty bang. Then nothing. There were survivors from the Aguilla. None of them were Wrens.

The shock spread through the whole of the Service. It was immediately decided that women should not sail in escort vessels but only with the main destroyer in future.

Pamela was so upset that the First Officer sent her on compassionate leave, even though she was not related to Jean. It helped her to be with her own family and to share her memories with Jean's parents. She told them more about life in the Wrens than they had gleaned from their daughter's letters and it seemed to comfort them. 'It's good that she enjoyed it right to the end and had that brief time of happiness with Douglas.' Mr. Dixon reached for his wife's hand.

'We heard from him yesterday,' Mrs. Dixon explained, 'and he said his time with her was short but so completely happy.' But here Jean's mother broke down and Pamela went to make a cup of tea.

* * * * *

The news hit Margaret hard. Jean had been her first friend in the Wrens and the last letter received from her, just before she sailed, had been enthusiastic about Margaret's decision to save her marriage. She had written, '*Only you can run your life and no-one else knows what is right for you. Now that you know your own mind I am sure that all will come right.*'

But there was still no news of Brian.

* * * * *

Jo was getting increasingly frustrated. She had not been offered a post as Boatscrew Wren in spite of the half-promises, and the competition was still fierce. Too many of the girls from wealthy homes had plenty of experience of crewing and even competing in races in civvy street.

She complained to Margaret, 'Signalling doesn't stretch me. I know it's important, but ...'

To her the news of Jean's death came not only as a shock, but also as a spur. She must do something about this war. She wanted to be involved, to make a difference. She asked for an interview and stated her case.

'I only joined up to be working on boats and I was a volunteer. I do think I've earned it.'

The young woman interviewer smiled at her. 'I'm not unsympathetic, but there are plenty of others who can say the same. Would you be willing to take another course if it would help?'

'What sort of course?'

'I was thinking of Ordnance. You'd be servicing the guns on boats and, with your signals training as well, you should stand a good chance of becoming a Boatscrew Wren. In any case, you would be working on boats all the time.'

Jo didn't hesitate. 'That's all I want – to be on the boats. I ought to have done that first.'

'It's not too late. You won't be far away. The gunnery course is on Whale Island.'

'In Portsmouth harbour? HMS Excellent?'

Jo was surprised. Whale Island seemed to be inhabited by senior Naval personnel. There was something hush-hush about it. But she discovered no secrets when she went to the Ordnance Depot and was taught to dismantle, clean and check 20mm Oerlikons on Tank Landing Craft (LCTs).

She had done some game shooting at home and had a good eye for a target. Using the ring-sight presented no difficulties to her. By the time she had completed the course she could hit the target sleeve, towed by a plane, every time.

Violet heard of Jean's death at the Admiralty. They had just got the casualty list and she read the name with disbelief. She remembered vaguely that Pam had mentioned that Jean was going abroad and had thought no more of it. A Wren standing next to her caught the sharp intake of breath and said sympathetically, 'Someone you know?'

'A girl I did my initial training with. She'd only been married a few months. Her husband's regular Navy.'

'Poor devil. I bet he thought it would be him rather than her.'

Violet shrugged. 'Can't tell in this war. It might be one of us any time.'

202

'You can say that again. There was a land mine dropped quite early last evening. I don't know what the damage was, but the Jerries were at it all night. I never got a wink of sleep.'

'Where was that?'

'Putney – or perhaps more Hammersmith way. It's difficult to tell. Sometimes I think I'd be safer sleeping here. But you know what they say – if a bomb's got your name on it, it'll get you, no matter where you are.'

They grinned and parted cheerfully.

Violet thought that Pamela would be most upset, then she forgot about it. She had not lived in London without seeing the devastation wrought by the bombing and had even helped, on one memorable occasion, to dig people out of the wreckage. Jean was just one more casualty.

And so was the girl whose place she was now taking on the Oxford run. Three weeks earlier she had been told that a Wren driver had been injured by an 'incident' as she approached London. She had been on an important job and Violet was to take her place for the time being.

Violet did not think that driving a Humber shooting brake daily from Oxford to the Admiralty was important enough to take her away from her family and friends in London, even if she was driving a courier with boxes of secret codes and ciphers. Unfortunately, he was a singularly solemn and self-important young man who took his duties seriously and was always worried that they wouldn't be able to get through London.

'It seems the East End caught it again last night,' he would say, almost every day, and she would invariably reply,

'Don't worry, sir. I know scores of routes in London. Lizzie will get you there.' She called all her cars Tin Lizzies as most of them rattled despite all her maintenance.

The rating who rode shot gun behind them was usually asleep with his revolver in its holster on the floor and the boxes containing the precious secrets gently coming undone as they bounced over the atrocious roads. She had been given to understand that Harry didn't get much sleep at nights because he knew a lot of girls who liked sailors.

Violet had been in the Wrens too long to be prudish. He was a single man and might have a short life. Besides, his cockney good humour made her laugh.

'Just give us a shout before we get into the smoke,' he had said. 'As long as I'm awake before any of the Officers start getting nosy.'

Today, after she had dropped her passengers, she picked up a couple of assignments which would keep her busy until early afternoon. She had come in along High Holborn, but the Officer who she picked up at Euston warned her that there was some sort of blockage at the station end of Waterloo Bridge and she should avoid it.

'Is it bomb damage?' she asked.

'Haven't a clue. I only know because someone in the train mentioned it.'

Violet dropped him at the Admiralty and found herself free for a couple of hours. She decided to see if Aunt Ruby was all right. The house was untouched but there was no-one at home and she guessed her aunt would be at the WVS canteen, making herself useful.

It was as she was passing the Adelphi that she was stopped by an Army Officer in battledress. He had looked worried, but brightened as she stopped.

'Could you get me to the Elephant? It's urgent.'

'Well, I could ...' She sounded doubtful, and he said quickly, 'I could make it all right for you. It's an unexploded bomb. '

'Get in. Were you on your own?'

'My oppo's with the jeep, stuck on the bridge. He'll follow me as soon as he can but I have all I need.'

He climbed in beside her, parking a heavy rucksack carefully on the back seat. It was only then that she noticed the crown on his shoulder and realised that she was driving a Major. He was a fair, stocky man, with a pleasant 'dark brown' voice. He asked, 'Were you on duty?'

'I'm free for a couple of hours, as it happens.'

'Joe will catch me up long before that. He's a resourceful chap. If necessary, he'll bale out and direct the traffic himself.'

But Violet was too busy thinking of her best route to take much notice. Blackfriars Bridge was the obvious alternative, but so it would be for everybody else. She was startled when the Major said sharply, 'What's the delay?' but she was used to impatient passengers and he had more excuse than most, so she replied, 'I was wondering which was the best way to go. Blackfriars will probably be choc-a-bloc.'

'We'll have to risk it. And look – I'm sorry. I ought to be used to it. UBs are always in badly bombed areas and I know you can't hurry getting to them.'

It was the first time she had ever had an apology from an Officer. 'It's all right, sir.'

He laughed awkwardly, 'I'm always like this till I'm there.'

'And then you have to be cool.'

'Oh, that's easy. You get so absorbed in what you're doing, you don't have time to think of anything else. You don't mind if I talk? It helps me relax.'

So she let him talk and even listened when she wasn't concentrating on the tricky driving conditions. The bridge had not been too bad but the East End had received a pasting and she was soon avoiding burst and twisted pipes, pools of water, bomb craters and piles of bricks.

He explained that defusing a bomb was like solving a puzzle and it engaged the mind completely, like playing chess. They knew a lot about several types of bombs now, but the Jerries were always coming up with extra complications.

'Jolly clever, the Jerries. You have to give them that. I met a lot of them before the war – nice fellows, too. Shame about Hitler.'

'What were you doing before the war, sir?'

'Scientist. What about you?'

'Useless debutante, I'm ashamed to say. I think this is it.'

She dodged round a large police van and pulled up near a crater which was roped off and bore the legend 'Unexploded Bomb.'

The young Officer reached for his tools, said, 'Thanks' and strode off. She saw a policeman stop him and then lift the rope. She watched him kneel and undo the rucksack. There was no reason for her to stay, but she didn't move. His jeep hadn't turned up yet – she might be able to take him back to base if this should prove to be quick.

When the jeep arrived an hour later, she still hadn't moved and wasn't aware of it until a carroty-headed man peered in at her and said, 'Hello. What are you doing here? Did you bring our boffin? He said he'd try and get a lift. Trust him to pick a good-looking girl.'

Violet ignored all this and said, 'I've never seen anyone so totally focused on what he's doing. Shouldn't you go and help him?'

'Not likely. He'd have my guts if I broke his concentration. He'll signal if he needs help.'

It occurred to Violet that she was due back on duty, but she could not move until the job was done and the man safe. It was another hour or more before that, but then there was no more excuse for delay.

When she saw the Major stand and give the thumbs up to the young Lieutenant, she drove back to the Admiralty and picked up her passengers for Oxford. She explained the delay, but Harry grumbled all the way. He had had a date at seven and he wasn't going to make it.

In her bed that night, Violet relived those long hours and thought, 'Why was I silly enough to say I was a deb? It sounds like boasting, though it's nothing to be proud of. He probably despised me for it.' Then later, tossing and turning and not finding sleep: 'What rubbish, I don't suppose he ever thought about me – and, anyway, what does it matter? I'm not likely to see him again.'

But over the next few days, the image of a fair head and broad shoulders crouching over a hole in the ground, totally oblivious of all else, would appear before her eyes at odd times of the day and night even though her thoughts were elsewhere. She told herself that the presence of danger was what had made such a strong impact on her mind and shook herself impatiently when it occurred.

It took Joe of the ginger hair over a week to find her. Then she received a letter which read:

'Dear Miss Allen,

I left this at the Admiralty for forwarding. They wouldn't give me your address, of course, so I can only give you mine and hope you will respond. The Major asked me to thank you for him if I found you.

Would you meet me for dinner at Browns on Wednesday at 7.30? I'll be there anyway and I'll understand if you can't make it as I don't know where you are, or what your duties are.

Joe Anderson.'

This required an immediate reply to explain the situation. She would have gone, if possible. She didn't meet many men these days who would give her dinner at Browns Hotel, and who would be as pleasant as Joe. She wrote to Lieutenant Anderson, explaining why she could not meet him, and added, *'This is not an excuse. I would have enjoyed dinner with you.'*

Two days later, there was a telegram.

'*The Mitre at 7.30 tonight – please.*'

The oldest hotel in Oxford was full of charm and more intimate than Browns.

'Can we dance afterwards? Have you got a late pass?' he asked when they had ordered.

'I can't be too late. I have to be up at six to check Lizzie before we go. She mustn't break down with all that secret stuff on board.'

In the event they found so much to say that they sat over drinks in the lounge until she had to leave.

'Boffin asked me to thank you for driving him. He was disappointed you didn't stay.'

'I was horribly late. The Corporal who rides shot gun for us was furious because we got back to Oxford too late for his date. Do you always call the Major "Boffin"? What's his real name?'

'Oliver Anderson – yes, it's the same, we're cousins. The family have called him Boffin since he was ten because he was always into science. Experiments that went wrong were a hazard of every holiday with him. You never knew what was going to blow up next. He got me working with him, but I don't know how long he'll get away with it.'

'I can't understand why you aren't too worried to watch him – especially if you're close.'

Joe shrugged. 'There's a risk whatever you do and I trust him to know what he's about. I can help quite a lot sometimes and once you're involved there's no time to think about anything else.'

'I should think his wife would be out of her mind. I would if it was my husband.'

'I hope there isn't a husband,' Joe said. It was a statement, not a question, and Violet, to her annoyance, felt that she was blushing.

'No. Just a figure of speech.'

'Boffin's not married. I think there's a girl, but he wouldn't have told her what he does.'

She felt they had talked enough about the Major and set herself to draw Joe out about his own life. He was quite willing to talk about his Aberdeenshire home and was thrilled to find that she knew the area.

'I love Scotland,' Violet said. 'So are you one of the hunting, shooting and fishing set?'

'No. We don't like taking life. Golf is our game.'

He began to talk about Scotland's wonderful golf courses, but there were many allusions to his cousin, who had been a hero to him from childhood.

'He was always the leader and a marvellous planner – not impetuous, like me, and I thought him very brave, even then. Of course, he was four years older and that makes a great difference when you're young.'

They sat in companionable silence, watching a young couple who were absorbed in each other. The girl, who was in a smart suit, was wearing a wedding ring .The young man was in khaki. It seemed they were on honeymoon.

Joe said, 'It's hard on them. He's probably on short leave – perhaps embarkation leave. This is no time to be married. I wouldn't do it until this is over.'

'Have you got a girl, Joe?' It was not a loaded question. Violet did not feel involved with this man.

'Heavens, no! I wouldn't be dating you if I had. It wouldn't be fair.'

She laughed at him. 'How nice and old-fashioned that sounds. Scotland's a long way and, after all, you're only giving me a meal.'

He grinned back at her, his long mouth mocking himself.

'I suppose it's the Presbyterian in me. But it's one thing I wouldn't do. I wouldn't expect my girl to go out with anyone else. And I intend to see you again if you'll let me. When do you get a day off?'

'I'll be free on Sunday and I'll be in town to have lunch with my aunt and uncle.'

'Great. Then can I call for you in the afternoon? Duty permitting, of course.'

Violet agreed and gave him the address. It was the beginning of many dates with Joe, and on one of the early ones she met the Major again.

There was a dance at the Army barracks where the men were stationed. He came towards her and she held her breath for a moment, willing herself to calmness as he took her hand and said, 'At last I can thank you myself. You got me out of tight spot. You didn't get into trouble?'

'No – and of course, anyone would have given you a lift at a time like that.' Violet managed to speak with a composure that she did not feel. What was it that was so disturbing about this man?

'Ah, but it takes Boffin to choose a lovely girl, even when he's in a hurry,' Joe said.

208

'Insolent pup! I'll get you transferred if you're not careful, and I shall take your girl away from you!' And he led her on to the dance floor.

Violet had had plenty of practice and was a splendid dancer. She found her partner a little wooden but she soon had him relaxed, her natural flair and pleasure in her skill helping her to behave normally, so that they were soon talking and laughing together.

And that, she told herself firmly as she drove back to Oxford, was how it would have to be. Joe had warned her that his cousin had a girl – and a dangerous job. That, as the Yanks would say, was two strikes against her.

But it was not the face of the smart, smiling man holding out his hand to her, but the old picture of the still figure, bending over the bomb crater, which haunted her dreams.

On several occasions, both Violet and Joe had had to cancel meetings, so she did not think it strange when, towards the end of 1943, she received a telegram which read, *'Sorry, not tonight. Writing.'*

But there was no letter and Aunt Ruby, who liked Joe, was beginning to be curious as to whether they had fallen out.

'No, and I can't understand it myself. They surely wouldn't have sent him abroad with the work he's doing. Perhaps he's met a girl and really fallen in love.'

'Wouldn't you mind?' Ruby was surprised at Violet's detachment. The young people were too good-mannered to display affection in public, but she had thought that they would probably marry.

'Not if she was the right girl for him. I hope he and Oliver are both safe, though.'

It was about ten days before she found a letter waiting for her in London. It had a Scottish postmark and was not in a Forces envelope. She had a sense of foreboding as she opened it.

'My dear Violet,

I have the most shattering news. Boffin has been killed by an unexploded bomb. It went off just as he reached it. It should have been me as well, but I had gone to get something he wanted and only caught some shrapnel splinters.

I am on sick leave at present. I will write more when I can.

Love, Joe
P.S. Is there any chance you could come?'

She sat very still, then silently handed the letter to Ruby.

'Oh, my dear, I'm so sorry. Joe idolised him, didn't he? I think he'll need you. Could you go?'

Violet felt frozen. Oliver was dead. She felt that some final hope had gone. She needed to mourn him and where better than with his own family, where it would not seem strange. She said calmly, 'I could try. If I said my fiancé was wounded ... but I'll ring his people first.'

It was Joe's father who answered. She said, 'It's Violet from London. Joe asked me to come but I thought I'd better ask you first.'

It sounded so like Oliver's deep voice that replied warmly, 'Oh, my dear girl, can you come? He's so shocked. I think you would help.'

'I'll apply for leave tomorrow and let you know what time I can arrive – only, I expect the train will be very late.'

'No matter. We'll find out this end and pick you up at Aberdeen Station. It's less than half-an-hour from here. And thank you, my dear, we'll all be grateful to you for coming.'

So she applied for, and was granted, a week's leave, and received a railway voucher to Aberdeen.

In the train, squashed between two sailors and with others standing in front of her so that she could hardly move her feet, Violet started thinking of Joe for the first time.

What a terrible experience it must have been to see someone he loved blown to pieces. Poor Joe. Then she thought – and he is one among so many to whom that must have happened in this awful war, and on both sides. It seemed to her that she had done so little, had been wonderfully protected from the horrors, and she longed to take a more active role.

Without warning, she was in tears before all these strangers. The whole compartment went silent, its occupants shocked and uncertain of what to do. She struggled to stop, but a soldier who was almost standing on her toes bent down to her and said, 'No, don't try to stop – let it all come. You'll feel better for it.'

His kindness had the effect he intended and she gave herself up to her emotions, crying for all the bereaved, the dispossessed, the young men lost, and for her country which would feel the need of them in the years to come. She cried until she was drained of all emotion.

It was Joe's father who met her at the station. The man who had Oliver's voice was a smaller version of Joe, except that the once ginger hair was so sprinkled with grey that it had dulled to the colour of pepper.

'Thank you for coming, my dear. You'll cheer Joe up enormously.' His smile was wide and welcoming, but Violet had a sudden stab of fear .

'He wasn't well enough to come?'

She was heart weary. She had had plenty of time to compose herself after her outburst on the train, but it had been a long journey and she had had no sleep. The young man who had been so sympathetic had slipped into a vacant seat at Edinburgh and had offered her a shoulder to rest on. But it soon became obvious that the offer was not without conditions. The wandering hands and an attempt to kiss her as the darkened train sped through the night had resulted in her moving away from him. She had spent the rest of the time rigidly upright and determined to stay awake. That part of the journey had taken long hours as the passenger train was continually halted to give way to troop and freight trains.

The only bright spot had been that she had been met without the necessity of finding a telephone and waking Joe's people. She looked at Mr. Anderson with the tiredness and concern plain for him to see.

'He can't stand for long yet, but he's going to be all right. Lassie, you're dead tired, let's get you home.'

There was a battered taxi waiting, with a driver who looked as old as Methuselah, but he was very competent and the inside of the cab was more comfortable than it looked. Violet relaxed for the first time since the start of her journey.

'Hamish,' Joe's father addressed the driver, 'this lass is dropping with tiredness. Let's get home quickly.' They continued to talk, leaving her free to gaze out at the scenery. Scotland was as beautiful as she had remembered. On her left was a heather-covered hill, crowned by three silver birches.

211

'I will lift up mine eyes unto the hills.'

The psalm came into her mind unbidden and the words comforted her. No matter what devastation came out of this war, surely these would remain – hills, valleys, peaceful woods, all the spiritual refreshment that a loved place could bring. This was worth fighting for and it would have to be jealously guarded for ever.

The men's voices with the Highland lilt were subdued and seemed part of the peace and she would have slept if the journey had gone on for much longer. She scarcely saw the village as they drove down the long street of terraced houses with the small general shop and the bakery. Then they turned left into a road of larger Victorian houses.

'We're here,' Mr. Anderson murmured as the taxi stopped.

They were certainly expected. A handsome, tall woman came running down the steps to meet them. She had finely-chiselled features which, together with her short fair hair, gave her an elegance that might have seemed cold were it not for the warmth of the smile on her lips and in her eyes.

Behind her, at the top of the steps, stood Joe, leaning against the door frame, and Violet realised with a pang that he could not walk down.

'You must be shattered,' Emma Anderson said. 'I've organised a big breakfast, a hot bath and a bed. Does that sound about right?'

'Wonderful,' breathed Violet, kissing the proffered cheek. They went up the stairs together. Joe held out his arms and said, 'I hope you've got a kiss for me?'

She replied, 'Of course.' Then, aware that his arms could not hold her tight, she hesitated for a moment, then kissed him on the lips.

Violet slept blissfully until mid-day. Joe had come to her room and was looking down at her. 'My mother says you're to have a tray in bed. Are you ready for us to bring it up?'

'Certainly not. I'm getting dressed this minute. Out you go.'

She watched him shuffle away and wondered at the determination that had made him climb the stairs and how long it would be before he had fully recovered – if, indeed, he ever did.

It was Emma who gave her the details. 'Joe's always made such a hero out of Oliver, ever since they were children. Everyone

212

thought so highly of him and I used to resent it a bit because I thought it stopped Joe getting his due. Oliver overshadowed everyone. But as they grew older, I saw that he realised this himself and would do all he could to see that Joe got proper recognition. He really was a lovely man – we shall all miss him.' Her eyes clouded for a minute. 'Luckily, Joe didn't see the explosion. He passed out himself when he got a back full of shrapnel.

'They got most of it out – Charing Cross Hospital was wonderful – and they tell us that there's nothing left in that can do any damage. The muscles are taking their time to get strong again and, of course, the waiting frets him.' She smiled. 'I've never come across a Scotsman who was a good patient.

'We're thrilled to think he's got you and that you value him for what he is. I've always thought a girl who married Oliver would have too much to live up to. Women don't want husbands who are up on a pedestal, we want an equal partner if we've got any character ourselves.'

This was going rather far and Violet had no intention of being rushed, so she just nodded and said, 'I'm only too relieved to know that he hasn't got any lasting damage. Poor Joe. Even if he didn't see Oliver buy it he must have had a dreadful shock when he came round.'

'Yes, he's not over that completely. I think he feels guilty to be alive.'

'Oh, Mrs. Anderson, that's so common. We all feel like that sometimes. Why them and not me? That's how I came to join the Wrens.' She explained about her brother's friend and concluded, 'I often thought how worthless I was in comparison, but this war will take the brightest and the best, and we can only accept it.'

She spoke with authority. This was something she had experienced herself and seen many times with other girls.

Emma's face lit up. 'You hearten me. We've had so little trouble up here. I've often wondered how the London people were taking it – and Coventry – places like that. How can they bear it?'

'We comfort each other,' said Violet simply.

Violet was just dropping off to sleep. It was bliss to realise that she could relax utterly, instead of sleeping with one ear open for the first sound of the siren. Then, without warning, the familiar image of Oliver came before her eyes – a crouching man, totally engrossed in the task before him.

The next moment she was wide awake and sitting up. With total clarity she knew that the feeling she had mistaken for love was nothing more than hero worship. What was it Emma had said? 'Women don't want husbands who are up on a pedestal.' That was it. Everyone had put Oliver on a pedestal – and perhaps he deserved it. Those whom the gods love die young, she thought – but what an effort it would be to have a paragon for a husband. Of course, she would want a man whom she could respect but she certainly didn't want to feel that he was superior to her in every way.

As the certainty that she had never loved Oliver became real to her, she gave a little sigh of relief and was soon deeply asleep for the second time that day.

The next morning, Alec Anderson told them, 'I'm taking the day off so I'll take you anywhere you want to go – as far as I can with the petrol ration I've got.'

Violet already knew that Joe's father was an advocate with a firm in Aberdeen. She said warmly, 'That's very kind of you, but you don't need to do that. I'll be quite happy here, talking to Joe.'

'Don't spoil his fun,' Joe said with a grin, 'he's itching to be seen driving a pretty girl around. I could do with getting out of the house, anyway. I ought to be walking more.'

They drove along the coast road as far as the Bay of Nigg. It was a golden day and one that Violet never forgot. Granite buildings sparkled like points of diamonds in the sun, its light turning the sands golden and edging the white waves with brilliance. Then they turned towards Stonehaven, finding a pub where they had a lunch of cheese and pickle sandwiches washed down with cider. It was a wonderful combination, born out of the sunlight, good company and healthy appetites, and Violet thought no meal had ever tasted so good.

'Where are we going now, Dad?' Joe asked, getting to his feet awkwardly. 'I ought to stretch my legs a bit.'

'I hear the salmon are leaping just now. Would you like to see them, Violet?'

'I d love to. I know a bit of Scotland but I've never seen salmon leap.'

So they drove through Cults and on towards Peterculter. At the Brig of Feugh there were already a few people gazing into the rocky waterfall.

They spent the next hour leaning over the parapet and watching the silver streamlined bodies make the effort to leap the boulders of rock above them. Time and again the fish would be knocked back into the pool below by the force of the current but each one persisted until they had jumped to the top of the waterfall and could swim on up the river. It was spellbinding to watch them, but Joe was tiring and his father was on the alert.

'Plucky little devils, aren't they?' Joe said, straightening up off his elbows which had been resting on the bridge.

'Come back to the car now and we'll go and find some tea,' Alec said. 'I'm sure Violet can do with some.'

But Joe would not sit down until he had walked over the bridge and back. Violet and Alec sat in the car, aware that he wanted to go on his own.

'His legs really are getting stronger. It's all seemed very slow to us and I think he was too depressed to care at first. He's already made more effort since you came,' Alec said with satisfaction. 'He'll get on quickly now. I'm sure of it.'

Violet had had no idea of how exhausted she had been until she fell into the routine of the Anderson household. To go to bed and sleep without fear of being awakened by the scream of the air raid siren and having to rush to the shelter, half-awake and half-dressed; to wake to a leisurely breakfast and have nothing to do but laze and talk to Joe – these were like taking deep breaths after insufficient oxygen.

She thought of her home in Richmond and wondered how all the people of London and the cities that were regularly bombed would cope after the war. Would they all be too worn out to take on the daily chores of living and have the energy to rebuild as well? She decided that she should cut short her time here and spend a few days with her parents.

'It's been a real tonic' she assured Emma, 'even these few days have done me so much good.'

'We've loved having you, and Joe has perked up so much. Have you told him why you joined the Wrens? I think it might help him.'

'I haven't yet. We haven't been alone very much, but I'll try to talk to him before I go.'

After dinner that night, they found themselves alone in the living-room. Violet wasted no time. 'Joe, I want to talk to you about Oliver,' she began.

'What is there to say – the best man bought it and I'm left. A poor substitute.' He smiled but the smile did not reach his eyes. She was suddenly very angry with him.

'For God's sake, Joe, stop being so bloody sorry for yourself. I'm not sorry for you – you've been lucky. Do you think you're the only one who feels like that? I lost a friend who went down in the Aguilla – a lovely girl, woman really. The sort who'd help anybody – and she'd only been married a few months. My brother lost a good friend – he's the reason I joined the Wrens '

Joe interrupted, 'Were you in love with him?'

'Me? I hardly knew him, but I was so damned furious at the waste of his life that I went and joined up. And, God knows, I've done little enough, but I suppose it all helps. Now there's Oliver – someone else we both mourn, as everyone who knew him must. A fine man. But so are you. And you're still here and will be a comfort to all your people, so pull yourself together and stop putting yourself down.'

She paused, out of breath and flushed from her outburst. Joe thought she had never looked so lovely. He said gently, 'Tell me – how did you get leave to come here?'

Violet hesitated, but he was regarding her steadily as though compelling her answer. 'I said my fiancé had been wounded.'

'I thought it might be that. Before you tell any more whoppers don't you think we'd better make it the truth?'

She had seen it coming. And he needed so much to have something to hope for just now. She said, 'Well, just so it won't be a lie any longer.'

The smile that lit up his face made her think that she might not even regret it.

Jo drew in her breath sharply and the young rating eyed her warily. This was not the first time he had caught the rough side of her tongue.

'This gun is a bloody disgrace!' she exploded. 'You ought to be shot, getting it like that. If it gets any rustier, I'll have to write it off. Get it clean – and I mean sparkling – before I see it tomorrow.'

'Oh, hell. Give us a chance. I got a date tonight.'

'Too bloody bad. Do it. I'll report you if I see it like that again.'

His eyes followed her as she left the ship and he muttered, 'Damn butch woman.' It was already five o'clock and he had several hours' work if the gun was to pass her standard in the morning.

No-one would have guessed that she was too happy to be really worried about the state of the Oerlikon, which would have had her raging six months ago.

But that was before she met Celia.

The little fluffy blonde with speedwell blue eyes had been a revelation to Jo. She had no idea that friends could be as close as they were. From the moment that their eyes met in the YWCA they had both known that here was someone special.

Celia, in a blue summer dress that showed her slim figure to perfection, had smiled at her and said, 'There's a seat at my table. My friend's over there.'

The YW was crowded as usual and Jo picked up her tray and followed the girl gratefully.

'This is Maureen and I'm Celia. We're both in the NAAFI at the Army barracks at Southsea. What's your name?'

Jo introduced herself and told them what she was doing.

'I applied for Boats crew at first, but I've withdrawn that because I enjoy the job I've got. I get on as well with the men as I do with the girls.'

'I bet you have to repel boarders. Fancy climbing over them boats in a skirt with all the sailors watching!' Maureen's expression said that she would quite enjoy it.

'I wear trousers on the ships and the men accept me as one of themselves now – once I proved I could do the job as well as them.'

Celia was watching her with undisguised admiration.

'You must be clever. I wish I could do better than washing teacups.'

Maureen started to laugh. 'We had a new intake yesterday. They'd just had their jabs. One of them – ooh, such a nice-looking

217

fella, cheeky grin, you know – well, he put his hand in his pocket to get some money and couldn't get it out again. We've seen it before. Their arms stiffen up. Celia went round to him and jerked his arm out. He gave one yell then he put his other arm round her and wouldn't let her go till she let him kiss her. Lucky old thing.'

Celia blushed at the thought of it.

'All the men were laughing. I felt very embarrassed. I don't like men messing me about.'

'What did you do in civvy street?' Jo asked them.

'I was a waitress in a teashop in Bournemouth, 'Maureen replied. Celia seemed anxious to tell Jo her story.

'I've always been at home. My Mum died when I was twelve and I was left to housekeep for my father and two older brothers. When the war broke out they all joined up – Dad as well – so I didn't have much choice but to volunteer too. Then it was a case of more housekeeping in the ATS or cookhouse, so I thought the NAAFI might be a bit more fun.'

Maureen excused herself and wandered off to talk to some girls and men who were at a nearby table. Jo watched her sit down and plunge into animated conversation, then she turned her attention to Celia once more. They were still deeply engrossed in each other when Jo was due back on duty.

They had met every time that they were both free since that day, finding much in common so that they were never short of topics. They both admired the acting of Leslie Howard in *49th Parallel* and *Gone With The Wind*. They both liked the same music and spent one perfect evening when Leopold Stowkowski was playing in a short film.

Inevitably, they discussed what they wanted to do after the war. Both wanted to live and work in the country, but beyond that their ideas were vague.

'Perhaps,' Jo said tentatively, 'we could do something together.'

Celia opened her eyes wide. 'Do you really think so?'

'Well ... it's early days, but we've got on so well, haven't we? If we decide it would work out, we might try it. Of course, you might marry before long. You're so pretty, I'm surprised you're not engaged already. The men round here must be blind.'

'I'm fed up with men. All they expect you to do is wait on them – and hardly a word of thanks. My brothers took it for granted that I would look after them all when my Mum died, and Dad wasn't much better. Though he did say, when I joined the NAAFI, "Now you'll have a life of your own". I don't think he'd given it a thought before though. I'd think twice before I shackled myself to any man.'

'I know what you mean. Most of the sailors take you for granted – think women were invented to make tea for them,' Jo laughed. 'I've sworn at a few since I had a bit of authority. They admit, grudgingly, that women can do some of the jobs as well as men but I bet we'll have to do them better after the war if we're to get anywhere. I'm determined to be my own boss, but won't your Dad insist on you going back to look after him?'

Celia shook her head vigorously. 'He can insist till he's blue in the face. The Army should have taught him to look after himself. I shall make my life to suit me, so there.'

Jo had to smile at the look of determination on that small face, but she only said, 'Well, we'll see how it works out. We might both change our minds and, if not, it would be fun to go into partnership.'

Margaret was not dependant on Jo for companionship, but they had got into the habit of going out together from time to time. When Jo had turned down two of their dates and had made no attempt to fix another, she decided that she had enough to worry about with Brian's silence and that she would 'have it out' with Jo.

The next time that she finished a day shift she strolled round the shipping in the harbour and saw Jo coming towards her.

'Oh, hello. Were you looking for me?' Jo asked innocently.

'Yes. It's just that I haven't seen you lately. I wondered if everything was all right – your home, or anything?'

'Oh, I see. Yes, everything's fine. Couldn't be better. Have you heard from your husband?'

'No.' And then, in a rush: 'To tell you the truth, that's why I'm here. I don't want anything else to worry about, so I want to know why you're avoiding me.'

Jo's eyebrows shot up and she began to flush. 'I haven't been avoiding you. At least, not on purpose. It's got nothing to do with you. The truth is, I've met a rather special person, who's been taking up all my time. I didn't mean to desert my other friends.'

Margaret smiled warmly. There was no gainsaying the radiance of the girl in front of her.

'Oh, so that's it. Well, I shan't butt in or worry you again. I can see you're in love. That's wonderful. There's nothing like it.'

219

Her face crumpled suddenly and tears blinded her. She patted Jo's arm and turned away. Stunned and shocked, the girl gazed blindly after her.

It is not difficult to pick up the facts of life on a farm and Jo was no fool, but there were things which were never discussed. Like most of her generation, Jo had gone into the Forces with great gaps in her sexual knowledge. She was vaguely aware of men, who her brothers called 'cissies' and laughed at, who appeared very effeminate, but she had no idea of other implications.

That there were women who were attracted to other women was a completely new concept to her, but Margaret's assumption that she was in love had seemed outrageous and then, suddenly, no more than the truth.

'I must be a freak – a man in a woman's body,' she thought that night. She looked back at her life and could see the pointers. Her father had always called her a tomboy, because she wanted to play with her brothers rather than other girls, but he seemed to think it was natural in a girl who had no sisters and who was no trouble to the boys. They accepted her as one of themselves and she had never heard them complain about having to play with a girl. She knew she was a sore disappointment to her mother because she showed no interest in feminine clothes.

'It isn't natural – never wanting to dress up,' she had said when Jo refused to consider 'coming out' and being presented at Court. Her father had been on her side over that.

'It's a great waste of money for nothing. Can you see her enjoying the season? All those parties and balls and doing the rounds. She might enjoy Henley and Wimbledon, but not all the rest of it.'

But it was her mother's words, 'It's not natural', that haunted her now.

When Margaret was summoned to see the Welfare Office she went icy cold. This would be about Brian. Well, she had prepared for the worst a long time ago. She only hoped that her letter had reached him so that he would have known she had not deserted him. She went slowly, head down.

But as she passed the galley there was a burst of music from the radio. Someone was singing with it. '*There's a boy coming home on leave.*' Her heart suddenly lifted and she was filled with the certainty that the news would be good.

The Welfare Officer was all smiles.

'Sit down, Lawson. I've got some good news for you. Why didn't you tell me your husband was missing?'

'I didn't know – only that none of the family had heard from him. We thought a mail ship might have gone down.'

'It's a bit more dramatic than that, I'm afraid. His ship was torpedoed somewhere off Singapore, but there were survivors and we know now that he was one of them.'

'Was he hurt – or don't you know?'

'I think not, but he had pneumonia afterwards. He's on his way home now, so I expect you'll hear from him very soon and we'll see about some leave for you when he arrives.'

Margaret went home as soon as she was off duty .This news would not keep. She let herself in with her latch key and found her mother in the drawing room, nursing her cat. Tibs was a recent acquisition, brought home by her father to keep her mother company. Mrs. Mann had said that she didn't need it and that she had plenty to do, but, seeing her with it now, it occurred to Margaret for the first time that her mother was lonely. She had heard the door and looked up with a pleased smile.

'This is a lovely surprise. Are you on leave?'

'Not yet. Only a flying visit. I came as soon as I finished work to tell you that Brian is on his way home. He was torpedoed, but he's safe. Oh, do be pleased for us, Mum.'

'I'm glad he's safe, of course, but I suppose this means we've lost you now.'

'Of course you haven't lost me.' Margaret felt, and sounded, exasperated. 'Did you think I'd stay at home all my life? I certainly won't go back to my old job after what I've been doing.'

Her mother went into the kitchen without answering, carrying Tibs with her. Margaret followed, but a rigid back was turned to her as Mrs. Mann put the cat down and filled the kettle.

'Mum, I love you and Dad. You know I do, but you couldn't have thought I'd be your little girl for ever.'

She took the kettle out of the woman's shaking hands and held her in a warm hug. Not until she felt the body relax did she let go. Then her mother scooped up the little cat and buried her head in his fur. There was a gush of tears and through them came broken words.

'My only child ... so longed for ... so proud of our lovely little daughter ...'

It was Margaret who made the tea and brought her mother a cup, then she said thoughtfully, 'I understand. You thought I belonged to you – and so I do. But I have a right to my own life, just as you have a right to yours. Some of it was my fault. I never stuck up for myself, in fact I was a silly little fool who wouldn't say boo to a goose. The Wrens have changed all that. I have responsibilities and work I know I'm good at. You know I'm a Petty Officer now. You ought to be proud of me.'

Unexpectedly, her mother laughed. 'Oh, I am. You should hear how I boast about you at the Red Cross. I bet they get fed up with me sometimes.'

They were discussing Brian's escape and making plans for his homecoming when Mr. Mann came in. Over the meal he said, 'He's a good lad in spite of everything. I always liked him. Well, I could see how much he thought of you. I suppose you'll be giving us grandchildren soon?'

'I hope so, but I don't want him to stay in the Navy. I've no wish to be a sailor's wife.'

Her mother looked up with a brilliant smile. 'Do you know, I never thought of grandchildren,' she said.

Margaret had returned in great content and was surprised to find a note from Jo.

'*Could you meet me tomorrow night at the YW? I'll be there from 7pm. Please come if you can, it matters a lot to me.*'

It was puzzling and Margaret hoped it didn't mean that Jo was in trouble, just when she had nothing to worry her for the first time in months.

As soon as they met Margaret saw that the radiance was gone. Boyfriend trouble, she thought. Oh, well, there was plenty of that about.

'You look better,' Jo greeted her. 'I hope it means you've had good news.'

'The best. Brian's on his way home. They were torpedoed and he was lucky to be among the rescued. Now what did you want to see me for?'

'We can't talk here – not for what I've got to ask you. Let's have a coffee and then a walk.'

Margaret agreed, weighing up a Jo she had not known. This was a tense girl, gripping her cup with both hands, her head bent over it.

When they came out into the twilight they walked for some time before Margaret broke the silence.

'I can't help if you don't tell me, Jo – and whatever it is, it won't be unique.'

'Unique – that's the word. Freak is another.' Then in a rush, 'Look here, Margaret, you're a married woman. What do you know about those – you know, effeminate men?'

'What? No, it's all right, I heard you, but what on earth ..? Whatever I expected it wasn't this. Do you think your boyfriend is ... unnatural? Has he been bothering you to do weird things?'

'No. Look.' Jo grasped Margaret's arm, none too gently, and brought them both to a halt.

'I misled you the other night. My special friend is a girl.' She swallowed, but went on determinedly: 'I never thought anything about it until you said I was in love. That's what it feels like. There was so much joy in it. I was shocked when you made me realise. Am I a freak? I don't know anything about this and I'm going mad with worrying. It would help if I knew there were other women like this. Could you find out for me?'

'Let me think.'

They started walking again in silence, Margaret trying to come to terms with the revelation. It had revolted her, but her sense of fairness made her recognise that it was no fault of Jo's. She had done nothing wrong and was appalled at her discovery. What bad luck to be born with such a problem.

After a while, Margaret said, 'I'll tell you what I think I could do. Suppose I went to the Welfare Officer and made out I was worried about one of my own girls. If it's not unusual, she would know.'

'Oh, would you really? It would be such a help. I'm sure Celia doesn't know anything about it either – and I shan't tell her, unless she realises.'

When Margaret saw the Welfare Officer it was assumed that she had heard from Brian and was applying for leave.

'No, Ma'am. In fact I'm worried about one of my girls. She asked me to see you but not to give her name. I feel I must respect her

223

confidence. She's very upset and I think you may be able to help.'

'If she's pregnant,' the Officer said dryly, 'she can't keep it a secret for long.'

But when Margaret had explained, she exclaimed, 'Well, that's a new one on me. I've never been asked about it before but, of course, it's not unusual. We don't get much of it – not that we know about – in the Wrens. We have our suspicions sometimes, but it's illegal and anyone caught would get dismissed from the Service.'

Caught? Doing what? thought Margaret, but she only said, 'It will be a relief to her to know she's not alone. She's a nice girl really.'

The Officer smiled and suddenly became confidential.

'As a matter of fact, I come from a little village where there are a couple of women living quietly together and causing no offence to anyone. They are an asset to the community and are respected. I doubt if most of the villagers realise that they're lesbians – no-one thinks anything of two women living together. It's unfortunate for such people, as society doesn't consider them normal, but you can reassure your friend that she's not alone.'

So it had a name. Then it could not be so very unusual. The main thing, apparently, was never to admit it. As the Officer had said, people were not suspicious about two women living together, when ignorance on the subject was so widespread.

Jo's reaction was the same as Margaret's when she heard all that her friend had discovered.

'But what is it that I'm not supposed to do? I can't drop Celia without an explanation and that might be worse. I don't want her to worry like me – and perhaps she isn't like me, anyway. It may be more like a schoolgirl pash in her case. But it's a relief to know I'm not a freak.'

* * * * *

When Pamela was told that she had a male visitor she thought that it might be her brother, Jack. His unit had been evacuated early from the shambles of Dunkirk and he was still somewhere in England, fretting, like all the rest of the Army, because he couldn't take a crack at Jerry. But the person waiting for her was a tall man in the uniform of a Naval Officer. Douglas. He came to her with a warm smile and hand outstretched. For a moment neither spoke.

224

They had not met since Jean's death and it was difficult for both of them to know what to say.

'Douglas, I'm so sorry about Jean,' she said at last.

'Yes, I know. They told me how upset you were. I'm sorry I didn't see you, but I was in Norway at the time. I'd like to talk to you. Could you come out with me when you're free?'

'I'd love to. Tonight would be possible.'

She was going to the pictures with some of the girls. Deanna Durbin was on, but she could go later in the week and she would easily find someone to go with her.

He took her to an Officers' Club in Liverpool, where she had a meal such as she had not had since the war started. There might be a shortage of food, but all the best was reserved for the Forces personnel who were in the gravest danger.

It soon became apparent that all he really wanted of her was to hear about Jean. Well, she thought, I owe him that this time.

'I know, roughly, what her work was. Did she ever talk about it to you?' he asked earnestly.

'Not much. Just said that it was interesting, and sometimes quite exciting. But, of course, anything they got in cipher would be hush-hush anyway.'

'As you say – and she would have been good at keeping secrets. What did you do when you went out together? You saw a lot of her, didn't you?'

'Yes, whenever we were both free,' said Pam. 'Mostly we went to the pictures, but if there were ENSA shows – or even amateur ones – on our ships, we both went.'

'Didn't you go dancing?'

'I did. I love it. But Jean wouldn't.' Pam eyed him speculatively and wondered if she should continue. She decided he would probably be pleased, so she went on, 'She'd never been used to it at home. I think the church frowned on dance halls, and she said she didn't want any man's arms around her but yours.'

The colour burned up in the handsome face and the eyes looked unnaturally bright. After a minute, he said, 'Thank you for telling me. It sounds like Jean. We went to the Tower in Blackpool when we were on honeymoon. She was reluctant at first, but I persuaded her that it wasn't a den of iniquity and she was really enjoying it by the time we left.'

'I'd love to do that. I haven't been as far as Blackpool yet.'

225

'You haven't? Why ever not? It's not that far. I'll take you on my next leave.'

'Would you really? I'll look forward to that.'

And even though the talk went back to Jean, Pamela clung to that promise as they said goodnight.

Celia and Maureen were just closing up the NAAFI when the siren went. For some reason it sounded louder than usual. The high-pitched wavering shriek seemed to go on and on. There was a sudden 'crump' as a bomb hit the ground some distance away. Then they heard aircraft getting nearer.

'Hell, Pompey's going to catch it tonight.' Maureen had hardly got the words out when a Staff Sergeant put his head in the door and shouted, 'Get down to the shelter, you girls – *now*!'

They grabbed their tin hats and ran.

The shelter was dark and crowded with ATS who were off duty. There was dead silence as they listened to the noise going on overhead – and it did seem to be right overhead. Their own guns had opened up and the ground shook.

Someone said, 'The boys'll be pleased they're getting a crack at Jerry.'

Several voices said 'Shush', as if their concentration and listening could make a difference.

Abruptly, Maureen began to scream. After a few seconds of shocked silence, they all turned on her.

'Shut up. Do you want to panic the lot of us?' and then a clear voice began to sing, 'Run, Hitler, run Hitler, run, run, run', and others took it up gratefully. It was better to hurl defiance at the enemy than to sit here listening to him.

Through her gulping sobs, Maureen muttered, 'Sorry – don't know what came over me.'

Celia squeezed her hand and said, 'You're probably better for letting it out. God knows what bottling it up will do to the rest of us when this is over. Oh, I do hope Jo and her lot are OK'

Jo, coming late off duty, collected her supper and carried it back to her cabin. One of the perks of being a Petty Officer was that she had one to herself, because she was not in the mood for company.

226

She was not an imaginative woman, but it seemed to her that the night held a special menace of which she had not been conscious during any other air raid.

Listening to the now familiar drone of heavy planes, the screeching of engines, the barking of guns and the frequent sickening sound of bombs whistling down and then hitting masonry, she was increasingly sure that she would never see Celia again.

As the all-clear sounded, the girls poured out of the stuffy shelter, taking grateful gulps of the air and finding it far from fresh. The reek of smoke and cordite hung over the whole area, but it seemed that nothing on the camp had been hit. The Junior Commander called for silence.

'We appear to have come through that with no damage to the camp, but we haven't had time to examine every hut. You may go back, but look carefully for any sign of trouble. Open doors gingerly and stand well back before going in. If you find anything that looks dangerous, report to me. I'll be in the Command Post. There will be breakfast in half an hour and then report for your usual duties.'

As they dismissed and began to drift away, Celia grabbed Maureen's arm.

'The NAAFI's been open all night! I hope nothing has disappeared yet. I'll go and lock it.'

She ran to the building and Maureen watched her open the door. The whole block appeared to totter, then it fell inwards. Mercifully for Celia, the first blow had killed her.

Jo wrote a careful letter to her parents, after much thought:

'Dear Mum and Dad,

I have something to tell you. I think you should know, but I shan't mention it again and I hope you won't either.

Someone I was very fond of has been killed. If you are hoping for grandchildren you shouldn't count on me. No doubt the boys will make it up to you.

We weren't officially engaged, so I can't get leave. I think it's probably better to be here, doing my job. I'm not very good company at the moment, but I'll see you soon.

Love, Jo.'

It was a misleading letter, but none of it was a downright lie, and it would spare them a lot of grief. Celia's death was a way out of her immediate difficulty, but never one she could welcome.

If I have to live my life without love, she thought, I must make up for it in other ways. I won't be the only one when this awful war is over.

* * * * *

Margaret, coming out of the stuffy workshop, stretched herself and took a few deep breaths of the fresh air. She had been painting all day and was generously streaked with the colours she had been using, mingled with the dust of the shop. She wanted nothing so much as a bath and a stretch out on her bunk before taking part in a ship's concert, where she was part of the chorus line. So she was not best pleased to find a signal waiting for her. She was to go at once to the office. Very well, she would go just as she was.

There was just a niggle of fear in her mood of defiance. Neither she nor his parents had heard from Brian. Surely his hospital ship would be safe? She put the worry out of her mind, but unconsciously quickened her step.

Outside the door, a man's voice behind her asked 'Margaret?' and then as she turned: 'Margaret. It *is* you.' And there was Brian, holding out his arms.

The next moment she was caught in his close embrace and he was murmuring endearments into her hair. She clung to him equally tightly, tears running down her face, so that when he eventually held her at arm's length, saying 'Let me look at you', the streaky dirt and patchy paint made him laugh aloud.

Realising what a sight she must be, Margaret laughed shakily too and murmuring, 'You might have let me get cleaned up first', went back into the comfort of his arms.

It was much later that he explained why no-one had heard from him. He had written to his parents and to her, only to hear that a mail boat had been sunk. When he received no reply to either letter, he assumed that it was his mail that was at the bottom of the sea and decided that he might as well wait and surprise them.

He had been disembarked at Liverpool, where he was

pronounced fit to proceed, fully kitted out, granted leave and given a rail warrant. He had sent his parents a telegram to say that he was safely back and was heading for Pompey first.

'So there's nothing to stop us having a long, gorgeous honeymoon. Where shall we go?'

'Do you think the Lake District would be quiet? I've always wanted to sail on Windermere. Of course, it rains a lot up there,' Margaret finished, doubtfully.

She looked up into the familiar face. He was bronzed and healthy, with a finely-honed edge about him that she found irresistible. They hadn't spoken about 'beginning again' or trying to make their marriage work. From the moment they had met again, the old magic was back, and now they had both acknowledged that the partnership was more equal than it had ever been.

He grinned at her, his eyes alight with mischief.

'Don't take that tone with me. You know perfectly well that if you want to go to Windermere, that's where we'll go. And anyhow, I don't care how much it rains. It's the perfect excuse to go to bed and make babies.'

And that was what they did.

This is Now - 6

'How do you know?' I asked Pamela at the end of our second session.

She laughed. 'Margaret told me herself. We kept in touch more than any of the others because of Jean. Then after the war most of us joined the Association of Wrens and we were able to trace people through them. But Margaret was carrying her twin boys when she came to my wedding, and she told me they had been conceived on that holiday.

'We met Violet later and that's when Margaret told us about Jo.'

'I wonder what happened to her,' I said.

'As it happens, I can tell you that too. Years later, Violet was touring Devon and she found Jo running a garden centre there. She had set up a craft centre as well – one of the first in the country – and Jo's partner was in charge of that, a pretty girl called Beryl. They seemed very content.'

'Well, thank you for your time and telling me all this, but I haven't heard much about your own war.'

'Not much to tell,' mused Pamela. 'I spent all my time servicing the radios for the Fleet Air Arm. We had one or two dicey incidents – plenty of bombing round the docks, but lots of fun too. I wouldn't have missed it for anything. I fell for a married pilot but he didn't survive all his operations. Not unusual – it happened to scores of girls.

'Then Douglas came home on leave and asked me to marry him. I was still missing Frank and I thought – no, I don't suppose I did think, it was all feelings then – so I felt we might as well console each other. I didn't kid myself that he was over Jean, so I didn't think I was cheating him. It was a mad time, you know – fellows and girls in such close proximity all the time – and just when nature goes rampant, and there was always the thought that you or he might have a very short life.

'So I married Douglas. We got one of the 48-hour licences that you could get then. I felt quite excited and very proud to have such a handsome man. Then I discovered that he was also kind and considerate. By the end of the war, I was glad he had survived and we ended up having a happy marriage – perhaps happier than the ones who were madly in love. He died fourteen years ago and I still miss him every day.

'There – that's as much as I'm going to tell you about me.'

'I suppose you wouldn't come back to Norfolk with me and meet Helen?' I asked. 'She was so anxious to know what happened to Jean. I'm sure she'd like to see you.'

Pamela shook her head. 'Oh no, she wouldn't. I couldn't tell her any more than I've told you. It would only make her unhappy.'

I got up to go, but a sudden thought struck me. 'You have a gift for telling a story. Did you ever do anything with your writing?'

'I've had a few children's books published. I write under the name of Elaine Woods.' She smiled as she saw recognition in my eyes. 'Why, I do believe you've heard of me.'

'Heard of you? I was brought up on the Star Bush stories!'

On the train from Liverpool Street to Norwich, I thought about the books that Pamela had written. They were set in the countryside of my childhood. It seemed idealised now, but would have been valid for when she started them. Even twenty years ago, when I was reading them, there was enough rural life for me to find them authentic.

The children who had found the magic Star Bush and learned so much more about their surroundings than the grown-ups knew had taught me a great deal about my heritage – all forgotten now, and most of it gone. Or so I told myself. Yet my spirits rose with every mile as the train left the suburbs behind.

When I returned from London, the local paper was full of a story about two men who had had a run-in with three badger diggers. One of them was Simon. He was still sporting a multi-coloured right eye and a sprained wrist when he delivered some trees for Aunt Julia. Seeing him wince as he lifted his burden from the truck, I went out to him.

'Can I help?'

'Thanks. My shoulder's a bit stiff still.'

I picked up a pear tree and a cherry tree and asked, 'What happened?'

He grinned. 'Didn't anybody tell you I'm the hero of the hour? Look, let's get these into the back garden then I'll give you the whole story.'

Aunt Julia came out as we went through the side gate with the trees. 'Oh, Simon. Thank you. How are you? Come and have some tea and you can tell me what to do with them. Well, of course, I know we've got to plant them, but tell me how to treat them ...'

But Simon interrupted her flow. 'I'm filthy. It's good honest muck, but you don't want it in the house.'

So once again, it was to the summerhouse that we went. Uncle Reg got his instructions about the fruit trees and then asked, 'Now tell us what really happened the other night. I heard something from Ronnie, but he was on his way to the doctor and couldn't stay talking.'

Simon thought for a moment, then said, 'Jan doesn't know the area, so I'd better explain. We are next to the Woodhouse Farm. There's a badger sett in an old orchard which borders their furthest field. Ronnie Woodhouse was coming back across the fields late one night. He'd taken his girl back home to Holt, where he had left his bike, but he got a puncture on the way back, so he was pushing it across the short cut to the farm when he heard a noise. He stopped and crept along till he saw two young badgers digging out a new sett, so he sat down and watched them. Then he could see that their parents were outside an old sett, further up the bank. He told me about it and we arranged to go the next night. It was so fascinating that we stayed till it was nearly light. The two young cubs seemed ever so pleased with themselves, playing and bickering, but still getting on with the job and quite nasty to the parents if they came near. That was three or four months ago and we've been back a few times since then.'

He paused. His lips tightened and his eyes looked menacing, then the expression was gone as quickly as it had come. He relaxed and continued: 'Ronnie came and knocked me up about two on Monday morning. He'd seen lights over by the orchard and guessed someone was out after the badgers. He had a pair of sporting guns, but we thought they might have dogs with them, so we phoned the police and the RSPCA before we left. Good job we did.

'We found a car under a stand of trees and it had gun cases in

232

it. We thought of waiting for reinforcements, but when we heard an animal cry out in pain, we both started forward, shouting at the top of our voices to get them to stop. There were three men with lanterns and nets, but they were just about to run off – I suppose not knowing how many we were. Then one of them turned and took a pot shot at us. Ronnie was quick. He got the man in the arm and he dropped the gun, but by then the others had realised that there were only the two of us and they came back.

'Then I saw the badger. It was a big old male with its stomach ripped out. I was so mad – I don't remember what happened really. I know I sprained my wrist when I wrested a gun away from one of them, and I'm sorry to say I shot one of the lurchers, but it was him or me. They were men of about forty – no-one from round here. Poor old Ronnie ended up with a broken arm, though he did knock one of them out.

'The two others belted off and we heard the car start up. When the man came round we tied him to a tree. By the time the RSPCA turned up they had nothing to do but bury the badger. They took the nets as evidence and they're going to prosecute the man we caught.'

'What about the car? Did you get the number?'

'Yes, we took that when we first saw it, but it had been stolen and the police found it abandoned in Birmingham. They've got a good description of the men and they'll have a few distinguishing marks on them, so they may be found – though I doubt it. Ronnie did most of the damage to them. I suppose I was lucky to get off so lightly.'

I took a deep breath, then I said, 'But you're crazy – both of you – risking your life for animals. It's stupid.'

Simon said in a toneless voice, 'My God, you're hard. Have you ever seen a badger?'

'No, and I don't care how cuddly they are – they're still only animals and not worth a man's life.'

Uncle Reg said gently, 'You'll have to forgive her, Simon. She's been in London too long.'

'They're animals, they're not all sweet and cuddly – not by a long chalk,' insisted Simon. 'They have to learn to survive in the animal world, but it's obscene that so-called human beings should be their worst enemies. We have so much more power than them – and for what? A few pounds for a badger skin – perhaps a good bit for a stuffed one. Blood money.'

I turned indignantly to Uncle Reg. 'London has nothing to do with it. It's a matter of common sense. Most people in this country are silly about animals – we've got a name for it, haven't we? Other people think we're mad and I'm inclined to agree with them.'

Simon got up, thanked Aunt Julia for the tea and strode off without a backward look. Uncle Reg gazed after him and shook his head.

'That man amazes me. He sounds so calm, even when he's furious, but Ronnie told me he went mad when he saw the torn badger. It was Simon who knocked the man out – not Ronnie – and using the most original language he'd ever heard.'

'Simon swore?'

'Like a trooper – and then some – or so Ronnie says.'

'Well, that makes me think a bit better of him,' I conceded, 'but I still think they were fools to have gone.'

We were having tea when the peace was disturbed by a harsh, loud croaking. Uncle Reg inclined his head and Aunt Julia said, 'There he is.' I watched in disbelief as a handsome pheasant came running across the lawn towards us. My uncle went out of the french windows and bent down to the bird, making little clucking noises and saying, 'Are you hungry? Come on then.'

The bird retreated, then stopped as he passed it on his way to the bird feeder at the end of the garden, then it went after him with quite a turn of speed and waited by the food bin. Uncle Reg scattered some seed on the ground and the bird started to feed.

'What a beautiful creature. I shouldn't think he'll stand much chance when the guns come out,' I said.

'We don't know of any being bred round here. Reggie thinks they may be wild ones. He's brought a couple of hens down with him, but they'll only feed if he's on his own. It's been going on for a few days now and Reggie is as pleased as a mother hen.

'Oh, and I've got a message for you from Helen,' added Julia. 'There's a speaker on at a WI near Norwich tomorrow who she thinks you should hear. A woman who flew Spitfires during the war.'

'What! I never heard of such a thing.'

'Well, I don't know. But Helen says she's talked to them before about her life abroad after the war, and she's quite lively, though she's over ninety. Doreen says she'll take us and Helen.'

Betty White was tall and slim. She held herself upright and the pure white hair framed a healthily tanned face. Only a slight scragginess round the neck showed a sign of her age. The word that came to my mind as she rose to speak was 'indestructible'.

The chairman had said, 'Betty needs no introduction' and she didn't bother with one, going straight to the beginning of the story. Her voice was surprisingly clear and a little harsh for her age, but she was obviously used to public speaking and soon had us laughing.

'It was in 1935 that the Government announced a scheme to train young people to fly. It was something I had wanted to do ever since I went to an air show with my father when I was about sixteen.

'I don't suppose any of you here are old enough to remember Clem Sohn?'

'Oh yes, we are!' said all three of my companions.

'Oh, good. Did you see him come out of that plane and fly with his artificial wings for quite a while before he opened his parachute? The Birdman, they called him. I saw him several times and it was always exciting when you got the first glimpse of him. Of course, he killed himself in the end. I don't know whether his experiments helped the progress of aviation, but he certainly gave me the flying bug.

'The only snag was that lessons cost five pounds an hour in those days and I was earning twelve and six a week. What's that in new money? About sixty two pence, I suppose.

'Well, when they announced that the Civil Air Guard would train us for two and six an hour, I jumped at it.'

Betty looked round us all and seemed to realise for the first time that there were men in the audience, which happened sometimes if there was a good speaker on and the women had been allowed to invite their menfolk. A mischievous smile lit her face.

'Well, gentlemen, I'm sorry if I offend you, but I'm certain in my own mind that the powers-that-were had meant to specify Young Men, but they had said Young People, so the flying instructors got the shock of their lives when some girls turned up. Most of them were horrible to us – Army Sergeants had nothing on them – and they said to our faces that girls wouldn't be any good.

'I told one of them straight that if he couldn't teach us it was a reflection on him. I was always one to speak my mind. It didn't make me popular, but it stood me in good stead when there were so many bloody-minded little pip-squeaks about. They had power for the first time in their lives and behaved like little Hitlers.'

She paused and there was a murmur of agreement from Doreen and some of the men.

'Ah, some of you know what I'm talking about. Well, we were given dungarees and forage caps and learned to fly on high-wing planes. I used to cycle six miles to the aerodrome. The Government subsidised the little flying clubs – they were all on grass, of course, but the Piper Cubs were literally tied up with piano wire and it often happened that there were none operational for miles around. I've spent many an afternoon grinding valves to fix them when I should have been flying.'

She paused briefly, but not to consult notes. I could see only one, very yellow, piece of paper in front of her. She was trained to do circuits and bumps, which I took to mean flying round the airfield and landing, and was supervised to do cross-country flights. After eight hours, she went solo. To get her licence she had to fly a figure of eight between two church towers with observers at these points. After fifteen hours' flying time she was licenced to fly any single-engined aircraft at between 1000 and 2000 feet.

Here she picked up the yellow paper.

'This is my full pilot's licence, and it's never been revoked. Theoretically, I could fly Concorde.'

She waited for the murmurs of appreciation to subside and then continued: 'All very well, but it was followed by years of frustration. When the war broke out, I went up to the Air Ministry in Kingsway to volunteer for flying duties and met the snootiest WAAF Officer I've ever encountered, before or since. She informed me in an icy voice that the RAF had plenty of pilots and that no woman would *ever* be allowed to fly.

'Suitably chastened, I went back to my life as a typist, but I wasn't going to let one supercilious woman put me off and I kept bombarding the Air Ministry with applications at regular intervals.

'At first they only wanted people with a thousand hours' flying time and I had just twenty-one. But their need was increasing and their flying time requirement was gradually reduced. As they came down, I kept crediting myself with more time and we met around two hundred hours, when I was accepted as an Air Training Auxiliary.'

Here she threw up her hands in a gesture of triumph and we all applauded.

'Well, that was all right, but I still wasn't flying. Oh, no. We had

236

to learn all the theory before they would let us loose on aircraft. Meteorology, orienteering and all about the insides of the engines – and a fat lot of good that did me! Just you wait and I'll tell you what we had to help us – or rather, what we didn't have.

'We were licenced to fly all single engined aircraft, though it was mostly Tiger Moths and Piper Cubs at first. Then I went on to Harvards and did my solo on a Hurricane – circuits and bumps again. I had one Instructor who was a first-class bastard.'

There was something between a gasp and a laugh from the audience. Such language from such an old lady!

But Doreen murmured, 'We all learned to swear like troopers in the ATS. I had to watch it when I got home.'

Betty White was unmoved. 'Well, he *was* a bastard. He used to carry a ruler and rap you over the knuckles with it if you made a mistake. Anyway, I qualified as a Class Two ferry pilot and was able to fly anything except four-engined jobs – I didn't want to go on them, too much like driving a bus.

'So I might get an assignment to pick up a Spitfire from a workshop in Manchester and fly it to an airbase in the Cotswolds. Which was fine, only I'd never flown a Spit. before. I was always scared rigid anyway, on all the assignments. There were so many hazards. Now I'll tell you what we had. An Ordnance map and a compass. No radio, no contact of any kind once you were off the ground, until you landed.'

She paused and Julia said, 'That took some guts. Better her than me.'

'The drill was that you went to the office and marked your route on your map with a bit of string. Then you found out how much you had to adjust for magnetic north. Lastly, you went to the Met Office to see which way the wind was blowing.

'Take off was a nightmare. You had to open the throttle, get the wheels up and get your map out, all at the same time and with only one pair of hands. Then you prayed that little wood you'd seen on the map was still in the same position – otherwise, especially in Spits. and Hurricanes, you could get very lost in three minutes.

'They were lovely planes to fly – the old Spitfires and Hurricanes. You knew they'd never let you down and they never did. I'm not surprised our Fighter pilots got so fond of them. No, it was only yourself with dicey maps, foul weather and only two hands that got you into trouble. Strictly, we weren't allowed to fly unless the weather was clear and we could see the ground, but the Met Office didn't have all the answers and I've been caught in a sudden fog over hilly country and come out not knowing where the hell I was.

'That's when you started worrying about petrol. You were only supposed to take enough for the journey – I imagine they didn't have so much they could afford to allow for mistakes. What a relief it was when you spotted a well-known landmark. The Fosse Way was the best because you could follow it for miles. I've thanked Julius Caesar for it more times than I can count – though I don't suppose it's done him any good.

'Mind you, there's nothing to beat flying all by yourself on a glorious day when you know your way and haven't a care in the world. And if you have cares, you lose them up there, what with concentrating on the job and the sheer exhilaration of flight. The sensation of being solely in charge of your plane and being full of confidence in it and in yourself – that was the best thing the war gave me.'

This was the first time she had sounded serious and it was all the more impressive for that. I thought of Florence and Margaret and all of the other girls who had found confidence in themselves during the war.

But Betty was back to her racy tone which denied her age and made you see her as a young woman again.

'Ooh, the Polish boys were lovely! They were so pleased when they got a new plane and they thought we girls were wonderful. The Brits would probably greet us with "What are you bringing us now – we've got plenty already" and then ignore you, but the Polish boys would lift you down, take your parachute and the rest of your clobber back to the mess and make a fuss of you.'

She was back in that world again. She rolled her eyes in ecstasy and was rewarded by our laughter.

'I've had to land a few times because of shortage of petrol, but I usually found my way all right. But then we had the fear of invasion and they started camouflaging everything.

'The first time I got really lost was over a field in Lincoln. I was flying a Hurricane and the petrol was a bit low. I knew I couldn't be far away, but all I could see was a field of cows. I looked at my map and then at the petrol gauge and decided I'd better land anyway.

'Suddenly, from a barn in one corner the RAF appeared – and started to move the cardboard cows!'

238

She sat down to laughter and warm applause.

In the interval I spoke to her. 'No, they didn't all operate like me. I knew one girl who was in a squadron of eight, operating Tiger Moths, but that was at the beginning. Later on, she used to requisition parts and then fly them out for the ground crew to mend their own planes. The Yanks couldn't understand that. If they pranged one, they just got another – never bothered to even try to fix them. "Plenty more where they come from," they used to say. The most wasteful country on earth.

'I had a boyfriend who used to go over to the American bases, looking for spare parts. They thought he was mad.'

There was a little group waiting to speak to her, so I hurriedly explained about my novel. 'I haven't written about the WAAF yet. Do you know anyone I could interview?'

But she said that she didn't, so I moved away.

There was a beautifully groomed woman, tall and fair, who looked about sixty. She moved with me, took me by the arm and said, 'Will I do? I was on barrage balloons, if you're interested.'

'You?' I said, and then, 'Sorry, that sounded rude, but you look far too young.'

'Thank you, but I'm seventy-five. My name is Kate Raybould.'

That Was Then - Kate's Story

It seemed to the three girls that they had always been together. Living in the same backwater near Wimbledon Common, they had gone to the little church school near the golf course. Then they had joined the Brownies and, in due course, the Guides. They belonged to the Girls' Bible Class at their church and, together with other members, they started the rambling club. In the 1930s everyone rambled or hiked. Together they explored most of Surrey; Guildford, the Hogs Back, Friday Street with its beautiful lake, Abinger Hammer, where watercress grew in the river. Then there were Box Hill and Leith Hill and Epsom, where there was a steep climb from the railway station and then the reward of the windswept Downs where you could walk right across to Headley.

On this Saturday in June 1939 they had hiked across Wimbledon Common to Roehampton on their way to Richmond Park.

Judy Mason, tall, long-limbed and with the rangy body of an athlete, strode out ahead with some of the older girls. Kate and Eve didn't mind. She would wait for them at the 'grub stop'.

Little Eve, inclined to plumpness, stumped along resolutely and turned her big, brown eyes on Kate.

'Isn't Judy marvellous? She's got so much energy and she's so good at sports. I wonder if that's what she'll go in for.'

'I think that would be a waste of her education. But you're right. She's a marvellous runner and swimmer – and bright too. Not fair, is it?' But Kate didn't sound at all perturbed.

Judy had won a scholarship to a secondary school and had just taken her School Certificate. They were all waiting for the results, but the girls knew there would be no question of her going on to university, even if she got Matric. Her parents just couldn't afford to support her after she was seventeen.

They were all working-class girls and Eve was an under-housemaid in one of the big houses on the Common, where her father was employed as a chauffeur. Kate had managed to get a job in a hairdressing saloon, where she was supposed to be getting training. Her fair good looks had got her the position, but the training was sketchy and she had really wanted to work in the open air.

'It's nice that Judy hasn't gone off with her other clever friends at that school – a lot of them are toffee-nosed,' Kate mused, 'but she hasn't got a bit like that.'

'Oh, Kate, could you see her father if she did! He'd soon cut her down to size. I never knew anybody so proud of being working-class as him.'

'My dad says that's because he's a good tradesman. He did his seven years as an apprentice and he's entitled to call himself a bricklayer. Dad says he wishes he had a trade.'

Kate's father sold insurance and collected the payments every week. It wasn't the easiest of jobs with money so tight that he dared not miss a week or he would never have been paid, but Eve thought he was clever to be able to balance his books and said so.

They turned in to Richmond Park and came up with the leaders by the pool, where they were preparing to eat their sandwiches.

'Slowcoaches,' Judy teased them, tossing her long auburn hair out of her eyes as she looked up at them affectionately. 'Mary and Grace have been talking about joining up as soon as war is declared.'

'Perhaps it'll all blow over, like last year,' Eve said, but there was no conviction in her tone. Nobody thought we could go on appeasing the Germans for ever.

Mary said, 'My brother's been teaching me to drive. He says they'll want women drivers for all sorts of jobs when the men start to go. I think he was thinking about grocery deliveries, but if I'm going to do that I'd sooner do it in the Forces.'

Eve squeezed Judy's arm. 'My dad's teaching me, but I don't know if I'll ever have the nerve to drive in traffic.'

'Of course you will. Aren't you lucky to have somebody who's got the loan of a car? I wish I had the chance.'

Kate was silent. She was wondering how soon the three of them would be separated.

None of the trio was eighteen when the war was declared, but Judy had already heard that she had gained her School Certificate and, shortly after, that she had also passed the Civil Service entrance examination. She went into the Ministry of Health at Acton in November and found that all the talk was of the office being evacuated out of London.

Reluctantly, she had opted for a job with office hours, feeling that it would leave her ample time for sport, but within a few weeks she was having to work overtime, getting home at about 8.30pm and with no time to do more than see Eve or Kate.

'Gosh, you've got a shiner! Mum told me you'd had a fall – what happened?' she asked Eve one night.

'Fell over a kerb in the blackout.' Eve lifted her determined little chin and Judy saw that half the square face was covered in bruises. The right eye was surrounded by a purple-going-yellow stain which had prompted her comment.

'Lucky you didn't break your nose,' Judy said.

Eve looked at her ruefully and raised a bandaged hand. 'Only at the expense of a sprained wrist. I put my hand out to save myself. Well, it is better than a broken nose – and there are plenty of people worse off than me.'

Despite the judicious use of torches, there were many accidents in the pitch dark during that first winter of the war.

When she had commiserated with Eve, Judy told her about the arrangements for the office evacuation.

'We're going to a place known as XJ and Lord Haw Haw says it's Blackpool. Some of the older girls have been there on holiday and they hope he's right. They say the beach is lovely and there's the pleasure beach and two big dance halls, but nobody knows whether they'll be open if we start getting bombed.'

'What does your mum say? You're too young to leave home?'

'No. She says I've been taught what's right and wrong and I'm not daft, so I'll be all right if I use my commonsense. I was a bit surprised, but it's nice to know she trusts me.'

'And your dad?'

'Oh, you might guess. He says I should try it for six months and if I hate it, I can resign, but it's a good job with a pension and he thinks I should stick it. Can you imagine – thinking of pensions at our age – and with a war on!' The girls laughed.

Kate's reaction was similar and she said, 'Well, I expect they think you'll be safer out of London, but it looks as if you'll be the first to break up the trio.'

As it happened, she was very nearly wrong.

Maud Bishop was the cook at the house where Eve worked and

they got on well. Eve enjoyed cooking, having been taught by her mother, and she was never averse to giving Maud a hand when there was a big 'do' on. Maud was twenty-six and it seemed to Eve that she had been engaged forever to Leslie Head, who had been employed by the gas company until he had joined the RAF as soon as the war broke out. Now it seemed that the two were affected by the sense of urgency that was hitting the country, where marriages were taking place in unprecedented numbers and all the local papers were full of wedding pictures.

Just before Christmas, Maud told Eve, 'Leslie's due for leave in January and we're getting married.' She waited for Eve's congratulations, then continued, 'and you'll never guess what comes next. Go on, have a guess.'

'He's going to take you somewhere exotic for your honeymoon?'

'Yeah. Like Ramsgate. No, I'm going to join the WAAF.'

'What for? You won't be able to stay with him, will you?'

'Shouldn't think so, but he says it's a good life. Plenty of company, good food, and he's better off than he was in civvy street. I reckon I will be too. I know I get the rate for the job, but it's pretty awful if you stop to think of it.'

'Have you told Mrs. Rose yet?'

'No. I'll let her have her Christmas in peace. How would you like me to put in a word for you?'

Eve laughed. 'Can you see Marjorie's face? The head housemaid, having a cook my age over her! She'd have a fit.'

But when she broached the subject at home, her mother encouraged her to try for it.

'There's one thing. If Mrs. Rose is awkward, you needn't worry about your dad's job. He won't be staying after Mr.. Rose gets his commission in the Army. I don't know what's going to happen to us. It's hard enough now.'

'Maud says Leslie's better off in the RAF. P'raps Dad should think about joining up as a driver – they're bound to want them,' Eve said thoughtfully. 'Would you hate it too much?'

'I'd hate it, I suppose, but he's under forty. He might get called up anyway.' She looked wistful and then said truthfully, 'It would be nice not to have to scrimp so much. Both the boys grow out of clothes and boots so fast. I don't think we'll ever be straight till they stop growing – and even then.'

'I wish I could help more, Mum. You're not in debt, are you?'

'No. Well, only to the tallyman, but I do hate paying him so much a week – and only able to go to a few shops with the Provident cheque. I'm sure I could get clothes cheaper if we could afford to pay for them outright.' Then she smiled up into Eve's troubled face. 'But don't worry, dear. We'll manage – we always have. I know you would help more if you could, but that few shillings you get are little enough. You ought to have some pleasure at your age.'

When Maud gave in her notice, Mrs. Rose sent for Eve. She was a slight, rather nervous woman whose one object in life was to keep up with her friends.

'Maud tells me you want to take her position, Eve, but I've told her it is quite out of the question. You're only seventeen – you must see it's impossible.'

'I'm eighteen next month, Madam – and Maud will have told you that I can do the work.'

'I'm sorry, but we couldn't possibly employ someone as young as that as a cook. It wouldn't look right.'

She's imagining what her friends will say, Eve thought, but I won't stay on now Maud's shown me another way. She said spiritedly, 'Well Madam, there's a war on and you may find it difficult to get another cook, but if you're sure you don't want me, I'll give you a week's notice now.'

'But ... but, you won't stay on as you are? I didn't expect this. What will you do? I can't give you a good reference if you leave me like this.'

'No matter. I shall volunteer as a cook for the WAAF and join up with Maud.'

She turned away and made for the door. Behind her, Mrs. Rose was moaning quietly, 'But what shall I do with both of you gone?'

When Kate heard Eve's news, she had no hesitation.

'Well, that settles it. I'm fed up with Caroline. I should be on perms by now, but I'm still doing shampoos and washing basins. I'll come with you.'

1940 had come in with the worst weather for forty years, so it was in a blizzard that Maud, Eve and Kate went to volunteer for the WAAF, but their spirits were high when they learned that they would all go together to a camp near Gloucester.

244

The journey was painfully slow, the railway carriage freezing and there was only a snow-filled sky and the white fields to be seen. Maud, who was thin and had little in the way of winter clothes, was shivering for most of the journey.

'I hope our uniform will be warmer than the one I wore at home. Those big coats look as though they weigh a ton, but I could do with one now.'

'Go on,' Eve said teasingly, 'don't tell us Leslie never put his coat round you. You must know how much they weigh.'

Maud blushed, then laughed, 'As a matter of fact we put it on our bed. It doesn't sound very romantic, I know, but we were glad of it. What a day we chose to get married. My father looked like a snowman by the time he'd finished snapping us.'

The girls all loved the uniforms once they had smartened them up. Though they laughed at the 'blackouts' – knickers with elasticated legs – and the heavy lisle stockings, even these were acceptable as the freezing cold weather continued. But, without exception, they detested the heavy lace-up shoes which were stiff and cold.

'These blooming clodhoppers have given me chilblains,' Kate complained. 'I never had them in my life before.'

Soon several of the girls were afflicted as they were forced to march everywhere with shoes that rubbed the affected heels raw and left them bleeding. The MO was unsympathetic and told them the trouble would disappear as soon as the shoes got worn in.

'After we've got worn out,' Maud said. 'I wonder if the men have this problem.'

As Gloucester was only an initial reception centre, they were just there for a few days. After they were kitted up and taught how to clean their buttons and badges the rest of the time was spent attending lectures. These ranged from air raid precautions to the dangers of VD, which left some of them feeling sick and even more puzzled. Most of the younger women had never heard of it before and when they understood the majority felt insulted.

'How dare they assume we aren't respectable girls. It's disgusting!' the redhead exploded as soon as they got away from the lecture room.

'Maud,' Kate asked, 'do you know if we're in any danger? Could decent girls catch this?'

Maud swallowed her embarrassment and let them all ask her questions. She was the oldest of the group and the only married woman.

'I don't know all the answers,' she said frankly, 'but I'm sure no decent girl would come to any harm. Kisses are allowed if you're fond of the person, but don't let it go any further until you're married.'

'I suppose,' Eve said tentatively, 'it doesn't seem so disgusting when you're in love.'

'It's not disgusting at all, Eve. Far from it. It just seems natural to be together and to give each other ... no, I can't explain it. Love is the key and respect for each other. I expect your mothers all told you that men won't respect you if you're too easy and they certainly won't marry you.'

Chris, a fresh-faced girl with bright blue eyes, laid her hand on Maud's arm.

'I want to thank you for myself, and I should think, for everybody. My mother told me something, but I hadn't the nerve to ask her questions.'

There was a chorus of agreement as the session broke up.

Kate said to Eve, as they prepared for bed, 'I'm sure Maud is right and that the men respect decent girls, but personally, I hope I've always got too much respect *for myself* to fall into any traps.'

After Gloucester, the girls were posted for their initial training to Morecambe. If anything, the journey was even more trying, with unexplained waits along the line and two hours stuck at Preston. They were in compartments and corridors crammed with other troops and hemmed in with full kit, but at least it helped to keep them warm until they all bailed out at Preston station. By the time their train came in they were all thoroughly 'browned off' and even the usual comedians had given up trying to raise a smile. But Eve and Kate had a consolation.

'Do you realise,' Kate said when their destination was known, 'that we'll only be a few miles from Blackpool? Judy, here we come!'

She had beaten them by just a few weeks and they had her address.

'She'll get the surprise of her life when she hears from us.'

But nothing prepared them for the ferocity of the snow-laden wind coming straight off the sea. The journey to camp had them huddling up together for warmth, while they kept their heads well down to protect their faces and eyes.

The mess hall was bleak and the reheated food unappetising. The cooks had prepared it for the time the train was due to arrive and they were nearly as browned off as the new arrivals, having waited around for them for so long.

It was left to the Corporal to cheer them up.

'You'll be billeted out. They are mostly boarding houses, used to taking visitors, so they'll be comfortable. If you get a duff one, let me know. We pay them well to look after you, so you should get hot baths without any argument. Don't let them charge you extra.

'You report here every morning and get your meals in your billet. Within reason, we try to keep friends together.'

She added a few general instructions and then took them into town.

Kate and her friends were joined by Chris and her sister, Lena. They were as close as twins and their one dread was that they might be separated. They were both rather shy and no-one had got to know them yet, but since the night of Maud's question session, they seemed to regard her as a mother figure and had asked whether they might join her.

'Five of you?' The Corporal consulted her list. 'Mrs. Pendry, Sea View – she's still got some commercial travellers in, but she can do two double rooms and a single.'

Their landlady was on the watch for them. She took one look at their frozen faces and quickly ushered them into a large room where there was a blazing fire.

'I was beginning to think you wouldn't arrive tonight. Warm yourselves up before I show you your rooms.'

The girls crowded round gratefully. It was the best welcome they had had since they left home.

By the time Judy knew that her friends were in Morecambe, she was beginning to get used to her new life. Like them, she was in a small bed and breakfast hotel and had been told that she was free to find other accommodation if she wished. Apart from stopping twenty-one shillings from her weekly wage of two pounds, ten shillings, the Civil Service took no other interest in her domestic arrangements. Her lodgings were near the Cliffs Hotel where she worked and this, she decided, was a bonus in the bitterly cold weather.

She shared a bedroom with Beryl Davis. They had been friends since they started work on the same day and found that they shared several interests, especially walking and skating.

'I wonder if there's a skating rink here,' Beryl said, as they settled into their bedroom on the first night.

'Bound to be,' Judy replied absently. She was busy testing the beds and making sure the light worked. 'These beds seem comfortable, but I think we'll have to take it in turns to put out that light by the door. I don't fancy getting out of a warm bed to do that.'

'I brought my torch. Didn't you bring one? You'll need it if you go out at night.'

Beryl sat on one of the beds and looked round the room. There was a white painted chest of drawers and, across one corner, a rail with coathangers behind a floral curtain. The two single beds took up most of the rest of the room. Judy caught her eye and smiled.

'It's a bit sparse, but we might be able to find somewhere nicer later on.'

'If the landlady's reasonable and the food's good, this will do me.'

The next morning they went to see their office. It was quite an imposing hotel, with a wide foyer and several black radiators against the walls. They made straight for one of these and warmed their hands, while they waited for someone to tell them which room they were in. But some of the bedrooms had not yet been converted to offices.

Alerted by a sudden movement of heads as everyone gazed upwards, they looked towards the wide staircase. Coming down it were three men, all looking embarrassed, as they clutched a bouquet of chamber pots in each hand. There was a shocked silence, then someone tittered and suddenly there was a roar of laughter in which the men joined. It made a good start to their first day.

As soon as they could, Kate and Eve went to Blackpool. It had stopped snowing, but the wind was still fierce. Gladly, they turned off the sea-front and into the road where Judy's billet was situated.

'I know, the wind's awful,' agreed Judy when she saw them.

'Come and warm up. I came up this road and on to the sea-front yesterday and couldn't move. Luckily, there were some soldiers there, for the sole purpose of catching us as we came round the corner. Golly, it may be all right in summer, but it's diabolical just now.'

She wanted to know all they had been doing and commented, 'Better you than me. I hate the idea of being regimented. It's quite a good set-up here. You can find your own digs and share with who you like. This is good. My landlady's a motherly type with two daughters younger than us, and both nice girls. We work in a hotel along the front – oh, I must tell you – such a hoot! They were still clearing some of the bedrooms when we arrived. Talk about timing. Just as we went in the door, three men came down the stairs carrying chamber pots. I don't know who was most embarrassed – them or us. Then someone started to laugh and we all howled.'

'What are you finding to do? Are any of the seaside attractions open?' Maud asked.

'They all are – except the summer ones. I went to a variety show at the Palace. That changes programmes every week and they get some top people. I saw Cyril Fletcher. You can dance at the Palace too, on the same ticket.'

'You haven't been to any dances though, have you?' Eve sounded shocked. Her evangelical church tended to look on dance halls as haunts of the devil.

'Well, no, I haven't yet, but all the girls here do. They think I'm weird. I might try it once and see what I think.'

They talked until it was time to catch the tram back to Morecambe.

'It's a pity you're only here for three weeks,' said Judy. 'We could have some fun when the weather gets better. I'll tell you what though. We've found a nice little restaurant in town – I'll treat you to a meal before you go away.'

Despite the weather, the girls enjoyed their stay in Morecambe, but they realised that, being off camp, they were not experiencing service conditions.

'And a good job, too,' Eve said, surveying the scene outside from the window of the warm dining-room where they were having breakfast. This was being served by Mr.. Pendry, a thick-set, balding man, who was used to working with his wife in the guesthouse all summer. He spent the winter making repairs and renovations and sometimes picking up an odd job. They also went abroad for part of the winter, usually to Spain, as he told the girls at length.

'That'll be over now for the duration,' he said, 'but mustn't grumble – we had some good times. Once—'

'Sorry, we've got to rush,' Kate interrupted him. 'Get jankers if we're late on parade.'

The days were packed with lectures, drill and PT. In the evenings, they wrote letters home, washed their hair and their undies, saw Judy and, weather permitting, went to the Palace of Varieties in Blackpool. They enjoyed the aptitude tests, which ranged from reading to quick reaction exercises. Eve did well in the driving test, sitting in front of a simulated fast moving road and driving a pencil along it without hitting the sides as it curved and cornered sharply. Maud, to her surprise, was commended for her clear, well-modulated voice.

They had been allowed to express preferences, but without any guarantees that they would get what they wanted.

'Somewhere warmer than here,' prayed Maud, as their postings became nearer.

'Volunteer for cooking, like me. It's always warm in the cookhouse,' Eve urged her.

'Not on your nelly! Now I've got the chance, I want a change – something where I'll be of real help to the lads. I'd like to go to a squadron eventually.'

It was virtually certain that Eve would get her wish, so it was no surprise to find that she was to go on a catering course before being posted as a cook.

'Well, that'll do me,' Maud commented. 'I'll be with a squadron as soon as I've finished training.' She was to be a radio-telephonist.

Kate had told the Officer at her interview that she rather liked the idea of an outdoor job, but her jaw dropped when she saw her posting.

'A Barrage Balloon unit! Well, I certainly didn't bargain for that.'

'You'll get plenty of open air there,' Eve teased.

'Cardington for training – where's that anyway?'

'Bedford way,' Maud told her. 'I've got an aunt there. I'll write to her and I'm sure she'll invite you home.'

The two sisters, Chris and Lena, were happy with their postings. Not wishing to split up, they had both volunteered for duties as mess orderlies. At least they would train together. Like so many other friends they had made, none of the others ever saw them again.

Initial training was followed by a week's leave and Judy had arranged to go home for the weekend. They would have one last reunion before they all went their separate ways.

'Thar she blows!'

'Hooray!'

'Piece of cake!' The shouts of jubilation as the barrage balloon settled sweetly into the wind were interrupted by the cutting voice of the Flight Sergeant.

'All right. Never mind the congratulations. You've got to do it like that every time.'

'All right for him. He doesn't have to do it at all,' grumbled May as they headed for the Naafi. Kate had already put her down as the team's Jonah. There was very little grumbling on the whole. Flight might be strict but they were there to learn, and they appreciated his expertise and concern for their safety.

They were nearly at the end of their training and the weeks had been packed with learning new skills. At first they learned to handle ropes and rigging, patch the fabric of the balloons and splice wires – a practice which left their hands cut and sore. They knew how to inflate and deflate their charges, how to winch them in and put them to bed and they also knew what the inside of a balloon looked like. They had crawled into an air-filled one to see where the valves were.

Now they were on the training site for two weeks and they were under canvas. Their kit was the heavier by another kitbag, battledress, oilskins, souwesters and heavy boots.

'I don't think I'll ever be warm again,' Kate said, beating her body with her arms and looking disgustedly round the cold tent. 'It'll be good to be posted if only to get back in barracks and have a fire.'

The well-named June Jolley grinned and dived into her kitbag. 'Here, have a drop of this. Warm you up.' She thrust a half-bottle of brandy into Kate's hand and added, 'and don't let anybody else know and, for Pete's sake, don't get near Flight and let him smell your breath.'

'Where in Heaven's name did you get that?'

'My Dad gave it to me – medicinal purposes only, he said. Well, it stops me freezing to death, and I've been sparing with it as you can see.'

Kate took a sip and gasped. She had never tasted spirits before. Then as she felt the warmth coursing through her, she handed the bottle back, saying, 'Thanks a lot. I could get addicted to this stuff.'

'Not on our pay,' June grinned. 'I don't know what this cost, but it was twelve and six a bottle before the war.'

They were to have yet another lecture on safety after dinner, so they hurried with their meal and grabbed seats near to the radiator in the lecture room. The girls were already aware that the work they would be doing was potentially very dangerous and they had all been given the opportunity to remuster but no-one had taken it.

Today, the Officer departed from the well-known text and fired a series of questions at them.

'What are the barrage balloons filled with?'

'Highly inflammable hydrogen.'

'What is your worst enemy?'

'The weather,' they chanted, with feeling.

'All right. One at a time. Jolley, which weather is the worst and why?'

June stood up. 'Lightning, because the cable is a good conductor and the electricity will earth through it and the winch gear.'

'Good. So we bed the balloons whenever thunder is forecast. What is the other reason? Stagg.'

Kate answered, 'It could set fire to the balloon.'

Stage by stage they were taken through the safety procedures. By the time the lecture ended, the Officer was satisfied that none of these girls would ever be so foolish as to descend from the winch without jumping. One foot on the winch and one on the ground would ensure that her body would make a perfect conductor for lightning.

They went back into the original training site to take their exams.

'Well, at least it's warm enough to be able to write – and to get a good night's sleep,' June said. In fact the late April sun was beginning to have a touch of spring on its breath at long last.

After the exams came postings. Kate and June were to go to Sheffield after their two weeks' leave.

* * * * *

Eve was in the mess, clearing up after the midday meal. Most of the men had gone to enjoy the rest of their break in the late spring sunshine, except for one group who were ribbing one of their number and making enough noise for a zoo. She would have

252

to move them on in a minute if she was to get out herself, but her eyes were continually drawn to the solitary AC plonk who was seated at a table near the door.

She knew him slightly – one of the maintenance men – a nice boy called Mike, whose fashionable moustache only emphasized his youth. Just a kid, to be a husband and father, she thought. Now there must be something wrong at home. He was chalk-white and was gazing into the distance, clutching an envelope and turning something over and over in his other hand. Well, there was a war on, and people had all sorts of troubles. It was nothing to do with her. She shrugged and went over to the occupied table.

'Come on, boys, some of us have got work to do.' She scooped plates from under their noses, adding, 'You know you're supposed to bring these back.'

'Wash 'em up for you, if you give me a kiss.' One of the airmen caught her round the waist and got a wet dishcloth in his face for his cheek.

When they had gone, Mike was still sitting there looking so forlorn that her heart went out to him.

'Sorry, Mike, I'll have to move you out.' It was no good, the soft voice had not roused him. She put her hand on his shoulder. 'Is something wrong?'

He glanced up then. 'Oh. Aah, summat's wrong all right.' He held out his open palm and showed her a wedding ring. 'She sent it wi'out a word.'

Eve pulled out a chair and sat down beside him. She thought for a minute, then said, 'Your little baby hasn't been born long. Maybe she's just depressed after the birth. It happens sometimes.'

'Nay, she were fine after that. Happy enough when I were on leave and real upset when I come back.'

'Well, you'll have to go home and sort it out, won't you? Go and apply for compassionate leave.'

His face brightened. 'I'm not long back – and it's not like she was ill.'

'I should think she must be, to do this to you. Anyhow, go and ask. Go now.'

She sounded commanding and he went out obediently.

The Welfare Officer asked, 'Where's your wife living?'

'Doncaster. We'd just moved when I got called up.'

'Is there a friend or relation who could go and see her – find out what's wrong?'

'No. Her mother's in Hull and there's nobody nearer.'

'Well, for Pete's sake, why move there?'

'I was offered a job. A man I knew opened a place up there. Now he's doing war work and needed more mechanics.'

The Officer sighed. 'I expect she's bloody lonely, that's all. Well, Squires, I'll give you a week and a rail warrant. See if you can find her some company while you're home. Ask the local vicar. Hope you can sort it out.'

Christine Squires was indeed lonely. She was in an area where she knew no-one and was virtually tied to the house with her young son. She was trying to save from the meagre amount Mike was allowed to send her so that she could afford the train fare to Hull. She wanted her mother and she wanted to show off her baby, but Mike had said that Doncaster was safer than Hull and she didn't want to take him into danger.

Unexpectedly, her husband had proved to be a good letter writer – in fact he seemed to spend all his evenings writing to her – until this last time.

The expected letter was late and when it arrived Christine was hugely relieved. He was still safe – or had been when he wrote. She opened it with joy. Five minutes later, she was crying bitterly.

Mike had written, '*Sorry I missed writing to you yesterday, but I went to a dance last night at one of the WAAF camps – can't tell you where. It was the best night out I've had since I joined up. There was a good band and plenty of WAAFs to dance with ...*'

It went on to say that he had shown them all his picture of her with the baby, but Christine didn't read that far. She had already burst into tears.

He could go out and dance with other girls, enjoy himself, while she sat alone here with nothing to do but mind her baby and worry about him. If that was all he thought of her, their marriage was as good as over. She knew that was what her parents would think. Why, her father would have had fifty fits if she had so much as glanced at another man after she was married.

After she had stopped crying, indignation took over. Very well, if

254

he thought he could treat her like that he would find out that she had her pride. Without a second thought, she snatched the wedding ring from her finger and put it into an envelope. Buoyed up with indignation and deadly calm, she gave no thought as to whether it would reach him in this unprotected state, but addressed the package, got the baby ready to go out and pushed his pram round to the post office.

It was some time after she returned home before the enormity of what she had done began to dawn on her. I must have been mad, she thought miserably. Perhaps I am going mad – I ought to have someone to talk to. But there was no-one. She could only wait now and see what his response would be. If there was a letter in the morning it would have been written before he received her ring. But there was no letter in the morning.

Wearily, she dressed and fed her son, cuddling him to her as if to reassure herself that she had someone who needed her. She took him out to the park from a sense of duty, but the day seemed particularly cold and she spent the afternoon huddled over the fire, listening to the wireless and trying to take her mind off her great trouble. That night she got no sleep and welcomed little Leslie's wakefulness because it gave her something to do.

There was no letter the next morning, but about midday she saw a dreaded figure. A boy got off a motorbike at her gate and came up the path with a telegram in his hand. At the sight of the yellow envelope, her heart stopped. The boy looked at her with a question in his eyes and she nodded that he should open it. He did so and glanced at it then handed it to her with a wide smile.

'It's good news, Missus, he's coming on leave,' he said.

Mike came to find Eve as soon as he got back.

'I want to thank you. I was so shocked, I didn't know what to do until you told me.'

'And everything's all right now?'

'Aye. Poor little devil, I never realised what an awful life it is for her. I know it must be hell for a lot of women, worrying about the men, but she been so alone. Well, I fixed that. There's people going to see her regular and some of 'em will take her to a club for mothers and babies, so she'll soon get to know plenty of women.'

He went away confidently. Eve watched him go and thought, I

255

hope he has enough sense not to tell her in future if he's been enjoying himself.

* * * * *

Judy celebrated her eighteenth birthday by going to see Luise Rainer and Paul Muni in *Tales From the Vienna Woods* and then going on to Neville's restaurant for a meal. She had been accompanied by seven of her friends and this was one of the things she loved about Blackpool, there was so much to do and plenty of company.

Even so, while the cold weather lasted, she decided to take a correspondence course. She had taken Latin and French for her School Certificate and found that she had an aptitude for languages so she made up her mind to study German. She was often indoors on her own as nearly all her friends went dancing.

Like Eve, she had been brought up to believe that dance halls were riotous places where people got drunk, and where there might well be white slavers. Beryl urged her to come, saying that it was all great fun and there was no danger as long as they all came home together. Later they had suitable escorts (and became adept at handling those who weren't) but at the moment all the Civil Service girls went out in groups and stayed together.

'Judy, put those old books away and come to the Winter Gardens with me,' Beryl pleaded one evening.

'Who else is going?'

'Nobody. And if you don't come I'll go on my own.'

Judy looked up at that. 'You wouldn't, would you? Anything might happen in the black-out – oh, Beryl, don t go.'

But her friend took out her best dress and threw it on the bed before disappearing into the bathroom. Knowing how stubborn Beryl could be, Judy was worried and decided that she would go rather than let any harm come to the girl.

Blackpool was awash with trainee airmen, Polish Officers, heavily pregnant women (who had been evacuated from more dangerous parts of the country) and, of course, Civil Servants. Not only was there no shortage of partners, but the girls had plenty of choice. From the moment she entered the Winter Gardens all Judy's prejudices melted away. The warmth, the lights, the gaiety and laughter seemed to hold her in a spell. She had always loved physical activities and had a natural sense of rhythm, and she had danced at family gatherings. Within minutes she was invited on to the floor by a shy young airman who seemed no older than herself.

'It's my first time here. It seems a nice place,' she said, as they danced a waltz in silence.

'Mine, too,' he replied, 'I only came up here last week.'

'Are you out at Squire's Gate?'

'No, we're billeted in town. We don't go onto a base until we leave here.'

'And what are you hoping to do?'

'Spitfire pilot, like everybody else,' he replied with a self-deprecating smile. 'It's a case of whether I can make the grade.'

They chatted on, their self-confidence increasing as they talked, so that when Judy was asked for the next dance by a much older man, she felt able to carry on a conversation without a hint of shyness.

Beryl was delighted to see her enjoying herself and both girls were engaged for every dance. After that evening Judy was as keen as any of her friends to go to the Tower Ballroom or the Winter Gardens. Both places were packed every night and could afford to keep their prices low. A ticket to the Variety Show at the Palace also gave admission to the dance hall downstairs. The girls scrimped and saved on everything, especially lunches, so that they could go dancing once or twice a week.

The sum of twenty-one shillings a week was deducted from their salaries to be paid to their landladies for bed and breakfast and one hot meal a day. As the payments came direct from the Ministry and not from the girls, the guesthouse owners believed (or professed to believe) that the girls were paying nothing. They had no qualms about charging sixpence for a bath and the same for the use of an iron, so it was a constant battle for the girls to make their money stretch. As Judy had foreseen, there was no question of sending money home. She couldn't even afford to have a bath every day.

Clothes were a constant problem. The girls longed for nice dresses, especially as the weather warmed up and the beach called them whenever they were free. But Blackpool was not exactly full of cheap dress shops and Beryl had already had the humiliation of going to the Tower Ballroom in a new summer frock, only to find that at least six other girls were wearing an identical model.

'Beryl, when you're home next week, could you find me a dress? I've managed to save ten shillings for it,' Judy said, handing over the money.

She was delighted a week later to receive, not one, but two cotton dresses.

'You owe me eleven pence on both of them' Beryl told her. 'One was four and eleven and the other was six and eleven.'

The dearer of the two was patterned all over in blue daisies on a white background and had a dirndl waist. The other was peach and light green. Both fitted perfectly and Judy thanked heaven for her stock size figure.

She was a pleasant-looking girl, with hazel eyes and a snub nose, beautiful fair skin and auburn hair. One of the Polish Officers had been overheard to say that she was a typical English rose, but she begged his companion not to repeat it, knowing that she would only get teased by her workmates.

Both she and Beryl were happy with their fellow boarders and also with the group of girls with whom they worked. Some of these were Blackpool girls and they got on so well that many of them invited the girls to their homes and, in turn, were invited out with them when the London girls were celebrating. One of the older women who was popular with them all was Carrie Gregory. Her mother owned a guest house and all Carrie had ever done until the outbreak of war was to help her with the work and do all the accounts. But now Carrie had been taken on as a temp. by the Ministry and was thrilled by the change in her circumstances. For one thing, she had her own money and could do what she liked with it and, for another, she had all the company she wanted. As time went on, she had responsibility for a group of girls, supervising their work and generally acting as a shoulder to cry on, all of which she relished.

Almost without realising it, all of the younger girls were growing up fast and becoming confident in running their own lives. There were romances galore as time went on, engagements to celebrate and sometimes a wedding, which meant that the London girls reverted to temps, as there were no married women allowed to be permanent Civil Servants.

The only constant anxiety was for their families as the phoney war gave way to bombing over London and other large cities. Neither Judy nor Beryl could telephone home, as with few exceptions only the wealthier people had phones, but her father's boss would allow

258

a call at weekends and would always take a message. Beryl's sister could take an urgent message at her office and could be relied upon to ring their boarding house if there was any news. As they were free out of office hours, they went home for weekends as often as they could afford the fare.

Most of their dancing partners were young airmen or their instructors. The Polish boys preferred to take their girls out to dinner and there was a lot of amusement about the way they insisted on carrying their handbags.

'There's a gorgeous restaurant in the Pleasure Beach grounds,' Lena said. 'Benek took me there last night and we had this stuff called corn-on-the-cob. You eat it in your fingers and it's drenched with butter.'

'That would get you in a nice mess,' Beryl teased, 'and your handbag, too.'

They were getting a bit fed up with Lena, who was beginning to put on airs since she had hooked a Polish Officer.

'Oh, you have some little forks to put in each end of them,' she explained, tossing her head and marching out of the room.

Judy and Beryl laughed. They knew that she thought they were jealous of her conquest, but their ideas were quite otherwise.

'Where's the future in it? Does she want to go back to Poland after the war? And suppose he's married anyway. I'm not starting to go out with any of our gallant allies.'

'Especially the ones who can't speak English,' Judy said.

The trio had done it again. Eve had got 48 hours' leave in order to see Kate, and Judy had arranged to come home for the weekend. They were gathered in Kate's house early on Saturday morning.

'How's it all going?' Judy wanted to know.

'It's been freezing so far. I got my open air job with a vengeance. Now it remains to be seen what Sheffield is like,' Kate replied. 'How about you? Are you still having the time of your life in Blackpool?'

'Yes, it's wonderful. We all go dancing and skating and last week I saw Hutch at the variety show. What about you, Eve?'

Eve said quietly, 'Well, I'm a properly qualified cook, so I'll be able to get a job in civvy street when this is all over. I suppose that's something. But the training course didn't teach me anything I didn't know, except how to do meals in big quantities.' She flushed. 'As a matter of fact the Training Officer commended me and asked if I'd like to work in the Officers' Mess.'

'That's great.'

'Oh, I said no. I'd rather be with people my own sort. All the young Pilot Officers seem mad to me – always showing-off and talking nonsense – wizard prangs and going for a Burton,' she said scornfully, 'and the older ones would treat you just like they treat the maids at home.'

Kate was instantly concerned. 'Why don't you remuster if you're not happy? They can't make you stay as a cook.'

'I'm not unhappy. Besides, what else could I do? I'm not built for physical things like you – and I haven't got Judy's brains. The camp's lively enough and there's always something going on. I don't mind dancing with the boys I know.' She smiled. 'One of them even persuaded me to play Housey-Housey the other night.'

The other two nodded their approval. Eve was beginning to come out of her shell.

'Well, what shall we do today? A ramble? It's not a bad day – considering what it's been like.'

They agreed, and Eve asked, 'Who else of our lot is still around? Gillian? Muriel?'

'Gillian's out in France, nursing. Didn't you know? Muriel went to the Midlands with her class of evacuees three weeks ago. I saw her last weekend and thought she was less than enchanted by the place – I shouldn't be surprised if she makes a move soon. There's no-one else – unless you want to see Madge and her baby.'

'No, I don't think we ought to spring all of us on her. I've got plenty of time before I go back,' Kate said. 'Let's just have a wander on the common and see where we get to. Hang on while I see what Mum can spare for sandwiches.'

Mrs. Stagg came in presently, carrying a packet for each of them. 'I'm afraid it's only jam. There isn't a bit of the cheese ration left, but I'll make you some soup when you get back.'

'If that's your home-made jam, it's good enough for me,' Eve said. 'Would you like us to come back through the village and see if there are any queues worth joining?'

'No, thank you, dear. I'm going out early myself. I've got Kate's rations to collect and that'll make a big difference.'

The three set off across Wimbledon Common in the direction of the windmill, their spirits rising as they saw the new spring green on the trees. Passing the first of the big houses they could see right through to the back garden. It was brilliant with numberless daffodils.

'I wonder what they're doing for the war effort. You'd think they'd be growing vegetables,' Kate mused.

'Perhaps they'll be ordered to eventually,' Judy said, 'but we do need something to cheer us up too.'

'Oh, look, ducklings!' Eve pointed.

They stood on the banks of the Rushmere pond and gazed as the babies followed Mum and Dad, looking like a flotilla of tiny ships following the big ones, in line astern. As they watched, the drake dived and Eve said delightedly, 'Up tails, all.'

Judy nodded, 'Yes, but I like the other one – you know – "From troubles of the world, I turn to ducks" and he goes on to say, "and ducks are soothy things, and lovely on the lake" – I wish I could remember who wrote it.'

'Sensible man, anyway,' said Kate, 'just what we've done.'

Kate gazed about her in disbelief. They were expected to work in this place? She had been looking forward to getting her permanent posting, but not on the site of a cemetery. She thought wryly that some of the girls would not be too happy about their sleeping companions.

It was a very basic site, lit by oil lamps, and Sarah Davison, the Corporal in charge, was just explaining to them that they would cook their own food on the solid fuel range and heat their water in the boiler outside.

'It's not the best camp in the world, but it needn't be the worst if you pull together. You should take turns to do the cooking and light the boiler and kitchen stove.' She bit her lip, and continued, not very hopefully, 'Do any of you understand the oil lamps? They're a bit tricky if you're not used to them. They have to be cleaned and filled every day.'

One of the girls laughed. 'I was born on a farm – I've coped with oil lamps all my life. I'd be glad to do it all the time, if it earns me exemption from cooking. You wouldn't thank me for what I'd produce anyway.'

In the relieved laughter that followed, Sarah said, 'We might agree to that provided you still take your turn at lighting and stoking the fires. OK then, let's get down to making the duty rosters.'

By the time they had finished all 24 hours of the day were covered as the balloons had to be guarded at all times. It worked out at two guard duties a week for each girl, as well as standby duty in case the balloon had to be handled in the night.

As she left them, the Corporal remarked, 'Oh, by the way, you can go over to HQ for a bath once a week.'

'Blimey, what do we do the rest of the time?'

'You carry your own bowls of hot water over to the ablutions. They've been freezing cold, but it's beginning to warm up now, so it won't be too bad.'

She showed them where the fuel dumps were and left them to it.

'What we do for England,' Kate said. 'I thought this was going to be a piece of cake after being in tents.' She had dumped her kit on one of the beds and now turned to the girl next to her and added, 'I'm Kate Stagg.'

'Sheila Bundock.' The owner of the pleasant voice was a well-built girl who looked as though she could cope with the balloons – and everything else – without any trouble. She was perhaps three or four years older than Kate and there was something about her that inspired confidence. Now she raised her voice to address the whole room.

'I think we need heat first. Do you agree? Shall we tackle the kitchen and the boiler?'

'Good idea. I'll get some fuel. Who'll come with me?' June asked.

The girl who was to be in charge of the lamps said, 'And I'll go and get some paraffin – nothing like it for getting a fire going – only watch your eyebrows.'

Over the next few days they settled to the routine. The weather was warming up, but there were still a few gales left over from March.

One night when the wind was howling the girls on standby were called out. Kate, half-way up a ten foot high ladder, was reaching up to the stabilisers at the sides of the balloon. Above the noise, to her disbelief, she heard shouting.

'Put that light out!'

An officious Air Raid Warden, who should have been aware of what the girls were trying to do.

What followed, from at least two of them, was a reply so shocking that Kate felt her freezing ears redden and get hot. How could girls say such things?

'Well, that's him told. Stupid man. There won't be anything flying on a night like this.'

It took Kate a long time to realise that some of her team, who were so reliable and helpful, thought nothing of swearing like men when provoked, and that this in no way prevented them from being good companions. Nor did it mean that they were 'bad girls'. In fact, they were more likely to despise the men who tried to belittle women undertaking men's jobs. As time went on, she learned more and more to value people for what they were.

*   *   *   *   *

'My God, What's that?' Maud sat straight up in bed and looked round the hut. Anita opened a sleepy eye and mumbled 'Wasser matter?' Then she heard it, too. Not a raid. Not so near, but an unmistakable crump-crump-crump of continuous gunfire.

There were only three of them in the beds. The others would be on duty, except for Gladys, who had a 48-hour pass. Winifred was just stirring. They looked at each other, unwilling to admit their suspicions, but at last Anita said, 'It's German guns – across the Channel.'

'So near.'

With one accord, they dressed and went out to gaze in the direction of the noise, but there was nothing to be seen – yet.

By April 1940 Maud was a qualified Radio Telephone operator. Her course had not been a difficult one and she had enjoyed becoming proficient at working her switchboard. Then she was posted to the fighter base at Dover where she shared a Nissan hut with six other girls and had made a friend of the New Zealand girl, Anita.

There was not a lot of activity in Britain just then, but people were no longer talking about the 'phoney war'. There had been great losses in the Navy and Germany had invaded Norway and Denmark. But in May the Dutch and Belgians surrendered.

The Blitzkrieg was amazing. 'Lightning war' was a good name for it. The Germans moved at an incredible pace and the British held their breath and prayed that France would hold out until we could hit back. Girls from all the services were hastily evacuated from the continent.

As the month progressed the Allies were being pushed steadily back to the coast. When the girls heard the gunfire they knew that our Forces must be on the beaches. On May 27th the evacuation of Dunkirk began.

During that week, when any of the girls were not on duty they made straight for the depot where the troops were being received and offered their help to the WVS and Salvation Army.

At first Maud and Anita were shocked at the state of the newly-arrived men. They looked like a defeated rabble who had been through hell. They were soaked through and hungry and many were wounded.

The voluntary workers moved among them with trays of tea and sandwiches, shouting 'Any more for any more?' and only a short time later, when they were fed and dry, and on the first trains home, all their old spirit returned.

Against all the odds, they had survived and they knew their luck. There were thumbs up over steaming cups of tea and assurances to the girls, 'Don't you worry – we'll be back.'

They took many messages from the men to pass on to their families – they might just get through before the official notifications and before the men themselves arrived home. Maud and the rest of the girls on the base spent a lot of their spare time writing letters.

Gradually the news filtered through that 340, 000 men had been rescued, but the girls were more concerned that a hundred planes had been lost, many from their own base.

'We're for it now,' Maud said. 'I bet Leslie will be worried about me – funny to think it's me in the front line and not him.'

All of Britain thought that an attempt at invasion was imminent and there were those who thought it would succeed, but June came and went with nothing more significant than a declaration of war on the Allies by Italy, which most people shrugged off, having no opinion at that time of Italy's fighting capabilities.

In July, the Germans invaded the Channel Islands. Although it was a severe blow, the Allies were heartened by the arrival of Australian and New Zealand troops.

Anita was very proud. She told everyone, 'I knew the Anzacs wouldn't let you down. They don't get angry quickly but, boy, when they do ...'

The fighter planes were nearly back to strength and had been flying daily sorties, mostly for reconnaissance, and this gave the girls plenty of practice. They could hear what the boys in the planes were saying on the intercoms and often knew where they were before anyone else on site.

The bombing raids commenced in August. The Battle of Britain had begun in earnest.

Although the bombing was mainly concentrated on the ring of Fighter Command stations around London, Dover was a first line of defence, and the pilots were alerted to 'scramble' many times a day.

The WAAF manned the R/T equipment round the clock, going off duty ostensibly to sleep, but more often to gaze out and watch the dogfights over the Channel.

'I thank God all the time that Leslie's not flying,' said Maud. 'I know he'll still be in danger servicing the planes, but no more than us. These boys – I don't know how they keep going – and, oh, Anita – poor Winifred.'

Winifred had been on duty when her boyfriend's plane was shot down. She had heard his voice telling them he was hit, then 'bailing out', followed by a burst of gunfire – and silence.

She had passed out and Maud, who was on standby, was summoned to take her place. After less than two hours, she had returned to duty and pleaded to be allowed to continue.

'I want to hear ours get back at those bastards,' she said venomously, 'and you needn't worry, Ma'am, I'm not going to have a nervous breakdown just to please Hitler.'

Nor did she. The sheer amount of work was a great help. There was just no time to brood.

Maud and Anita were on duty when there was a dogfight right above the base. The German fighter came in with a Spitfire on its tail. The Spit was well above and diving. As it straightened out it caught the Messerschmitt with a burst of fire in the engine. The plane burst into flames immediately and the girls raised a cheer which was stopped abruptly as they heard the German pilot screaming in the inferno. They were to hear those screams in their nightmares for many months.

Day after day the same patterns were repeated until all the personnel were dropping with exhaustion. Then, in early September, Hitler decided to concentrate the might of the Luftwaffe away from Fighter Command to concentrate on the wholesale destruction of London.

Dover station was granted a respite from the constant orders to scramble, though they still had the job of intercepting the Nazi bombers on the way to the capital.

* * * * *

Judy and Beryl had found some better accommodation in a house where they were the only two boarders. They still saw their friends at work and spent much of their leisure time in a group, but they enjoyed having their evening meal with the family. Their landlady, Lily, had a husband in the Army and there were two young children, Bobby aged ten, and June who was nearly twelve. It was obvious to the girls that Lily was lonely and that she was glad to have them there. She had even allowed them to use the portable gramophone and was delighted when they brought in a new record. Judy came in one evening with a sixpenny purchase from Woolworth of Caruso singing 'Only a Rose', and asked if she might buy some German language records and play them in her room. The request was granted and the girls felt that they had made a good move.

One night Beryl came in early from a date and found Judy studying.

'That's the last time I go out with him,' she said, pulling off her coat and moving to the fire.

'Trying it on, was he?' Lily asked sympathetically.

'And I thought he was so nice. That's the third time I've been out with him. Judy, what are you doing here? I thought you'd got a date.'

Judy looked up and laughed.

'So I had – and with a handsome airman, too. But didn't he know it. Thought he was God's gift to women and talked of nothing but himself. So I told him I'd got better things to do than listen to all his self praise and I came home.'

Beryl heaved a sigh. 'They can't all be rotters. Can they?'

'No,' Lily said, 'there are plenty of decent ones and I'm sure you'll both find one.'

After a few weeks the girls began to notice that the quality of their food was not so good and that the family had eaten before they came home. Lily explained that she had taken to giving the children their main meal at midday as it seemed to keep them awake if they ate later.

'I expect she's finding trouble making our rations stretch. The meat's down to next to nothing, Mum says,' Judy said.

Beryl looked thoughtful. 'Maybe if we told her that we would eat out once a week it would help. Shall we do that?'

When they broached the subject, Lily seemed vastly relieved.

'That would help a lot,' she said, 'only I can't afford to charge you any less.'

266

They assured her that they had not expected it, assuming that she had less money than when her husband was earning.

It was a shock to find that they still came back to nothing but potatoes one night a week, especially as they were rarely in for Sundays because they were usually invited out by some of the Blackpool girls.

Judy began to nurse a horrible suspicion, so that the next time Beryl went home for the weekend she stayed in to Sunday lunch. About noon, Lily's aunt and uncle arrived, followed a little later by her mother. They sat down to dinner, five adults and the two children, to a roast joint of beef, Yorkshire pudding and vegetables. Judy looked grimly at Lily, who had the grace to flush. It was a subdued meal and Judy knew that they were all realising that Lily would never be able to make such a Sunday meal for them again. They tried to preserve some semblance of normality, asking Judy questions to which she returned the briefest of answers. Yes, she liked Blackpool for the dancing. No, she didn't think she would come back for a summer holiday after the war.

As soon as possible, she went to her room after telling Lily that she would be out for tea.

Judy felt completely deflated. Was no-one to be trusted, man or woman? It was difficult to believe that Lily, who had seemed so warm and welcoming, had been robbing them of their rations. Must she now look for ulterior motives in everyone? She was angry, but her anger was suffused with sadness and at last it gave way to tears.

She and Beryl both agreed that there was no question of them staying in the house.

'Do you think we could go back with the others?' Beryl asked, but they both felt that it would be impossible.

The office heard all about it the next morning and it was Carrie who said that her mother had room for them, though they would have to share the living-room with any commercial travellers who happened to be staying.

'And,' she added fiercely, 'mother was horrified. No decent woman would do that to young girls who needed all the nourishment they could get – that was what she said.'

They accepted gratefully and moved in during the next week. They were to stay there for the rest of their time in Blackpool.

A few months later they had reason to be glad that they had not gone back to their original digs. For some weeks the girls who were still there had been talking of a new maid from Wales who was very kind to them. She was a buxom woman of about forty and they were soon telling her all their troubles and showing her all their new purchases.

'She took such an interest in all of us,' Myra told them, 'but she's going back to Wales today. We realised she'd been crying and then she told us her mother is very ill and she doesn't know if we'll ever see her again.'

Nor did they. When they returned from work that night it was to find that their kind friend had vanished with the contents of the gas meter and the best of everything from their wardrobes. A new hat from one, a birthday brooch from another, handbags, stockings, dance dresses – they were still discovering missing items weeks later.

'I won't give up on people,' Beryl said stubbornly. 'You and I know lots who we can trust. Oh, Judy don't be like that.' For Judy was stamping round their room repeating that she would never trust anyone again.

'It's this place,' Carrie said. 'There are people who always regard seaside towns as easy pickings. People on holiday have a bit more money and aren't too careful with it. That's why we have to disclaim responsibility for anything that goes missing from the bedrooms.'

By the time that they had been there two years, Judy thought that Blackpool had completed her education.

1942 saw a great many changes in Judy's life. Beryl was away almost every weekend, either at home or visiting friends she had made in Fleetwood. They were farming people with a son employed in the family business. Bruce's rugged good looks, fair hair and freckled face were combined with a down-to-earth ease of manner which had won Beryl's heart immediately. It was no surprise to Judy when they announced their engagement and she was pleased that Beryl had found someone who was not a combatant and was likely to survive the war.

There was a spate of engagements about the same time and the section decided to celebrate them all together. Their supervisor was a man who they all called Uncle George. He was nearing retirement age and seemed delighted to have a bevy of young girls around him, nor did he mind that they gave him no respect, preferring to have their affection.

'Uncle George,' Carrie said, putting a hand on his shoulder, 'there's all these lovebirds wanting to have a big engagement party, and they've invited both of us old fogies. Only they haven't got much to spend and they would like to have it here in the office – do you think you could get us permission?'

'I can only ask. Tell you what – I'll take you with me and we can tell them a sob story. All these young girls away from home – you know the sort of thing.'

One of the newly-engaged girls was Betty, who they all liked very much. She was sweet-natured and rather shy. She had come in from the adjoining office to show off her ring, blushing mightily but with a radiant happiness which was good to see. Her fiancé, Bob, was a Petty Officer in the Royal Navy and she had known him all her life. He was stationed at Portsmouth but was home on leave and he promised to supply the drink for the party if the girls would provide the food.

George got them permission on condition that he would be responsible for locking up, and Judy looked back on that time as one of her best memories of Blackpool. She prayed that Bob would survive the war and that he and Betty would have a happy marriage.

But she was getting restless and not because she saw less of Beryl. The contrast between her life of work and pleasure and the other life she saw every time she went back to Wimbledon played on her conscience. She ought to be doing more for the war effort.

Her mother, like those of her friends, slept in the Anderson shelter in the garden every night – if she could get any sleep with explosions going on all around her. The windows of the house had been shattered so many times that they were now criss-crossed with so much scrim that daylight hardly penetrated.

Mrs. Mason had taken to keeping hens to supplement their rations and spent much of her time in lines at the food shops and listening to all the wartime recipe programmes on the wireless. Money was not a problem any longer. Her husband had been drafted into war work and was in Norfolk during the week, building aerodromes for the American airforce, and she had an allowance for her son, Andrew, who was maintaining aircraft on a fighter squadron.

Judy's mother was a neat little woman who had always kept herself well-groomed, but now her hands were getting rough and her hair seemed dull. Seeing how much she looked forward to the weekend, when Dad would be home, Judy realised how very alone she was.

'I wish Andrew wasn't in such a dangerous place,' she said, 'but I suppose I should be glad he's not flying. It's a blessing you're out of it. I thank God every day that I don't have to worry about you. And your father is so proud of you – such a good job, and now getting promotion.'

This was a sore point with Judy. All her friends had got it, including the lazy one who sat on her unanswered post whenever there was an inspection. Promotion in such circumstances meant nothing. She thought again that she ought to be doing more for the war effort.

'Do you think Dad would still be proud of me if I was in uniform?'

'Heavens, no, child! Don't add to our worries. Besides, he wouldn't like it at all. Throwing away a pension, too. Ah, you may laugh now, but when you get to our age you'll be glad you can look forward to it.'

Then she laughed at herself.

'I suppose it's stupid to talk like that. You'll probably be married in the next year or two.'

'I don't know,' Judy said thoughtfully, 'Thank heavens I'm not serious about any of the RAF boys – a good many of their girls will end up with no husbands.'

Even her sheltered life did not keep Judy from realising that every plane lost on a bombing raid meant the deaths of seven young men, and plenty of planes were being lost however much the authorities tried to disguise it. Eve and Kate both knew the truth and Judy always arranged to come home whenever one of them was on leave. They both looked so smart in their uniforms and talked about all the good times they had. She had a great urge to join them, but she knew it would mean a row with her father and give her mother another cause for worry.

Eve spent most of her days with Judy when they were home together as her house was empty much of the day. Her father had gone into the Army as a driver and her two brothers were evacuated.

The result was that her mother had found a job as a fitter, working in the railway workshop at Wimbledon. Eve was inordinately proud of her.

'She repairs signal equipment and puts replacements in signal boxes when there is bomb damage. Don't you think that's great?'

'Everybody's doing more than me. I wish I could join the WAAF too.'
Judy went back to Blackpool even more dissatisfied.

* * * * *

In the early days of the war, Carrie Gregory had been more than pleased by the change in her circumstances. She had been born in her parents' guest-house in Blackpool and had known no other life. By the time she was twenty her mother was a widow and for the last eighteen years, Carrie had taken her father's place in the business. It had been accepted that she would stay there until she married and she had enjoyed meeting the people who came to stay.

She and her mother loved each other and had got on well together, and as she saw Carrie gradually drifting into the position of the spinster daughter, Mrs. Gregory thought that this was eminently suitable. The girl would inherit the business in due course and her future would be assured.

But the early days of the war hit the trade hard and Carrie had taken the job with the Ministry of Health, knowing that her mother could cope without her.

Going out to work had come, unexpectedly, as a liberation. Only then did she realise how circumscribed her life had been. It wasn't just that she was earning for herself and proving that she could survive in the outside world of work, what was best of all was that she was making friends.

One of the London women, Harriet Baker, who was slightly older than her, had asked Carrie out several times and she had accepted with pleasure, and even a feeling of excitement. But she began to dread returning home afterwards, as her mother made it obvious that she had spent a lonely evening. Of course, there was no reason why Mrs. Gregory should not have made one of the party, but she was of tough Scottish Presbyterian stock and held that a widow should not 'go gallivanting'.

Judy and Beryl soon realised the position and did their best to persuade her that she could safely leave the house long enough to come with them and Carrie to see the latest film, but she would have none of it.

In the summer of 1942, there came a change. Mrs. Gregory's younger sister lost her rented house in a daylight raid. Her husband

and both her sons were in the Army, so Carrie and her mother agreed that Aunt Mabel should be offered a home with them. She accepted and, within two weeks, the forceful and indomitable little woman was making herself useful. Carrie felt redundant – and rejoiced.

It took Mabel Tarrant no time at all to realise that Carrie was straining to get more freedom and she was already saying, 'Of course you must go out and enjoy yourself with your friends. I'm here to keep your mother company now,' and to Mrs. Gregory she said privately that it was a great opportunity for Carrie to catch up on some of the pleasures that she had missed as a young woman.

Meanwhile, Judy was getting more determined that she would join the WAAF. A week before she had danced with an Army recruiting Sergeant who had said to her, 'I don't like to see all you young girls having the time of your lives here and doing civilian jobs when we need you so badly.'

And she had agreed with him.

The situation resolved itself one night when Carrie and Judy returned late home from a dance, escorted by two young airmen. Mrs. Gregory had been tight-lipped and rigid with disapproval.

'Carrie,' urged Judy as soon as she could speak to her privately, 'you are going to have to leave home if you're ever to have a life of your own. I'm going to join the WAAF. Come with me.'

'If only I could, but there would be such a row with Mother.'

'And so will there be with my father, but if we join up without telling them they can't stop us. Once we've done it, they'll have to accept it and probably start boasting about 'my daughter in the WAAF' like all the other mothers and fathers. Haven't you heard them?'

'Yes, I heard some woman talking about "my soldier girl" the other day,' Carrie laughed. 'Let's do it.'

* * * * *

Shortly after Hull started getting a pasting, Mike came to tell Eve that his mother-in-law had moved out of the danger area up to Doncaster, so his wife would have her company.

'I'm right glad I moved her now. Hull's caught a packet all over the place.'

Some of the men seemed a bit subdued that morning. Two of

the planes from the base were still missing. None of the others had seen them shot down, so there was hope that they might have landed elsewhere, but the chance was fading by the minute.

The men's mood affected Eve. She tried to keep her spirits high for their sakes, but she felt depressed and restless. Kate and Judy were doing important work – she was cooking. There had to be something more she could do.

Less than two weeks later, she was told to report to the Section Officer. Now what? she thought. There had been no difficulty with her work or conduct, or with any of the kitchen staff as far as she knew. 'Don't let it be bad news,' she prayed.

'Come in and sit down, Wade – and don't look like that – it's not serious.' The Section Officer was smiling. 'In fact, we want you to do something for us. There's no compulsion, but I think you might like it – as a change from the cookhouse.'

'I wouldn't mind,' Eve admitted, 'but I didn't think I was qualified for anything else.'

'Oh, I'm sure you could do this, after you've had a go under supervision. I expect you know that we're losing Corporal Biggs – for the happiest of reasons.'

Eve nodded. Patsy Biggs had been married about six months ago and had made no secret of the fact that she wanted to get out of the Service and would get pregnant as soon as she could.

'It leaves us short of a tractor driver and HQ can't promise a replacement yet, so I looked for someone who could drive and I found you. It would include taking the bomb loads out to the planes. Will you do it?'

'It's true my father taught me to drive, but I never did much and I haven't for ages. I'd do it if I could.'

'Oh, we'll soon show you how to manage a tractor. It's very simple – even I can do it.' The Officer smiled again. 'Thank you, Wade. What's Harlow like? Can she handle things until we get another cook?'

'No trouble there, Ma'am. She's been a very competent assistant.'

So Eve had some leave and returned to her familiar camp as a Corporal.

Until then, she had had little contact with any aircrew, but that soon changed. She was taught how to drive the tractor and supervise the loading and unloading of the bombs so that she could transport them to the planes in safety. Ground staff would load the planes, but more often than not, some of the crew would be there.

'B. for Bertie' had one member of the aircrew who was always present.

Fred Abell, a Flight Sergeant, was a Wireless Operator and Air Gunner who was very particular about his equipment. Although he had to let the maintenance boys do their jobs he always checked his wireless and gun meticulously before every operation.

Eve liked his thoroughness and the fact that his speech was free of the jargon she had so despised in the young Pilot Officers. They fell into conversation easily and when he asked her to go out with him – always with the proviso that any arrangement might have to be cancelled at the last minute – she agreed with a feeling of excitement.

They went to the pictures and saw Walt Disney's *The Reluctant Dragon*, which amused them both and had no emotional scenes which might have been too intense for these first days of getting to know each other.

Still laughing about the picture, they went into a tea-shop and it was then that Eve said, 'I do hate hearing some of the air crew carrying on like arrogant little boys with their "wizard prangs" and "PO Prunes". Why do they do it? Do they think it's clever?'

'No. You've got it all wrong,' Fred replied in his slow drawl. His brown eyes looked intently into hers, willing her to understand. 'They do it to keep each other's spirits up. To hide the fact that they're scared to death most of the time. It's like people being bombed and singing to drown the noise – a kind of defiance. Most of them are only kids and haven't learned any other way of doing it.'

'So what do you do, Fred? Or aren't you scared?'

'Oh, I'm scared all right. You'd have to be an unimaginative idiot not to be. When you hear where your target is, if it's a long distance, or a place that's hell for flak – and usually it's both – your stomach turns over. I may not use their jargon, but we older ones still fool around and kid each other – and get drunk when we lose our mates.'

'Have you lost many, Fred?'

'A few. You get hardened.' He brightened. 'My best mate's one of the ground crew. Hey, he's got a girl in the searchlight battery. Why don't we make up a foursome when we can?'

Eve smiled, and the man thought it was the loveliest smile he

274

had ever seen. Both knew that they wanted to go on seeing each other.

Eve liked Colin Morris from the moment she met him. He was a tall man who had answered to the nickname Lofty ever since he was at the same prep school as Fred. They had volunteered together, both hoping to be pilots, but Colin had failed the medical, having less than perfect eyesight. It was pure coincidence that he had been posted to Fred's squadron.

He had clear blue eyes surrounded by laughter lines and he told the most original stories, keeping his face so straight that Eve was not always sure he was not serious.

His girl, Babs, was on a women's searchlight battery, where she had spent the awful first months of 1940 under canvas. As her duties were from sundown to sunrise she could only see Lofty when she was completely free of all manning, standby and guard duties.

When she was free, the four of them went out happily together and Eve warmed to the girl who reminded her so much of Judy with her enthusiasm for everything suggested. Judy's common expression as a child had always been, 'Ooh yes! Let's do that.'

One evening towards the end of 1942, Babs came to a dance with them wearing an engagement ring.

'It's so nice to be able to wear it,' she said, showing them the modest diamond circle. 'I can't wear it in camp, and I wouldn't let Lofty buy me a more expensive one in case it gets pinched.'

There was a feeling that the tide of war was beginning to turn in the Allies' favour and a new note of optimism was creeping in.

'Well, the war can't last for ever,' Lofty added, accepting their congratulations, 'so we thought we might as well – I don't want any other bloke pinching my girl.'

'And at least Lofty's not flying, so I don't have to worry about that,' Babs said happily to Eve. Then in a rush, 'Oh, my God – I shouldn't have said that.'

'It doesn't matter. I know the score and I don't intend to get serious.'

The girl looked at her with a knowing little smile. If Eve didn't want to acknowledge that she was in love, that was all right. But Babs was under no such illusions.

Nor could Eve fool herself for long. Fred had been restless ever since Lofty's engagement. He had realised from their first date that Eve was the girl he wanted to marry, but he was in the usual dilemma of all the Servicemen who were in dangerous jobs, and his was the most dangerous of all, where casualties were high. Was it fair to ask her, or even to tell her that he loved her? But he longed to know that Eve felt the same – and she hadn't given him any idea. In the local, alone with Fred, Lofty raised his glass and said, 'What's bugging you, old man?'

'I'd like to get engaged. Like you, I don't want anybody else muscling in on Eve. But I don't know how she feels and – well, is it fair? I've still got several ops to go.'

'Babs says Eve's fond of you and won't admit it. If she is, and I'm sure my girl would know, it's not going to make any difference to how she'd feel if you bought it.'

He looked at Fred's frowning face and picked up both glasses.

'Have another one – and cheer up. You're with a good team. You'll make it.'

But Fred was already beginning to smile. 'You're sure? Babs said that?'

'She said so – and I think it's pretty clear anyway. Go on. Ask her.'

The next morning, Fred was watching for Eve as she drove her load up to B. for Bertie.

'Have you got time? I want to talk to you.'

He looked solemn and Eve wondered what had happened now. Her heart sank at the thought that he might have been posted. They drew away from the plane, not even hearing the catcalls of the bomb loaders.

Without preamble, Fred said, 'Eve, if we both survive all this, will you marry me?' Then, as she stood dumbfounded: 'I'm not sure it's fair to ask you now, but I need to know. I love you so much, I'd be a dead loss without you.'

She smiled up at him. 'Not you. You'd carry on regardless. No, I'm not being flippant, only it's a surprise.'

'But do you love me?'

'I think so. Give me a little time.'

'Tonight? Tomorrow?' His arms ached to hold her, but it was broad daylight and they were both in uniform. 'I'm sorry – it's not very romantic – first thing in the morning. But when?'

'Soon,' she promised him as they parted.

When she was free to think, Eve said a prayer for guidance then she examined her own feelings. Yes, if it was left to her the answer would be that she loved him and would be his wife. If he didn't survive then she would know it was not meant to be and would accept it as God's will. Either way, she would have the answer to her prayer.

She had come a long way from the eighteen-year-old who thought that dancing was wicked because her church told her so, but her natural instinct was caution and a quick repulsion of anything which threatened her innate dignity. Fred had recognised this in her and had been careful not to give her offence, but now he could hardly wait for her answer.

Nor did she keep him waiting. Once her mind was made up, she realised that it would have been cruel. That night, safe in his arms, she said, 'The answer is yes, to both questions.'

'Thank God, my own love. I'll really have something to live for now.'

There followed a strange time for Eve.

There was pure joy in their meetings, followed by deep anxiety every time that he was on an op, and relief when B. for Bertie reported back safely. She got very little sleep when the planes were away and always counted them as they took off, and often five or six hours later counted again as they returned. If one was missing she got no more sleep until she could check that he was home.

At the bomb depot, the men who loaded up her tractor would often pretend that they were dropping a bomb. After the first time, she learned to ignore their horseplay and would have a laugh with them, but one morning she burst into tears. She soon pulled herself together and apologised to the shocked men.

'I'm sorry — it's not your fault. I'm just overtired.'

She drove her load up to Fred's plane and smiled at him. But one look at her face told him something was wrong. When she explained, he threatened to thrash the life out of the men who had frightened her.

'Oh, Fred, no! They were only larking about — they've done it before. It was just me being silly.'

The Flight Sergeant said no more, but he went to see one of the women Officers.

'Corporal Wade, please report to the MO immediately.' The message reached her as soon as she returned from loading up.

Her first thought was for her family, but surely it wouldn't be the MO who would break bad news to her – or would it? If it was very bad, perhaps they did have a doctor there. She washed hurriedly and went to the medical block.

'What's up, Jeff?' she asked the orderly.

'Routine medical check, I think, Corp. Hang on and I'll let him know you're here.'

But the MO told her to sit down and said, 'What happened at the depot this morning? You told the men you were tired. Were you on the town last night?'

'Certainly not, sir,' Eve said indignantly, 'I just haven't been sleeping too well.'

'Hmm. Why not? This place getting you down? Lying awake to hear the planes coming back? Want a transfer, do you?'

'Oh no. I like being here.' Then honesty broke in. 'It's true, I often do hear the planes, but so do most people.'

'But they go to sleep again. Why don't you?'

She didn't answer, but he had no difficulty in guessing the cause.

'Well, we'll have to break the pattern. Go home and get some sleep. A week's sick leave and I'll see you when you come back.'

It was the worst leave she had ever spent. Her mother was still working at Wimbledon railway station, the two boys were enjoying themselves in Dorset and showed no signs of wanting to come home and her father was somewhere on the south coast, presumably preparing for the invasion of Europe.

But, mercifully, she did sleep. She was more exhausted, both physically and emotionally than she had realised. The enemy was not likely to drop bombs on Wimbledon Common and she slept in her own bed every night, scorning the Anderson shelter in the garden. Sporadic gun fire from a nearby battery and the sound of distant bombing did nothing to disturb her, but in the daytime she felt guilty because she knew that so many others went sleepless every night and were still carrying on.

Kate's mother invited her to share the midday meal and to listen to the Home Service news, and Eve accepted with gratitude. One day, she was sitting in Mrs. Stagg's warm kitchen, listening to *Workers' Playtime* when she picked up the *Daily Express*. There had been a raid on Dusseldorf and '*all our planes returned safely*'. She ignored the whole article, knowing how unlikely it was.

The second page grabbed her attention at once. A news reporter and cameraman had been allowed to attend a debriefing. The air crews had to report to a debriefing Officer immediately they returned from a raid – and there, sitting across the table from the Officer, was Fred. He was flanked by two other members of the crew, but the angle of the camera had caught him full face. It was his eyes – huge with tiredness – that held the girl in their stare. Everything he had been through settled there. A type of blank horror was in them. This man had been to hell and back and was holding fast to his sanity – just.

Into the room came a burst of laughter from the wireless, followed shortly by someone singing cheerfully,

'*What a show. What a fight.*
Guess we really hit our target for tonight.
And we sing, as we limp through the air,
Look below, there's our field over there ...'

But Eve didn't hear the end of the song. She reached over and switched the wireless off, crying, 'Oh, no. It's not a bit like that. I'm sorry, Mrs. Stagg but I'm too upset to stay.' She would have gone back home, but she was held in a firm grasp.

'No. I don't suppose it is, my dear. They try to keep our spirits up that's all.' Neither of them heard the midday news.

Kate thought it was her lucky day. There were three letters for her. Letters meant so much when you were away from home and her mother realised this and always wrote once a week. Her friends kept in touch but might go weeks before writing and she could not blame them, knowing how little time was available for letters. It was especially true for her, with the extra work of keeping fires going and doing cooking, though this last chore was falling more and more on one girl who actually enjoyed it and did marvels with the rations they were allowed.

She opened her mother's letter first and read with growing concern about Eve's last leave.

'*I think she is in love with one of the men flying on these bombing raids. It must be a constant worry for her, being on the same station. I hope you won't fall for one of these fliers.*

Eve knows too much about their work. She got very upset when the wireless was playing A Wing And A Prayer, she said it was glorifying the job and it wasn't like that at all. Perhaps you can help to cheer her up, but she only just went back from leave, so I don't suppose she'll get any more yet. I did feel so sorry for her.

I'm afraid we are very selfish and only think of our men. Now I wonder just what danger you are in. I don't suppose you will tell me.'

Kate read the rest of the letter quickly. There was no doubt that Eve's breakdown had upset her mother. She would have to write straight away, with a few more of her anecdotes to prove she was having a good time.

In the two years that she had been in Sheffield she had coped with her balloon in all weathers, from using a line to scrape the snow off it to fierce tussles in high winds, and she had great satisfaction in keeping it flying, nose to wind, for the protection of the skies. She had not told her mother about the most frightening time when a Messerschmitt had shot it down in flames, so that the girls had to avoid the burning material while trying to douse the fire.

In between her work, she enjoyed the company of the other girls, the dances at various camps, the shows they put on for their own amusement — one group had even formed a fife and drum band — and the visits of show business personalities.

These latter, travelling under the banner of ENSA, went all over the world to cheer up the troops, often in considerable discomfort and in areas of great danger.

Although the Forces referred to ENSA as '*Every Night Something Awful*', the boost to morale when the likes of Joyce Grenfell and Gracie Fields appeared was undoubted. When they turned up in the Middle East and Far East, the 'forgotten Army' knew they were not forgotten. Many of the artistes brought messages from home and, in some cases, had gone to the trouble of visiting the senders. These women deserve to be included in the record of war heroines.

Something of this went through Kate's mind as she read the letter from Maud. She said that they had had a visit from Anne Shelton and the boys had raved about her for days afterwards.

'She looked incredibly young in uniform and very pretty. Nearly all the lads have got a pin-up of her somewhere. I hear Vera Lynn is in Africa. They certainly get about.

I've got involved with a group who are putting on a pantomime for Christmas. We are doing Cinderella and 'she' is a 6ft Flying Officer. I am one of the beautiful sisters and Cinders fancies us both, so you can guess the implications. It gets more outrageous, and I have to say, crude, every time we get together, but you can't help laughing and that's what matters.

I get very cheesed off sometimes without Leslie so this keeps me going. At least he's in no more danger than the rest of us and we'll be due some leave together shortly. Won't it be wonderful when all this is over and we can get on with our lives?

Have you heard from Eve? She seems to like her job better than the cookhouse, but I haven't heard from her for a while.'

Kate's lips tightened. Something would have to be done about Eve.

The third letter was from Judy. She had completed her training and was on a bomber station. As usual, she was full of enthusiasm.

'I wish I'd done this years ago, Kate. It's just so exciting and you know you're doing an essential job.

I am engaged in plotting planes out and back. All the Big Bugs are there some of the night, so we have to be on our best behaviour, but it's counted a great honour to have this job.

The boys are a grand crowd, but I realise the odds are against them completing all thirty missions – though some do – and I don't intend to get involved. One of our girls was engaged to a Pathfinder Navigator. We knew he'd got into Berlin because the fires were alight for the men following, but he didn't make it back. I'll never forget her face as the others started reporting in, and how it became bleaker and bleaker. So – not for me.

Now to much more cheerful news. You remember Carrie from Blackpool who joined up with me? Well, she's engaged to a Sergeant! They are both about forty and neither expected to get married. I saw it happen. He asked her for a dance and they spent the rest of the evening just talking to each other – and that before she'd been in the WAAF five minutes!

She's been offered a chance to go on a Cadre to train as an Officer. I went down to the station with her and who should be there but her Sergeant. Neither of them knew the other would be there and their faces just lit up! She's like a teenager – all excited happiness and trying to pretend that it's because of this course!

I wondered how long it would be before she told me. Well, I've just had a letter with the great news. She keeps saying "at my age" as though no one over forty had ever got married before. Remember how the old dears at church used to say, "You don't want to go to those nasty dance-halls. How many people do you know who met their partners at a dance?" Now I know several and I bet you do too. Carrie is just the latest. She says they'll wait till after the war, but I wonder.

Have you heard from Eve? I hope we can arrange some leave together again – more difficult now we're all in HMF.'

Kate folded the letters. At least, everyone she cared about was safe for now. She must write to her mother first and then to Eve.

*   *   *   *   *

'I wish I could come and see your panto. It sounds a riot,' said Leslie.

'Yes, it would have been lovely to be together for Christmas. We're lucky to have this leave though. Leslie, surely we must be planning an invasion soon?'

'Oh, I think it'll come next year – and then we'll finish 'em off quick. We're stronger than they are now .'

Maud clung to him.

'I'm getting fed up with this war. I want us settled in our own home. What wasted years it has taken out of our lives.'

'That may be true for us and for all the women at home, but for many of my mates it's been a kind of freedom they would never have had. Lots of them will go on to better jobs after the war and some have met girls they would never have met. I'd like to keep in contact with some of them. I've made some good friends among them.'

Maud knew this was true for the girls, too. She couldn't see Eve back in domestic service, or Kate in a hairdressing saloon, unless she was working for herself. They had been forced to grow up quickly and the result was that they were poised, confident girls.

Maud enjoyed playing her part in Cinderella, chiefly because it gave so much pleasure to the audience, and Christmas Day had been better than any she had ever had at home. The food was marvellous – all the three Services went to town at Christmas – and there had been lots of laughter as the Officers served the ranks. But afterwards she felt decidedly flat.

282

'I'm cheesed off,' she complained to the girl beside her in the pay queue. Then her name was called out. She heard 'Head', but stepped forward, saluted smartly and signed 'Bishop'.

Immediately she realised the mistake.

'Sorry, Ma'am. I forgot. I just signed my single name. Can I cross it out?'

The Officer laughed. 'Here's a WAAF who doesn't know whether she's married or single.'

There was some giggling and a few ribald remarks. Maud never heard them. It had just dawned on her that she was pregnant.

With the certainty came an enormous excitement. Her service days would soon be over. Then she could make a home for Leslie and their child.

*   *   *   *   *

It was at a dance at an American base that Kate met Buddy, a quietly spoken country boy, who told her at once that he was engaged and showed her a snap of his girl.

Kate was not too enamoured of the Yanks, many of whom were brash and thought any girl was theirs for a pair of nylons or a box of chocolates. Unfortunately, it was true of enough of the English girls to encourage them in the belief. Buddy, lantern-jawed and unprepossessing, was certainly not in this category and she danced with him happily, then accepted his invitation to a drink.

'I'll have a cider – only half a pint. I don't drink much,' she told him.

He spoke to several men round the bar and then brought the drinks back to their table. It seemed that the men had been watching what he ordered for, while Kate was still sipping her cider, she found glass upon glass appearing in front of her. She thanked the first man politely, then told the second, and subsequent ones, that she wouldn't be able to drink any more and they had better have it themselves. After that, she let the full glasses mount up and ignored them.

Her attitude seemed to annoy some of them. 'Aw, c'mon, sister. Do you good.'

A red-faced airman, who looked as if he had already had enough, turned to his mates.

'These limey girls can't drink. Would you rather have a pair of nylons, honey?'

He brought his face down to Kate's with a leer. She got up. On her feet, she topped him by half a head.

'I'm not yours, or anyone else's, for anything you could offer me,' she said quietly. 'Sorry, Buddy, but I don't like the company you keep. I'm going.'

He had stood up when she did, and with a murmured apology, was escorting her back to the dance floor, when she heard one of the Yanks say loudly, 'Typical – you'd think they were winning the war by themselves, instead of having to fix everything to keep going.'

She turned then, her eyes steely. 'Oh yes. I've heard you don't attempt to mend anything – not even your planes.'

'Ain't got time, Ma'am. Plenty more where they came from.'

'And who do you suppose flies the replacements over here? Our girls – that's who! Every time you requisition another plane you put one of my friend's lives at risk. Very clever, aren't you?'

The young man looked bewildered. 'Can't be right,' he muttered.

'You find out – and think about it.'

After that she was too upset to stay any longer and let Buddy take her back to camp.

On a stormy November night, Kate's balloon came to grief. There was a strong east wind blowing when she went on guard duty and every so often it veered north-east. In fact most of the team had been out all day, trying to keep it with its nose to the wind. The squally rain had added to their discomfort and they had come back to their quarters thoroughly chilled and with hands that had lost all feeling.

In the kitchen, Eveline who did most of their cooking, kept soup, sandwiches, tea and cocoa going all day. This was a marathon as she had also helped with the balloon. The girls fell on the hot drinks gratefully.

When Kate took over, the girls on standby stayed with her. It seemed that they were battling for hours and as fast as they got it correctly aligned the wind changed and the balloon tugged at its moorings and swung wildly.

'God, it's going again!' Kate was almost crying with frustration. At last the wind seemed to make up its mind to stay in the east. When they relaxed, they realised just how cold and tired they were. June Jolley grabbed Kate's arm.

'A drop of something in your tea. You can't do guard all night like this – you'll catch your death of cold.'

Kate hesitated. Guards were forbidden to leave their post. But there was something in what June said. She didn't want to get pneumonia.

'I'll risk it – just for a minute.'

It was so nice and warm in the kitchen. They thawed out gradually with hands coming back to life as they cupped the bowls of thick lentil soup – almost a meal in itself.

'Eveline, you're a wonder. Where did you get the lentils?'

'New lot. Just come in. Stores clerk's a friend of mine.'

They grinned. Eveline might be taciturn but you could rely on her to cultivate the men who would be most useful. Everyone who had anything to do with food was a friend of hers.

Kate, accepting a cup of tea with a dash of the 'little something' from June's endless supply, thought grimly that she must soon return to the cold and rain out there. But she was too late.

'Guard! Who's supposed to be on duty tonight?'

The Duty Officer's frosty voice preceded her. Kate jumped to her feet. 'I am, Ma'am.'

'Then you'll be pleased to hear that the balloon has nearly broken loose and is torn. You'd better bed it as best you can, then you can stand down. I'll see you in the morning, Stagg.'

She went, stony-faced. The girls had never seen her so angry before.

'Oh God, Kate. I'm sorry – now I've got you on a fizzer.'

'Not your fault. I knew I shouldn't have come in. At least I'll get a few hours sleep when we've put the bloody thing to bed.'

But of course, she didn't.

The next morning she stood in front of the same Officer, who wasted no time.

'I'm disappointed in you, Stagg. You've let yourself down and your team. I had you down as one of my most reliable girls. Have you anything to say for yourself?'

'No, Ma'am. I was in the wrong.'

'Very well. You are fined three pounds ten shillings towards the cost of repairing the fabric. Dismiss.'

Kate saluted and went out. The fine was steep considering the little she earned and she felt aggrieved. Surely they could have confined her to barracks, which was what she had been expecting. She was rather surprised that the fine was the only penalty.

Three days later she found out why. Kate, June and Mary were posted to Harwich.

'Well that's a dead loss,' Mary complained. She, like June, had been on standby on the fateful night. 'Just as I was getting on so well with one of the Brylcreem boys.'

'It won't be so bad. If it's a proper site we won't have to get our own meals and cart fuel about. And we'll get hot baths whenever we want,' June pointed out.

Kate hardly heard them. Surely Harwich was near Felixstowe, and Eve was stationed there.

* * * * *

Judy enjoyed her life in the WAAF. She was a girl who was always willing to accept a challenge and a chance to do or learn something new. She adapted to a different way of life immediately and got on well with her companions.

She could not help but be affected by the number of planes which did not return from ops.

Working in the plotting room, she always knew how many were missing, but it only made her more determined not to get involved with any of the crews. She would happily dance with them, but never accepted a date. Without lying, she managed to leave the impression that she already had a boyfriend, so that they did not feel slighted.

She was already beginning to wonder if there was anything more active she could do when she went home on two weeks' leave and met an old friend. Yvonne had joined the WRENS and was stationed in London, serving in a Minewatch unit. Judy was intrigued. 'How do you watch mines?' she asked.

'There are observation huts in the middle of the London bridges and, as soon as the siren goes we have to get to them – we've got about two minutes to do it. Then we have to watch for anything dropped in the river and note its position and direction. On the All Clear we run to the nearest phone and ring the Port of London

Authority and they close that part until they're sure it's safe. It's not a bad job, but you need to be able to run fast – right up your street – speed is of the essence, as they say.'

'What about getting dressed?'

'Oh, no time for that. The Wrens on duty sleep with all their clothes on. We have to get cracking, I can tell you.'

A few days after this, Judy received a telegram from Carrie.

'Wedding on Saturday. Can you come?'

So they had decided not to wait until the war ended. Of course, Judy thought, he would be going overseas as soon as we could get back into France. Surely, it couldn't be long before the attempt was made. What luck that she could go.

'Beryl, how lovely to see you. When are you getting married? I thought it would be before Carrie.'

Judy had come from the church and met a group of old friends outside. Talking and laughing, they made their way to the reception.

'Oh, we're all trying to persuade Bruce not to enlist. After all this time farming, and knowing he's doing a vital job, he suddenly got restless. Says all these men in uniform give him an inferiority complex. I told him he should wear a label saying "I'm a farmer", but I understand how he feels, so I'll wait until he decides what to do.'

Carrie had intended to have a quiet wedding, but her mother and aunt had other ideas. Except that the bride refused to wear the traditional white gown, saying that she was too old to make a fool of herself by trying to look like a young bride, no-one would have known that there was a war on. It must have helped that they owned a boarding house and knew all the local suppliers, but it seemed to the girls that nothing was lacking at the reception.

'This is right up my street,' Beryl said happily, with her nose in a second glass of champagne, 'I haven't swanned around like this since before the war.'

Carrie and her new husband came to say goodbye before setting off for an unknown destination. They both looked quietly content. There were hugs all round and then Judy said that she had better think about getting a train home. Mrs. Gregory said, 'Nonsense, Judy. There are plenty of empty beds here. Surely you can stay until tomorrow, at least.'

So the girls stayed on in the hotel lounge, happy to spend the rest of the day together and catch up on all the news.

As she walked along the prom next morning, Judy saw two girls in the distance and one of them looked familiar.

'Why, hallo Betty. I didn't recognise you for a moment. How are you?'

The face which was turned to her had coarsened, and the 'hallo' Betty gave in return was sullen. Judy thought she looked like a tart, but put the thought away and asked, 'How's Bob?'

The other girl gave Betty a nudge and they both giggled.

'All right – as far as I know,' Betty giggled again.

She's playing the field – and Bob in danger on the seas, Judy realised. She turned away, sickened, then, with sudden resolution, turned back.

'I'm sorry we met again, Betty. I would have liked to remember you at your engagement party when you were so much in love and we were so pleased for you. Bob deserves better.'

As she turned away again, she heard more ribald laughter and then Betty shouted after her, 'Suit yourself – pious bitch.'

This marriage, Judy realised, was just another casualty of the war.

Back in camp, Judy began to make enquiries as to whether there was a Minewatch unit in the WAAF. The Officer to whom she spoke considered her in silence, head on one side, then she said, 'Getting restless, Mason? You know you're doing a vital job, don't you?'

'Yes, Ma'am. Of course. I'll stay where I am, if that's really where I'm needed.'

'Well now – I shouldn't even drop you a hint really – but just keep patient for a while. We might be able to offer you something more exciting.'

In the autumn of 1943, Judy was summoned to report to the Air Ministry. Her interview took place in a boardroom and she was seated at an imposing long table which smelled strongly of polish. Opposite her were two women Officers, some high ranking RAF Officers and two older men in civvies. The preliminaries over, the questioning began.

'Miss Mason, you have fluent French and German?' This from one of the civilians.

'I don't know about the German. I've only taught myself from books and records.' He shot a sentence at her in German, and she shook her head. 'I couldn't follow all of that so quickly.'

He said another sentence more slowly and she was able to answer him. He nodded and immediately switched to French and she answered him just as quickly. Then one of the women Officers asked, 'You are something of an athlete, I understand?'

Judy gave them a list of her achievements at school and in the WAAF.

'Have you ever done any acting?'

As the questioning continued, she understood that they were probing both her knowledge and her character. When it seemed to be coming to an end, one of the senior RAF Officers asked, 'How would you feel about doing a parachute jump?'

'Parachute? From a plane? Oh, great! Sorry, sir, I should have said I'd like it very much,' she concluded demurely, but they were all smiling at her. Judy was almost sure that her last questioner had muttered "at a girl!' under his breath.

She went into Kingsway, crossed the Strand and collapsed onto a seat in Lincoln's Inn Fields where she tried to take in what had happened.

She was to receive intensive training to polish up her French and German, followed by instruction in surveillance, combat, radio transmission and parachute jumping. At any stage they could turn her down and send her back to base. If she wished, she could also opt for this. Because they could not tell her about her assignment until the last minute, she had the option to refuse it.

Nothing had been put into words, but she felt sure that she would be going to France as soon as, or possibly before, the Allied Army.

Glowing with excitement, she walked over Waterloo Bridge and went home to Wimbledon for the night.

* * * * *

Eve went back from her short leave feeling more rested and aware that she must appear fully operational. She was sorry that she had broken down in front of Mrs. Stagg and hoped that Kate wouldn't get to know. Now she must steel herself to hide from Fred any worries she had about him. Just as you never wished the boys 'Good Luck' before a mission, so you never gave them any cause for anxiety. She had not missed the MO's hint that she could be posted and this was the last thing she wanted. She would not worry any less about Fred if she was away from him.

So she met them all with smiles and assurances that a few nights' sleep had done her a power of good. She reported to the MO and was given permission to resume normal duties.

'I've only got six more ops. to go, then I'll get some leave. What about getting married then,' Fred asked, 'or would you rather wait?'

The old practical Eve replied, 'Let me think about it,' then quickly, 'no – let's do it – who knows how long this caper will last. We can't let life pass us by. And let's tell everybody. They'll be as pleased for us as Colin and Babs were.'

He lifted her off her feet and swung her round.

'Darling girl! Now I know I'm going to make it.'

'Of course you are.'

She was suddenly sure that he would.

It began at midday with what looked like a dogfight off the coast of Felixstowe, but even as they watched the planes kept coming towards them, looking like skeins of migrating birds. Almost before they had grasped the situation, they were running for the shelters.

'Thank God it wasn't this morning when we were loading up,' Eve said.

'That's all very well,' replied one of the girls, 'but it means that all our planes have got their full load of bombs on board.'

On her words came the first sickening sounds, thuds that shook the shelter, explosions and noise to shatter the eardrums.

It was all over in half-an-hour. Some of the R/T girls had stayed at their posts and were still in touch with HQ. Miraculously, the wires to it had not been affected, though there was a tangled mass wound round one of the radio masts. They were told to stand by and report all damage as soon as it had been assessed.

The girls came out of their shelter and looked about. In front of them, their own quarters seemed to be untouched. In fact, very few of the buildings were damaged. The raiders had been intent on destroying the planes, most of which were in the open. There were great craters in the ground, one with the best part of a plane in it.

Most of the Lancasters were damaged and four were complete write-offs. One of these was B. for Bertie.

As she walked towards it, Fred came to meet Eve. She looked at him disbelievingly. He looked shrunk into himself, smaller and old. She wondered that he should feel the loss of a plane so much. Surely none of his crew had been killed?

'Lofty's bought it,' he told her and his voice was a thread of sound. 'Him – not me.'

'Oh, Fred, no! Not Colin. Oh, poor Babs! How did it happen?'

'He stayed with his plane too long – working on something he wanted to finish.' He added bitterly, 'There won't be much to bury.'

The whole airfield was cleared up and the damage reviewed, then Eve asked permission to go to the searchlight battery and break the news to Babs.

'I think she probably knows by now, but it may help her to have a friend near. Yes, you may go.'

Eve found her just about to finish a shift in the Command post. The camp was cock-a-hoop because the adjoining gun battery had brought down one of the Nazi planes, but Babs was tight-lipped and controlled. It was no time to give way to her own grief. Back in her hut, she hugged Eve warmly and thanked her for coming.

'They're arranging some leave for me and I'll go and see Colin's parents, but I don't know that it'll do any good.'

Eve was a good listener and Babs needed to talk, if only to make the tragedy real to herself.

'Do you know what I regret most, Eve? I expect you'll be shocked, but I wish I'd slept with him. I was brought up to be respectable and I didn't intend to give myself to any man. But Colin was different – what was between us was different. I'm sure in the eyes of God we were man and wife. Colin wanted to after we got engaged, but he respected me too much to persuade me when I said no. Oh, God, I wish he had!'

She broke down at last and Eve held her while she wept. When Eve went back to her own site, she felt drained of all emotion, but she was very thoughtful.

That evening Fred told her that he was going on 48 hours' leave, pending the delivery of more aircraft. He looked older and his eyes were remote.

'I've just written to Colin's mum and dad. My family will be shocked too. We've all known each other for years.'

'My darling, I'm so sorry.'

She held him close and he clung to her.

'I wish you were my wife and could come away with me.'

'I am your wife,' she said simply.

In was on Fred's second mission after Colin's death that B. for Bertie failed to return. Some of the others had seen it coned by searchlights and reported that the wing had been shot off. It did not immediately burst into flames and parachutes had been seen. There was a hope that some of the crew might be prisoners of war.

But weeks went by before they got news of two prisoners from that raid. Fred was not one of them.

Before then, Kate had been posted to Harwich and came to see her. All their lives they had told each other everything and this was no exception.

'These last weeks we've been living like man and wife whenever we could. It's one thing I'll never regret.'

Kate was aghast.

'But, Eve, what a risk to take! Why, you might have got pregnant.'

Eve burst into tears. 'Oh, Kate, don't. You can't know how much I want his child. I only wish it had happened.'

* * * * *

At the end of January 1944, Judy was home on indefinite leave.

'So what is this in aid of?' her father asked.

'Sorry, Dad – can't tell you. Don't know much about it myself.'

She had completed all her training and was awaiting the summons, which would surely come soon. Now she had a difficult decision. How much could she tell her parents? As Mr. Mason looked at her quizzically, she made up her mind. Surely she could trust him.

'Dad, I shouldn't even say this, but don't worry – or let Mum worry – if you don't hear anything of me for quite a long time. In fact, no news is good news, the Air Ministry would let you know if there was anything wrong.'

He shook his head. 'You should have stayed in the Civil Service. Your mother will have kittens if we don't hear from you regularly.'

'Then you'll just have to tell her as much as I've told you.'

* * * * *

292

The telegram came in mid-February, and that night she stood on a small private airfield in the Midlands. The sky was pitch black and the shapes that moved about had blackened faces and were clothed in black. That cold air and the sharp smell of the wet earth stayed with Judy all her life. It took her a little while to realise that there were five of them, and as they moved closer together she recognised a woman from one of the training courses. They moved towards each other and clasped hands without a word.

A short briefing told them that they would be dropped in two pairs, on different parts of the French coast, though within easy contact by radio. Then the pilot said, 'Veronique and Jean will be dropped first, then Estelle and Phillipe.'

A man came to her side with a long loping stride. 'You are Estelle? Phillipe is my real name – I'm French-Canadian.'

'Do you know any more than I do?'

'Not a sausage – only that we'll be met and taken to a farmhouse. The rest is up to us.'

Abruptly, in a nearby field, a horse threw up its head and whinnied. They all froze, but there was no other sound. They climbed into the little plane, making room for each other and all their gear which would be dropped by separate parachutes.

Judy – or Estelle, as she must now think of herself – was suddenly gripped by a wild excitement. This would be the adventure of a lifetime, with only her own wits to outsmart the Nazis and stay alive. And she could do it.

Their object was to find out where the Germans expected the invasion to be made and what preparations they were making to meet it. She had been trained never to reveal that she understood their language, but to get as close to them as she could with safety and listen to their conversation. The least little rumour might be very useful intelligence for the Allied Command, planning for D-Day.

After she was airlifted home in May, she was still sworn to silence and always remained reluctant to talk about that time.

'It's all so boring to tell. Such a lot of it was just waiting. The best thing was being in partnership with Phillipe. He held me back a few times when I would have gone blundering in – well, no, not that. I'd been trained too well to do that, but he stopped me taking some pretty awful risks.' Judy's face lit up in one of her radiant smiles, as she continued, 'We were such a good team that we are going to make it permanent.'

'You're engaged? What's he like?' Kate asked.

'Practical, courageous and very ordinary looking, which was just as well for him several times. He'll be good for me and stop me – no, not stop me, he says he loves my enthusiasm – but make me think first.'

And that was almost as much as they heard about Judy's great adventure. It was years afterwards before they knew that she had received the MBE.

This is Now - 7

'I didn't understand then how Eve – of all people – could have done such a thing. Just about the worst behaviour for a woman in those days. I would have thought it despicable if it had been anyone but her. Of course, when I saw her sadness, I couldn't help but sympathise – and she was still Eve, who I had known all my life, and who patently felt no shame.

'It wasn't until I fell in love myself that I understood,' Kate said.

'You haven't told me anything about that,' I said softly.

'Well, it was after the war –1946 to be exact. I could have lost my heart a few times but I was determined not to get involved until I knew we had a future. I had seen too many heartbreaks by that time. Did you know that one in every seven of the war casualties was an airman?

'Anyway, about 1943 we got some new neighbours who had been bombed out of a house in London and by the end of the war they were part of our little community. In fact, I think it was Mrs. Raybould who organised the street parties.

'We knew they had a son who had been a prisoner of the Japs and they were expecting him home any time, so when I saw this young man in khaki coming along the street and peering at all the house numbers, I realised it must be him. I knew Mrs. Raybould had gone shopping, so I took him in and gave him a cuppa. That's all.'

'Oh, come on. You must tell me a bit more than that. What was he like, after that awful experience?'

'Well, he looked very thin, of course. His face was gaunt and it made his eyes look huge. Hazel eyes – very serene, as though he had come to terms with what had happened. He told me later that he hadn't expected to survive and he would regard the rest of his life as a bonus.'

Kate was back in those days, gazing into space with the beginnings of a smile on her lips. I said nothing and presently she continued.

295

'I thought him very well adjusted considering what he had been through, and so he was. Never any nightmares or depression. He said that one of the nurses on the ship that brought him home had talked to him a lot about the future – how you could dwell on the past all your life and end up an emotional cripple, or put it behind you and think about what you wanted to do in future.

For him that included a wife and family. I can't tell you any more except that we were very happy and had two lovely daughters. Bill lived to see his first grandson, but the prison life had taken its toll and he died of diabetes when he was only sixty. I was lucky to have him for so long.'

She smiled, but her eyes were too bright. I said quickly, 'What about the others, Judy and Eve?'

'Judy married her French Canadian and went to live in Montreal. It seemed like the end of the world in those days, but they have been back often since travelling became so much easier and we've been over there several times. We had a great holiday when Bill was still alive when they showed us the Rockies and Niagara.

'Eve was about thirty when she met a man who had lost his wife during the war. She married him but didn't have any children of her own – only a stepson. She still lives in Wimbledon and I see her often. She seems just the same to me, as though we had never been apart. We never mention Fred, but I m sure she still remembers. She's slowing down a bit now but she's done a lot with her life. At one time she and her husband, Roy, worked in a Dr Barnardo's Home and she still takes an active interest in children's concerns.'

I thanked her warmly for spending so much time with me and telling me so many intimate details. Then I said, 'Do you mind if I ask you? – the WAAF got a bad name for promiscuity. I suppose all the women's services did. Do you think most of the girls went wild when they got away from home?'

'No. Only a minority. I was in from 1940 to 1945 and I only ever knew two girls who weren't married and went out pregnant. One would sleep with any of the men, but the other was a sad story.

'She was a Corporal who we all liked – a nice girl in every way, and she was engaged to a soldier who was in the Middle East. She had a lovely voice and was taking the lead in The Dancing Years. We were collaborating with an Army unit nearby and one of their Officers was the male lead. He was a fair, handsome man. I can see him now. Oodles of charm.

'While rehearsals were still going on, we heard that her fiancé had been killed, but she carried on bravely and they gave a stunning performance to a whole lot of mixed troops and civilians. Some weeks after, one of the Sergeants guessed that she was pregnant. The father was this Army Officer, who was married. She had intended to say nothing and go AWOL eventually. There was a lot of sympathy for her. It wasn't difficult to guess how it had happened, with her grieving and looking for comfort.

'I expect there were a lot more girls like Eve who were really in love and felt they had little time to be with their men, but I still say the majority of them were decent girls.'

She smiled and said lightly, 'I expect it all sounds frightfully old-fashioned to you. It's a whole different ball game today, isn't it? And of course, the risk of pregnancy was a factor in keeping girls virgin till they married, but I think there was also a sense of pride in themselves. They considered that they were entitled to the respect of the men. Proper pride – that was what they had. Some of them had come from homes where the father treated the womenfolk badly and they were determined it wasn't going to happen to them.

'That was one of the things that the Services taught them. They saw a different way of life and they weren't going back to the old ways.'

During October, Doreen and George sold their house and were preparing to move to Castle Acre. With the news, Doreen sent details of other houses from Norfolk estate agents 'in case Jan might be interested'.

One or two of these looked very suitable if I should decide to buy and the prices were a huge incentive. I had never taken any interest in the cost of houses and I was amazed to discover that I could get a very nice property for half the price of the London flat. The only snag was that it would be irrevocable. It was unlikely that I would ever be able to afford a nice place in London again – unless, of course, I wrote a bestseller, but I wasn't holding my breath for that.

What decided me was finding the perfect house. The Hollies was modern and compact without a lot of ground which I would never have time to cultivate. It was on the outskirts of the market town of Dereham, which had spread out so much that my suburb was completely built-up and had everything I should need. It felt like a good compromise between the country and the town. Best of all, I should have enough money to spend on it to make it superb. I could afford to get a state of the art computer with all the equipment I needed to make me self-sufficient without access to an office.

I put in an offer which was accepted and agreed a price for the flat with Myrtle.

Soon after this, I got a mysterious phone call from Robert.

'Can I come and see you on Sunday? – just a flying visit.'

'Yes, of course – but why?'

'Tell you all about it when I see you. Till Sunday then', and maddeningly, he rang off. I went to find Aunt Julia in the garden.

'Can Robert come to lunch on Sunday? Don't worry if not – I can take him to the Buck and Hare.'

'Of course he can come. You can't hear yourself speak at the Buck, even if the food is good.' She regarded me quizzically, head on one side. 'He can't keep away, can he?'

I said shortly, 'It's not like that' and went back to my novel. I felt ruffled and unable to concentrate. Between Aunt Julia's knowing eye and Robert making a mystery for nothing, I was decidedly put out. I changed my shoes and went for a walk.

It was an early autumn day, bright and dry, but with a faint coolness in the air. I thrust my hands into my pockets and strode along, enjoying the sight of lines of swifts sitting on the telephone wires. I was sure they were debating whether it was yet time to leave us. They looked so like notes of music on a score that I stopped in front of one group and started to whistle the tune that they made, though it wasn't very melodious.

'Nice happy sound,' said a voice I knew. Simon was standing at the entrance to the nursery.

'Damn fool thing to do – and even worse to get caught.'

'No. It was delightful to hear someone whistling. Something we lost when the errand boys disappeared. Were you coming here?'

'Well, I wasn't, but it's Aunt Julia's birthday next week and I was wondering what I could get her that she hasn't already got. Are there any tools you can think of?'

He was silent for a moment. I was meant to think that he was considering an answer, but I was only too aware that he was looking at me with pleasure. It was not an unusual experience for me but I didn't kid myself that it meant anything more than admiration.

'You look so much better than when you first came here – especially this morning, with the colour in your cheeks. Country life suits you.'

'Just as well. I'm buying a cottage here. Did Aunt Julia tell you?'

'Yes. She said you were going to get everything installed so you could work from home.' He changed the subject abruptly. 'What about a bird bath for your aunt? I've got a good selection, some of them locally made.'

I couldn't resist the temptation to walk round with him. The nursery was a pleasant place at any time of the year, but just now there were pots of geraniums still putting up a show, dahlias in all the colours from yellow to deep mauve, winter heathers just beginning to show colour and all the autumn tints of shrubs and trees. But the bird baths defeated me. They came in such variety that it was impossible to choose.

'I don't know,' I said helplessly. 'There's no saying what she would like. I'll have to bring her to pick one for herself.'

That evening, I asked Aunt Julia if she would go to the nursery to choose herself a bird bath. I might have known that she wouldn't hesitate. On the following day she took about five minutes.

'It has to be the right height so that I can see the birds from the kitchen window. Deep enough for them to bathe, but not to drown. No fancy ornaments on it. Yes, this one.'

'Right. I'll deliver it tomorrow,' Simon promised.

When he came, the local papers were full of letters about the hunt, both for and against. Aunt Julia asked, 'What do you think, Simon?'

'I don't know,' he said. 'They say the hunt helps to keep the countryside in good nick and so on. Certainly, foxes can be very destructive if they're hungry or their numbers get too great. And they say it's better than shooting them in case they only get injured and die in pain.'

'Can't the farmers and gamekeepers shoot straight any longer?' I asked.

He shook his head. 'Jan, I don't have any answers. The hunting people may well be right – but, still, it goes against the grain when you put yourself in the fox's place. One thing's for sure – they always leave enough foxes in the area for the next hunt. They'll never hunt them to extinction.'

'It gives employment to a lot of people,' Uncle Reg said.

'Oh yes. There's no doubt about that – and keeps the old crafts alive – saddlery, breeding and training dogs, livery – no end of jobs would go if hunting went. Blacksmiths would lose a lot of work, too.'

'I can see there are arguments for and against, but my sympathy is with the fox,' I said.

Aunt Julia broke in then. 'Your sympathy might have been different if you'd ever seen a hen roost when a fox has been in. I saw it once when I was a girl. My mother had some young pullets – they would have been laying by the next week – but a fox got in and killed all thirty of them.'

* * * * *

Robert arrived just after 11am and whisked me off into the summer house.

'What's the big mystery?' I asked.

'All in good time. How's the book going? Or shouldn't I ask?'

'It's going well, but slowly. I get so carried away by all I'm finding out – and then there's the difficulty of having so much material. I'm used to having to choose and edit, but I feel so guilty about having to leave out so much. I've made up my mind that I should concentrate mainly on the three Women's Services – even with them it's a constant battle about what I really must include – but it means I hardly mention the nurses or the voluntary services, or the munitions workers and I'm only too well aware of what a terrific amount they contributed.'

Robert grinned. 'If you don't leave out some of it you'll end up with a tome which will make a useful doorstop. Why don't you start thinking in terms of doing a second book, including all the unknowns?'

'Heavens above, Robert, let me get this one finished first!'

'All right, but I bet you've got quite a lot of material for another already.'

'I suppose so. I haven't even mentioned the girls who served abroad. Anyway, you didn't come here to talk about that. Give.'

He was looking as I had so often seen him, when he was trying to decide the best way to approach a client – weighing up the possibilities.

'It's like this. I don't think I'll be seeing out my year's contract. They aren't satisfied with me and I don't like their ideas. I'm going to talk about resignation and I think it will be by mutual consent.'

'I knew you weren't happy, but surely they can't fault your work?'

'That's the trouble. They don't want what I want to supply. There's an atmosphere – no, a belief – that the audience are not very intelligent and can't handle anything that stretches them. My sort of attitude scares them stiff. They can see their ratings falling. I really do think they've got it wrong, Jan. I'm sure most people – not just us media moguls – want better than they're getting.'

'Quality,' I nodded, 'I believe that's right. So, what are you going to do about it?'

'I'm hoping to start a company to make decent programmes. There are a few people who think like us. Some of them will join me, and some will take the programmes when they see them. Will you join us?'

'Doing what? I'm planning to work from home. I don't want to go back to London.'

'Write for us. Work from home. You wouldn't have to come up often. What about all that material you haven't used – 'Unsung heroines' – there's your first subject. How about it?'

'Let's see how it goes, shall we? I'd like to get this book launched first.'

'That's fair enough. At least you haven't turned me down. And I expect it'll be some time yet.'

Six weeks later, I took possession of my house. Robert was great. He drove my treasures down from the flat and helped me to hang curtains, then we caught up with each other's news over coffee.

'Sorry, I've got nothing stronger to offer you. I haven't got around to stocking up yet, but I'll take you down to The Nelson before lunch. You must have got up at the crack of dawn – I'm so grateful.'

'I get up at the crack of dawn most days. I find it's my best time for writing.'

'Oh, Robert, are you going freelance? What are you writing about?'

'I had a bit of luck – went to a boring book launch and met a talented photographer and illustrator. She works a lot for the

American market and we're doing a book together on English churches. There's a lot of interest out there in all our history and we've got a good deal.'

'But that's great. Have you given up the TV job?'

'No, I'll see the contract out now. Thank God it was only for a year.'

He smiled and it was a peculiarly sweet, secretive smile. I recognised it at once and said, accusingly, 'Robert! You're in love. With this girl who's doing the book with you?'

He nodded. 'I never thought of it happening, but she's the one I want to spend the rest of my life with. I'll ask you to the wedding in due course.'

'Robert, I'm thrilled. Of course, I'll come.'

It was true, too – and I had never fancied him, yet I felt a sudden pang, as if I had suffered a loss.

'Your cottage seems well furnished. When are you moving in? And what have you been doing? Your turn to spill the beans.'

'It was so easy, because I sold the flat with all the furniture – none of it would have looked right here. So then my mother and I had a marvellous couple of days going out and buying all the new stuff. My sister, Claire, found the reproduction desk. Aunt Julia would have wanted me to get everything from antique dealers or auctions, but I couldn't afford the one and hadn't got time for the other, so it was done very quickly. And the book's finished. I'm doing the first revision.'

Early in the New Year, I bought a new car, but I had no intention of driving it in London, so one day I took Uncle Reg into Norwich while I caught the London train. We arranged that I would pick him up when I arrived back if he was at the station. Otherwise, I would assume that he had caught an earlier bus.

As I got on the 2.30pm at Liverpool Street, I hoped fervently that he would be there to drive me back.

The day had begun well, with a promising interview with my agent. She had liked the book and thought she knew a couple of publishers who would like it too. Then I had gone to Robert's office to deliver some work and discuss future subjects. I was pleased to see him still looking so happy about his engagement and full of plans for his future.

Then he took me to lunch and that was when the day turned sour. We had gone to an Italian restaurant off Greek Street – nothing elaborate, and there was no reason why either of us should meet anyone we knew.

And then this obnoxious man had come over to Robert, rudely barging into what was obviously a private conversation. He pulled up a chair and sat down at our table. 'Hello, old man. Haven't seen you for ages. How's tricks?'

I felt myself flush with annoyance, at the same time that Robert touched my arm warningly.

'Hello, Gregory. I'm fine thanks. Jan, may I introduce Gregory Fisher. He buys programmes for intercontinental TV. Gregory, this young lady is one of our writers. She worked with me on the mag. until we decided to make a move.'

This was formal language and I noticed that Robert had not told him my name. Surely he would take the hint. But he leaned forward and bent his head. It was meant to look deferential, but I knew he was trying to look down my blouse and was glad I had dressed formally for a first interview with the agent.

'And what have you been doing with yourself since – or shouldn't I ask?' He looked archly from me to Robert.

'Robert is an old friend, engaged to a talented American,' I said coldly, 'and I came up to see my agent. I've just written a book about women's work during the Second World War.'

My tone had made no impression whatsoever, but the old goat almost licked his lips as he said, 'Oh, we know what work they did, don't we? They kept our boys happy.'

I got up and addressed myself first to Robert.

'Sorry, but I'll leave you to talk. This conversation is not to my liking. I'll ring you tonight, shall I?'

Robert nodded, and made no attempt to stop me.

Then I let my temper loose. I turned to Gregory.

'There are a proportion of those women everywhere, but most of the girls in the Forces were respectable. Your sort always think the worst, but you have no right to denigrate the marvellous work they did – to keep this country safe – even for people like you.'

I think it was the scorn in my voice that sent the blood to his face. He began to mutter something, but I was already making for the door and did not hear him.

Once on the train, I felt exhausted. London was always tiring after Norfolk, but this drained feeling was a mixture of fury and exasperation. How dared that ignoramus denigrate the effort my girls had made. I acknowledged that they were 'my girls' now and I felt fiercely protective of their reputations.

Well, if my book ever saw the light of day, Gregory and his ilk would be confounded.

In Norwich, it was mild but drizzly. I saw Uncle Reg in the back of my car and sighed with relief. I opened the front door and sank into the passenger seat.

He looked up from the evening paper and as I turned my head, he said, 'Been like that, has it? OK, I'll drive.'

We were nearly home when he saw the hedgehog. He stopped, got out and came back carrying it.

'It's alive and I can't see any injuries, but it was just lying there. I'll stop and let Simon see it.'

'Does he know about them then – more than you do?'

'He knows more country lore than I ever learned and I've forgotten a lot with being in the City. Look, I know it needs warmth. Would you take it?'

My first thought was fleas, but there was something pathetic about the little animal, gently breathing and with its tiny feet working. I took it on to my lap and as I felt its warmth and life I was suddenly protective and willed it to live.

Simon came quickly, striding towards us as he saw what I carried. He took it from me and examined it briefly.

'No obvious damage and no fly maggots, so it hasn't been there long. Probably had a shock of some kind.' He turned to me and ordered, 'Go into the cafe and tell them I want a bottle of hot water.'

When I came back, he had lined a box with straw. He picked up an old sweater and wrapped the hedgehog in it, put the bottle beside it and carried it into one of the greenhouses.

'OK Thanks for bringing it in. I'll keep an eye on it.'

'Will it survive?' I asked.

'Depends – shock can kill and there may be internal injuries.'

'Can I get you some milk to give it?'

'No. Milk's bad for them. Water and meaty cat food when he's awake.'

'Most people seem to think they like bread and milk,' Uncle Reg said.

'So they do – love it – but it gives them the runs. You can come and see it in the morning, but now I must get on.'

We were dismissed. As we got back into the car, Uncle Reg said, 'Proper countryman. Does what he can then leaves it to Providence and gets on with his work.'

I thought of the hedgehog often during the rest of the evening and was surprised by my own concern – a maternal instinct, I supposed, for all dependent creatures. There was no doubt about it. My time back in the country and the stories I had heard had mellowed me. Other writers have often said that you get involved with your fictional characters, that they become real to you, and that they teach you a lot about yourself. And my characters were not fictional – oh, I had altered names, mixed up characteristics, changed locations – but the people and their experiences were real enough. All the war time incidents had happened to someone. What wonder if I was changed?

Just before I slept, I saw a clear picture of Simon. He was coming towards me with his arms held out – but only for the creature I cradled in mine.

The morning was crisp and clear. The country would have beckoned me anyway, but today only one walk was possible. I covered the half mile to the nursery and Simon, determined to be practical, friendly, of course, but not ... Not what? Not admitting how much I wanted this man who would ruin my career and turn me into a country wife – and, anyway, I reminded myself, he had shown no sign of wanting me. I straightened up and strode in to see my hedgehog.

Simon came to meet me, his face sombre. He said, 'I'm sorry, Jan. I've just buried him.'

It was a shock. I had not expected such an outcome from this man's capable hands. To my own amazement, I started to cry.

And now his arms were round me. He said quietly, 'Don't grieve. He's better off than suffering – nature knows best. He's only one of hundreds that die every year.'

'But he was mine,' I said.

'Oh, my dear love, none of them are ours. They belong to themselves. We have the privilege of sharing the world with them. That's all.'

His arms had tightened round me, and I realised what he had said. I raised my tear-stained face to Simon's smiling eyes.

That was nearly a year ago. And, of course, our marriage has not put a stop to my career. Simon encourages me and points out that writing is something that can be done through marriage, child-raising, illness and anything else I may have to cope with, even if it has to take second place sometimes. And as for being a country wife – I love it. Every time I have been to London recently, the traffic and the noise get worse.

I find in this rural community something of the same spirit that the Servicewomen found in wartime. Everyone knows everyone – they either get on well together or tolerate the awkward ones. Their problems tend to be the same and they help out where they can. Their generosity to local causes always astounds me.

So tomorrow, I'm going on the Countryside March with Simon and Jerry. A coachload are going from this village alone. I still don't know the rights and wrongs of fox hunting, but I do know that I want our way of life to continue forever. And what you want and know to be right, you must fight for.

The women who went to war taught me that.